GRANT'S INDIAN

A NOVEL

BY

PETER JOHNSON

Peter Johnson
134 West 93rd Street #7D
New York, NY 10025
www.peterjohnsonbooks.com
www.grantsindian.com

Cataloging-in-Publication Data for this book is available from the Library of Congress.
Library of Congress Control No. 2009903517

ISBN 978-0-9819842-0-9

Book design by Yvonne Vermillion www.magicgraphix.com
Printed in the United States of America.

For Sally

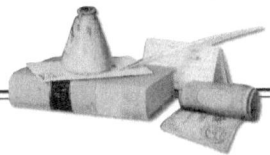

CONTENTS

Chapter I

AN INDIAN AT
APPOMATTOX

Appomattox 1865

I T COMES BACK TO ME NOW WITH THE PONDEROUS clarity
of a dream, the figures larger than life, big and grainy as they loom and
fade, now close, now far, their actions determined and purposeful as
gods, as if they had conned by rote the parts they would play in American
history's most perfect moment. They ride slowly out of the noontime haze
of a Virginia Palm Sunday in solemn procession, five uniformed men, two
blue, three gray.

First comes Tucker the sergeant, his cap in tatters, the crown flapping
like a chimney-lid, his gray coat buttonless, a white handkerchief nodding
before him on an apple branch, his hands easy on the reins of Champ,
his dead commander A.P. Hill's dappled gray – stragglers killed Hill a
week ago today. "Tell Hill to come up *now*!" shouted Stonewall Jackson
as he died two years ago, and Lee would cry the same before his order to
"Strike the tent" on his own deathbed five years hence. Then comes Lee's
aide Marshall in borrowed gloves and clean paper collar, a brave stab at
gentility *in extremis*. Then our own Babcock in full federal fig, from his
fresh-trimmed beard down to his bright and jingling spurs, his dress kit
somehow salvaged while the rest of us had abandoned ours in the pell-
mell week-long mad pursuit from Richmond. Beside Babcock rides Lee,
in a fresh uniform unpacked from thin paper this very morning, complete
with red sash, snowy linen, and a magnificent dress sword with a lion's-

1

head hilt, wrapped in gold wire and sheathed in a gold-filigreed English-leather scabbard – the gray fox brought to bay and sitting Traveller as grave and massive as a cathedral. At a discreet distance in the rear rides Lieutenant William Dunn, Babcock's orderly, soft and unobtrusive, head down, wrists crossed over the pommel, so silent and workmanlike that history will soon forget he was there.

The group pauses at the bridge, and after a brief conference Tucker and Marshall spur forward into the little town. Lee urges Traveller down to the stream to drink. Babcock and Dunn sit fidgeting and silent, until Tucker returns and leads them clopping over the bridge and up to the porch of the two-story brick farmhouse Marshall has found for the meeting with General Grant.

History droops an eyelid. The house's owner is Wilmer McLean, who moved here after shells crashed through the windows of his previous house at Bull Run during the war's first battle four years ago. He moved west and managed to ride out the rest of the war unmolested, hunkering down in the remote Virginny hills while the thing runs its course. But history must have its symmetry. The war, begun in Wilmer McLean's old back yard, has sniffed him out to finish in his new parlor.

Lee enters, removes his gloves, sits at a small table and waits. Colonel Marshall shifts from foot to foot. Babcock tries to make conversation, moving furniture around so the room is how he thinks Grant will want it. Tucker and Dunn wait outside with the horses, showing the white handkerchief. The clock ticks a slow half hour, the loudest sound in the room, as history awaits General Grant.

Oh, did I want to eat Lee's brain that day, as we used to say, to get into his head and look around. One thing I wanted to know was where his surrender uniform came from, that beautiful dress gray with all the brass and the dress sword with all that gold. We, after all, had been pelting after him so fast we just had the clothes on our backs, and he'd been in even direr straits. I've thought about it often, sitting here thirty years later at my desk and shuffling my papers, and I've begun to think maybe he had it with him the whole war, packed away in his traveling trunk, waiting for just such an inevitability as this.

Sometimes in an antic reverie I imagine the outfit, empty, following him, its legs and sleeves flapping, up from Richmond after the Seven Days, to Manassas and Antietam, where he would have needed it if our

2

Burnside hadn't wasted the afternoon trying to fight his way across a bridge over a river that he could have waded, and if McClellan had figured out he was winning and renewed the attack next day. I see it trekking back with him down to Fredericksburg, where maybe it was in his saddlebags that December day while he sat astride Traveller on Marye's Heights and watched his riflemen make windrows of Burnside's troops and history has him muttering to Longstreet, "It is well that war is so terrible. We should grow too fond of it." Did it then battle with him through Chancellorsville, where Jackson lost his way, his arm, and his life, and up to Gettysburg, where it would have had to be aired and ironed double-quick if Meade had dared to come down off Cemetery Ridge? Did it then fight backwards, shadowing Lee through the Wilderness and Spotsylvania and Cold Harbor, staggering back over all those rivers all the way to Richmond, where it got unpacked and hung up for the long siege, then packed up again for the final dash west which brought it to rest, finally with Lee's elusive body in it, here in Wilmer McLean's parlor, sitting, one elegant, creased knee crossed over the other, boots polished, brass buttons tapping on the little marble table-top?

Grant didn't have a surrender uniform. He barely had a uniform at all. When he met General Lee that day he was wearing what he always wore, a private's blues with three stars on the shoulders so you'd see he was a general if you looked hard enough. His coat was misbuttoned and his boots were muddy. "In my rough traveling suit, the uniform of a private with the straps of a lieutenant-general," he later wrote, "I must have contrasted very strangely with a man so handsomely dressed, six feet high and of faultless form."

It was all an ingenuous accident, of course. "When I had left camp that morning I had not expected so soon the result that was then taking place, and was consequently in rough garb." Me? General Lee wants to surrender to me? Why, I haven't a *thing* to wear! Grant had been in touch with Lee for two days. Lee's army was surrounded, cut off from rations, deserting and yielding in droves. What other "result" could there be?

It's true, those two West Pointers could go on and on about proprieties, sending white-flagged couriers through the lines all day, trying to get the right twist on things. For three days at Cold Harbor, they argued long-distance about whether to call a "truce" or a "pause," while five thousand boys bled and puked their destinies into the mud. Maybe, Grant figured, if it took him and Lee three days to work out a simple truce, a full-blown surrender might take a month.

Don't believe it. Grant told us last night if once he got Lee face to face, Lee wouldn't get away without surrendering. Despite that, he lit out early this morning, rode overland through streams and mud when he didn't have to, crossed the river twice, almost as if he was teasing Lee's messengers to catch him, so that when they finally found him at noon he had neither time to change nor fresh clothes to change into. There were accidents at Appomattox that day, but this wasn't one of them. Sam Grant, frank, scruffy, and muddy, arrived at the McLean house looking just the way he wanted to, just like Lee did.

Grant is in the room, shaking hands with Lee. He doesn't make an entrance, send in orderlies or aides. One minute, just Babcock, Marshall, and Lee are there, and then there's Grant, cigar lit, gravely shaking Lee's hand and pulling up a chair. It is *echt* Grant. All his life he's had a way of just *showing up*, of just *being there* without anybody noticing how he got there. His non-entrances were the stuff of legend, and this was one of his best. A year ago, arriving in Washington to take charge of the army, he slouched up to the desk at the Willard with his son Fred, registered as "U.S. Grant and son, Galena, Illinois," and got shunted off to an alcove under the eaves. That night he walked alone over to a White House reception, stepped in the front door, and waited for Lincoln to notice him, which he eventually did, crying, "Why, here is General Grant! Well, this is a great pleasure!" His first command to his surly Illinois regiment in 1861 was a dismissive, "Men, go to your quarters." Even later on, as ex-general and ex-president, arguably the most famous man in the world, when invited to call on Bismarck in Berlin he just stepped out of his hotel, lit a cigar, walked to the palace, tossed the butt away, and had his plain republican fist raised to knock on the door when it swung open quick to admit him.

Grant and Lee look at each other, trying to fathom what planet the other rode in from. They embody nothing less than the past and the future. Lee is military tradition, Marlborough and Wellington and Napoleon, not to mention Scott and Dumas and Stendhal. Grant is nobody's heir, a military orphan who just growed like Mrs. Stowe's Topsy, an autochthonous creature of the frontier and the war, a product of no imagination but his own, a purely American breed that history and literature haven't caught up with.

4

As Grant makes himself comfortable in his chair, does Lee's nose twitch? Why, he wonders, does this strange little man smell of mustard? Last night, struck with a killing headache, Grant agonized, awake till dawn, bathing his feet and forehead, his wrists and neck, in mustard water and mustard-soaked cloths. He hasn't changed clothes, and the home-remedy scent still clings to his ragged cuffs and beard.

Oblivious to the smell, Grant is talking now, while blue officers file in and line up against the wall, shuffling and sniffling and quiet, like people tiptoeing into a sickroom to hear the last words. Grant talks about the Mexican War, says he remembers Lee from then, and Lee nods and says he remembers Grant too, though he probably doesn't. Captain Robert E. Lee, Winfield Scott's caparisoned aide, the soldier's *beau ideal*, remember quartermaster Lieutenant Sam Grant? I doubt it, but Lee has nothing to lose by being polite. Grant chatters on, more voluble in the presence of a stranger than I've ever heard him before or since until, he later claimed, "our conversation grew so pleasant that I almost forgot the object of our meeting."

Not quite *our* conversation. I was standing there against the wall with the rest of them, and I can tell you Grant was the only one talking. Lee was nodding and grinding his teeth, staring at this strange, chatty, mustard-smelling little man, wondering what was going to happen. Was he Grant's prisoner? Did Grant want his fancy, lion-headed sword? Grant didn't say anything about that, just prattled amiably on until Lee cleared his throat and suggested he was here less to swap stories than to surrender his army and perhaps they should get on with it. Relief passed from face to face that the foreplay was over.

"Oh yes," says Grant, "surrender." And without breaking stride he motions to me, and I hand him an order book with two carbons in it. I kept one of the carbons and had it framed. I'm looking at it now, thirty years later, as I write at my desk at 300 Mulberry Street, New York City Police headquarters. Grant later authenticated and autographed it for me. But the sheet is blank when I give it to Grant, and it stays blank for awhile as he looks at the air and thinks. The smoke of his cigar, which has been curling gently away, starts puffing like a locomotive, and when it has built a full head, Grant commences writing, blowing up a storm. You can imagine the room. Nobody talking, people coughing behind their hands, the jingle of spurs as men shift from foot to foot, the clock on the mantle slowly ticking, so slowly that each tick feels like it might be the last.

Outside, men tending the horses are throwing a ball around and shouting until someone goes out and tells them to stop. It's pretty hard, though, to quell all the noise outside. Men keep arriving as news of the surrender spreads. Hooves thud in, stones skid and scatter, there comes a question, a reply, then an abrupt "Whoop–!" broken off by a sharp "Sh-sh-sh!" and whispered voices. Then another rider arrives, then a flurry of them, and the whole process repeats. And always in the background, the neighing and snuffling and jingling of the horses as they too greet old friends.

"When I put my pen to the paper," Grant later wrote, "I did not know the first word that I should make use of in writing the terms." But Grant, for a man of few words, had a way with those few. "No terms except an unconditional and immediate surrender can be accepted," he wrote at Fort Donelson, and the electrified country gave new names to his initials, *U*nconditional *S*urrender Grant. "I propose to fight it out on this line if it takes all summer," he wrote from Spotsylvania, and the country clasped him to its bosom as the soul of manly grit. (My wife and daughter and I went to vaudeville last week. "Are you demanding unconditional surrender, sir?" gasps the belle. "I propose to fight it out along this line if it takes all summer," leers baggy-pants. So quickly does drama squeeze down to farce.) Now, called on to write the surrender terms, Grant huffs and puffs and licks his pencil and scribbles, puffs some more and scribbles some more and comes up with something that, as Huck Finn might say, sure did knock the spots out of any surrender document ever *I* see before. Just two hundred or so words, in which Lee's army is told, in effect, to stack arms and go home. Once there, in another of those memorable phrases, they are "not to be disturbed by United States authority so long as they observe their paroles and the laws in force where they may reside."

That was it. No mention of the Confederate States of America, which Lincoln had never acknowledged to exist at all. No mention of punishment or confiscations or "conquered territories," or anything else beyond the scope of the immediate armies. "Not to be disturbed by U.S. authority" is what it says, and what it does is in one stroke put the entire Army of Northern Virginia, *including General Lee*, out of reach of any official reprisals *in perpetuity*. Lee winds glasses on to read the document, looking suddenly aged and scholarly, like the schoolmaster he will soon become. "This will have a very happy effect on my army," he murmurs.

There's some hemming and hawing about the terms – Lee borrows a pencil to caret something in – and Grant gives the document to Colonel Joe Bowers, one of his two secretaries, to make a copy, while he and Lee discuss getting rations to the Southern army.

The conversation trickles off. Grant lights another cigar, watches the smoke for awhile, turns, and seems for the first time to notice us standing against the wall. Oh, he says to Lee, let me present my officers and my staff. So he does – first Sheridan, who just that morning bottled Lee up, then the rest of us.

They go down the line, Lee shaking the hands of those that offer them and bowing to the others. He shares a private moment with Seth Williams, who was adjutant when Lee was superintendent at West Point. The last officer in line, the one closest to where Bowers is scratching out the surrender, is a surprise to Lee, a dark-complexioned man with high cheekbones and a flat nose. Lee takes one look at him and, I swear, jumps back a whole step. It's the only spontaneous move he's made since he entered the room, and it's a comic-opera jump like he's seen a snake. He turns to seek advice but finds himself alone. His aide Marshall is at the table with Bowers. Had they dressed up a Negro in uniform just to rub it in? Play a joke? No, somebody whispers, that's a Seneca Indian from upstate New York, chief of his tribe. Well, that's another matter entirely to General Lee. He extends his hand to the Indian and says, "I'm glad to see there's one real American present."

And the Indian takes Lee's hand, looks him in the eye, and in perfect unaccented English tells him, "We're all Americans, General." Lee nods solemnly, looks wise, and resumes his seat. Beautiful.

"Damn!" mutters Joe Bowers at the secretary's table, and all eyes, having no place else to go, turn to him. Joe is in trouble. He stayed behind to staff our base at City Point when we all left a week ago. Unable to stand the suspense, he lit out on his own and has been pounding after us for days, just barely managing to catch us at the last moment as we walked up to McLean's porch. He's nervous, sweating, and breathing hard. His hand is trembling and his pen is dripping. He's already blotted one copy of the surrender and thrown it away. He put the wrong date on the next one and had to throw *it* away. Now he's almost through a third, but he's spilled the inkbottle on it. Even *Grant* hands him a handkerchief to help mop it up.

(Bowers was proof that character is destiny. All through the war he was late for things, always rushing to catch up to Grant. After the war he tried it once too often. Less than a year later, as Grant's train was pulling out of Garrison, N.Y., Bowers ran to catch it, leaped and missed and died under the wheels.)

Time is heavy in the McLean parlor. The introductions are done, and people are having trouble making small talk. The air is heavy too. Though the windows are open and a fine spring breeze is wafting through, there are more than a dozen large, hairy men in the little room, all of us sweating and ripe from days on horseback and nights on the cold, cold ground. The place is getting gamy. The one thing that's got history held up is the simple secretarial chore of making a copy, which looks fair to take Joe Bowers till sundown. The drama has been stretched to the sticking point, and it's time to go. History is twitching its lips and farce is in the wings.

Helpless, Bowers scrapes his chair back, turns to the officer behind him, Grant's other secretary, and whispers, "Parker, you'll have to write this, I can't do it." So who steps forward to save the day? Who brushes Bowers aside, sits at the table, pulls out his sheaf of papers and his trusty pen, borrows an inkbottle from Marshall and starts writing? Who, upright and imperturbable in the swirl of history, sits solidly at the table and in a big, round hand, rips off the immortal document that brings an end to four years of suffering and slaughter? Who ensures that the two armies can stop fighting each other and turn west to clear the country of the pesky redskins who are the last hindrances to its manifest destiny to sweep from coast to coast? *The Indian!*

That's right. The document that reglued the Union and made it stick, that ended the fighting and confirmed Lincoln's "new birth of freedom," was inscribed by a man whose native language wasn't English, who was kept out of the army long after even Negroes were welcomed, who was there by accident because he used to hobnob at Grant's father's harness shop in Galena and was the only man in the room whose ancestors back to the first generation were born in America.

His task accomplished, the Indian sits back and pockets his pen. He hands the surrender terms to Colonel Marshall and receives Lee's acceptance in return. The Indian and Marshall are history's children as much as the two generals. Marshall is the grandson of John Marshall, Chief Justice of the Supreme Court. The Indian – "Grant's Indian" they call him at headquarters – is no slouch himself. He is Ely S. Parker, born Ha-sa-no-an-da, now called Do-ne-ho-ga-wa, grand-nephew of Red Jacket and Grand Sachem of the Six Nations of the Iroquois Federation, chief of state of his entire nation and so, in strict diplomatic terms, the highest-ranking man in the room.

Now Lee is on his feet. He shakes hands with Grant, pulls on his gloves and goes out. The officers on the porch come to attention and salute, Lee returns the salute and calls for Traveller, whose bridle has been slipped to let him graze. Everyone agrees Lee struck the palm of his hand absently with his fist not once, not twice, but three times. He watches Traveller being bridled, reaches up himself to free the horse's forelock from the brow band and mounts. History, though not Grant, has Grant coming out the door, seeing Lee and removing his hat. Everyone else uncovers, Lee raises his own hat briefly then passes through the gate and down the road to the river.

As soon as Lee is out of sight, all hell, as Milton would say, breaks loose. Locusts descend on the McLean house. Everyone wants a piece of furniture or a piece of a piece. Wilmer McLean, trying to assert possession, stands in the middle of the room, grabs things from people, refuses the money that men shake in his face, but the furniture goes and money piles up willy-nilly at his feet. The tables and chairs the generals used vanish, then the candlesticks, the inkwells, the mirrors, the clock. Most of the prize stuff is grabbed up by people of rank, those who were in the room throughout and want mementos. Then the lower orders sweep in, and their motive is loot plain and simple. They strip the cane off chairs and divvy up the splinters, they tear sofa fabric into rags for sale and profit, they grab handfuls of horsehair from the innards and stuff it in their pockets. McLean's house, spared by the war, is devastated by the peace. In later years you could furnish a good-sized town from all the scraps claimed to have been liberated at Appomattox that day. It was like a rehearsal for Grant's presidency.

And through it all, that Indian officer sits at the table, then stands at the mantle, imperturbably copying out orders Grant has given for tomorrow's deployment and dispersal of arms, rations and prisoners. He has to stand because Sheridan whisked the table out from under him and carried it off. Out on the lawn Sheridan ran into George Custer, rolling around on the ground wrestling with Fitz Lee, General Lee's nephew, and enjoying a West Point reunion. Sheridan gave Custer the table to take home to his wife Libby, and Custer rode off from Appomattox, guiding his horse with his knees, the marble-topped table upside-down on his head. Eleven years later, the centennial of the country's birth, when I heard how Custer had charged the Seventh Cavalry down toward the Little Big Horn shouting "We've caught them napping, boys!" and blundered into Crazy Horse and the Sioux nation, I imagined him doing it with his hands off the reins, holding that little marble-topped table on his head.

I see this all clearly now, though it was thirty years ago, a cloud-vision etched against the sky. The gray-bearded rider and his gilded sword. Grant with his misbuttoned tunic and the smell of mud, manure and mustard. The officers shifting from foot to foot. The solemn bows and handshakes. The reverential departure, the descent of the relic-hounds, and Custer riding to his fate with a little table on his head. And the Indian. "We're all Americans, General," he tells Lee, and then, when Bowers's hands are shaking, he takes the pen in the midst of the tumult and the tension and enshrines the surrender.

That's the way it happened. I know, I was there. The pen still works, and I'm using it to write these words.

I'm the Indian.

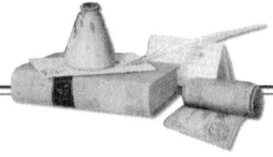

Chapter II

USELESS GRANT
AT DIRTY DAN'S

Galena, Ill. 1860

I FIRST MET GRANT IN 1860 IN GALENA, JUST UP FROM THE Mississippi on the far northwest edge of Illinois, which at that time meant pretty much the far northwest edge of the U.S., the last of civilization before the plains. Galena was a boom town, a lead-mining center, named for and fueled by the galena ore that honeycombed its slopes and fed by the deep-water Galena River that swept through on its way to the Mississippi ten miles downstream. The town boasted all the appurtenances of wild-west prosperity. Saloons and whorehouses, tack shops and feed stores lined the muddy streets, which led up from the river at precipitous angles, and the citizenry were kept wary and entertained by the runaway drays that periodically broke loose and careened down through the mud and cobbles, spewing crates and barrels and sending folks to cover under the balconies. Irish navvies rubbed elbows with Swiss and German metalsmiths, Southern lawyers and Yankee gamblers mingled at the bars, Cornish and Welsh miners dined in shirtsleeves next to elegant merchants' wives and Negro waiters streamed in and out to serve the whole crowd. Fistfights spilled out of drinking and sporting establishments, and the thud of gunfire enlivened Saturday nights.

I had gone west, as I had had hankered to do all my life, as Superintendent of Federal Building Construction, both for Galena and for Dubuque, Iowa across the Mississippi. I cut a respectable figure in town, not hard to do, respectability not being the keynote of Galena or anyplace else in the west in the late '50s. The customhouse rising on the riverbank and the mariners' hospital on the hill were my main projects, and it was a pleasure to calculate their progress, as story rose on story, as a measure of how far I had risen in the world.

It was far from the way I'd imagined going west when I was a boy, when I spent nights picturing myself as a Fenimore Cooper Indian, trekking west with moccasins on my feet, a handkerchief on a stick and a gleam for the main chance in my eye. My schoolchum Henry Flagler had left school at fourteen and done just that. He was now busily cornering the grain market back in Cleveland. But by the time I managed it I was close to thirty and no longer the "young man" whom Horace Greely exhorted to "go west."

Fate had brooked no other choice. The necessity of earning a living with one hand and keeping my Seneca nation intact with the other had made my formative years a shuttle between my home reservation of Tonawanda (near Buffalo), the state capital at Albany, and the power centers of New York and Washington. I came early to the responsibilities of adulthood, and by the time I lit out for the frontier I was already a solid citizen, an easterner to boot, and the hard-drinking, bare-knuckled town of Galena didn't charm the man as it might have the boy. I quickly got impatient with the wildness, the incivility, the boisterousness, drunkenness, speculation, gambling, buffoonery – all the things that made the west the west. The locals barely considered me an Indian at all, so greatly did I differ from the wild Plains Indians of their night-sweats, and when they called me "Chief" it was more from respect than foolery. I was a Mason and a captain in the local militia, with a room in the DeSoto House up the hill.

One of the more prosperous shops in Galena, on a corner of Main Street just before it ascends the hill, was J. R. Grant, a harness store owned by Jesse Grant of Cincinnati, an outlet for his Ohio tannery, run by his son Orvil. Orvil, like the old man, was a canny sort. He knew the value of keeping the shop full, of paying customers or no, so he established a social center just inside the front door, with a pot-bellied stove, comfortable chairs and a supply of local and distant papers and magazines to stir conversation. I sniffed the place out soon after my arrival and started dropping in.

In the spring or early summer of 1860, when I had been in residence for three years, there was a new arrival in Galena. I can't be specific about the date, because even then Grant had that penchant for making a non-entrance that later became so celebrated. I just remember that over the course of a few weeks, we in the front became aware of a new presence in the back of Orvil Grant's harness store. A new *absence* was more like it. You'd walk into the store and catch, out of the corner of your eye, somebody scuttling into the back room. He didn't talk to anybody, didn't wait on customers, just hovered in the shadows, beady eyes shining like a rodent.

We heard he was Orvil Grant's older brother and assumed he was the family idiot. It trickled out that he was a West Pointer who'd fought with distinction in the Mexican War, married, moved from post to post, gone to ground in California, where he'd washed out of the army on drink, come back east and tried to make a go of it farming, failed at that and been bailed out by Papa Jesse, who'd stashed him in the back of the Galena store to keep the books. Grant was no idiot. But he sure was useless, and that's what people started calling him not-so-far out of earshot. Useless Grant. His shy, skittering manner, though not the behavior of a simpleton, was near enough as to make no difference. In the summer of 1860, thirty-eight years old, with a wife and four children stashed in a house father Jesse rented for him at the top of a muddy street, Ulysses Grant was plain beat – as beat as I've ever seen a man before or since.

I see my younger self now, a strapping buck of thirty-two, toiling up High Street at the end of a hot mid-summer day. I was dusty and parched after wrangling with the carpenters at the still-uncompleted customhouse and making good headway uphill toward the cool of the DeSoto House bar, when I heard a rumpus from one of the saloons that lined the lower street – "lighthouses" they called them, and there were some fifty-odd of them on the few wild streets of "downtown." I knew some of them, but not this one, whose name a rough board plank announced as Dirty Dan's. I was about to pass by when something – Fate, or perhaps a flash of Seneca *on-din-nonk*, a prophecy dream – slowed my uphill progress and drew me toward the sounds of conflict. I peered over the swinging doors into the darkness.

I've never seen a bear-baiting, but as my eyes adjusted to the interior I thought that's what was going on here. A semicircle of men stood in front of the bar with their backs to me, stomping their feet on the board floor, clapping hands and hooting, raising dust and setting the lamps flickering.

They were pushing some creature in the middle back and forth, grabbing him by the neck, spinning him around and shoving him staggering across the ring. Each side grabbed him in turn and flung him back, the circle sagging and reforming, raising shouts and guffaws as the creature, off-balance and desperate, ran itself ragged.

"Hey! Useless!" some were shouting, amidst heartier epithets. I eased through the doors, gained the back of the crowd, stood on tiptoe and used my full six feet to look over them. The victim was none other than Orvil Grant's brother Ulysses. How he'd got up the courage to venture into society, and why he'd picked this venue for his debut, I didn't pause to wonder. An underdog all my life, I had a sympathy for the breed, so I turned sideways, lowered a shoulder and bulled through the crowd to the center, arriving just in time to intercept the staggered prey on a rebound. He spun round and flailed a fist at me, but I plucked it out of the air, grabbed his shirtfront, and looked him in the eyes. "Let's get you out of here," I told him.

His eyes held mine, and the wild look dissolved, replaced by something sharp and grateful. He nodded once, I let go my grip on him, and we turned to face the crowd. I took a step toward the door, expecting, I suppose, by sheer force of personality to part the waters, but a big fellow with a blue-checked shirt and an eye patch blocked my way.

"Hey, boys," he grinned. "Now we got us a drunk and an Injun too!"

A growl arose from the throat of the mob, but for a moment they held back, recalculating the odds. We stood that way for a few seconds, us in the center afraid to move out, them around us not quite daring to move in. It was our moment. When they're in doubt, attack. But I was in doubt too, and as I wavered, Grant took charge. "Back-to-back, toward the door," he muttered and spun round behind me.

I followed his lead. With me the van and him the rear, he meant for us to fight our way out, and as he emphasized it with a backward kick of his boot on my leg I jumped into action. I feinted a shoulder at the big, eye-patched guy, and as he dove for where I wasn't, elbowed him in the kidney, moved past him, grabbed the littlest guy I could find, and flung him broadside into the crowd. The fight didn't last long, but it must have been a sight – me in front like a chesty plow-horse, a head taller and fifty pounds heavier than the runt behind me – and him back there swishing and whisking like the tail of Gargantua's horse, brushing flies aside and knocking down the whole wood. I kept grabbing people and throwing them out of our way as the light of the swinging doors loomed closer, and all the time I felt and heard grunting and scuffling behind me as Grant fended off stragglers. Not a word passed between us, but we stayed in touch, ass-to-ass, belt-to-belt, matching pace as we bulled ahead, me stopping if we lost contact until the shove of his butt urged me to proceed. Organization was our key to victory. That and, no doubt, the comic spectacle of a big Indian Falstaff inching forward with scrappy little Prince Hal in tow soon confused and demoralized our foes and sent them searching for other sport while we reached the door and burst into the sunshine of High Street.

We dusted ourselves off and cast a backward glance at Dirty Dan's, through whose doors the enemy were making noises and gestures of dismissal. Assured that there was no pursuit, Grant eased his shoulders back, drew his head up out of his collar, tugged down the corners of his vest, blinked at me, stuck out his hand and opened a corner of his mouth.

"Grant," he said.

"Parker," I told him, and we shook on it.

He continued to size me up, beard twitching as if he was chewing it over. It wasn't really a beard at this point, just a thick stubble. He tossed his head back at Dirty Dan's and asked, "Military?" My fighting skills had impressed him.

I shrugged. "Militia," I said, dismissing it, and when he nodded I asked him, "You?" Monosyllables. We were a vaudeville team.

"Hm!" he said, and it wasn't really a laugh or a chuckle, just a grunt through his nose. That was the way he mostly expressed amusement. I only heard Grant laugh full out maybe three times in my life. "Mexico," he said, looked like he was going to say more, then rolled his hand and flipped the thought away.

I lifted my chin at the hill up ahead, and he nodded, so I set off again and he fell into step with me, walking in a sort of tipped-forward way, his chin in the lead, as if, as one of Meade's staff later said, "he had determined to drive his head through a brick wall and was about to do it." Abruptly, as if afraid he'd lost something, he stopped, and his hands danced around his clothing until one of them patted a vest pocket and emerged slowly drawing a long cigar. It was bent from the ruckus at Dirty Dan's, and he straightened it with uncommonly delicate fingers for such an uncouth creature, stuck it in his mouth without lighting it, and in that hunched-forward walk with the cigar in his teeth it looked like the cigar was drawing him like a dowsing wand, pulling him up the hill.

When we reached the DeSoto House I motioned him to come on up the steps. "Drink?" I said, and chuckled to myself. You'd have thought he was the Indian and I the white man, coaxing him along with simple words I hoped he'd understand. It sure looked like I was the civilized one and he the savage, me in my jacket and cravat, my stick pin and watch chain, and him in a ragged vest and tattered shirt, further mussed from rough usage at Dirty Dan's.

At the word, "Drink," Grant looked up at me, standing as I was on the first step of the DeSoto House in an attitude of welcome and gave a half-grin with the side of his mouth that wasn't clamped on the cigar. He scanned the veranda and broad windows of the hotel, looked down at his shabby kit and peered suspiciously up and down the street. Then, with a short nod, he tugged down his vest, smoothed his hair and beard with one hand, stuck the unlit cigar back in his pocket with the other and strode up the steps. A sort of dignification overtook him. His shoulders straightened, his head elevated, his chin rose, until by the top step you'd have sworn he'd acquired a pearl-gray vest and spats, so much did he look like there was no place on earth he now belonged but on the top step of the DeSoto House in Galena, Illinois. Once he decided to move forward, the sad-sack vanished. That's the way he was in the war. As soon as he decided, hesitation fled, a spring came into his step and ice into his eyes, and by the time he got where he was going you'd swear that nobody so perfectly belonged there as he.

He paused on the veranda, as I indicated a preference for sitting outside, and for a moment that furtive look flashed in his eyes. Reluctant, apparently, to drink in the open, he left me behind and strode through the main doors, turned left, and had himself seated at a polished mahogany table in the main lounge by the time I caught up. We ordered whiskeys and he raised his glass to me in thanks for the rescue, and we sat for awhile in silence, him nodding and pursing his lips, his eyes growing soft and receptive, taking the place in.

I liked the silence, which he seemed comfortable with too. There was something of the Indian about this man, with his recessiveness, his diffidence, and his penchant for melting in. He drank like an Indian too.

16

To the Iroquois, drink is anathema and therefore as tempting as any other forbidden fruit. Some of my earliest memories show me lying at the top of the stairs of my parents' house with my brother and sister, hearing my grandfather hold forth downstairs on the evils of drink. His voice rising in a high quaver, he would tell of the prophet Handsome Lake's journey on the sky-road to the house of the Evil-minded. "There he saw the Tormentor," the old man would say, "dipping red-hot liquid from a cauldron and forcing it between the teeth of a drunkard, saying 'Drink! For this is what you crave!' As he drank his breath turned to fire that all the waters of the earth couldn't quench, and the Tormentor further goaded him by commanding, 'Sing and dance! For you claim that drink makes you merry!' The fire-water does not belong to you," my grandfather insisted. "It was made for the white man." So, naturally, as I eased more and more into white society, I learned to drink like a white man.

The drunken Indian was already a stock music-hall figure, and, having discovered a little inclination that way myself, I had learned to drink moderately. The problem, I found through early painful research, is not that the Indian has some racial defect that makes him susceptible. It's just that when an Indian starts drinking, he's likely to keep on drinking till he's done, same way he does everything. Time is at the Indian's service, not *vice-versa*. We joke that the white man needs a clock to tell him when he's hungry. Not so the Indian. When he's got time and a bottle, he drinks it till it's empty, and he's passed-out, pissed-out drunk. I learned to keep my head by matching my sips to the pace of the slowest white drinker at the table.

I'd never met a drinker as slow as Grant. After the first salutatory sip, he just sat there with his glass on the table, revolving it slowly between two fingers, as if he wished he could take more. As I wouldn't let myself drink until he did, we bade fair to sit unquenched all evening. Finally, as host, I broke the standoff by lifting my glass. As soon as I did, Grant's fingers curled around his, and we raised our glasses to our lips, eying each other as if drinking in a mirror. It was comical, as with caution and some amusement, we raised and lowered our glasses in tandem, matching each other sip by slow sip until both glasses were empty and we ordered more.

Grant's silence was like an Indian's too, the way he let it gather around him. Some men's silences make you nervous, as if either they're too shy to speak, or, as happens more often, they're waiting for you to start gabbing so they can size you up. Grant was just silent. After we'd established our drinking rhythm, he patted his pockets, retrieved the cigar and examined it, straightened it with those soft fingers and set about lighting it, his actions so slow and self-absorbed that I got mesmerized. It took him a good long time to get the thing lit and glowing to his satisfaction. The diminishing lucifer was about to singe his fingers when he shook it out and threw it on the floor, leaned back in his chair, sighed and exhaled a comfortable cloud. He lit a cigar the same way he'd fought his way out of Dirty Dan's. Same way he'd walked up the steps of the DeSoto House – with total absorption. He was a man in a fight, then he was a man walking up the steps, now he was a man lighting a cigar.

"So you were in Mexico, Captain Grant," I said, breaking our skein of monosyllables.

He looked at me with interest – maybe it was the "Captain" – nodded and waved a hand. "Quartermaster," he said, as if he'd worked in the kitchen the whole time, though he'd been cited twice for bravery. He didn't then – or ever – feel like talking about battles. "Did you see much of the country?" I asked him. "Apart from the war, I mean."

That opened him up. Yes, he replied, he traveled extensively in Mexico and liked the country very much, the land and especially the people. "They're not to blame for their government or their leaders," he said. "Unlike us at home."

His speech was simple and direct, and, like the man, short and to the point. He started off talking in short bursts, like an engine raising steam, often leaving off the subject, especially when the subject was "I." "Spent a lot of time in Monterey after the battle," he said. "Beautiful city, enclosed by purple mountains. Orange and pomegranate trees so thick you can hardly see the houses until you're right on top of them."

I thought back. While Grant had been in and around Monterey the summer of '46, I had been sweltering in Washington City, only eighteen years old, but already the Tonawanda Seneca ambassador, meeting with President Polk and Secretary of War Marcy, trying to protect Indian lands from the same government that was gobbling up Mexico's.

"Climbed Popocatepetl," said Grant. His eyes softened at the recollection, and he raised a corner of his mouth. "Treacherous climb on narrow ledges. On the way up one of the mules, a white one, lost its

18

footing and tumbled over the side. Off a big cliff. Just vanished, and all the baggage with it." He waved the mule away with his cigar smoke. "That night we were just about to turn in, fires were banked down, when there's a noise out beyond the fire. Who's that? Who's coming? We grabbed guns, maybe it was a wolf." He sat back and snorted at himself. "I tell this story to my children," he explained. "Anyway, it's true. As we're all trembling there, who comes wandering into camp? Not a bear or a wolf. *The white mule!* He'd survived the fall, hadn't lost a pack off his back. We felt him all over, no broken bones, just tired and hungry. Next day we struck out for the summit, but had to turn back. We all got snow-blind. Couldn't see our hands in front of us. Some of us, me included, had to bandage our eyes they hurt so. Had to trust the animals to lead us back down, following along like blind men, clinging to their tails. And who do you think took the lead? Who led that whole sorry troop down off the mountain?" He jabbed the cigar. "That white mule. True story," he said, and watched smoke laze toward the ceiling.

He was turning his glass between his fingers, so I raised mine, took a sip, and he followed. "Always had more confidence in animals than in people," he muttered, again leaving the "I" off. Read his *Memoirs* and you'll never read an autobiography in which "I" appears so seldom. When he was dying up at Mt. McGregor ten years ago, his throat so corroded by cancer he couldn't talk, he wrote to his doctor, "The fact is I think I am a verb instead of a personal pronoun. A verb is anything that signifies to be, to do or to suffer. I signify all three."

The conversation continued on desultorily, with more silence than chatter, as we made our slow way toward the bottom of our glasses and the butt of Grant's cigar. At length he raised his glass for a final time, discovered it empty, glanced toward the bar as if considering another and saw something he hadn't expected.

"Hello, Fred," he said. I followed his eyes and saw a berry-brown, tow-headed youngster, maybe ten years old, wearing single-galussed overalls, no shirt or shoes, standing by the door. "What are you doing here?" Grant asked gently.

"Mama wants you home," said the boy, clinging to the doorjamb. "I went looking for you." He frowned at the glasses on the table.

"Come here," said Grant, holding his arm out. The boy sidled into the room, keeping the table between him and me, and eased up to Grant's side. Grant ruffled his hair, and the boy tried to smooth it. "This is my son Fred," he told me. "Say hello to Mr. Ely Parker, Fred."

"Hello," said Fred quietly, clinging close to his father. I extended my hand, which he just looked at.

"Go ahead, Fred," said Grant.

Fred reached his hand out and just barely touched mine, pulling it back and staring at it, then at me. "You're an Indian," he said.

"A tame one," I said solemnly.

Fred looked at his father, saw that he was smiling, and smiled too. "Eel-ee," he said to me. "Is that an Indian name?"

"No," I told him. "It's English. There's a cathedral in England called Ely cathedral. My Indian name is Do-ne-ho-ga-wa."

Fred's mouth moved, trying out the name. "Donny, um," he said. He twisted his shoulders and laughed. "Ely's better. Like a fish."

"Mr. Parker to you," said Grant, pushing back his chair and standing up. He stuck out his hand and I took it. "Thanks, Parker," he said. "See you again."

"Bye Mr. Parker," said Fred. Grant looked at me like he was going to say more but didn't. He tightened his mouth, nodded, shrugged and walked out the door, his hand on little Fred's shoulder.

I'd like to say that as a result of that encounter we became lifelong and inseparable friends, but we didn't. What did result was a certain easing of Grant's skittishness. Now any time I'd enter the livery store, which was often enough, Grant would acknowledge me with a grunt, a nod, a perfunctory "Parker" before fading into the back, and I'd respond with an easy "Mornin' Captain." It was comical, addressing him as Captain, since he was certainly the least captain-like individual we who gathered around his brother's stove ever did see.

As 1860 turned to fall and to winter 1861 those gatherings became more animated and urgent. Our own Illinoisan Abraham Lincoln was elected president, and South Carolina seceded, followed by the other deep south states, and the south armed while the north dithered. Lincoln got inaugurated March 4 while sharpshooters lined the capital roofs. The attention of the nation, and of our little group around the Galena stove, turned to Fort Sumter in the harbor at Charleston, South Carolina. Lincoln resupplied the fort, Beauregard's batteries roared and on April 13 the stars and stripes came down. On April 15, four years to the day before he rattled his last breath on a cornshuck mattress across from Ford's Theater, Lincoln declared an insurrection and called on the loyal states for 75,000 three-month volunteers. Virginia, Arkansas, Tennessee and North Carolina joined the Confederacy.

"Three months? That should be enough, shouldn't it, Congressman?" John Rawlins flourished his newspaper at the rest of us around the stove on a spring evening and addressed Congressman Washburne. Not yet thirty, Rawlins was already the town's leading attorney and moral conscience. The door was open, and warm breezes wafted in, mingling lilac and horse manure with the oily smell of harness.

"I should think so," said Congressman Elihu Washburne, unfolding his long arms and reaching for Rawlins's paper. He was in his constituent-visiting garb, farm trousers and suspenders over a flannel shirt but with polished boots that said Washington. "With Virginia in, Richmond becomes the capital. That's only a hundred straight-line miles from Washington?"

"Less," said Rawlins.

"Make it a hundred," said Washburne, examining the newspaper. "So. A month to train the troops. A month to march to Richmond. Another month to send the rebels packing. What, Rowley?"

Will Rowley, town clerk and Rawlins's neighbor, was a healthy skeptic with fiery red hair, but as mild as Rawlins was volatile. "Three months!" he scoffed. "They'll be lucky to find Washington in three months, heck with Richmond."

Rawlins glowered. "Damn you, Rowley. I say three months and the rebels slink home buggered with their own ramrods." People smiled. We called Rawlins "Black John" because of his black eyes and hair and also because of his astounding fits of profanity. "That your thinking, Parker?" he asked me.

I was sitting with arms folded and eyes half-closed, somewhere between inscrutability and slumber. I usually tried not to commit myself in subjects I was ignorant of, a habit that, followed generally, would keep most of us silent most of the time. But I knew something about this.

"I was in the Fifty-fourth New York back in Rochester," I allowed, "as captain of engineers. That, of course, was just militia."

"That's what's being called for," said Rawlins, peppery. "Militia. Think they can do it?"

21

I smiled. "After two weeks of drill," I said, "a militia regiment with decent officers can march in step, form from column into line and snap off a volley or two."

"How about after a month?" asked Washburne.

"I have no idea," I said. "After two weeks, we always went home."

Washburne and Rowley chuckled, but Rawlins had fire in his eyes. "But you see it, don't you?" he bristled. "We have trained militia companies all over the north. That's what the president has called for." He flung his arms wide. "All that's necessary is to form them into an army."

"*All* that's necessary," echoed Will Rowley. "As God said to Noah, 'All that's necessary is to build an ark and get all the animals in. I leave the details to you.'"

We all chuckled except Rawlins, whose eyes were black as agates in his pale face. "You can joke, Will, but it's as mortal a matter as we'll see in our lifetime."

"Yes, yes," drawled Rowley. He stretched his hand forth and intoned, "We must stand by the flag of our country and appeal to the god of battles!"

Rawlins shot up, color in his cheeks, and took a step toward Rowley. "I said it and I meant it, Will. Keep your goddamn sarcasm to yourself." Hands reached out to calm Rawlins, and he brushed them off and settled back into his chair. Congressman Washburne had chaired a town rally last night, at which Rawlins, in an impassioned speech, had used just those words.

"There, there," said Washburne. "I'm with you, John. But Rowley has a point. Gather seventy-five thousand men, they'll spend more time fighting each other than the enemy. It's a huge logistical problem. A health problem too."

"Logistics be damned," sputtered Rawlins, slamming his fist into his palm. "What matters is what's *right!* If we have the right, then the might will follow, and so will your damned logistics. It's will first, logistics second."

"Well, let's take that as a hypothesis," said Congressman Washburne smoothly. "Suppose that the various regiments *can* be molded into an army in a month, and that sentiments like Rawlins's can keep them from killing each other. What then? Can the thing be done in two months, before enlistments run out? Who knows the territory down there? What's it like?"

There was more than concern for the nation in Washburne's questions. At last night's meeting he had whipped up support for Lincoln and the cause by apotheosizing the "bloody flag" hauled down amid the "carnage" at Fort Sumter, where, in fact, only one man had been killed and that in a freak explosion during the surrender. Tomorrow the congressman had to address an actual recruitment meeting, at which he'd have to tell enlisting men exactly what to expect. He needed facts.

He searched our faces for them. When his eyes reached mine, I shrugged, unfolded my arms and spoke. "It's wet and swampy, full of yellow-fever and cross-hatched by rivers." I had spent 1855-56 in and around Norfolk, building a ship canal into North Carolina and getting sick.

"To hell with rivers and fevers!" said Rawlins. "What it takes is *will*. The issue here is moral, not logistical. This damn nattering about terrain and equipment is beside the point."

"Yes," agreed Washburne, trying out phrases. "This is what I need. An army armed not only by might but right. A foe so lazy they don't know one end of a rifle from the other. So demoralized by sin they'll flee at the first whiff of grapeshot. Free labor and industry can raise and equip an army better than a country grown slack from slavery." He leaned forward, elbows on his knees. "But three months? Can I really tell people that?"

Washburne looked around the circle as if counting votes, and most of us nodded, me lowering my eyes to half-staff and looking wise. Rawlins, his point won, pounded his fist on his knee. Watches emerged from pockets and chairs scraped as the party began to break up. We had won the war around the stove without a shot fired.

"Whoever controls the water controls the land," said a new voice behind us, flat and even. "The war will be fought on land, but won by water." The voice had a certainty that none of ours had had. We looked around and saw to our surprise that Orvil Grant's brother Ulysses had been hovering around the edges of the group listening. He stood there unshaven, unremarkable, arms folded across his vest, pipe in one hand, squinting his eyes slightly and nodding his head, as if he had caught the edge of a vision he was coaxing into focus.

"What's that?" said Washburne, snapping his head around. He'd likely never heard Grant's voice or set eyes on him before.

"The rivers," said Grant, his diffidence gone. "It's all going to be about the rivers. Look here." He held up his hand, the sleeve of his shirt rolled up to the elbow showing a thin forearm. He spread his fingers and pointed his pipe stem to them one at a time. "The rivers lead to the heart of the South." He drew the pipe stem down the outside of his little finger. "The Mississippi," he said and pointed to the other fingers in turn. "The Tennessee, the Cumberland, the Ohio. And over in the east," he paused with the pipe stem bending his thumb, "Richmond and the rivers that protect it. And look here." He wiggled the four fingers. "In the west, all the rivers run north and south, directly *into* enemy territory. In the east," he wiggled his thumb, "they flow west to east *across* the line of march. The way to Richmond is down the rivers of the west and through the back door, not across the moats and through the front."

Our circle eased back into our chairs. Grant was talking about a war and a country none of us had seen before.

"The Mississippi," Grant's pipe pointed to the knuckles on his little finger, "is guarded by St. Louis, Cairo, Memphis, Vicksburg, Natchez, New Orleans. We'll need to take them all. The Tennessee," he isolated his ring finger, "drives straight through Kentucky and Tennessee to Mississippi and the inland routes to Vicksburg and Mobile, then swings across the top of Alabama all the way to Chattanooga and Knoxville, with the Shenandoah Valley and the kitchen door of Richmond just beyond. The Cumberland," his middle finger, "winds down from the Ohio through Kentucky and bends to Nashville, where rail lines converge from all over north and south. The Ohio," his index finger, "is our lifeline. Free navigation of the Ohio from Pittsburgh to the Mississippi keeps all the other riverheads open and drives men and supplies into the enemy's vitals." He waggled the three outer fingers, the rivers of the south. "These three, and the forts that guard them, must be our first objectives in the west. The south will fortify the Cumberland and the Tennessee at the Tennessee border. At that point the rivers run close and parallel, so that if we take one fort by water the other will fall by land. In one stroke, the river routes to the south and east will be open, and Nashville, Knoxville, Chattanooga and Vicksburg will be in our grasp, with New Orleans threatened by river, land and sea. Only after these strongholds fall can we turn our back on them and reach out to pluck Atlanta and finally, Richmond."

Grant nodded slowly and examined the middle distance, as if reading a map he'd drawn in the air. All of us stared at him. The dumb had been made to speak and the blind to see.

Grant waggled his thumb, oblivious to the spell he was weaving. "Over here in the east," he said, "the rivers run athwart your path. You must build up your forces on the far bank, throw bridges across, make exposed crossings, fortify a bridgehead under fire then march out. A day's march away is another river, then another, then another. Your supply lines depend on bridges, which must be protected. No. The eastern war must be won on the rivers of the west."

He continued in that slow, quiet, confident way, each sentence laying down a certainty, his analysis salted with names that now were just dots on the map, but would enter the language with bloody emphasis in the next four years. Nashville, Vicksburg, Chattanooga, Rapidan, Rapahannock, Mataponi, Petersburg. He might as well have been writing a history right there of what would become the markers on his own path to victory. There were, of course, other names he couldn't yet know – Belmont, Donelson, Fort Henry, Shiloh, the Wilderness, Cold Harbor, Appomattox. But what started to emerge in the little man's voice as it curled around us in the dark and smoky harness shop was a map of the country and a vision of war none of us had seen before, a country with waters coursing through it like a bloodstream, a war of riverheads and railheads and supply lines, war as a discrete endeavor, divorced from politics or rectitude or ideology or slavery or the glory of the coming of the Lord. We saw our pipedreams of a quick victory dissipate like smoke by the cold breeze of Grant, as his steady murmur drew a new picture of the vast country, its mountains and valleys, its riverbends ripe for ambush, its unmapped cataracts and whirlpools. He offered no visions of victory or defeat, he just laid out the terrain as a matter of fact, seeing the land as something to be used, or if it thwarted him, bent to his advantage. The little man in his vest and apron would spend the winter of '63 trying to force the Mississippi to change its course, because it didn't flow where he wanted it to in front of Vicksburg.

There was silence, and we realized that Grant had stopped talking. He hadn't made a speech, he'd just told us what he saw, and when he was done he stopped. I saw him drifting toward the back of the store, nodding quietly to himself. Chastened amateurs, we made a few more stabs at conversation, but it was a stagnant brew after the clear spring that Grant had given us. We pushed back our chairs and said good-bye. As Rawlins, Rowley, I and the others went out the door to walk up the hill, I looked back and saw Congressman Washburne in the back of the store talking to Grant and Grant looking up at the tall congressman, lips pursed, eyes unblinking, nodding his head slowly.

I would have been damn surprised if someone told us then that, four years later, Rawlins, Rowley, Grant and I would be four of nine Galena generals and Grant the biggest general of them all. I wasn't surprised, though, the next night at the great recruitment meeting to find "Captain Ulysses Grant of West Point, distinguished veteran of the Mexican War," and the only professional soldier in town, proposed by Washburne as chairman of the session, nor to see him, day after day thereafter, drilling raw troops with strips of lath for guns on the riverbank green. Said Grant later on, "I never went into our leather store after that meeting, to put up a package or do other business."

Chapter III

HECK OF A JOB, BROWNIE!

Washington 1861

THE WAR GOT GRANT A JOB AND LOST ME ONE. AS A government engineer I was a political appointee, and when Lincoln's election washed the Democrats out, out went baby. I didn't grudge the loss. I'd tossed my lot into the federal grab bag, and that's the way the game went. As I cleared my desk, packed my bags and prepared to leave Galena I had no doubt I'd get my lot picked again. The army needed engineers, I was an engineer, and the twain would soon meet one way or another.

I toyed with just joining Grant's volunteers, but it seemed like a mug's game. I had clawed my way up through years of scrambling and politicking – hard work for a white man, let alone an Indian – and I wasn't eager to let go. I would set my sights as high as possible, using my connections and reputation to gain an army commission in the east, where the main action figured to be. So while Grant set off for Springfield with his recruits, I lit out for Washington with my résumé.

On my way, I detoured to Bellevue, Ohio, just west of Cleveland, where my old schoolmate Henry Flagler was beginning a commercial empire. I had known Henry at Yates Academy in western New York, which he fled at fourteen to seek his fortune while I stayed on. And fortune came to Henry Flagler. His grain-and-distillery business flourished, and he kept branching and sub-branching into areas of commerce and finance I had little understanding of. On my trips east and west, I always dropped in on him in Bellevue to see what new scheme he was up to.

After Galena, Bellevue was civilization itself. The railroad, passing through from Cleveland to Sandusky, had brought prosperity and respectability, and the town's manicured lawns and hedges, white houses and quiet streets, were far from the snarl and holler, the mud and mayhem of Galena. The last time I had passed through, two years ago, Henry and his wife Mary had just moved into a magnificent place on Southwest Street called the Gingerbread House for all the ornamentation that dripped from the porches and eaves. They had then been knee-deep in crates, boxes, and wallpaper, breathless at becoming master and mistress of such elegance. Now they looked settled and comfortable, and after polite preliminaries Henry and I settled down in his oak-and-leather study with drinks in crystal glasses.

"Forget the army, Parker," he told me. Through the open door I could see Mary in the drawing room, genteel leisure in a white gown, nodding over a book as the sun streamed in through the slatted windows. Children's voices drifted in from the yard. "Why not throw your lot in with me?"

I smiled. This was Flagler. Every time I told him what I was doing, he would top it. "I'm surprised, Henry," I said. "I thought the army would be a natural for you. Seize time by the forelock, you always say. Well, what else but the army are the times offering?"

Flagler smiled smugly and leveled his gaze at me. His eyes, an extraordinary lavender, were seductive and clear, and with his clean-shaven good looks he'd always struck me as a cavalry officer manqué. "The times haven't offered the army, Parker. They've offered a war. And it's war, not the army, that makes money."

He sipped his drink and I matched him. "But here," I suggested, "the two dovetail. The army may not bring money, but it will bring fame. And where fame leads, fortune follows."

He smiled condescendingly and shook his head. "Very neat. But no, no, no, Parker. Fame is public and ephemeral. But fortune," he rapped his knuckle on his polished desk-top, "that's real currency, made in the dark. The men who make money in the war won't ever see a battlefield or hear a gun."

"Assuming, of course, that making money is the point."

He stared at me as if I'd farted. "Well, of course it is, Parker. Why else are we in the game?"

28

I smiled and raised my glass. It was no use trying to convince Henry that there are realities other than financial realities. "So what's your game, Henry?"

Flagler's lavender eyes looked canny, darting at the door. In the drawing room Mary was drifting around examining her hanging plants. He leaned forward and spoke low. "It's so simple it's larcenous. There is a substance, Parker, that the army can't do without. It lies under the earth's crust, free for the taking. There are vast, untapped deposits of it throughout the country, the most accessible of them not far from here. All it takes is drilling tools, simple refineries, cheap equipment and labor, and the rest is pure profit." He rubbed his fingers together. "You see what I'm talking about?"

I saw. Rock oil, petroleum, had been known to us Indians since time began. It bubbled to the surface and floated in slicks on the ponds and rivers of northwest Pennsylvania, where the richest stream of it was now called Oil Creek. Indians used to soak it up with blankets for medicines, for paint, for fires, and the white man, when he first sniffed it out, called it "Seneca oil," because it seemed only we Seneca could stand the smell. (They pronounced it Se-NAY-ka oil, whence "snake oil.") It was more a curiosity than a commodity until recently, when a Pennsylvania experimenter named Kier learned to distill it to kerosene. Then, just two years ago, Edwin Drake sank a well into the aquifer below Oil Creek, and the stuff gushed up so much that an "Oil Rush" was on. The swamps north of Pittsburgh grew derricks where trees had failed. Flagler and a grain merchant named John Rockefeller were sniffing out the possibilities and had made several trips to the oil fields. The war, it seemed, was nudging Flagler to make his move.

"Petroleum," I said.

"Petroleum?" Flagler looked as if I'd talked Greek. "Don't be a fool, Parker. I mean salt!"

"Salt."

"Of course. Salt." Flagler shook his head at my dullness. "Petroleum's a fad. It has no commercial possibilities. But salt!" He laid his finger beside his nose. "Salt is the life blood of an army. Every ounce of meat must be salted, and an army consumes many, many ounces. And I know where to find it. Saginaw, up in the thumb of Michigan. I've made inquiries and bought property. It's only a matter of sitting tight, waiting for shortages, then pulling up stakes and moving when the time is right."

"Salt," I said. Flagler, as usual, was way ahead of me. In my naïveté, I'd assumed that oil was the business where fortunes would be made. It offered clean, cheap fuel, and its by-products, such as lubricating oil and medicines, seemed endless. With a small investment now, I thought someone with Flagler's drive could stretch a small fortune almost to infinity. Shows how little nose I had for business.

"Find something people need, use and need again!" said Flagler. "Sell lots of it and sell it cheap! Volume, Parker, not ratios, that's the way to go." He rattled on about tax-exemptions for salt, bonuses for local production in Michigan, projections of wartime demand, salt drills, evaporation kettles and a litany of technical terms that left me dazzled. "You should cast your lot with me, Parker," he said, sitting back and tapping his glass with a smug finger. "I'll make you rich. In the army, all you'll get is sick from the beef I've salted and sold you!"

Flagler looked about as if to see who was listening, leaned forward and tapped me on the knee. "I'm serious, Parker," he said in a low voice. "A small investment now will be worth a fortune later." He looked at me earnestly, his lavender eyes never leaving mine.

"An investment," I said. "You have a prospectus drawn up?"

Flagler brushed it away. "Investment, loan, call it what you will."

I smiled at him. "You haven't the capital, have you, Henry?"

Flagler looked offended. "I have some of it," he said. "More would help."

"How much more?"

Flagler cocked his head, assessing me as if calculating what he could get away with. "A thousand dollars now will make you rich after the war," he said.

I sipped whiskey and let him wait. Somehow, rich Henry Flagler was always short of the ready. Just a little loan here, a little there, I'd lent him over the years, and he'd always repaid. But never a thousand dollars.

I smiled at him and reached into my pocket for my note-case. "I'm feeling flush," I told him, and, as he virtually slavered over my moving fingers, wrote him a draft for a thousand dollars.

I blew on it and handed it to him, and he accepted with such thumps on the back that I thought I'd never escape. But I did, and spent much of the train ride to Washington City ruing my gullibility. I had no notion whether Flagler would pay me back, but it was worth almost the thousand dollars to put him in his place. Besides, I was rich from my government contract, flush with rents from my Tonawanda land and bright with my own future in the coming war. Let Henry have his thousand – I would have glory!

As soon as the train pulled into Washington City and I was able to walk in the sunshine I felt the excitement. A militia company detrained with me, assembled under the station canopy, and marched smartly off to their encampment, band playing and guidons fluttering. Up the hill the roof of the Capitol was splinted with scaffolding where its new dome was rising. I hadn't seen the building since the new House and Senate wings were unveiled, so I hiked up past daffodil fields and lilac groves to have a look. The new wings gave the once-compact Capitol a new sprawl, and it now seemed to lounge atop the hill like a Sphinx. Bullfinch's old dome looked like a fraternity beanie atop it, but the new one would give it a proper crown. Lincoln had ordered construction to continue despite the rebellion, to show the government was still in business.

I gawked at the construction tarps and timbers inside the rotunda. "Hey, Chief," said a voice.

"Mr. Brown." I turned to shake hands with George Brown, the Senate Sergeant-at-Arms. With his tight mustache and straw hat, Brownie was already a fixture around the place fifteen years ago when I arrived as an eighteen-year-old lobbyist. "Heck of a job, Brownie," I said, waving at the dust and rubble.

Brownie chuckled. "Still standin', at any rate."

"Standing and growing, like a lot of us," I said, patting my stomach.

Brownie chuckled. "Come here, lad," he said. "I'll show you around. Mind your step." He led me under the construction ropes, past buckets, barrows and piles of debris toward the Senate wing. The grand column in the foyer, behind which I used to linger and buttonhole senators, now seemed insignificant, shrouded in cloth, and the old Senate chamber itself had become just an ornate lobby. Was it possible that the Webster-Hayne debates, the Mexican War debates and the Compromise of 1850 had been fought out in this dark and cramped little space? Brownie led me down a marble hallway and through the door of the new Senate chamber, where he stood waiting for my reaction. My bag slipped from my hand. The place was full of soldiers.

"Yessir," said Brownie. "It's a barracks now. Meet the 6th Massachusetts."

Soldiers lounged everywhere, on the speaker's dais, in the aisles, the cloakrooms, and on the senators' desks. Senator Sumner's desk, where, in the old chamber, he had been caned nearly to death by Preston Brooks of South Carolina, now held a fat and snoring sergeant, his blue blouse hanging open over a hairy belly.

"They're actually not bad tenants," said Brownie. He nudged the sergeant, who opened an eye, snorted, reluctantly lowered his feet from Sumner's desk and slept again. "They chew and spit less than the senators. They've even taken over the basement and started cooking there. Fresh bread every morning. Hell on the furniture though. Senator Davis and some other Southern gentlemen's desks, we had to take them out and put them in storage or they'd have smashed them to splinters."

"Passions are running high," I noted.

"That they are," said Brownie grimly. "As you'll find soon enough. Where you headed, Chief? Time for a drink?"

Brownie kept a nice bar in his hideaway office overlooking the west terrace. Parched though I was, I declined. "I'll get some ice cream on the street," I told him. "Better stay sober for Mr. Seward."

Brownie's eyebrows went up. "Secretary Seward is it now? Come up in the world, haven't you, Chief?" He made a show of straightening my lapels and brushing dust away. "That's all right, so has Seward. Don't let him cow you, lad. He still pisses in the same pot."

I left George Brown, hefted my bag, and walked down Pennsylvania Avenue. I had spent much time in Washington over the past fifteen years but I had never, even during the Mexican War, seen so much urgency, bustle and military. Tent cities billowed on the Mall and on every vacant lot, and the whole place felt like a county fair. Pennsylvania Avenue blossomed like a carnival, with banners and bunting on all the shops and no shortage of customers. Pedestrians strolled, the women in new flowered hats. Ice cream shops and outdoor cafes did a brisk business, while in backstairs streets and alleys, "tobacco shops" were open. They offered tobacco out front for anyone who asked, but their main commodity was girls-by-the-hour, who leaned provocatively out of second-story windows. I checked my watch. No time now. Perhaps later, to celebrate the commission Seward would surely give me. The doors of Willard's and Gadsby's hotels swung with brisk comings and goings, and important-looking men had important-sounding talks in the lobbies and bars. Troops streamed in and out of the White House itself. Behind the White House rose the truncated pyramid that would one day be the Washington Monument. Construction winches with long ropes gangled from its innards.

I was sweating when I reached the State Department building just east of the White House. Security was tight, but I knew my way in and eased down to the basement washroom, where I splashed water on my face and straightened my tie. In the mirror I caught my mouth twisted in a smirk. "Here we go again," said my resigned face back at me. I had spent hours in that washroom over the years, as well as in other washrooms around the capital, in waiting-rooms, lobbies, and shoe-shine parlors, always waiting for something to happen, always powerless to *make* anything happen. I had sat in chairs and on benches, leaned against walls and pillars, cadged newspapers and tobacco and gossip from fellow lobby-sitters, always alert for those few magic moments when an inner door would swing open, a hand would beckon, and my name would be called. For days and months I had stood and sat, washed my face and straightened my tie, watching my youth trickle away as I fought for the Seneca's treaties and our rights to our remaining acres of homeland. Much of the fight had gone on right here in the State Department building, though more in the War Department building across the way, a fitting place for my bureaucratic blooding, since Indian affairs, until recently, fell tellingly under the Department of War.

The new secretary of state, William Seward, had just moved in, and I didn't have to wait today. I had an actual appointment. I was Grand Sachem of the Iroquois Nation, with official diplomatic standing, and as long as we maintained the fiction that the Iroquois were a "nation," the secretary of state was bound to see me. Whether he would actually listen remained to be seen, but I knew Seward from his days as New York governor and senator. In both offices he had been, if not our friend, at least not our enemy, which was all we asked from him as our land case wound through the courts. The reform crowd in New York had been our allies, disinclined to savage the Indian while at the same time arguing for Negro emancipation, and Seward had found it politic to speak mildly in our favor. I had always found him a bland and easy hypocrite, like the best of his breed, an amiable patrician, insulated by wealth from life's hard facts, but with a sympathetic ear and a worthy sense of *noblesse oblige*.

The State Department anterooms were crowded with an even larger than usual crush of office-seekers. A new administration combined with the new war to lure the feeder-fish in spring numbers. But I was ushered with encouraging dispatch into Seward's office, which had gilt damask wallpaper with *trompe l'oeuil* wainscoting woven into the fabric and green carpeting on which Seward's oak desk floated like a prairie schooner.

"Parker," said Seward gravely. He came from behind his desk, clasped his bony hand around mine, clapped me on the shoulder, looked at me down his toucan-beak of a nose and sat us down democratically in matching wing chairs by the fireplace. "How are things on the Tonawanda?"

I told him I was on my way there, and as far as I knew things were fine, but I was here on other business and opened my portfolio.

Seward frowned. "I understood this was an official call."

"Yes, sir," I said. "As official as can be. As you know, I am a government engineer, with military training. I want to offer my services to the country." I drew from my portfolio a sheaf of recommendations from all over.

Seward, still frowning, barely glanced at a few as I pressed my case. When I took a breath, he raised a hand. "I'm familiar with your qualifications, Parker. But let me understand this. Are you offering your services *on behalf of* the Iroquois nation?"

"Why no," I said, surprised. "I'm just offering me. I'm a free agent. My office with the Iroquois is largely . . ."

"Ceremonial, I know." Seward waved a hand. "But it is an office nonetheless. Tell me this. Good heavens, I've never thought of it before. Do you imagine that other Indians will want to follow you into the army?"

"I have no idea," I said, nonplused at the tack Seward was taking. "Those who are qualified and believe in the cause, I suppose will answer the president's call. As to the others. . ." I shrugged. I had no brief to speak for other Indians.

"Lord, Lord." Seward shook his massive head. "I'd never envisioned this. It's terrifying. Imagine a whole Indian regiment, a whole Indian brigade, going into battle. It's too bizarre! Entirely too bizarre!"

I tried to call him back from whatever picture his mind was forming. "Mr. Secretary, I'm sure it won't come to that. And even if it should, that's not why I'm here." I indicated the papers dangling from his limp hand. "I'm here as an engineer looking for a commission. There are bridges and roads to be built, barracks to be constructed. That I'm an Indian is of no consequence. That I'm an engineer, and prepared to go to work, is."

Seward shook his head, looking at the ashes in the fireplace. "I don't know what we're coming to, Parker," he said sadly. "It's one thing after another. This whole sorry business started out as a quarrel between gentlemen. Gentlemen of the north and gentlemen of the south. New York, New England, Virginia. The people who founded this country. Left to our own, we'd have cleared it up. Now what do we have? This new president, a foreigner from the western frontier, unversed, no feel for our heritage. Gangling, rawboned men with law books and bibles. And now a regiment of Indians sweeping down from Niagara wanting their own part in it."

"I'm not proposing. . ." I reminded him, but he shook me off and stood, handing my papers back to me.

"I know you're not, Parker, but it will come to that." He put his hands in his pockets and walked to his desk, leaning back against it, looking at the floor. "A quarrel among gentlemen must not turn into a brawl between frontiersman and Indians. And as long as I have something to say about it, it won't. Our southern brethren are dismayed enough as it is. If it gets bruited about that savages are being turned loose on them they will never return." He made a fist in front of his face, as if he had the whole situation in his hand. "If I can contain this thing, Parker, it will be very short. We'll make up as we always have, and then there will be plenty of peacetime work for all. In the meantime . . ." He waved his hand in a vague circle.

I stood, taking back the papers he handed me and stuffing them into my portfolio. "What do you recommend I do, Mr. Secretary?"

"Recommend? It's not my place to. . ." He shrugged. "Go home to your farm. Wait it out. Let the white men settle their differences and leave the Indians alone for once. I'll find work for you when it's over." He tipped me a confidential wink as if I was a member of the old boys' club.

"But I have no farm," I protested. "I mean, I do, but I've never farmed it. I know nothing about farming. I'm an engineer." Seward was no longer listening. He put his lordly arm on my shoulder and escorted me smiling to the door. I kept jabbering, looking to drive a wedge in, but the meeting was over and I'd lost. I was about to protest that there was a scruffy little soldier in Galena who didn't think it would be a short war but stopped myself. The last thing Seward needed was yet another unschooled western ruffian ruffling his smooth eastern machine. Before I knew it I was out of the room, Seward was blandly shaking my protesting hand and wishing me well, then the door closed in my face.

I stood, dazed and blinking, in front of the double oak doors, my useless portfolio in my hand. To my left and right, flanking the entrance, two secretaries sat in black suits at identical desks, scratching their pens and ignoring me. In the far corner, wedged between two file cabinets and almost hidden from view, was a third desk. I heard a "Pssst!" from over there and saw the occupant crooking his finger at me.

"Hello, Quentin," I said, walking over to him. Quentin Winslow was a veteran bureaucrat, who had arrived in Washington during Polk's term, just before I did, and had managed to survive five changes of administration. "Always take the third desk, Parker," he once murmured to me. "When the new broom comes in it sweeps away the first two, but the third desk, the one in the corner, is always safe." He looked the same as he always did. Maybe the blond hair combed straight across his scalp was a little thinner, maybe the soft, cleft chin was a little softer, the purse of his lips a little sourer, but it was the same Quentin.

He patted his soft fingers on his desk blotter to warn me to talk quietly. "Parker," he murmured. "What news?"

"Nothing good." He nodded for me to sit on the corner of his desk, and as I did so he adjusted his chair slightly so that I blocked the other secretaries' view of him. "I'm fishing for a job and getting no bites."

Quentin nodded as I reviewed my interview with Seward, his small pink-rimmed eyes now and then meeting mine but mostly darting here and there, alert for eavesdroppers.

"Yes," he said quietly when I finished. His lips barely moved. "Our new secretary has grand visions. He thinks he should have been president. Thinks he *is* president, in fact, and Mr. Lincoln will be a puppet." He sighed. "They never learn, Parker. They always think a new president will be their tool. Until he actually *does* something. Then they find they're valets. They have to hold the president's coat just like the rest of us."

"And what is Mr. Seward's grand design?"

Quentin leaned forward and looked past me. "Mexico," he whispered. "Cuba. San Domingo. Some foreign adventure that he can sell to the South. Unite the two regions for a big foreign campaign in which their differences will be forgotten. A crusade. Drums and bugles. Flags and trumpets." His soft hands fluttered.

"What do you think?"

Quentin pursed his lips and moved his head an inch one way, an inch the other. "Flummery. Persiflage. We have an army here now. Shots have been fired in western Virginia, in Baltimore, in Alexandria. There's no going back. The War Department's already putting out bids for clothing and machinery." He licked his thumb and paged through some papers. "Shoes from Lynn, Massachusetts. Tinned milk from Borden's in Connecticut. Canned oysters, crab and fish from Baltimore. Corn, salt." I thought of Henry Flagler's salt mines. Quentin squared the papers and looked up at me. "Once the bureaucracy is involved, and it is, there's no turning it back. The war is the *status quo*. We'll defend it with all the inertia we've got."

"What do you think I should do?"

"Wait," said Quentin, raising his thin shoulders slightly. "But not for the reason the secretary says. It will be a long war and there will be room for all. It's in a lot of people's interest to keep the war going. But at first," again he looked past me for prying eyes, "your being an Indian works against you."

"I'm not applying as an Indian, I'm applying as an engineer!" I protested, too loudly for Quentin, who leaned forward and patted his palm at me.

"Hs-s-s-t!" He settled back in his chair and toyed with a pencil. "You see, Parker, we do need officers. God knows there aren't enough in the regular army. But the officers will be appointed not for their qualifications but for their influence. Every mayor and county commissioner, every alderman and assemblyman, every selectman and leather measurer wants a commission. They want war records. What they get and how soon they get it will depend on how they stand with the government. Votes, Parker. How many votes can you deliver to the man that gets you a commission?"

"None, of course," I admitted. Indians, not being citizens, don't vote. I had made the mistake of thinking that, in this emergency, appointments would be made on merit. Clearly, it would take more than a mere rebellion to change the government's ways. "So I'm out for the duration?"

Quentin frowned. "Perhaps not. If the thing lasts long enough it will chew up all the politicians, and they'll need actual professionals to finish it. But for the moment, it's Christmas time in patronage city, and the plummy tree holds nothing for you, Parker. Go home. I'll keep you informed."

"There's another possibility," I said. I told him that there was a soldier out west who also thought it would be a long war. Maybe I should head back and sign up with him.

"Grant?" said Quentin. He squinted and searched his mental files. "Oh," he said, startled, as the card popped up. "No. Grant's a drunk. He'll go nowhere." So much for Grant. "No, stay in the east, Parker. Send letters, petitions. Keep the paper flowing, across my desk especially." He tapped his blotter.

"Shall I write to you directly?" I asked, baiting him.

Quentin gasped, as I knew he would. "Good God, no!" he hissed. "Never use my name!" He had the bureaucrat's horror of his name appearing on anything. "Write to the secretary at least once a month. I'll keep tabs. What the secretary sees, I see. When things open up, we'll get you a post. Meanwhile. . ." He rolled his hand and shrugged.

I trudged down the steps of the State Department, shaking my fist in passing at Seward's brick town house across the way in Lafayette Square. Four years later, simultaneously with Lincoln's assassination, Lewis Powell would storm up the stairs of that house and nearly slaughter Seward in his bed – not what my feeble fist-shake hoped for. I fretted and stewed my way north by train to New York, then to Albany and west on the slow boat out the Erie Canal to Tonawanda. It was as ironic as could be. Here was a war to end slavery, fought, as Lincoln would declare at Gettysburg, for the proposition that all men are created equal, and I, though American born and bred, couldn't join up for the odd reason that my ancestors were ancient here when everyone else's ancestors started arriving.

And there was a deeper irony. The war was about the union of the states, a concept, so hard for some Americans, that no Iroquois would have trouble with. The idea of little sovereign states riding within the great sovereignty of the nation is something we understand from the cradle, when we're taught the legend of the Longhouse and the origin of the League of the Iroquois.

My grandfather would tell the tale, sitting by our fireside, reciting it for assembled visitors. "The six nations that comprise the Iroquois League were once, like the states that comprise the union, separate autonomies, each with its own boundaries, dividing New York State from the Hudson to the Niagara. The Mohawk, Tuscarora, Onondaga, Oneida, Cayuga and Seneca were happy as separate tribes, hunting, fishing, cultivating our own lands, warring with each other. It was the arrival of the white man, the

French, then the Dutch, then the English with their industry and firepower, that drove us together in a league for the same reason the thirteen colonies united – divided we'd perish.

"Envision," my grandfather would say, stretching his arms out. "A great Longhouse with many families under one roof. Each family has its entrance, its skin walls closing it off from other families, its own fire at the center. They can come and go as they please, have great or little commerce with their neighbors. All live under one common law. A family, if it chooses, can move away, join another Longhouse, or move to the woods, build a tepee and live alone. But the one thing no family can do when it leaves is *take its own part of the Longhouse with it!*" And my grandfather would shake both fists and fold his arms, while others nodded and muttered "Heh" to each other.

The Iroquois Longhouse embraced all of New York State, its roof beam the ridge of mountains, its eastern door the Hudson and its western the Great Lakes, with each of the six nations assigned a strip of territory among the lakes and rivers of the interior. When I introduced myself to young Fred Grant I had used my name as Grand Sachem of the Six Nations – Do-ne-ho-ga-wa, or "Keeper of the Western Door." The Seneca are the westernmost of the Iroquois nations. It's the western door, the one to the outside world, that I'm doorman of, as the Mohawks, to the east, are keepers of the eastern door.

It's no great a leap to picture the whole United States as a Longhouse. Your Founding Fathers did just that when they used our Iroquois League as a model for their Philadelphia Constitution. For the south to lop off its portion of the roof and walls was to destroy the structure itself.

Much good this knowledge did me, as I rode the rails and rivers back to Tonawanda, the one place on earth I didn't want to go, the place I'd fought to get out of since I was a boy but kept bouncing back to like a misaddressed letter. Tonawanda was quicksand; the harder I struggled to get out the deeper I sank.

Chapter IV

THE CARPENTER ENCOURAGETH THE GOLDSMITH

Tonawanda, NY 1828-43

I CAN SEE MY GRANDFATHER NOW, RISING FROM HIS CHAIR by the fire in my parents' home. Jimmy Johnson was his English name, but in Seneca we called him So-se-ha-wa. My brother, sister and I would huddle together at the top of the stairs, hoping nobody would see us. "The Iroquois once ruled from Canada to the Carolinas, from the ocean to Illinois. Then the white man came and his settlements first chipped at us, then logged us, lopping limbs, tearing out roots until now we are confined to these few pockets in western New York and Canada." The old man's voice coursed like a river through the room, and visitors, both Indian and white, fell silent, each one certain that he spoke to him alone.

"Our demise as a nation, which was probably inevitable from the landing of Columbus, was hastened in the last century by our picking the losing side in every white man's conflict." People nodded and shook their heads. "We sided with the French against the British, with the British against the Americans, until finally we were a defeated nation with no allies and only the charity of the victors. Much charity might we expect! During the Revolution the Americans, harassed by Iroquois raids, decided, in their whole-hearted way, to have done with us for once and all. In 1779 General Washington, the Destroyer of Lands, sent General Town-Burner

John Sullivan and his four thousand on a swath that cut us to pieces, torched our villages, destroyed our orchards, turned corn and grain to ashes, killed hundreds, starved hundreds and drove the rest of us to huddle with the British at Fort Niagara. After the war we trickled back to find our lands scorched and blighted, and of that we were allowed only a small portion, the Seneca restricted to reservations on four rivers around Buffalo – the Allegheny, Cattaraugus, Buffalo Creek and our own Tonawanda."

Walking among the guests, holding his shawl to his shoulders, my grandfather continued. "Along the Tonawanda we languished between survival and extinction while the new nation puzzled out what to do with us. Then a great orator arose, Red Jacket, who in 1792 went to the white man's capital at Philadelphia and smoked the pipe with Washington and received from the Destroyer of Lands a paper declaring that thenceforth the Americans and the Iroquois would live in peace, the Iroquois to keep their remaining lands forever. We sealed the pact in blood in 1812, when finally, we picked the winner, joining the American General Winfield Scott in his battles around the Niagara River. Many of us," he pointed out my father, uncles and other veterans, "saw service with Scott, and the Six Nations emerged victorious and secure, finally at peace with their triumphant host, the United States of America, who had entered the Longhouse uninvited and hogged most of the meal." To a chorus of murmured "Heh's" my grandfather would sit down.

Red Jacket was my grandfather's brother, my great-uncle. He, with the rest of my family, settled on the Tonawanda reservation, astride Tonawanda Creek, a stream with many falls and rapids that enters the Niagara River just above Buffalo and joins the larger stream to rush from Lake Erie, over the great falls of Niagara, down to Lake Ontario. It's fertile land for farming, for timber, and for children, and it was there in 1828 that I was born.

"When you were a baby in my belly," my mother would say, tickling my own baby belly while I giggled and squirmed, "I had a powerful dream. I was standing in the streets of Buffalo. It was snowing, and as I reached to brush the flakes from my hair, the skies opened up as if a giant hand had swept the clouds aside, and what did I see?"

"A rainbow!" I'd shout.

"That's right. A great, broken rainbow, one foot of the arch resting here on the Tonawanda and the other far away on the little shops of the little streets of Buffalo. The rainbow brightened the land from horizon to horizon for as long as I could count to ten, then vanished as quickly as it had come, and the dream vanished with it."

"And what did you do?"

"In the morning, I rushed to the council house, where our dream-man lived, and do you know what he told me?"

"Yes!" I would cry.

"What?" she asked. "What was the dream?"

"*On-din-nonk*," I would carefully pronounce.

"That's right. A prophecy dream. A dream that revealed the desire of my soul for the baby that was in my soul. And what was that desire?"

I would recite for her what the dream-man said. "I will live with one foot in the white world and one in the Indian world," I'd solemnly lisp, as my mother nodded solemnly back. "I will be warrior and peacemaker to both. I will live among white men but never forsake my tribe."

"And?"

"My name will reach from east to west, north to south, as great among my Indian family as among the whites," I'd tell her, and she'd hug me proudly and feed me maple sugar.

It was a good time for any Iroquois mother to dream hopeful dreams for the future of her child or for any Indian, child or no. White civilization was inching west, then further west, then just a little bit further, please, and axes rang in our forests. Andrew Jackson, Sharp Knife, was the whites' new president, who had slaughtered Seminole and Creek, uprooted Cherokee, Chickasaw and Choctaw, who had come to office pledged to move *all* Indians over the hills and waters and west to oblivion. Even as I gurgled and burbled my baby dreams, entire nations of woodland Indians were stripped of their ancient homes in Georgia, Alabama and Mississippi and "removed" beyond the Missouri, forest-dwellers condemned to the desolate plains.

Turnpikes crossed the mountains from Baltimore to Illinois. Steamboats plied the Hudson, the Ohio and the Mississippi. My mother had seen the Erie Canal grow from a dream, to a ditch, to a deluge. "The largest canal in the world," boasted a booster, stringing out superlatives like Henry Flagler. "Built in the least time with the least experience for the least money and to the greatest public benefit." Buffalo rose from a sleepy outpost to an entrepot of commerce and emigration, a turnstile on the road from New England to the Great Lakes and the farmlands of the west, where steel plows were being forged to break the plains that had lain untilled forever.

The first railroad was chartered in New York State in 1832, the Mohawk and Hudson line from Albany to Schenectady, the first of many that would leap, track on track, to our back yard. There was a constant flow of white men past my mother's door, and she knew that soon they wouldn't be flowing past, they'd be standing there telling her to move. There were only two options for an Indian then – assimilation or annihilation. So when my mother had the dream-man read my future, she was looking not only at cloud-paintings in the sky but at the writing on the wall.

It was a reflection not only of the fashion but of the temper of the times that I, like my grandfather and most other Indians, received two names, one Indian and one American, passports to two different countries. My Indian name was Ha-so-no-an-da, or "Leading Name," another *on-din-nonk* of my mother's, the embodiment of her desire to keep me striving for the limelight. My American name was Ely S. Parker, Parker being a name we'd taken from an English soldier we'd captured in the French war. These two names would follow me all my life, Janus masks, one looking inward and one outward, one forward and one back, the two occasionally catching a mutual glimpse and staring at each other like an ape startled by its reflection.

Our house was a social center for Indians from our reservation and from afar and also for traveling white men. Twenty people at dinner wasn't uncommon, and they'd stay and talk into the night then roll up in their blankets against the walls and be gone when we tiptoed down in the morning. They recited the song of Ha-yo-went-ha, Longfellow's Hiawatha, of how the Iroquois League was founded, how Da-ga-no-we-da uprooted a tree and held it aloft for the tribes to bury their weapons in the hole. They told of Heno, god of thunder, who lived behind the water-curtain at Niagara, who killed a great serpent ravaging the crops along Cayuga Creek, and how the serpent floated down the river and lodged from bank to bank, damming the waters to make Horseshoe Falls. Other voices sang a softer strain, the *Gai-wi-io*, the "good word" of Handsome Lake, the prophet whose wisdom and new religion brought us back from the brink of extinction after your Revolution. We heard of the prophet's journey through the cloud-realm like Ulysses through the underworld, whence he fetched our thou-shalt-nots: the evils of drink, of gambling, of intra-tribal strife, of yielding to the vices that were recreation for the white man but doom for the Indian.

But two big words dominated the adults' fireside talks, and so much a part of my nights did they become that I wouldn't be surprised if the first words I spoke were "treaty" and "land."

In the *Gai-wi-io* of Handsome Lake, the worst sin was to sell Indian lands – worse even than drink and gambling. On his trip on the sky-road, the prophet met an Indian condemned forever like Sisyphus. From a pile of sand, he was to remove one grain at a time and carry it away, then return for another, and another, and another, and yet the pile remained undiminished, his labor unslackened, through eternity. This was the punishment for selling land.

Drinking went hand in hand with selling land. As I lay with my ear to the floor, speculators swarmed Tonawanda, offering cash to Indians who would take a drink, "touch the pen" and yield up land. Inevitably, tragedy struck. One day the Ogden Land Company arrived at the door and, like the landlord in the melodrama, reached into its coat and flourished a "treaty" signed by various "chiefs" exchanging the entire Tonawanda reservation for a cash payment and a tract of equal size in Kansas. It was illegal of course. We knew the "chiefs" were renegades who had called themselves chiefs in order to get drunk and get paid. Any treaty required the unanimous consent of the Six Nations, and the Ogdens hadn't got it. But they had got something more important. They had got the U.S. Senate to ratify the treaty, and when they presented it to our council it was a *fait accompli*: by 1843, it dictated, when I would be fifteen years old, the Tonawanda Seneca would have to uproot and follow the other eastern tribes west.

I grew up in the shadow of this treaty. Despite our vehement objections, despite the intervention of Quakers and other groups, it remained undented law. All of my childhood, as I first lay listening on the floor, then hunkered in the chimney corner, then sat at the fringes of the adult circle, the treaty case went on, the *Jarndyce and Jarndyce* of a generation of Seneca. Motions got filed, affidavits got sworn and impugned, depositions taken, adjournments granted, courts held hearings, appeals got made to presidents and congressmen, petitions were taken under advisement, small flames of hope kindled in lower courts to be snuffed out by higher courts, until, with all appeals seemingly exhausted, our Tonawanda band settled into demoralized torpor. Fields went unplowed, orchards untended, houses unrepaired, fences and stone walls crumbled and despair spread like fever.

I was a young, active boy, however. I didn't spend all my growing-up time gnawing my innards over a treaty I didn't understand and whose effects were so far in the future. I just grew up, like all boys, a creature of yard and barn, of fields, forests and streams. Eventually they corralled me, slicked me down, and sent me to the reservation Baptist school, where, as Grant would say about his own schooling, I repeated "A noun is the name of a thing" until I came to believe it. We learned English, or thought we did, but it was two steps forward and one step back. The English we mouthed every morning got lost in the Seneca we chattered the rest of the day, and a winter's worth of irregular verbs couldn't survive an Indian summer. Still, I was pretty good at it (I got A's at any rate) and fancied myself quite bilingual, well on my way to fulfilling my mother's *on-din-nonk* dream of dual citizenship, until an event that soured me, forever I thought, on the white man's ways.

I was eleven years old. It was a Sunday, and at our Baptist church we had a guest minister, who spoke no Seneca. Ned Beaton, our usual translator, failed to appear, and there was confusion and scurrying around as our family arrived at church. We were late, and the church was full, so chairs got hastily arranged for us in front of the regular benches, right under the pulpit and the gaze of the minister. He, a Dr. King from Rochester, had dined at my mother's table the previous night, and I had showed off my English in a recitation of perhaps one too many memorized poems. Now Dr. King looked down at our family group and said to my father, "Mr. Parker, your son Ely speaks very good English. Perhaps he could translate for me."

If I could have crawled under the chair I would have. But sitting there beneath the pulpit, the minister's charitable eyes on me, his hand beckoning, and the entire tribe murmuring behind me, I was cut off. So I stood up, showing all the confidence I could above my quaking knees, and climbed the three steps to stand beside Dr. King. I hadn't got my growth yet, so my chin barely reached the pulpit, and Dr. King put his hand on my shoulder and gently urged me to the side, where all could see me. He kept his hand there, in what I'm sure he intended as reassurance, during the ordeal that followed.

"The words are very simple," he told me. "Even when Our Lord spoke of the deepest matters, His words were those of a child."

That was easy enough, and I translated into Seneca, speaking loud and clear. My voice came out a childish squeak in the crowded church. It wasn't a very big building – it was our one-room schoolhouse on weekdays, where I shrilled my lessons from deskside without a tremor – but today, from up on the platform, with so many people, it seemed to enlarge to the vasty depths of a cathedral. How could my piping little voice be heard in such a cavern? The congregation leaned forward in hushed expectancy.

"My text today," said Dr. King, his voice vibrating through the hand that rested on my shoulder, "is 'The Carpenter Encourageth the Goldsmith.'"

That too was easy. Words for crafts are plentiful in Seneca, and I felt my voice gain confidence as I spoke. The sermon, unfolding leaf by leaf, was a hymn to humility, the gravamen of which was that it is not the approval of one's betters that one should seek, but praise from the humble. After stating his theme and repeating it several ways, like restating a symphonic motif, Dr. King spun it out in variations, returning each time through avenues and byways to the dominant strain, "The Carpenter Encourageth the Goldsmith."

He chose examples from the Bible, of the slave who praised Daniel's singing and won his freedom. From legend, of the spider who encouraged Robert the Bruce to "try, try again." From history, of the soldier with the bloody feet at Valley Forge who gave Washington courage. I knew these stories from school and could paraphrase from memory when the going got rough, as it often did. Dr. King was using lots of words I didn't understand. But I plowed bravely on. It even got so that when he reached the appropriate point in the story, all he had to do was squeeze my shoulder, and without him saying it in English, I'd sing out in Seneca, "The carpenter encourageth the goldsmith." The congregation got into it and chorused "Nyoh!" – it shall be done, our Seneca "Amen" – each time I hit the refrain. My sister's girlfriends gazed admiringly.

Everything was going fine, and my chest was swelling fit to burst, when Dr. King, growing perhaps too confident from my success and swept up in his own eloquence, sailed off into dangerous waters. I made brave to follow, my sails full of wind and self-assurance, but with no charts for the shoals below the placid surface. "When I was a young divinity graduate, right out of seminary," he said, and I stumbled a little on "divinity graduate," smacked my head into "seminary," and stopped dead.

"When I was an, um . . . a *boy*," I stammered, finding a vague synonym, "right out of the, um . . ." I bit my lip and looked up at Dr. King for help. He smiled benignly, unaware of my plight, and gave my shoulder a squeeze. What on earth did "seminary" mean? "I stepped out of the *cemetery*," I said with some confidence and saw uncertain glances pass among the crowd.

"My first assignment was to a very small parish in the mountains," he said.

I didn't get all of that either, and I bit my lip and frowned. People leaned forward. I had to say *something*. "I was sent to the mountains to *perish*," I tried, realizing as the words left my mouth that they couldn't be right, but hoping they'd help me stall. My head began to throb and sweat broke out on my brow. My mother, seated just down the steps in front of me, twisted her shawl.

Dr. King went blandly on, oblivious to the disaster simmering beside him. "When the day came for my first sermon," he said, "I approached it with butterflies in my stomach, for I knew that in addition to my new congregation, who would be watching for any mistakes, there would also be several of my classmates, as well as my theological tutor from the seminary, who always traveled abroad to hear his charges make their maiden speech."

This was beyond me. I screwed up my face and tried to concentrate. My mouth was dry and my temples pounded as I reviewed the damage. So far I had a boy walking out of a cemetery and being sent to the mountains to die. "When I got up to speak," I said hesitantly. I looked up at Dr. King. As he nodded encouragement, the light flashed off his glasses and made his eyes disappear, so he looked like a grinning, nodding, eyeless monster. What had he said next? Something about "butterflies." Or maybe it was moths.

"A plague of moths descended," I said, and my sister Carrie hid her face in her hands and giggled so hard she shook.

I hurried on. "And my new congregation was full of my classmates," I said. What else had he said? Something about a theological tooter, a maiden speech, and somebody's charges. "So when God's trumpet blew, all the maidens spoke at once in different tongues and were blown to bits by gunpowder," I concluded.

The church was an uproar of confused delight. My family's and my neighbors' faces danced before my eyes, large, then small, and my ears roared with Dr. King's words as he continued to boom forth.

"And when my sermon was finished," he said, "my classmates praised me for my wit. My teacher praised me for my erudition. But I was still not satisfied. And then an old woman, who had waited patiently for the others to depart, came up to me, shyly shook my hand, and said, 'Dr. King, I've heard sermons for many years, and that was one of the best.' And that, my friends, was the praise I'd been waiting for."

Those words, finally, were simple enough for me to get right. I translated them with relief, like a shipwreck victim clinging to a spar. But it was only a dying man's last flash of lucidity. Dr. King's hand squeezed my shoulder, the cue for me to open my mouth and deliver the moral which would end my agony, "The carpenter encourageth the goldsmith." But his hand was made of lead, pressing me down, the room went bright, then red, then black, and the last words of Dr. King's sermon remain untranslated to this day, as his Indian translator fainted and dropped to the floor.

I stayed upstairs all afternoon, brooding and inaccessible. At dinner, I marched downstairs and stood behind my chair.

"Ely," said my mother pleasantly. "Sit down. *E-won-de-gah-ga* – eat something. You must be hungry."

"Don't call me Ely," I said. "My name is Ha-sa-no-an-da. I don't want to be a white man. I want to be an Indian. I want to go away to Canada and learn to be an Indian and never speak English again as long as I live."

There was a large Iroquois settlement – larger than ours – on the Grand River in Ontario, about a week on foot from Tonawanda. Since the Iroquois had fought on their side in the American Revolution the British in Canada were more charitable to us than the United States. It was to this camp that I wanted to go, and my parents let me. With Tonawanda in disarray and despair over the treaty and the deadline for our diaspora by the Ogden Company fixed in stone, everybody's future had become *sauve qui peut*.

"It's only important that you keep learning," said my father. "*What* you learn doesn't matter." I set off for Grand River and the woods forever.

As I changed my name and traveled west in 1839, a tanner's son from Georgetown, Ohio was changing his own name and traveling east.

About to set out for his first year at West Point, Hiram Ulysses Grant was staring at new luggage his parents had given him, embossed with his initials, "HUG." He shook his head, hefted the bag, and hauled it back for retooling. "Hug Grant" was no way to present himself. People always called him Ulysses anyway, or Ulyss for short. It was simple to reverse the initials, and so he registered at West Point as Ulysses Hiram Grant. But the army being the army, even that wouldn't do. His name had arrived on the plebe register as Ulysses *Simpson* Grant, his mother's maiden name tossed in, so Grant shrugged the first of many shrugs he'd shrug in the army and became U.S. Grant, inevitably "Uncle Sam" to his classmates, and plain old Sam Grant by graduation.

As Grant moved east with his new name by riverboat and train, I hiked off west with mine to Canada. There I spent two happy years becoming as much of an Indian as I could. The camp along the Grand River was a contrast to demoralized Tonawanda. All the old traditions were alive there in a new Longhouse with a new council fire and a forward-looking spirit. We hunted, we fished, we learned to find deer hoofprints even among dry leaves, to stalk them even in brittle underbrush without a sound. We floated our canoes like feathers on the waves of stormy lakes and zipped down rapids like an arrow. We read the surface of the water to see its depth, its warmth, its cold, its pockets of fish and patches of danger. We learned to kill a bear, to eat his flesh, to make knives and needles of his bones and sleep with his skin as a robe. We ate his brains for strength, as we ate the fox's brains for cunning, the trout's for stealth, the serpent's for guile.

We learned about ourselves as well, the different pulses that beat in us to make us individuals. I found two things I hadn't known before. One was that I have "perfect north" the way some people have perfect pitch. They could blindfold me, spin me around, take me to strange woods on starless nights, and I could point north. It's more than which side of the trees the moss grows on, more than the pole star, more than the sun and the moon and the shadows. It's something that tickles my hair like a magnet and pulls me round right. The other thing I could do without practice was a bee-line. Where men naturally walk a curving path when there's no road, my path was always straight. Lost people walk in circles – they really do – lost Indians too. But if you drop me in the woods and point – just once – toward home, I can get there. These faculties stood me well in the war. There's nothing like a man with north in his noddle to get you through the

Wilderness amid the smoke and flame. And nothing like a man with a bee-line in his brain for laying down a trench-line in the dark.

But even in Canada white civilization encroached. Commerce between us and them was part of survival. One of my jobs, when I was not in the woods, was driving horses and mules between the reservation and the military posts at London and Hamilton, where, despite my resolve to have nothing to do with white men, I mingled with soldiers and other white citizens. I hovered on the fringes of their horse-trading at the corrals, listening, understanding words here and there, as curious about them as they were oblivious to me. To the white man an Indian barely had substance. He might as well have been a dog or a cat – less than that, since dogs and cats get attention as pets. Indians might as well have been birds or squirrels, just part of the landscape, for all they noticed us. It's a good thing we're tough or, like the birds and squirrels, we might have got baked in pies.

After two years on Grand River, I was asked to drive some horses to the army post at Hamilton, along with two English officers. They were Lieutenant "Bully" Reardon, as mean as his name, a barrel-chested, dark-browed brute who, if not for the army, would, I suppose, have been in the prison-galleys, and another lieutenant named Smith, a lean, mean fellow with a face like he sucked lemons.

Trouble started our first day. Smith and Reardon were riding in front, with me following and the horses strung out on a rope behind us. We had gone about two hours from camp when Reardon, knowing I spoke some English, asked Smith, loud enough for me to hear, if he'd brought the circle-expander.

Riding behind them, I couldn't see their faces, but a smile must have flickered Smith's puckered lips. "The circle-expander," said he. "No, Bully, I don't believe I did." He turned in his saddle to make sure I was listening. "You sure it's not in your saddlebags?"

Bully made a show of searching his saddlebags and patting his pockets. "No, Smith," he said. "I was sure McMillan said you had it."

Smith shook his head. John McMillan was the Indian hostler whose horses we were driving. Bully looked back at me. "No, come to think of it," he said. "I believe McMillan said Hey-you-wanna back here had it. Hey-you!" he shouted.

I pointed to my chest. I was thirteen and gangly, riding in the dusty heat bare-chested and bony with just my buckskin trousers on.

"Yeah, you. Whatsa matter? Cat got your tongue?"

I shook my head. It was an expression I didn't know. "Cat?" I said.

"Never mind," said Bully, motioning me to ride up beside him. With a sidelong glance at Smith he asked me, very slowly and seriously. "McMillan. He-give-you-circle-expander?"

I shook my head again. "Circle expander?"

Bully spat and growled. "Well, damn it all," he said. "These Injuns have no brains. How are we supposed to tether these horses without a circle-expander?"

Smith pursed his lips, exasperated.

"Well, there's nothing for it," said Bully. "Hey-you here will just have to go back to McMillan and get one."

I pointed to my chest again. "Yes you!" roared Bully, and my pony shied. Bully grabbed the reins and put his face close to mine. "You-go-McMillan," he said between his teeth. "Get-circle-expander. Then-catch-up. Ride-like-hell!" He gave my pony a slap on the flank that made him rear up and almost throw me.

I rode back as fast as I could to McMillan's stable, pulled up in the yard and dashed into the barn, where John McMillan was currying a gray. "What are you doing here?" he asked me in Seneca.

"They sent me back," I said, out of breath. "They said I forgot the circle-expander."

Well, McMillan had a good laugh over that, and so did everyone else he insisted on telling it to while I waited for my pony to water and catch its breath. Humiliated, I pounded the road back to catch up with the Englishmen and the string of horses, which by now I was sure they'd stolen, leaving me to pay for. But they hadn't. I found them not far from where I left them, lying under a tree picking their teeth with their knives while the horses grazed and drank from a nearby stream.

"Well, it's about time," said Bully, rising and brushing crumbs from his shirt. "Let's get moving."

"No circle-expander," I said, my face stinging with rage. I was hot and breathless, covered with dust and streaked with sweat. I ached for the shade and the water.

"What's that?" said Bully. "Oh, yes. The circle-expander. Well, we decided we didn't need it after all. You probably don't know how to use one anyway, do you?"

I had no English to express my anger and humiliation. "No circle-expander!" I said again, louder.

"No need to shout, Hey-you," said Smith, leading the horses around. "No circle-expander. Well, we'll just have to get along without it. Let's move."

There were chicken bones and apple cores on the ground under the tree. "Hungry," I said, pointing to my stomach.

"Hungry?" said Bully, swinging himself into the saddle. "Oh, no. Thank you very much. We just ate. To bad you weren't here. We had to eat your share of Squaw McMillan's chicken." He licked his fingers and put his face close to mine. "M-m-m-m! Good!" And he threw back his head and laughed.

So before I could catch my breath and cool off we were on the road again. I made a grab-me lunch of biscuit and dried beef from my saddlebags as we jolted along, Smith and Bully in front laughing and burping at me.

The whole week of the horse drive went that way. They were forever sending me on wild-goose chases, until I learned not to bite. They made fun of my name, they asked me riddles I couldn't understand and made me do more than my share of the work. At a town we passed through, Smith hauled me into the general store and watched with sour delight as I tried to buy a left-handed hammer and a sky-hook that Bully swore we needed. One night they had me awake all night holding a bag, chirruping for a mythical snipe, while they secretly slept.

This was schoolboy stuff, of course, harmless, mean pranks played by a couple of bored young soldiers far from home. A few years earlier I might have laughed along and enjoyed the adult attention. A few years later I might have been wiser and not bit. But I was at just that stage of vulnerable pride to let it eat me up, and as the week progressed I grew more and more sullen, riding behind them as if under a private thundercloud, until I ceased to be fun and they gave up and ignored me.

At Hamilton we delivered the horses, and I left my tormentors at last, but instead of returning to Grand River I turned my pony over to another Indian for return to John McMillan and set out on foot for Tonawanda. That week was a watershed. Bully and Smith, I realized, were just two among many white men. There was no getting away from them. To think that I could hide from them forever was a hope as illusory as cloud-painting. However deep into the woods I went, however much of an

Indian I became, they'd hunt me down. Twenty years after the Civil War, in which he was wounded three times, Oliver Wendell Holmes, Jr. said "it is required of a man that he should share the passion and action of his time at peril of being judged not to have lived." It was clear to me now that the passion and action of *my* time would be determined by white men. If I wanted to share the action I'd better join them sooner than later.

It was late on a Sunday night when I arrived at my parents' door. They hadn't seen me in two years, and I had grown from a boy to a young man, but my mother knew me at once. "Ha-sa-no-an-da," she said. "Come in. *E-won-de-gah-ga* – eat something. We're just sitting down to supper."

I stepped across the threshold. "Don't call me Ha-sa-no-an-da," I said in English. "My name is Ely Parker. I'm going to speak English. I'm going to speak English so well that even the *best* white men will call me their equal!"

Chapter V

POLK STAYS AN INDIAN EXECUTION

Washington 1846

FALL 1842, AT AGE FOURTEEN, I ENTERED YATES ACADEMY, about twenty miles north of the reservation. I was on scholarship, a boarding student, and, to my delight, the only Indian on campus. Not only was I *forced* to speak English, but I became a celebrity, my status as a curiosity quite pleasant after the rotten treatment I'd got used to from whites. The white boys and girls were naturally open and charitable, unlike their elders, in whom prejudice had hardened. At thirteen and fourteen, everybody's a little strange, so my being an *Indian* adolescent only made me a little more strange.

I threw myself into school, joining the French Club, German Club, Classics Club, Pathfinders Club for genteel hiking in the woods, Whig Club, Democrat Club, Literary Club, various sports clubs, paving my eventual adult way into the Masons, the militia, and the Grand Army of the Republic. Join 'em if you can't beat 'em. To force-feed my English, I became an orator of the Euglossian Society, for whom I spoke with varying degrees of ignorance on a wide range of topics in a deepening voice that my schoolmate Henry Flagler likened to Niagara Falls – "It booms, it sprays, and it keeps going long after it's made its point."

Flagler was a couple years younger than me, but we became quick pals. Perhaps the attraction was that he looked like *such* a white man and I was growing into *such* an Indian. Flagler was angular and thin, with high cheekbones, aquiline nose, a thatch of light brown hair and the most extraordinary lavender eyes, while I was growing rounder and darker, my nose flattening and my eyes and hair black. In the two years we were together at Yates, Flagler claimed that I grew outwards as much as he did upwards. Flagler was a minister's son and relentlessly secular in consequence. He spent little time studying, sitting around the dormitory with his feet on a windowsill, the soles of his shoes unstitched and flapping, while he spun for us his waking dreams of fast killings in the west.

One day he finally got his chance. I found him in his usual window perch, pensive, a letter in his hand.

"What?" I asked.

"News," said. "Good and bad." He flourished the letter. "My father got the sack."

"Henry, I'm sorry," I said, sitting down with him. "What happened?"

Henry laughed. "Damn fool married a white woman to a nigger!"

He handed me the letter, from his mother. Henry's preacher father in Ohio had indeed married an Oberlin College student to a black man. The father had lost his position, and the parents were moving back to western New York to start over.

"That's the bad news," said Henry, grabbing the letter back and beginning to pace. "The good news is they're broke and I have to leave school!"

"Henry, how terrible." To me, leaving school was anathema. "You could get a scholarship," I suggested. "Like me."

Flagler looked at me with those lavender eyes. "I'm not like you, Parker," he said. "I'm not book-smart. I'm just smart. Besides, they need my income now. It's a chance! Seize fortune by the forelock!" He gave my bangs a tug.

A few days later I saw him off at the gates of the school, his carpetbag in his hand. The next I heard from him was a letter four months later. From Ohio!

> Parker: I barely greeted my parents
> when I realized they'd be better off without
> me and me without them. Didn't even
> unpack, just kept walking, got aboard a

freight boat on the Erie Canal and went to Buffalo. There I took a vessel for Sandusky Ohio to hook up with my cousin Dan and his father. I was on Lake Erie for three days in a dreadful storm. I believe I learned enough poker just from watching to best you all!

Am now in Bellevue Ohio, working at my uncle's store, using my one Biblical talent of buying cheap and selling dear. We have a single keg of brandy at the bottom of the stairs. From the same keg we sell fine brandy to the English at $4 a gallon, ordinary brandy to the Germans at $1.50 a gallon, and hoot-and-holler to the Dutch for whatever we can get! We sell more than any to the Dutch for far greater profit.

Two lessons from this. First, inquire closely into the merits of whatever's offered for sale. Second, find a product everyone consumes and sell as much as you can for as little as you dare. The profit is in the volume, not the ratio!

Later letters arrived from Henry like dispatches from the front, urging me to quit the east and get into the game. When I left Yates in 1846, Henry was already making $400 a year.

They were delightful, the years at Yates, and so much did I think of myself as an honorary white man – driving a borrowed coach, escorting white girls to dances – that vacations at the reservation seemed like backsliding into a pit of ignorance. The old Indians and Indian ways grasped at my pantlegs as from the grave. Even more than most youngsters I began to think of my parents as obsolete. In my case it was true. My parents – my whole tribe – had been declared obsolete and were being crated for shipment west. As the deadline for our removal approached, got postponed, and approached again, I withdrew from the tribe more and more, praying for every summer to end, for the days to get shorter and the winds to shake the trees and herald the start of school. Then, like a butterfly, I'd shed my moccasins and my buckskins, don my shiny leather shoes, my frock coat and string tie, and trip grandly off to Yates, which was only a few squat buildings, but which had come to represent to me all that was fine in the world.

I'd haunt the library, running my fingers over the volumes, sometimes sitting on the floor, devouring hundreds of pages on the spot until the librarian gently suggested I take the book out. I wore a path between my room and the library, as if in a race to read every volume before I was snatched away. I'd walk along, my nose in one book, two more under my arms, and with private delight hear other students call me "Chief Nose-in-Book, Sachem of the En-cyc-lo-pe-di-a." So many books and so little time, I thought, as every time I finished one volume, two seemed to arrive to take its place.

Inevitably, the elders of the tribe sniffed me out, a young brave who was mastering the white man's ways. They'd mistrusted me at first, with my lingo and fancy clothes, but now I was someone they could use. The Ogden Land Company was panting down our necks as deadline after deadline approached, and I, with my new knowledge of English, became a cog in the process. I was only fourteen when I wrote my first letter to President Tyler for them. I left school several times to go as interpreter to Albany for meetings with Governor Wright. I wrote petitions to the secretary of war. When a compromise treaty was drawn up in 1842, I translated it and explained it to the tribe. I was instrumental in pushing back our removal deadline yet again to April 1, 1846, when I would be eighteen.

Finally, in the winter of 1846 I was plucked from school and sent to Washington City as part of a delegation to throw ourselves on the mercy of the Great Father himself, President James K. Polk.

The delegation was small, two chiefs named John Blacksmith and Isaac Shanks and me. What a strange assemblage we made! Chiefs John and Isaac were old men, in their sixties. They'd been old men all my life. When I was younger they were towering figures, both in size and reputation, but now they seemed shrunk and shriveled, their faces wrinkled and hard as walnuts. At eighteen, at my full six feet, I towered over them. They insisted on wearing Indian dress – buckskin leggings and tunics – which I found embarrassing. In my frock coat and string tie, I felt like a reluctant nephew escorting his elders to a costume ball.

We arrived in Washington City on a Monday in March and took rooms at the Willard Hotel, just up the street from the White House. Washington at the time was a skeleton, its bones, only partly draped, poking fragile through the skin. Broad Pennsylvania Avenue, from the White House to the Capitol, was fully settled and lined with shops and boarding houses, but it was like the spine of a body without limbs. The Capitol, squat and modest with its old Bullfinch dome, crowned barren Jenkins Hill with a few out-buildings clinging to its skirts. Cows grazed on the Capitol's lee slope, woods and pastures spread out into Maryland. Bare, lifeless avenues stretched toward far horizons, the land unsettled, untilled, with lone surveyors' stones marking lot lines and expressing brave hope that someday, something might be built there. The few settled squares of brick row-houses huddled together, their backs to the wilderness, trying to ignore the mud and squalor that were the main features of democracy's capital.

On Thursday morning, the president's "public day," we presented ourselves at the White House (as people were already calling the President's House). It was easy to do in those days. We simply walked up the long drive, passed the statue of Jefferson that then stood there, and through the front door. I had tried to persuade John and Isaac not to wear their buckskins, even ordering them morning clothes from a tailor, but they were defiant so there we were – two stage Indians and their civilian handler. It was a warm day for March – there were crocuses at the border of the lawn – and a number of black workmen were tending the plantings along the mansion's front drive, two of them right in front of us, planting shrubs around the portico.

I stopped dead.

"Come on," said John Blacksmith. "What are you gawking at?"

I pointed a numb hand at the two Negroes. It had just hit me what they were. "Slaves," I said.

John looked and nodded. "That's right," he said.

He pulled my sleeve, but I had turned to stone. "The president's slaves," I said. "The president *owns* those men."

"Come on, Ha-sa-no-an-da," said Isaac Shanks, standing impatiently on the drive. "You know about slavery."

I did and I didn't. I knew about it abstractly, as a distant evil of the rotting South. It was even a consolation sometimes: however bad off

Indians were, at least nobody could buy and sell us like Negroes. But here was slavery in the flesh, not ten yards from me – an old, black, snowy-haired man in a blue flannel shirt, kneeling on the White House driveway, his thin, bare ankles poking from his shoes as he turned soil with a trowel and sifted it through his fingers. A younger black man stood by with a wheelbarrow. His son? A nephew?

"But they look," I said, "just like. . . like. . ."

"What?" said John Blacksmith.

"Like people!" I blurted.

"Come on," insisted Isaac, urging me up the drive. "There will be a crowd. We must get there early."

I wrenched myself away from the Negroes and let the chiefs drag me to the front door, looking over my shoulder all the time at the diligent, careful black men. In all outward respects they were men, working like other men. But these men didn't just *work* for the president. He was a southerner, he *owned* them. He had bought them, could sell them, could break up their families, punish them, do whatever he wanted with them, just as if they were horses, or less, as if they were the wheelbarrow the younger man was holding.

John Blacksmith virtually pushed me through the front door. At the porter's lodge, just inside, I registered for the three of us and looked up to see the steward, as the president's majordomo was called, looking past me at the two chiefs. I cleared my throat and said, as importantly as I could, "We represent the Seneca Nation of New York State. We've come to see the president with a most urgent petition."

The steward looked at me as if surprised that I could speak. He was a head shorter than me, with shrewd eyes that made me feel bearish and clumsy. "Who represents the Seneca Nation?" he said. "You or them?"

"Oh," I said. "They do."

"And you?" he said, his eyes level, a smile playing at the corners of his mouth.

"I'm their interpreter," I said, summoning more confidence than I felt.

"Ah," he said, nodded at me once, and turned his attention to John and Isaac, who were standing stiff and formal. "If you gentlemen will wait over there," he said, nodding toward a crowd of people scattered about the foyer, "I'll see what I can do."

He spoke through me as if I'd turned transparent. I translated, thanked him, and we retired toward one of the soaring pillars. People milled about, clutching papers and note-cases, many of them in whispered colloquies, all of them keeping an eye on the stairway that led to the president's office, up and down which various minions, dispatched by the steward, scurried with more papers in their hands. Now and then the steward would leave his post, approach a group, speak in a low voice, and they'd get wafted up to the heavenly precincts, where I imagined President Polk sat on a throne dispensing justice.

With so many petitioners clamoring for an audience, I despaired of getting to see the man at all. John and Isaac stood impassive and stoic in their buckskins while I fidgeted and sweated under my collar, unable to sit or stand still. We were attracting some attention, or John and Isaac were. "Seneca," I kept explaining in a low voice. "Seneca Indians from New York State." I was sure we looked ridiculous.

Evidently, though, the chiefs' appearance aroused curiosity upstairs as well, for presently the steward appeared before us, nodded at me, and addressed John and Isaac. "The President will see you now," he said, and a smile flickered as he looked at me, said, "You too," and ushered us toward the stairs.

At the top of the stairs, a fastidious young man who couldn't have been much into his twenties introduced himself as Knox Walker, the President's secretary. He got our names, repeated them to be sure he had them right, and stood with us for a minute or so, one finger raised, his eyes on the door across the way. When it opened, two men emerged backwards, bowing their way out, then the door closed and they turned, brushed past us, and descended the stairs whispering urgently, waving their arms. Knox Walker looked at the ceiling, seemed to count ten, then beckoned us to follow him. He opened the door, waved us in, and there sat President Polk, at a remarkably small desk, looking at a piece of paper.

It wasn't a very impressive office, no larger than some bankers' offices I'd seen in Buffalo or the Headmaster's office at Yates, certainly a comedown after the Grand Foyer. But the only thing that mattered, I guess, was that it was the president's office, and it was the man who made the office grand.

"Mr. President," said Knox Walker, "here are Chiefs John Blacksmith and Isaac Shanks of the Seneca Nation and their translator, Mr. Parker."

He motioned us to sit and we took chairs in front of the desk. Walker sat down at the president's side with a notebook and pencil.

Polk didn't stand but nodded briskly and folded his hands on the desk. He was gray-haired and serious, with dark eyebrows that gave his eyes a hooded look, like a gray falcon. Speaking to John Blacksmith, he asked, "What can I do for you, Chief?" His voice was flat and twangy, without the resonance I'd expected from someone so lofty.

I translated and was interested to see that Polk's eyes never left John's. Used to dealing with translators, the president kept his eyes on the man he was talking to and ignored me. In my frock coat and polished shoes, I faded into the woodwork, an invisible functionary like Knox Walker.

John Blacksmith, unfazed by the president's directness, responded in kind. "You can help us keep our lands," he said and launched into a history of the Ogden Company's usurpations. Well, I thought, as I translated the whirs and gulps of Seneca into plain, flat English, we're launched now. Instead of hemming and hawing, smoking and feasting, as Indians do before getting down to business, we're plunging into *medias res*. Cards on the table, that's the American way. After years of torment, we had the president's ear, and the issue looked fair to be settled by sundown.

Not so. The president heard John Blacksmith out, nodded, frowned, pulled his upper lip, looked about to say something wise, thought better of it, spread his hands on his blotter and said, "All this, of course, is the business of the secretary of war. He's the man for you to see." And he slapped the desk as if he'd solved the problem then and there. Of course we knew that Secretary Marcy was our man, but our protests had always met a stone wall in him. We were hoping, with Polk, to go over his head.

"How are the beds at the Willard?" asked Polk.

John Blacksmith frowned and blinked once as I translated. "Too soft," he told the president.

Polk nodded sympathetically. "So I've been told," he said. "Mrs. Polk and I always preferred Gadsby's. Before we moved here, that is."

We looked at the president, he looked at us, and with that stirring news the meeting ended. Knox Wilson stood, we stood and turned to go.

"Oh," said Polk. "Tonight is Mrs. Polk's weekly reception. I hope you can attend."

I accepted, and we all nodded, bowed and left, Isaac Shanks muttering about hotel beds. In the hallway Knox Wilson must have noticed our disgruntlement, for he took me by the elbow and said quietly, "Don't worry. The president would never countermand a member of his cabinet. The important thing is he saw you. Word will get around. Come to the reception tonight. Stay in view." He was eying the buckskins and beads of the two chiefs. "Do they have, uh, other clothes?"

"You mean. . .?" I ran my hand down my own lapel.

"Yes."

"I can get some."

"Don't," he said, ushering us toward the staircase. "Exotic helps. People like to be seen with Indians. Makes them feel daring." He shook our hands and we went down the stairs, through the foyer and out the door. Heads swiveled at us and whisperings arose among those who had waited longer than we.

Outside I breathed the fresh spring air, squinted in the sunlight and felt a swelling in my chest and a lightness in my step. We had seen the president. Heady stuff, however inconsequential the result. In my eighteen years I had grown from a naked savage to a hobnobber with the highest in the land.

Mrs. Polk's reception that night was a tepid affair. The Polks were Tennessee Scotch Presbyterians, embodiments of thrift and rectitude. No hard liquor, no dancing, in fact no music at all until everyone was assembled in the East Room. Then a brittle little drum-and-whistle band struck up a tune in the corridor and the Polks strolled arm-in-arm into the room. It was fairly comic. Mrs. Polk was so much taller than her husband and strode along so manfully that it looked as if he was on her arm rather than the other way around.

"It's called 'Hail to the Chief,'" murmured a voice at my elbow.

I turned to see a young man, as young as Knox Walker, but so pale he almost vanished, standing in the shadow of a pillar, his thin blond hair trailing across his scalp. "Nobody used to notice when the president walked into a room. He's so short, you see. So Mrs. Polk ordered the music played to give him a fighting chance."

"Who. . .?" I asked, but he shushed me and motioned me not to look at him.

With the Polks' arrival, things unbent a little. The president and Mrs. made a circuit of the room in what the town had dubbed their "Polka," and a string band in the corner played some tunes. President Polk held his head abnormally high, thrusting it out of his collar like a turtle, as if to match his wife's height, and scuttled along in a brisk little mince to keep up with her.

John Blacksmith and Isaac Shanks attracted a lot of attention in their buckskins, and I obliged with introductions most of the evening, trying through picture-associations to keep names on the faces that swarmed around us. Henry Clay, whom Polk had barely beat for the presidency, looked, with his death's-head cheekbones, like a skull molded from *clay*. Daniel Webster was splay-footed and shuffled as if his feet were *webbed*. Secretary of State Buchanan had a turned-down mouth, as if in re*buke*. Postmaster General Cave Johnson had deep-set eyes like *caves*. I looked for John Quincy Adams but was told he regarded the White House as his ancestral home and seldom visited the upstarts who now claimed it.

I had returned to the pillar where the thin young man lurked. "Pssst!" he whispered. "Here she is. Always makes a late entrance. Won't let even the president upstage her."

I looked toward the entrance, where all other eyes were turning, and saw a vision from a half-century ago. An ancient dowager wheezed through the doorway like a merchantman under sail, drawing just enough wind to keep her afloat. She paused under the arch and fanned herself as if flushed, though her face was powdered stark white. A turban wrapped her head, and she sported a gown of shocking pink with a décolletage that would get a woman half her age arrested. After waiting for the room to fall silent, she tottered across to the president and extended a regal hand. A murmur followed her wake.

"Who. . . ?" I said to the pale young man.

"Dolley Madison." he said.

My head whipped round to stare at her. Dolley Madison! I looked behind me at the pale young man, and behind *him*, I took in for the first time the painting I'd been idling in front of. It was the full-length Washington by Gilbert Stuart, the canvas that Dolley Madison had cut from its frame and saved from the British in 1814. Were those the scars her scissors had made? Dolley Madison was still alive? She had been the social arbiter of the capital for sixteen years, first lady both for the widower Jefferson and her own husband. It all felt like such ancient history, yet here she was, in very modern 1846, greeting the president, condescending brilliantly to him as if it was *her* house *he* was visiting.

"They indulge her," muttered the pale young man. A hand fluttered. "A national treasure."

I continued to gawk. The War of 1812, when my father and uncles had fought and Mrs. Madison had saved the painting, ended only thirty years ago. But the saga was so oft- and well-told that it might as well have been the sack of Troy, she Hecuba shielding her children from the Greeks. Yet there she stood in the flesh – quite a bit of flesh amidst the ribbons and the silks – laughing a whiskey-rich laugh from her jewel-spangled throat, an overage ingénue wandering onto the set of the wrong play. Here were the somber, sober Polks, with their simple dress and plain manners, mirrored by the blacks and modest colors around them. And here was Dolley Madison, three-quarters of a century old, in brazen pink, flounced and ruffled, painted and powdered and flirting, tapping men on the cheek with her fan like a Regency belle.

It took us a few days to get an appointment with Secretary of War William Marcy, busy as he was with the threat of war in Mexico. It was not a meeting we looked forward to. Marcy was an old New York hack, tough as nails. He was governor when the Ogden Company log-rolled their treaty, and, despite our petitions, hadn't raised a finger to stop it. He liked to call himself "General" Marcy from his service in 1812, when he'd destroyed a few villages of British-leaning Indians, and he fancied himself a sort of junior Jackson, riding the name of Indian fighter from office to office and now to the secretaryship of war. His chief fame lay in coining the phrase, "To the victor belong the spoils," to justify Jackson's wholesale office-cleaning, and now, as a beneficiary of the "spoils system" he was our major roadblock. We had tried to leap-frog him by going to Polk but had bounced right back.

He hadn't changed much from his New York days, a tall, square man with a square face, crouched behind his desk like a bulldog, both fists clenched as if he had a knife in one, a fork in the other, and we were lunch.

"The treaty is clear," he told us. "It has been ratified by the Senate and is the law of the land. Your people will have to leave."

"But the president . . . " I began.

"The president is far too busy to be concerned," he said. We continued to press, until, muttering something about "looking the matter over one final time," he waved us to the door. In the corridor, I saw the pale young man again, lurking in the shadows. He coughed lightly and raised a finger to his lips, then vanished through a door that was hidden in the wallpaper.

We returned to our hotel despondent, all appeals seemingly exhausted. After several days, when no word came, John and Isaac decided it was fruitless to wait any longer, and we were literally packing our bags when there came a discreet knock on the door. It was the pale young man again, the same I had seen at the Polk's reception and again in the corridor outside Marcy's office, standing there, his hat to his chest. His thin blond hair was combed straight across his scalp, and as he talked his soft chin quivered. "Yes?" I said.

"Message from the secretary of war," he said, his mouth barely moving. "You are Mr. Parker," he informed me.

"Yes," I said. "I've met you. You are. . . ?"

"Not important," he said. "But the message is. Come to Secretary Marcy's office at ten tomorrow morning. You're to meet with him and the president. That's all." He turned to go.

"Wait a minute," I said, plucking his sleeve. He looked at the offending hand with such horror that I let it drop.

"Yes?" he said, brushing his sleeve with nervous fingers. "Something not clear?"

"Do you have anything in writing?" I asked. "Some confirmation?"

"No," he said, looking trapped. "Just what I said."

I opened my hands as if to show him I had no weapons. "At least tell me your name," I said. "In case somebody asks where the message came from."

He frowned and conceded the point. "I see," he said. "Reasonable, of course. Quentin Winslow. Please don't use it if you don't have to." He was twisting his hat in his hands and looking down the corridor.

"I won't," I said, extending my hand. "My name is Ely Parker."

He looked up and down the corridor, looked at my hand and touched it with his fingertips. "I know who you are. I'm State Department," he said. "Come find me if you have trouble." And he faded down the hall and vanished as if into the wallpaper.

I closed the door, let out a whoop and translated for John and Isaac. They nodded thoughtfully and nothing more. Old hands at diplomacy, the chiefs were comfortable and patient with the crawl of such dealings, while I still veered between triumph and tragedy for every small advance and setback. But between Knox Wilson and this Quentin Winslow I was getting an inkling of how things worked. The fact of seeing people is more important than anything they say. We had been seen by Polk and by Marcy, and, perhaps more to the point, we had been seen by their functionaries, who had reported the meetings to each other and to other functionaries. These quiet young men, moving from office to office with papers in their hands, formed a private network behind the corridors of power. I began to see, just dimly, that government happens, not in great public declamations and decisions and papers signed with flourishes, but in whispers among smooth, anonymous young men in dark suits who meet in dark corridors with their own dark agendas.

The next day we met a different and smiling William Marcy at the War Department, who put on his hat and accompanied us down the long walkway between the buildings to the White House. It was not one of the president's "public days." The columned foyer was empty of visitors, and Mr. Marcy strode right through it to the stairway, led us upwards, brushed past Knox Wilson and ushered us into Polk's office.

"Ah," said Polk, looking up from papers. "Good! Good!" He waved at the chairs gathered around the desk and Knox Wilson got us seated in the right ones – John and Isaac in front of the desk with Marcy, me at a chair on one side of the desk with Wilson in a chair closer to Polk on the other side. Morning sunlight streamed through the long windows; we could glimpse the glittering, famous view down the Potomac. To our surprise *Mrs.* Polk was there also, in a chair behind the president near the draperies. She didn't speak but nodded as we entered and made our reverences, and she was similarly silent during the whole interview. Now and then the president would turn to her with a question on his brow and a silent communication would pass between them, a nod, a quick shake of the head, or maybe just something in her eyes letting him know she was up with him.

"I'm inclined to think this matter needs more consideration," began the president. His thumb riffled a stack of papers on his desk.

Marcy sat straight up in his chair. "The Senate has already decided. . . " he began.

"Yes, yes." Polk waved him down. "But under a different administration and under, uh, shall we say, different circumstances." He cocked an eye at Marcy. I was too busy translating to fathom what the "different circumstances" were.

The president picked up the sheaf of papers. "These letters, these petitions," he said to John Blacksmith. "You have powerful friends in New York State."

John nodded once, and his stolid face, which to a white man would have looked unchanged, to me became suffused with hope – just a slight change in the light in his eyes.

"Mr. Morgan, Mr. Warren," said Polk, flipping through the papers, "Mr. Martindale, Mr. Schoolcraft. . . ." Mrs. Polk nodded at the back of his head and the president seemed to feel it. He brandished the papers at Marcy. "This is testimony, Marcy, from reputable people, that the Seneca are being unfairly treated up there, that the treaties of confiscation were obtained and signed by fraud."

"But obtained and signed nonetheless," persisted Marcy. "The government can't be responsible for the *bona fides* of every signatory."

"The government also can't afford to be a party to fraud," said the president, and the two of them bandied legalisms for awhile. As I translated, I too saw a glimmer of hope. The chiefs' work at home had borne fruit, and petitions from our friends were reaching Polk's desk. Reuben Warren of Buffalo, whose son I was at school with, had collected signatures. Lewis Morgan and Henry Schoolcraft, well-connected friends and scholars, were awakening whites to the Iroquois as a separate and valuable culture. John Martindale, West Point man and district attorney at Batavia, was casting our protests into proper legalese. All this activity seemed to be giving Polk, or someone who had his ear, pause.

"So *I* have decided," said Polk with some emphasis as Marcy settled back, resigned, "to refer the whole matter back to the Senate." He looked at John Blacksmith. "I will *ask* them to look at the petitions and the evidence that have accumulated since the treaties were signed. Mind you," he added, "I can only *ask* that the Senate do this. I can't *tell* them to do anything. But," he leaned back and smiled slightly, inviting us to join his little joke, "I think I have a little influence where it matters." We all chuckled dutifully, Knox Wilson started to gather papers and end the meeting. "Is that satisfactory, um, Chief?" said Polk to John Blacksmith.

Polk clearly expected nothing more than a grunt of acknowledgement, and I expected the same as we rose to go. So it was as great a surprise to me as it was to Polk and Marcy when John Blacksmith rose, put his hand on Isaac's shoulder to keep him seated and started to make a speech.

"Great Father," he said, and I winced as I translated the feudalism. Marcy and Knox Wilson looked startled but eased back into their chairs. "I was born," said John Blacksmith, "when your nation was born, in the year when Washington became your chief. We Seneca fought against you in your revolution and paid for it with your General Sullivan's raid, which confined us to the reservations. I don't protest it. We chose the wrong side. But look here!" John reached under his buckskin vest and flourished a large medallion, an oval of silver engraved on both sides, that hung from his neck on a leather thong. "In 1792 your chief Washington met with our Red Jacket, smoked the pipe, and struck this medal as a symbol of peace between the United States and the Iroquois."

The medal got the white people leaning forward, and John Blacksmith pressed his advantage, displaying it to Marcy, to Knox Wilson and even circling the desk to show it to Polk. Mrs. Polk rustled forward from her chair and examined it with her husband. "On one side the eagle of your nation, in his talons the arrows of war and the olive branch of peace. And on the other," John turned the medal, "Washington himself sharing the pipe with Red Jacket. Behind Washington are the houses of your civilization, while behind Red Jacket stand the trees of our forest. Washington meant both our peoples to keep their lands and dwell in harmony."

John Blacksmith tucked the medal back under his vest and returned from behind the president's desk. "I, Mr. President, am Red Jacket's heir. My name in Seneca is Do-ne-ho-ga-wa, keeper of the western door of the Longhouse. And you, Mr. President, are Washington's heir. As he smoked the pipe of friendship, so by taking his office do you smoke with us and become the keeper of the promise he made." John tapped his chest where the medal hung, resumed his seat and, with everyone's attention still on him, drove the shaft home. "In our Indian heaven, Mr. President, there are no white men." He smiled and the corners of Polk's mouth went up too. "But the Great Spirit made an exception for Washington. By heaven's entrance is a walled enclosure, with broad avenues and many trees. At the center is a spacious mansion, more spacious even than this one. From all of nature the Great Spirit selected gifts of bounty to bloom and flourish there and please the great Washington. Every Indian, as he enters heaven, passes the gates of this mansion and sees Washington walking back and forth in quiet meditation, never speaking, but happy and content in his heavenly estate."

John Blacksmith leaned back and steepled his fingers. "Mr. President, I have often envied Washington his serenity and contentment, but I worry about his solitude. Surely the Great Spirit does not intend him to live alone forever. He merely waits for other great white men to appear, who by benevolence and justice will prove themselves his liege companions. Who knows, Mr. President?" continued John, and I wonder if I was the only one who saw the twinkle in his eye. "Perhaps you will be the second white man at the gates of heaven. Perhaps you, by your fairness to us, will have your name linked to that of Washington forever. Washington and Polk in heaven!"

I thought he laid it on a bit thick, but Polk absorbed it with great solemnity. He even came out from behind his desk to bid us farewell, and as he shook hands with John he rose on tiptoe and thrust his head out of his collar, as if to match the statuesque Washington on the Red Jacket medal.

On the White House drive I automatically turned toward town, but John Blacksmith stood there for a moment, sniffing the air. "I have a hankering for fields and streams," he said. "Let's visit the river."

We took a path that circled around the mansion and down the slope. In those days, before the Washington Monument, wild country stretched from the White House all the way down to the Potomac, and we walked along, enjoying the sunshine and watching the buds on the trees eager to burst. We passed stables and cowsheds, then fields where black men were tending the herd. Polk's slaves again. A wave of depression swept away the brief euphoria of John Blacksmith's speech. Polk's slaves. Washington had owned slaves. So had Jefferson, Madison, Monroe, Jackson, Tyler. Slavery ruled half the country. A country that could permit that could permit *anything* and find a reason for it. They weaseled around slavery by honoring "states' rights" and the "peculiar institution." They could just as easily countenance Indian slaughter by calling it "sanitary removal."

We passed from the White House grounds into the swampland that bordered the Potomac. What a mixture of grandeur and swamp Washington City was, and how quickly one gave way to the other! Some spring birds were settling in, looking bewildered at the absence of leaves and flowers. The river was in flood, and we walked along the towpath. The two chiefs moved easily, their moccasined feet sure and silent, while I sidestepped behind them, tripping through puddles in my city shoes.

"That was a very moving speech," I said, laboring to keep up with John. "About Washington."

John grunted. "Politics. They expect it. Any Indian who *didn't* invoke the Great Spirit and Washington would leave them unfulfilled."

"It was more than that," I protested. "He was genuinely moved."

"He's trained to look genuinely moved," said John over his shoulder. "He's as good an actor as I am."

Isaac snapped a switch from a tree and slapped it against his leg as he walked. "We have no idea what was going on behind those eyes," he said. "Whatever it was, no slop about Washington will tip the balance. Sorry, John," he said, touching John Blacksmith's shoulder. John shrugged it away.

It was hard to keep up with the two old men. Overhanging branches and pathside brambles, which seemed to part for them, plucked at my coatsleeves as at an intruder as I stumbled along behind them. My shoes were muddy and my collar felt stiff and prickly.

"It's the electoral vote, isn't it?" said Isaac.

"Partly that, partly Mexico, partly a lot of other things," said John.

I was puffing and sweating and confused in my woolen coat. "What about the electoral vote?" I asked.

"New York," said Isaac, as I hovered at his shoulder to hear. "Polk's election came down to New York. He won by only about five thousand votes and only because the Whig vote split between Clay and Birney. If Clay had carried New York, Clay would be president."

"So?" I had no idea Isaac had his fingers so firmly on the political pulse.

"So that's what will swing things for us if things swing at all. It's a congressional election year, and Polk wants to keep New York Democratic."

"I don't understand."

"Let's sit here," said John. A broad, flat rock jutted like a wharf into the river, and the two chiefs walked out on it and squatted down. Isaac pulled a knife from his belt and started whittling the switch. I peeled off my coat, folded it with the lining on the outside and sat on it to protect my pants.

"What does the election have to do with it?" I asked, rolling my shirt cuffs back. "Indians can't vote."

"No," said Isaac patiently. "But people who *like* Indians vote, and that's where our strength lies."

"I see," I said, beginning to.

"Mr. Polk has grand schemes," said John Blacksmith, looking out at the brown and rushing river. "He has annexed Texas, and he wants all of Mexico from the Rio Grande to California. He has sent his army to stare across the river until the Mexicans get nervous and start something. Then he'll declare the army has been attacked and order them to 'retaliate.' Like a wolf sitting outside a sheep pen. When the sheep get so nervous they break down the fence, the wolf kills as many as he wants. In 'self-defense.'" As we spoke Zachary Taylor and the U.S. Army, including Second Lieutenant U.S. Grant, were sitting on the Rio Grande ostentatiously cleaning their guns.

"But how does what happens on the Rio Grande affect what happens on the Tonawanda?" I asked.

"All rivers flow together," said John Blacksmith. "New York only weakly supports Polk and will only weakly support a war. Anything could tip the balance. There is a wave of revulsion now in the north against the way all the southern tribes were marched west. 'This isn't the south. It can't happen here,' say the upright northern folks, and now it *is* happening there. So they're disturbed, as witness the pile of petitions on Mr. Polk's desk."

"I see."

"So." Isaac, whittling, took up the thread. "There are two things in our favor. The conscience of the north and the war with Mexico. The northern conscience will permit a war with Mexico. It's far away and the people speak and look strange. But will it permit the simultaneous eviction of the Seneca from New York? That's too close to home and strains the conscience. Ah, say our upright New Yorkers, we see what you're doing to the Mexicans. The same thing you're doing to our pet Indians. Well, you just stop it. And like smoke, New York's support for the Mexican adventure disappears. Mr. Polk is calculating whether he can afford a brush fire in his rear while he's starting a conflagration in his front."

I picked up a handful of pebbles and flicked them one at a time into the river. "So we're pawns in a bigger game," I said.

"Oh yes," said John, standing and looking to the far bank, where three deer had come down to drink. From where we were, no sign of civilization was visible. "There are games within games within games here. Nobody gives a damn about us. They have their treaty and that's that. But now we have time and friends. Not friends, maybe, but people whose *interests* coincide with ours. They'll hold the treaty up yet again to see how the wind blows. Meanwhile we keep possession."

"Our strategy," said Isaac, "is not victory but delay. To delay so long that it's unprofitable for them to fight us. The ball is rolling our way for the moment. We must keep it so."

John put his hand on Isaac's arm. "Choose your words carefully, Isaac. 'Keep the ball rolling' was Mr. Clay's slogan. And Mr. Clay lost."

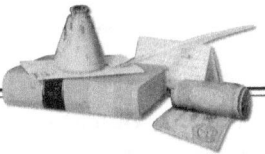

Chapter VI

DOLLEY MADISON
SAYS SELL!

Washington 1847

T HE BALL ROLLED, BUT OH, HOW SLOWLY. SO SLOW ARE
the wheels of government and the law's delay that I had to keep reminding
myself over the next months that delay was good – any obstacle we could
craft to deter the Senate from deciding on the treaty was in our favor. The
waiting wore out John and Isaac; by mid-May they were so pining away
for fields and streams that they went home and left me in charge, even
entrusting me with the Red Jacket medal. John Blacksmith's last words
to me as he boarded the homeward train were, "Delay and delay. Always
delay," hard advice for a young man who craves action. But I spent the
next months dutifully haunting the halls of Congress and discovering
how frustrating it would be actually to want something *done* in a process
designed to get nothing done at all.

It was delicate. My first job was to make sure that the Senate Indian
Affairs Committee took up Polk's suggestion to review the treaty. That
done, I had to return to the same senators and somehow convince them
that the treaty was of no great urgency, that they could take their time with
it. While the Senate diddled, we were safe. But if they came to an early,
hasty decision, our fate was a roll of the dice.

In those days there were no congressional or senatorial offices, no
secretaries or staffs. A senator's office was his desk on the Senate floor, off
limits to petitioners like me. We who wanted things hung around outside

and became what a later writer called "lobbyists," a "dazzling reptile," a "huge scaly serpent," that wound "in and out through the long, devious basement passage, crawling through the corridors, trailing its slimy length from gallery to committee room." Lobbyists would hover by the doors until a senator emerged, then pounce. I had a favorite pillar that I lurked behind and I soon found that my youth, my height, my girth and my complexion gave senators pause into which I could leap. Once I had them toe to toe these masters of the national scene were wondrously voluble. Henry Clay, Daniel Webster, John Calhoun, William Seward, all opened their mouths, if not their hearts, to me and said whatever they could without really saying anything. At the other end of the avenue I had more meetings with Secretary Marcy and President Polk. Between times I attended receptions and got fat eating white man's food on Indian money.

The big doings in Washington that spring were not the small matter of Indian lands in the near northeast, but the big matter of Mexican lands in the far southwest, which our government had grown tired of ogling and was now lusting for. As John Blacksmith had predicted, the provoked Mexicans panicked. On May 3 they attacked at Matamoros. On May 11, Polk sent a war message to Congress, and the nation's blood happily boiled.

Not everyone boiled in favor of it. In the House I listened as John Quincy Adams and John Calhoun wasted their waning breath against it. Illinois Congressman Abraham Lincoln, demanding to know the exact circumstances of the so-called attack, was hooted down. Grant, who was in it, later called it "one of the most unjust wars ever waged by a stronger against a weaker nation." Herman Melville wrote that Mexico was just a "Loose-Fish" for America to grab, as the Spanish grabbed America, the Czar grabbed Poland, the Turk grabbed Greece and England grabbed India. "Is not Possession the whole of the law?"

But in the spring and summer of '46, it all looked grand. Washington bustled, carriages clattered purposefully through the streets dispensing serious men who hurried up marble steps with dispatch cases. Crowds shoved and murmured at bulletin boards and newsstands. Knots clustered outside the Capitol and White House at all hours, just to rub close to the men who were close to the men who knew things. Army camps sprouted in the parks, and mothers locked up their daughters as volunteers in new army blue swaggered in and out of taverns and tobacco shops, where girls did a brisk hourly trade in thin-walled upstairs rooms.

To further preen the country's pride a national fair came to town that spring to celebrate our industrial might. What a number and variety of people showed up from all over, including some western Indians, my first glimpse of Indians from outside our Iroquois Federation. There were Osage and Comanche, as worried as we were about keeping their ancestral lands, which lay in the armies' path to Mexico. We spoke through interpreters, of course, and a wilder bunch than the Comanche I never hoped to see, covered with paint and decked from head to foot in brass rings, beads and shells. It was hard for them to understand that I was an Indian too, and that my white man's clothes and manners were donned for the occasion. They sniffed at me like purebreds at a mutt.

But if the Comanche made me effete, the exhibition made me a bumpkin. The progress the country had made in my eighteen years struck me with the awful truth that life was passing me by, looping skywards while I leaned against a pillar waiting for an appointment. Look what developed between 1828 and 1846. Photography. Polk was the first president to be photographed. Hot-and-cold running water, gas lights, duct-and-register heating, John Deere's steel plow, McCormick's reaper, the Buffalo grain elevator, multi-winged clipper ships, displaced as soon as they appeared by transatlantic steamboats that crossed the ocean in a month. Coal replaced charcoal in huge blast furnaces, there were rail-rolling mills, cast-iron stoves, sewing machines, screw propellers, electric printing presses, electromagnets, electric current, insulated wire and vulcanized rubber. In Hartford, Connecticut, Samuel Colt had invented the revolving pistol and a system of "mass production," which would doom handwork and make man the servant of machinery.

Belt-driven power was another innovation, generating torque for everything from looms to paper-rollers. I jammed my fingers in my ears against the din and watched a roomful of weaving equipment from Lowell, Massachusetts, belts and wheels gearing up and down, transferring power from one generator to a half-acre of machinery. Had I been a tribal augurer I might have read in the snap and whir of the leather belts, in their endless loops from drive to pulley, the destruction of the Plains Indians. The eastern machines ate leather belts by the wagon-load, the plains of the west were black with buffalo, leather-clad from hump to hoof. When eastern demand met western supply in the '70s, it roared its delight in gunpowder. Four million buffalo died for their hides, the herds dwindled, and the Plains Indians died with the buffalo. "Make and sell something that needs constant replacing!" as Henry Flagler said. Could he figure out how to replace the buffalo?

Above it all, in front of it all, sweeping all else before them, screamed and sang the twin engines that more than any other drove the nineteenth century – the railroad and the telegraph. It was the greatest leap forward since the wheel. Where wagon roads hugged the land, the railroad blasted mountains, filled valleys, leveled hills, and bridged once-mighty rivers in single, shining arcs. Telegraphed news got around the country faster than gossip got around town. From the dawn of man till I was born in 1828, human messages traveled no faster than a horse. By 1846 they reached the speed of light.

But the progress in commerce and communications didn't speed up legislation, and at the beginning of August Congress postponed the Seneca treaty one last time, adjourned, went home and after five months in Washington so did I. Before leaving, I wandered about the emptying Capitol with George Brown, the Senate Sergeant-at-Arms, as he checked doors here and there. "You never know who you'll find," said Brownie. "One year a Congressman set up a cot and camp stove in the cellar and lived there the whole recess."

In the basement he opened a door off a corridor and motioned me into a room I'd never seen. "The Supreme Court," he said. It was an unimpressive chamber, dark and much partitioned. Three long windows let in little light, and the profusion of irrelevant arches seemed a pathetic attempt at grandeur. Gas lights smoked and hissed.

"The Senate met here until the British burned the Capitol," said Brownie. "They moved upstairs after the rebuilding and the Supreme Court moved in."

On a dais in front was a long counter with nine chairs behind it, where the justices sat, and as my eyes got used to the light, I saw a figure sitting in one of them.

"Who . . .?" said Brownie officially, starting down the aisle.

The figure rose and spread its arms. "What hath God wrought!" it intoned.

Brownie stopped. "Oh. Hello, Chief."

For a moment I thought he was addressing me – he called me "Chief" as did many others – but he was talking to the figure on the dais, who now walked down the steps to meet us.

"This is a sketch," said Brownie, ushering me forward. "Chief, meet the Chief."

I shook hands with the man, who, on close inspection, proved to be old and wrinkled, but upright, like a Presbyterian minister with a hawk nose, bushy eyebrows and intense brown eyes. He wore an old-fashioned cravat and carried a stovepipe hat.

"I wanted once to get the view from Marshall's seat," he explained, in a voice that cracked like a whip.

"'What hath God wrought?" I inquired.

"Morse," said the other Chief. "First telegraph message was sent from this room in 1844. That was the message."

"Ely Parker, meet John Ross," said Brownie, and only the grip of the old man's hand kept me from falling down, as his eyes held mine like the Ancient Mariner.

"John Ross? The Cherokee Chief?"

"Ely Parker?" replied John Ross, "the Seneca prodigy?"

"What are you doing here?" asked Brownie.

"Revisiting the scene of the crime," said John Ross.

My breath leaving me, I sat down in an aisle seat. John Ross, the Cherokee Chief, was probably the most famous living Indian. Although less than a quarter Cherokee, he had grown up with them, farmed with them, fought with them and for them and joined them in exile when the fight was lost. The fight was lost right here.

John Ross took a seat in front of me and turned, chin on his arm, to study me. "So you want to keep your lands," he said, without preface.

"Well," said Brownie, rubbing his hands together and backing up the aisle. "I've got traps to check. You Chiefs can find your way out."

When he was gone, John Ross still studied me. "Why a crime?" I asked. "You won here." In 1832, the Court had ruled, with Chief Justice Marshall, that Georgia's confiscation of Cherokee lands was null and void. "John Marshall has made his ruling," President Jackson reportedly said. "Now let him enforce it." By 1838, the Cherokee were forced to follow the infamous "Trail of Tears" west to Oklahoma.

"We won nothing here," growled John Ross. "We won an illusion. Serves us right. We bought illusions from the start."

I shook my head. "Forgive me," I said. "I know so little. Choctaw, Cherokee, Chickasaw, Seminole and Creek was what I learned in school."

"Look at us." John Ross flipped his cravat. "Two tame Indians in our cravats. Yes," he continued, "The Five Civilized Tribes, as they called us once we knuckled under. We were once like the Iroquois in the north, inhabiting the south from the Atlantic to the Mississippi. We were fairly 'civilized' even before the white man arrived, settling in villages around rivers and streams. That's why the white man called the Creek Creek, because they settled along creek beds."

"Like my people," I said.

"Close enough," he said. "At least you're still in New York State, for now." He looked around the shadowy chamber. "Until you end up here. Then watch out. In the south, all that's left of us are names of rivers. Appomattox, Chickasaw Bayou. Chickahominy, Mataponi." He chuckled. "Except my home town. We called it Ross's Landing. The whites thought Chattanooga more picturesque."

"You saw it coming?"

"We saw, but didn't understand. It happened as the tide eats the shore. The English, then the Americans, signed treaty after treaty with us, each time chopping off a chunk. 'Could you give us the shore and stay in the swamps?' they asked, then 'We need the Mississippi,' they told the Chickasaw, 'We need your creeks, they told the Creek,' and took all the good landing places. The Cherokee fared the worst."

"I know," I muttered.

John Ross put his hand on my arm. "No you don't," he said. "I know. I helped. We were the ones that bought the blarney. We thought the way to survive was not to resist, but to imitate. The white man wanted to move us because we were savages? Very well, we became sophisticated citizens. We established schools, laws, a legislature, courts and bureaucracy. A Cherokee named Sequoyah invented an alphabet for our language, which he was soon teaching not only to children, but to their parents and grandparents. By the mid-twenties the whole nation was literate in one language. This was a higher rate than in the white nation, with its many tongues, German and Dutch and French. We had a Bible, hymnbooks, textbooks, a Cherokee newspaper. They said we were barbarians? I wrote a constitution. They said we were unproductive? We raised and sold more apples and peaches, corn, wheat, oats and tobacco than any whites. We wove cloth and blankets, gloves and stockings. We had blacksmiths, silversmiths, carpenters. I came to Washington to prepare the way for full diplomatic recognition by the United States of the whole Cherokee Republic . . . " John Ross waved his hand and trailed off.

"What happened?" I asked quietly.

John Ross swallowed and looked far off. "Jackson happened. Gold happened. Most of all, we happened to ourselves."

"What do you mean?"

"We were too good, too educated, too efficient. We became so like the white nation that there was no longer any reason for us to exist. Could the United States – could Georgia – tolerate a separate republic within its borders? They began to think not. And Jackson, now president, gave words to the thought. 'Let all Indians be given new homes west of the Missouri,' he decreed. I was there at the inaugural. 'Go west,' Secretary of War Eaton told me. 'There's no room for you here.'"

"But you didn't."

"Some did," acknowledged Ross. "And that was the beginning of our trouble. We broke into factions who wanted to leave and factions who wanted to stay. I stayed, but with a vastly weakened nation. Then gold was discovered on Ward's Creek, in the northwest of our republic, and that was the end. Land speculators and local cheats in Georgia made short work of us. In 1836, the treaty of New Echota, which I did not sign, gave us two years to leave."

"And those who stayed?" I asked softly.

"Winfield Scott sent soldiers. In the spring of 1838, the army rounded us up, closed our schools, burned our homes, allowed us only what we could carry and herded us behind fences. Families at dinner saw the sudden gleam of bayonets in the doorway, and were driven with blows and oaths to the stockade. Men were seized in their fields, women were taken from their wheels, children from their play. Turning for one last look, they saw their homes in flames. They dug up Indian graves in search of silver pendants and other valuables.

"When the order came for the march west, the ground was freezing, snow was falling. We civilized Cherokee, who had learned to live in houses and wear cloth trousers, to travel by wagon and read newspapers, walked, prodded by muskets, all the way from the Smoky Mountains across the Mississippi to the wastes of what the Choctaw call Oklahoma. Thousands died, most of the children, and we named the exile road the

'Trail of Tears.' My birthplace, Ross's Landing, was the starting point for the Trail of Tears. It's just as well they call it Chattanooga."

He seemed to notice me anew. "I spent more time in Washington negotiating than with my own people. As you look promising to do. Much good may it do you. Though you may succeed where I failed."

"How so?"

John Ross rubbed fingers and thumb. "Gold," he said. "Pray for no gold in New York State."

It was dark when John Ross and I walked outside. "Where do you go now?" I asked him.

"Back to Oklahoma. I have a new plantation there, Park Hill, bigger than I ever had in Ross's Landing. And I rattle around alone on it. My own wife, Quata, died on the Trail of Tears."

John Ross looked old, and we parted, shaking hands like white men.

I was never in my life so happy to rush home and see that old, run-down, smelly, ramshackle reservation that I had spent so much time trying to escape. After the heat and damp of Washington, I was finally among fresh breezes and clear streams, woodlands and meadows, horses and cows. I felt like a captive beast returned to his native habitat. I tore off my city clothes, my frock coat and collar, and if my mother had listened to my pleas she would have burned them within five minutes of my arrival.

Life, of course, had been going on without me, and I eased into the rhythm of things, relieved after months of brainwork and palaver to get some physical labor under my belt. In fact, the expansion of my stomach *over* my belt seemed to be the chief accomplishment of my months away. I determined to do something about that, so the second day home found me at my father's sawmill on the Tonawanda on the other end of a crosscut saw with my brother Nic. Nic was three years older than me, twenty-one that summer, and a real "Indian Indian." His home was the reservation. He had never heard the sirens of civilization, content to grow up in the old way, his only concession being a nodding acquaintance with English.

Nic kept up a steady rhythm on the saw while he talked. "So," he asked me, direct as usual, "you gonna keep up with this?"

We were talking Seneca, and it was as much of a challenge to get my tongue around the clicks and whirs as it was to get my back and shoulders into the saw. I was frothing and puffing like a blown horse.

"Till lunchtime, anyway," I said.

Nic laughed and drew the saw through. He was doing most of the pushing *and* pulling, with me on the saw just for the ride. "Nah," he said. "I mean all this. Travelin' around. Politickin'. Indian business."

I grunted and let go the handle as the saw broke through the log. Nic knocked the wedge out from under it with a mallet, and I nudged the log with a pole down the spillway into the mill. "Somebody's gotta do it," I said. "Seems like that's what they groomed me for."

We guided another log into place, and I retied the sweatband around my head. "Yeah," Nic grunted. "That's what it seems. Get you an education, now you're their pet diplomat. Seems a waste."

I spit on my hands and bent to the saw. The sun was hot, but we were in the shade of the mill, with the cool river just behind us. "I dunno," I said. "Seems to me I owe them."

"Yeah," agreed Nic. "But not for life. You missed a whole school year sitting in Washington getting fat."

I laughed, breaking my rhythm and letting the saw slip from my hands. I slapped my naked belly, which bulged out over the waist of my old buckskin pants. "Got any better ideas?"

"Maybe me," said Nic. "My English is pretty good now."

"Yeah," I said. Then in English, "See the dog. The dog is brown."

"Better than that," said Nic. He motioned me to start sawing again.

I tried to saw in Nic's rhythm, and my shoulders spoke sharply to me. In English again I said, "The treaty clearly devolves the obligation for assessment of improvements upon the purchaser."

Nic kept sawing, his eyes on me, construing the sentence. His mouth worked at it. "Well, all right," he said finally in Seneca. "Maybe not *that* good. I heard the word 'treaty' in there, but not much else. But they've got this idea for me and Carrie to go to school in Albany. A school for teachers. So I'd have to learn English. And then I could take over for you."

The saw broke through, and we sent the log down the spillway to the bandsaw. It was the last of a wagonload an Indian named John Cornplanter had brought to be sawed into boards. John chucked at his horses and drove his wagon around to the back of the mill while Nic and I sat on some rocks by the creek to await the next wagon. From inside the mill came the whizzing and whining of machinery. More leather belts from more buffalo.

"I been just thinking," Nic said. "It's such a waste, you spendin' all your education on Indian business. I always thought you were meant for higher things."

I smiled at my brother. He claimed not to have my "brains," but he had smarts that let him put his finger on things faster. "Like what?" I asked him.

"I dunno." He picked up dirt and sifted it through his fingers. "Doctor, lawyer. . ."

"Indian chief," I laughed.

"Gonna be that already," he said seriously. "I mean something *out there*." His arm made a wide arc, scattering sand into the river.

I untied the cloth from my head and mopped my face. I had been planning on being something *out there* since I started going to white school. But in the last year, with the treaty on the main track, my own plans had been idling. "Trouble is, I want too much," I said. "I want to finish school, I want to make a career. And I want everyone else to be safe here when I'm gone. I was supposed to start Williams College this fall. They're holding a scholarship for me. But . . ." I waved my hand helplessly, bent down, and dipped my bandanna in the creek.

Nic flicked a stone into the water. "Yeah. Gotta be on call when the treaty stuff starts up again."

"Right," I said. I looked across the creek to the hill, where a breeze was catching the tops of the pine trees. I'd spent the past year waiting for things, and the coming year offered nothing but more waiting, for Congress, for lawyers and senators, for letters to arrive, petitions to be signed, for the chiefs to send me instructions, waiting to go to college, waiting for *my real life* to begin. Henry Flagler, in his letters, was chaffing me as a "perpetual student" and teasing me to join him in Ohio, where he was already part owner of a store. There was stuff to be done *out there*, and I wasn't doing it. "You know what I really want?" I asked suddenly.

Nic squinted up at me. "What?"

"To go west!" I said, laughing, just realizing it myself.

Nic snorted. "Where? Indian territory? That's where we're trying to *keep* from going."

"No!" I said, as the thought took hold. "I mean *west*! Where everything's unconfined, and there aren't people crowding you and legislative bodies wanting this report or that. No land companies hemming you in, because there's plenty of land for everybody! You know what I saw in Washington, Nic?"

"What?" grinned Nic. "The future?"

"Sort of," I said. "What I saw was people. People from all over." I told him about the throngs at the national fair, the bustle that attended the war. "I tell you, there's more to this country of ours than just this little eastern chute, where I keep shuttling back from here to Albany, to New York, to Washington."

"Ours," said Nic.

"What?"

"You said this country of *ours*. Who's us?"

I had, hadn't I? I started to apologize, but Nic's smile told me it was all right. "Well, we're all here," I said, flinging my arms wide. "Just because we're Indians doesn't mean we *have* to stay on reservations. We can adapt, assimilate, like everyone else. Just because I'm an Indian doesn't mean I'm *just* an Indian, you see that?"

Nic nodded thoughtfully. "I thought from when you was little, you was different. Curious, you know? Always doing something new, learning something new."

"Yeah," I said. "I don't like there being things I don't know."

Nic squatted on a rock and propped his pole against his shoulder like a spear, a classic Indian painting. "I think you got it in you to be a big success. Whatever you choose to do. And I don't mean just among the Seneca, I mean something bigger. On a scale that's, you know . . ." His fingers climbed a ladder in the air. "On the *big* ladder. Not just an *Indian* lawyer or an *Indian* doctor. I mean success compared with it *all*." He frowned, having trouble finding words, groping for thoughts the Seneca language doesn't admit.

"Yeah," I said, helping him out. "Indian becomes a teacher, what do they say? He's a pretty good teacher . . ."

"*For an Indian*," we said together and laughed.

"You mean," I said, "I can just be a successful person, Indian or no."

"I guess." Nic frowned, not sure.

It was a hard thought for an Indian to think. There's no such thing as a successful Indian. Or, put it another way, *every* Indian is a success, because he's succeeded at being an Indian, and to succeed at being an

Indian all you have to do is be an Indian. Be born one. It's like being a successful horse or bird or cow. It's built in. White men rate success a little differently.

"What are you?" I asked Nic suddenly.

"What do you mean?"

"Just that," I said. "Somebody asks you what are you, what do you say?"

Nic shrugged. "A Wolf Seneca, what else?" he said, giving the clan name before the tribe.

"And what do you do?"

"Right now?" said Nic. "Right now I'm sawin' logs."

I nodded. "See? That's right. I bet ninety-nine out of a hundred Seneca or Kiowa or Comanche, any Indian, that's how they'd answer. What are you? I'm a human being. What do you do? I eat, I sleep, I breathe, I saw logs. But you ask a white man, what are you, what do you do? It means something else."

"Yeah." Nic squinted at me. "Means what's your job?"

"Right," I said. "Seneca have jobs. Father runs the sawmill. People farm. John Blacksmith is Do-ne-ho-ga-wa. Peter Wilson is a doctor. But you ask them what they are, they don't say, I'm a sawyer, or sachem, or farmer or doctor. They say I'm Seneca, Cayuga, Mohawk. But not white men. Them, it's I'm a printer, a tavern-keeper, a coachman, a lawyer. What they are is their jobs. It's different, see?" Nic was nodding in agreement, but I kept going, explaining it to myself as much as anything. "A white man thinks he's born as raw material, like clay that's just a lump until he molds it into something. They say make something of yourself, as if yourself wasn't something already."

A wagon with a load of logs backed up to the spillway. We shouldered our poles and walked over to it. "Don't worry, *little* brother," said Nic, putting his hand on my belly and giving it a shake. "I'll study hard. Carrie too. One day we'll set you free."

Nic meant well, but it would be awhile before anybody else but me could act as go-between. So all summer I worked at the mill, and all fall I helped with the harvest, while what should have been my freshman year of college dribbled away.

January of the new year, 1847, I was back in Washington for the reconvening of Congress. I made the rounds of the New Year's receptions, including the White House and Dolley Madison's, right across Lafayette Park. I even got a chance to shake (well, to touch, let's say) hands with the great dowager. Her skin felt like parchment.

Again I was the lone Seneca in Washington, but even though I wore the Red Jacket medal wherever I went, I still spent a lot of time sitting in anterooms while the important business went on in inner chambers. I resumed my "lobbying" and managed again to see all the senators on the Indian Affairs Committee. As the vote drew closer I got such fair and friendly hearing that I allowed myself to hope, against my native pessimism and John Ross's warnings, for a decision in our favor. Senator David Atchison of Missouri invited me onto the Senate floor and showed me a stack of letters, arriving daily from all over New York, and opined that half the state must have written to him for us.

But senators may smile and smile and be villains. On February 19, as I sat on a bench outside the committee room, ignored by the great and great-seeming that passed me in the hall, one of those ubiquitous and anonymous young men that run things in Washington – he wasn't Quentin Winslow – glided up to me, in funeral black, handed me an envelope, clucked sympathetically, showed a pained smile, and vanished. It was the committee's report on the treaty, and my face drained as I read it. It was against us right down the line. While expressing sympathy with the Seneca claims, admitting that the treaty had been obtained by fraud, agreeing that the lands were ours by right and heritage, the report stated in baldest terms that undoing the wrong committed in ratifying the original treaty would compound the error by admitting the fallibility of the Senate. It would "unsettle the whole of our Indian policy" and produce "interminable difficulty, embarrassment, and expense." In other words once the Senate was committed to a course, however erroneous, it could not be deterred even when it saw that the course was wrong, because to do so would call attention to the error. The error was now "policy," and to shift policy might cost money, time, and, above all, embarrassment. As the cowboy said, watching two trains barreling toward a collision, it might be an interesting idea on paper, but it was a hell of a way to run a railroad.

Numb with shock, grief and failure, I stumbled out of the Capitol like a spectre and down Pennsylvania Avenue toward the Willard, the committee's report dangling from my hand, heedless of the cold rain that had started to fall. My mind swam with bleak images of my family and my tribe, sitting around their fires in their sturdy houses along Tonawanda Creek, houses they'd built with their own hands on the last bits of land they'd salvaged from their ancestral wilderness, waiting for me, their trusted emissary, to bring back word that, yes, there was justice in the white man's world, they could keep their homes and their last shreds of dignity. And what had I to tell them? They'd have to move. They, like the Cherokee, would have to shoulder their belongings and walk the Trail of Tears to the west, where who knew what awaited them? Certainly not the fields and forests, the lakes and streams of our perch up there on the top of the world. We'd heard from Seneca who had visited our "new homes" in Kansas. There was nothing there but sand and sagebrush. We'd die. That's just what the Senate wanted. Rather than prove an "embarrassment," they wanted us to die.

"Young man," said a woman's voice at my side. I had been vaguely aware of a carriage in the muddy street keeping pace with me, and now one of the occupants pulled the blind aside and beckoned. I stepped off the curb and the carriage stopped. A footman jumped off the back, opened the door and stood at attention. Inside was Mrs. Polk!

As I gaped at her I saw her search her memory, and, politician that she was, produce my name. "Mr. Parker, is it not?" she said.

"Y-yes," I stammered, unsure what to call her. "Mrs. Presi- that is, Miz, um..."

"Mrs. Polk is just fine," she said. "Don't stand there in the rain. Get in. Where may we take you?"

Reacting automatically to the command in her voice, I climbed in. Another woman sat next to her, bundled in furs to her chin with a turban pulled over her brow, her face barely visible. I nodded absently to her as I took the backward-facing seat opposite them. "Um, my hotel is the Willard, ma'am," I told her. "I was on my way there. It's just a few blocks. I could easily . . . "

"The Willard, Jeremy," she said peremptorily to the footman, as if the presidential carriage were a common cab, and he closed the door and remounted. We lurched forward.

Mrs. Polk looked me over, assessing, her eyes active under dark eyebrows. She was a striking woman but not conventionally pretty by the standards of the time, which preferred its women evanescent, not strong-featured and *definite* like Mrs. Polk.

"You know Mrs. Madison, of course," she said, indicating the figure next to her. I shot upright and banged my head on the roof of the carriage.

As I fumbled to recover, Dolley Madison spoke, in a kindly and bemused voice that rustled like old paper. "I have that effect on people," she said.

"Mr. Parker," explained Mrs. Polk, "is a Seneca Indian. He's here to persuade the Senate to let his people keep their lands." She narrowed her eyes and thought. "In New York, is it not Mr. Parker?"

"Yes, ma'am."

She nodded, pleased to have got it right. "And how is the struggle going?"

"Oh," I said, trying to keep a good face on things, "as well as can be expected. You know the Senate."

"Ye-e-es. I do," she said, and cocked her head at me. Her sharp ears had caught something in my voice. "Have they, at length, come to a decision?"

I looked at the committee report, soggy in my hand, and back at the two ladies. Mrs. Madison was looking out the window, but Mrs. Polk's cool eyes were on me, expecting a real answer.

"As a matter of fact, they have," I said, and, to my surprise, I spilled out the whole mess to her. How hard we'd worked, the meetings, the trips to New York and Albany to get petitions and letters sent, the senators who'd betrayed us. Every time I'd catch myself and try to stop, Mrs. Polk would ask a question, which would open a new floodgate, and the torrent went on and on. I told her how frustrating it was to be polite and diplomatic when the life of my tribe was at stake, of my friends and family, and how the cool blandness of government managed to take flesh-and-blood, life and death, sheer survival, and reduce them to figures and numbers, bits of paper to be counted like so many ballots.

I let it pour out until there was no more, and I was in tears like a child sobbing to my mother. I half expected Mrs. Polk to take my head in her lap and murmur, "There, there. Sh-h-h. Mother will fix."

My face hot, I stopped and looked out the window, biting the insides of my cheeks. After looking at me for a moment to make sure I was finished, Mrs. Polk cleared her throat. "Well, there is always the courts," she said.

Expecting nothing but a cluck of sympathy, I was surprised to get something practical.

"The courts?"

"To be sure," she said. "That's the beauty of government. Nothing is final. Or almost nothing. My husband can do no further for you. The legislature has spoken. But that leaves the judiciary. You take your case to them." A twinkle appeared in her eye. "And if you think the executive and the legislature are slow, they are *nothing* compared to the courts. They can take *forever*! And meantime, the land is still yours while the case drags on."

The courts! As soon as the hope arose it vanished. John Ross, sitting in the Chief Justice's chair, "revisiting the scene of the crime." It was just one more place to delay our Trail of Tears.

Out of the corner of my eye I had seen Mrs. Madison more and more interested in the conversation, frowning, humphing, looking out the window, looking back at us, about to say something, deciding better, drumming her half-gloved fingers on the armrest, pursing her mouth.

Abruptly, she spoke. "I've never seen why men make such a fuss about land!" she declared, her face emerging from its swath of furs. "There's so *much* of it. The whole country's made of land. If you can't have one piece, why not take another? But no! They're always squabbling over the *same* piece!"

Startled, but with my tongue loosened by my confessions to Mrs. Polk, I explained as best I could that land, unlike people, is not created equal, and that our few remaining Seneca acres were bottomland, close to rivermouths, accessible to commerce, the perfect location for farming and transportation. That's why, as well as for their ancestral associations, we wanted to keep them, and that's why the white men were fighting so hard to get them. Mrs. Madison nodded as if she understood, but after awhile I think I got too technical, because her eyes clouded and went someplace else. When I paused, she shook her head as if to chase away bad thoughts.

"Men always want so much land," she said, as if personally affronted. "My husband Jemmy and Tom Jefferson! All they wanted, more than independence, more than being president, was land. And where did it leave them? Land poor. It was a contest. Tom got land, so Jemmy got land. Then Tom got more, and Jemmy wanted still more, and on and on it went. And then what did they do? Spend their last years selling off this parcel then that, at rock-bottom prices too, because they needed the money from some of it to pay the taxes and mortgages on the rest of it. It was a never-ending downward spiral, young man." She leaned forward and tapped me on the knee, her bony fingers trembling out from a fraying half-glove. "It was folly to begin with. As if you could *own* land! Hah! Land owns you. You walk around with this immense burden of property bending you down. I saw it! They became slaves to their property, more slaves than the slaves they owned, because they were responsible for the slaves *and* the property, and the slaves were responsible for nothing." She nodded sharply for emphasis, and her turban slipped forward. She adjusted it savagely with a gnarled hand, as if it were the very property she was railing against, and Mrs. Polk smiled at her indulgently.

Mrs. Madison sniffed, thrust out her chin, and continued. "And then, of course, the land shrinks until there's nothing left but a great, drafty manor house that takes dozens of people to maintain, and no money to fix the roof or do anything but put on a brave face for company. If you get any company, that is, for who's going to visit you when you're so down-at-heel? And they're all in the same boat, land poor without a clue, poor things, how they got there." She pointed out the window, as if to the country at large. "Here we are in the lap of nature's bounty, everything ours for the plucking, and what is the highest aspiration of man? To own land, mortgage himself and his family into the poorhouse, and when he dies, to leave behind nothing but debt, so that his poor widow has no choice but to become a public charge and depend upon the generosity of a lifetime of acquaintance. Jemmy's body wasn't even cold before they were at me with their liens and mortgages, waving them over the corpse like the flappings of the shroud."

She tapped my knee again. "Young man, the happiest day of my life was when I sold the last plot of that accursed land and moved to Washington City. Poor, yes, I know that's what they say. But unencumbered, let me tell you that! If you ask me, that's what everybody should do. Forget about the land, sell it all and move to town! We must stop owning and start renting!"

The carriage had stopped in front of my hotel some time ago, and the rain had lightened. Mrs. Polk looked at Dolley Madison, who was leaning back in her corner, pleased with having her views on land recorded, looking out the window again, placid and satisfied. Mrs. Polk smiled at me, nodded, and I bade my farewells and alighted, feeling somewhat better. Maybe it was unburdening myself to Mrs. Polk and her calm practicality. Maybe it was Dolley Madison and her chattery torrent. Maybe it was just the slackening of the rain. Somehow things didn't look as bleak as they had a quarter of an hour ago.

Just before the carriage pulled away, I saw Dolley Madison's face at the window again. Her half-gloved hand pulled aside the curtain and she stared out at me. "Take my advice, young man!" she crowed, and several passers-by thought she was talking to them. "Forget about land! Learn to travel light!"

The horses' hooves clattered, the ladies vanished down the avenue, and I entered the Willard with a little spring in my step. The world hadn't ended. The sun would rise tomorrow. There was always something practical to be done, as Mrs. Polk suggested. And one could also simply rise above it and move on, as Mrs. Madison so gallantly demonstrated. I laughed out loud as I imagined myself going back and telling John Blacksmith and my parents, "Dolley Madison says we should all sell our land and move to town."

Chapter VII

WHAT HATH THE SUPREME COURT WROUGHT?

Washington 1857

ON MY RETURN TO TONAWANDA I FOUND THAT JOHN Blacksmith and the other chiefs had the same idea as Mrs. Polk – appeal to the courts. They had never, in fact, had much faith in the Senate. I felt foolish, the point man on a mission the chiefs had already consigned to failure, and useless when the tribe's white lawyers stepped in and took things out of my hands. They even took back the Red Jacket medal.

Stuck for something to do, I looked within and searched my guts for a vocation like a seer reading his own entrails. There I found an Indian boy who knew where north was and could walk a bee-line in the dark. I liked the outdoors, I liked the land, so I took Emerson's advice to "do your thing." I got hired on as a sub-assistant engineer on the Genesee Valley Canal, a new feeder on the western end of the Erie Canal. Sub-assistant engineer is a joke – it's how Flagler addressed his letters. I started at the bottom, literally. In 1848, age twenty, I became a ditch-digger.

The world shambled on. We won the Mexican War, and Zachary Taylor became president. The troops came home, and First Lieutenant Ulysses S. Grant married Julia Dent in St. Louis. He and his bride got posted to Sackett's Harbor on Lake Ontario, the same lake whose backwaters I was dredging for the canal company. If I'd looked up I might even have seen his steamer pass, but our ships weren't destined to meet just yet. Then gold was found in California, and everybody but me went looking for it. Army posts sprouted on the west coast, and Grant got separated from his growing family and shipped via Panama to California and points north, where he went slowly drunk and broke trying to raise pigs and potatoes to supplement his army pay.

I dug deeper and deeper into engineering and finally found my trade. It was close to the earth (actually *under* it for the first few months), and its labors bore physical fruit. If an engineer works long enough, then looks up, he finds he's built a bridge, a lock, a canal. I advanced from ditchman to axeman, rodman, leveler, transitman, and eventually second, then first assistant engineer with an office on Main Street in Rochester. Rochester was completely civilized, much bigger than Buffalo. The Erie Canal and Genesee River spilled into Lake Ontario, where steamboats, barges, and freighters plied. Mills and factories belched smoke, and the woods and streams of the city's Indian past were far behind. In Rochester *Tonawanda* was the name of a passenger steamer, and the only Red Jacket was the saloon across from my boarding house. I settled into the routines of work, and the years passed quickly and uneventfully, except for the occasional Seneca alarms and excursions that called me to Washington or Albany. In 1851 John Blacksmith died, and the Iroquois Confederacy conferred his title on me. His ceremony of condolence was followed by my ceremony of investiture – I became Do-ne-ho-ga-wa, Keeper of the Western Door of the Long House, chief of relations between the Six Nations and the outside world, holder (once again) of the Red Jacket medal, and, as I was thereafter charged to sign my official letters, "Grand Sachem of the Six Nations of Indians in New York and Canada." I was twenty-three years old. Despite there being fifty sachems in our tribe, all of them equal, it pleased whites, including Flagler, to address me as "Chief of the Six Nations" or "Chief Sachem," a shorthand we allowed. White men like to know they're dealing with "the man in charge," so I became he.

But, apart from the ceremonial office, my practical use to the tribe diminished, as my brother Nic got out of school and back on the reservation as U.S. Interpreter for the New York Indians. He married a white woman, Martha Hoyt, and was more and more a paterfamilias, both for our family and for the tribe. Though I met with Presidents Taylor, Fillmore and Pierce, keeping my string of presidents intact, it was no longer necessary for me to be permanently near Tonawanda or even in New York State. "Travel light," Dolley Madison had crowed at me, so I traveled. My first direction was not toward the west of my dreams, but south, where I became chief engineer on the Chesapeake and Albemarle Canal, burrowing through the Tidewater from Norfolk to North Carolina. Then finally, in the winter of 1857, all the threads of my life wove together in my magic carpet to the future.

On Wednesday, March 5, 1857, I was once again outside what John Ross termed "the scene of the crime," the Supreme Court chamber in the Capitol. Mrs. Polk had been right, the courts are *extremely* slow. It was ten years since the Senate had refused our petition to prevent the Ogden Company from seizing Tonawanda, ten years of lower court challenges, victories, defeats, appeals, more victories and defeats, and here we were again. Eighteen and a prodigy when I first came to Washington, I was now twenty-nine and almost middle-aged.

"Quit pacing, Ely," said Nic from behind his newspaper.

"I can't help it," I said, but I sat down on the bench next to him, hands in my pockets, and tried to calm myself.

"Stop jingling your money," said Nic. I stopped that too and tried to breathe easily, looking inside me for the Indian calm that was still second nature to Nic, but that deserted me at critical moments.

"Stop looking at your watch," said Nic, hearing the rattle of my watch chain, but I looked at it anyway. Nine-fifty in the morning, ten minutes to go.

It was a big time in Washington. President James Buchanan was inaugurated yesterday, and Nic had just read me an editorial that dubbed him "His Irrelevancy," no match for the rivalries that seethed all over the country, from "bleeding Kansas" to righteous Massachusetts to sullen South Carolina.

Nic and I had viewed the inauguration only by the by. The real reason we were here was for this morning's announcement – the disposition by the Supreme Court of *Fellows v. Blacksmith and Parker*, the case that John Blacksmith had started in 1847 and that had survived the old chief by six years, now with John's daughter Susan and me as named defendants. Inch by inch over the ten years, court cases came down in our favor, as we challenged the Ogdens house by house and acre by acre. Yes, the treaty said they could have the whole reservation, but what about this house? What about that one? What about this stables, that barn, that apple orchard? It was slow but it worked. Our departure deadline was long past, and we were more dug in than ever.

Outside the Supreme Court were knots of people in various corners, some looking seriously at papers and chewing their lips, but most of them happy sightseers, in town for the inauguration and sneaking a peek at the Court, as if the Court, where our tribe hung in the balance, were just another tourist attraction.

When the doors finally opened, there was a rush for seats, and John Martindale, our lawyer, elbowed us to the front. It was still an unimpressive chamber, dark, partitioned, hidden away in the bowels of the Capitol. The one time I'd been there John Ross and I had the place to ourselves, two supporting players on an empty stage. Now the audience hushed, as a door opened at the side, a row of men in suits filed in and, to my surprise, took off their coats. It wasn't until they plucked black robes from hooks on the wall and pulled them awkwardly on that I realized these were the justices, dressing a little absurdly in public. "Oyez, oyez, oyez!" chanted the bailiff, and we all rose.

"Where's Taney?" I whispered to Martindale, as the justices took their places behind the long bench. He shrugged. Chief Justice Roger Taney's great central chair was empty. Flanking it, Justices McLean, Wayne, Catron, Daniel, Nelson, Grier, Curtis, and Campbell all looked very distinguished but also very *old*. I had ceased, by now, to equate age with wisdom, and I felt shaky at the thought of our tribe's future in their palsied hands. What could such old and cloistered men know of the world? An old, bewildered president and nine fossil judges. How could the country survive?

We chewed our nails while other cases were read, and, looking around as the justices droned on, I saw people quietly congratulating each other or looking resigned and defeated. Which group would we join? Finally, just when it seemed they'd forgotten us entirely, Justice Nelson cleared his throat, shuffled pages and announced *Fellows v. Blacksmith*. His voice was dry and unemotional, and he didn't look up as he read, so I had no way of knowing who was winning.

He began with a recital of the facts on both sides, and for awhile the players seemed evenly matched. Joseph Fellows of the Ogden Company had forcibly evicted John Blacksmith from his sawmill and yard, *quare clausum fregit*. Advantage whites. John had retaken and kept the property, the *locus in quo*. Advantage Indians. Fellows sued, and the case traveled through the lower courts. Advantage whites. Justice Nelson delivered a disquisition on the history of the Seneca treaties, beginning with the 1794 promise to leave our lands intact (advantage Indians) and the various modifications that ensued, ending with the 1842 treaty that gave Tonawanda away (advantage whites). "Compensation" had been paid us and "lands west of the Missouri" reserved for what Nelson ominously called our "new homes." Advantage whites again, and every time he repeated "west of the Missouri" and "new homes," I squirmed in greater agony as I felt the contest slipping away. Calculations revealed that our "new homes" reserved something more than three hundred acres for each of the three thousand Indians involved, implying that the treaty was more than generous. Big advantage whites, and the gas lights seemed to fill the room with smoke.

It was hard to sit there being patronized. According to Justice Nelson, we were a "dependent people," under the "care and superintendence," the "protection" of the U.S., "a ward to" the U.S. "guardian." Big and little brother. Please, sir, I want some more. I fiddled with my necktie. Nic, like a big brother, plucked my hand away and placed it in my lap, his face showing no emotion. Martindale scribbled in a notebook. For what, an appeal from the court of no appeal? His memoirs?

Justice Nelson licked his thumb, turned a page and cleared his throat. His tone changed subtly and I leaned forward. "Neither treaty," he read, "made any provision as to the mode or manner in which the removal of the Indians or surrender of the reservation was to take place." Was this it? "The grantees," he continued, meaning the Ogden Company, had assumed they were authorized to take forcible possession. Were they? This was the final point.

Nelson licked his thumb, had trouble turning the page, and licked it again, until I wanted to tear off my clothes, leap onto the bench, and turn the pages *for* him. He got the pages unstuck and cleared his rheumy throat. "The removal of tribes and nations of Indians from their ancient nations to their new homes" (I ground my teeth. "New homes" again!) "in the west have been under the government's care and superintendence," he read. "Indeed it is difficult to see how any other mode of removal can be consistent with the duty of the government towards these dependent people."

I chewed my fist. Advantage Indians? I ceased to mind the insult of "dependent people" if it meant the government was going to *protect* us. Nelson went off, with maddening deliberateness, into a parenthesis about how the Seneca were a *"quasi* nation, possessing *some of the attributes* of an independent people," which I, a chief of the "quasi nation" swallowed hard until I saw where he was heading. Surely, therefore, he said, the treaty could only be executed by "the government, which was a party to it," and not by the "irregular force and violence" of the Ogden Company.

Oho. Advantage Indians. Rather than ruling on the legality of the treaty itself, Justice Nelson was finding grounds for a reprieve in the language of the treaty as it stood, as he now made clear. For the government to allow a private agency to evict three thousand Indians "by irregular force and violence" would be, he said, in the one emotional term he used all morning, "appalling."

I leaned back and exhaled the breath I didn't know I was holding. "We think, therefore," Justice Nelson concluded, that the Ogden Company "derived no power, under the treaty, to dispossess by force these Indians, and that a forcible removal must be made, if made at all, under the direction of the United States." That was it. The Ogden Company, despite owning title to the land, couldn't kick us off it. Indians take the match. I looked at Nic, who stared straight ahead, but whose eye showed a tear and whose fists drummed softly on his knees. John Martindale leaned back and closed his eyes, a beatific smile on his face.

But I was unsatisfied. What about the fraudulent treaty itself? Wasn't Nelson going to throw out that bath water with the baby he'd just disposed of? As if he'd heard me, the justice cleared his throat, licked his thumb, turned another page, and read. "The court makes no opinion," he informed me, as to "the validity of the treaty," which was "executed and ratified by the proper authorities" and was "the supreme law of the land." And with that equivocal drivel, the ancient justice put down his papers, took off his glasses, and looked down the bench to see what was next.

So calmly it happened. In a cramped little room in the bowels of the Capitol, on a bright March morning, the Seneca nation was saved by the words of a frail old man who had probably never seen an Indian in his life.

When the Court recessed, John Martindale came across the corridor rubbing his hands. "Well, well, well," he said. "What hath God wrought!"

I was not so happy. "It's not a clean victory," I said. "It's just technical. The treaty still stands."

Nic grabbed my chin and pulled it up. "So, technically, we won."

I shook him off. "They didn't judge the merits. All they said was the Ogden Company can't evict us. But the government can."

"They won't," said Nic, grinning and brushing my lapels. "All we have to do is keep sending you down here every time there's a new president, you impress him with your manners and dignity, and we're safe for another four years."

John Martindale smiled. "The law is *all* technicalities. The Supreme Court has just said you can keep your land. That's the important thing."

"At the pleasure of the government!" I shot back. "That's not title, that's whim!"

"The government has a strong whim," said Martindale. "Once they get whimmed in one direction it's hard to whim them back."

Nic said in Seneca, "The government won't guard our hens with one hand and eat them with the other."

I at last agreed to join the congratulations. The Ogden Company's lawyers slinking out the door with fallen faces cheered me up too.

My other business in Washington, the next day, was a meeting with Treasury Secretary James Guthrie, in charge of assigning engineers to government projects, from whom, finally, I hoped to gain a commission in the elusive west. I had references from Governor Seymour of New York, Canal Commissioner Frederick Follett, State Treasurer Alvah Hunt, and State Engineer William J. McAlpine. I also had a specific post in mind, the superintendency of public buildings in Chicago. I had dug under the earth to build canals, scraped its top to level roads and site locks, now it was time to build into the air, creating courthouses, post offices, and other mighty edifices that would echo with the colloquies of the nation's business. Full of hope, scrubbed and fresh and eager, I strode through the door of the Treasury mausoleum, right next door to the White House, the lights of Chicago glittering in my eyes. A half hour later I stood again on Pennsylvania Avenue, deflated, staring at a brief letter that I clutched in disbelief, the lump of coal from my bright Christmas stocking. I was to be a superintendent, all right, but not of public buildings and not in Chicago. I was the new superintendent of lighthouses on the Great Lakes, bound for Detroit and the watery wastes of the North.

The State Department was right in front of me, so I trudged up the steps, up more stairs, down a couple of corridors, where I located my old pal Quentin Winslow squirreled away in a distant cubbyhole, stacks of paper sealing him from the outside world.

"Lighthouses!" I said, flourishing the paper at him. "I know nothing of lighthouses! Nor of buoys and beacons, which I'm also in charge of." I slumped into a chair by his desk.

"Sh-h-h!" cautioned Quentin, looking cautiously around. "What did you expect, Parker?"

"Certainly not this," I said, exasperated, reading from the paper. "Five hundred installations, dotting the lakes from Huron to Michigan to Superior." I'd seen myself a swashbuckling young man of the great western city, dispensing and refusing favors from my office on the square. Instead I was to be a lonely Indian in a canoe, paddling through the plumbless fog, foghorns lowing in my ears, searching through the soup for one buoy or beacon after another, my only shelter an occasional night in a keeper's cottage before slogging drearily on. Who would be my society? Lighthouse keepers, madmen, no doubt, driven cabin-crazy by the fog-bound nights and sodden days in the northern mists. I would soon become as mad as they.

Quentin let me blow. When I was silent he moved his head from side to side. "You reached too high, Parker. They'd never give you Chicago. Not to an Indian. We barely got through stealing it from them."

"A man's reach should exceed his grasp," I quoted. "Or what's a heaven for?"

Quentin looked blank. "Browning," I explained.

He blinked and shook his head. "I'm sure you are," he said. "But you didn't ask for heaven, just Chicago." He turned over some papers on his desk, licked his thumb and turned some more until he found something. "Would you consider something farther west?"

"As long as it's on land." I leaned forward to read the paper Quentin held, but he put it on his desk and covered it with an arm.

"All in good time, Parker. Watch that reach of yours," he said. "Go to Detroit. Wait for my telegram. We'll get you high and dry."

I hauled myself aboard the train for Detroit and read in the paper why Chief Justice Taney had skipped Court. He had been at work on the majority opinion in another case, announced the next day, March 6, 1857, of far more significance for the country than the disposition of Indian lands up near Buffalo. A slave of Dr. John Emerson was taken in 1834 by his master from St. Louis, Missouri, where slavery was legal, to Rock Island, Illinois, where it was not. Returning to Missouri in 1846, the former slave sued for his freedom there too, and was denied it by the state court. From there the case reached the Supreme Court. In the first place, said Chief Justice Taney, Dred Scott (the Negro) could not sue in Federal court, because he (and all Negro slaves and their descendants) was not a citizen of the United States or of Missouri or Illinois or Wisconsin Territory or anywhere. He was a slave, and once a slave always a slave. Furthermore, Scott's status in Missouri was determined by the laws of Missouri, where he was a slave whatever other states said. Furthermore, the Missouri Compromise was illegal, because it deprived people of their right to property (i.e., slaves) without due process. Thus Taney ruled almost all Negroes in the country non-citizens and subject to capture and bondage under the fugitive slave law. A Negro had no rights a white man was bound to respect.

This Indian, though, had got some respect, and I took off for the west, leaving the troubles of north and south behind. Before I even had a chance to unpack in Detroit, Quentin's machinations proved true in the form of a new commission. Superintendent of buildings not in Chicago, but at the other edge of Illinois in the boom town of Galena. So I bade Detroit hello-and-goodbye, caught the next steamer, and lit out for Galena, where destiny, in the shape of a shambling, unshaven, broken-down ex-soldier named Grant, would find me.

Chapter VIII

MULE TASTES
BETTER THAN DOG

Vicksburg 1863

IN THE SPRING OF 1861, WHILE THE WAR SPUTTERED TO start, I slunk to Tonawanda to work what Secretary Seward called "my farm," a farm I had never worked before, but I dutifully plowed seed and money underground and watched very little of it sprout. I was no farmer. Lucky the war kept going as long as it did or I'd have gone bust as a man of peace.

It was an oddly detached thing, farming up there at the top of the world while the country below was at war. Aside from an occasional troop of soldiers that passed through Buffalo, nothing but the newspapers told me there was a war at all. They and Henry Flagler, who wrote from the salt mines of Saginaw, Michigan that the war was treating him fine, and he "wouldn't be sorry to see it go on forever." He paid a substitute in the draft of 1862, which settled his military obligation. "My investment of $20,000 has returned one hundred fifty per cent," he enthused in December 1862, just days after windrows of northern troops were blown down at Fredericksburg.

> We have two blocks of 100 kettles for evaporating brine and a salt well next door. Costs are criminally low. Each block needs only three workers at $1.50 a day each. Barrels run about 30c in our own

cooperage, and we nail and pack for two bits. Total costs for a barrel of salt? Eighty cents, my friend, and at two-fifty a barrel wholesale, it's almost two dollars per of profit. Better than whiskey, even, and with the advantage that, unlike whiskey, salt is underground free for the taking. Fifteen thousand barrels this year, and we're not running close to capacity yet.

He didn't mention my $1,000 "investment."

The war soon reached capacity as well and started churning out casualties as if to meet a quota. The war in the west interested me most, but so transfixed were the papers by affairs in the east that I had to search the back pages for Grant. His November 1861 skirmish at Belmont, Missouri, rated scant mention. It wasn't until the capture of Forts Henry and Donelson and a whole southern army on the Tennessee and Cumberland in February 1862 fleshed out his initials to "*U*nconditional *S*urrender" that the country began to notice him. "Grant has forsaken his pipe for cigars," wrote Will Rowley to me from Donelson. "A newspaper man saw him sitting on his horse during the battle, scrawling out orders and puffing on a rare cigar, because you can't smoke a pipe and ride at the same time. But people read of the 'cigar-smoking general' and now boxes of them arrive daily. We of the staff have become confirmed in the habit as well."

I kept in touch with Rowley, now Grant's military secretary, as well as with other Galenans. "Black John" Rawlins was Grant's chief of staff and, according to Rowley, "babysitter and temperance lady too," keeping the general on the narrow path from which boredom and frustration tempted him to stray. As Grant ground ahead, I began to see him eating up the map exactly as he'd laid it out in his brother's store. Established at Cairo, the pivot of the Ohio and the Mississippi, he swung east to take Paducah, then south along the Cumberland and Tennessee to take Henry and Donelson and push all the way down the Cumberland to drive the rebels from Nashville before he outran his supplies and Washington's courage and got called back.

Then came April 6 and 7, 1862 and the first of those great set pieces, so awesome in their slaughter, that branded the war to the end. In the woods and flats between Owl and Snake Creeks and the Tennessee River, the Confederates attacked on Sunday, Grant counterattacked on Monday, and when it was done three thousand men lay dead on the field and under the peach petals that shivered down around Shiloh Church. Twenty-five thousand casualties on both sides in two days' fighting – greater than the whole Revolution, greater than the 1812, greater than the Mexican War. Three thousand dead was more dead in a few square miles than there were Seneca Indians alive in the whole world, more than the population of many of the places the dead men came from, more than the male population of Vicksburg and Gettysburg, yet so ravenous was the war the proud young nation had birthed that three thousand men was barely two days' rations. "I spent all of Sunday morning riding through the swamps looking for Lew Wallace's brigade," wrote Will Rowley. "When I found him, it took most of Sunday afternoon to convince him he was lost. We didn't reach the field until sunset. By that time you could have walked the space between the armies on a carpet of corpses."

Only the hollowness of old words in the face of new horrors allowed Shiloh the name of victory. The next year drained further sense from the language of war as Grant ground south toward Vicksburg in what people tried to see as "battles" but which were just slugfests in the swamp. Seven ways he tried to take the river fortress and seven ways he failed, "just like the labors of Hercules," Will Rowley wrote, but a year after Shiloh Grant was high and dry and so, still, was Vicksburg. Finally, Grant tossed his cigar aside, ordered up full steam, and in a spectacular night passage, Porter's ships blazed past Vicksburg's batteries. Grant ferried his troops across the Mississippi south of the town, and finally established himself, six months after he'd started and three days after his forty-first birthday, "on dry ground on the same side of the river with the enemy."

The battles that burned themselves into the nation's memory and later brought tears to the eyes of veterans' gatherings were just names then, rustling dryly from the newspapers that gathered in the corner of my porch. But the names gave the country a new self-awareness, as distant places rolled off people's tongues as easily as the town next door. A neighbor at the sawmill was as likely to speak of Corinth, Mississippi as he was of Buffalo, of Springfield, Missouri in the next breath after Niagara. "What news of the Peninsula?" we'd ask. Or Fredericksburg or Manassas, Brandy Station or Ball's Bluff.

It was a curious concatenation of tongues, the roll-call of America that spilled from the press. The Bible brought us Shiloh and Manassas. Rivers showed the fossil footprints of the Indians that had fished their depths and hunted their shores. But who knew any more who the Potomac were? Or the Rapahannock? What did Mississippi mean, or Tennessee or Shenandoah? Antietam Creek was a discarded shell that the new owners filled with new blood, as were Chickasaw Bluffs, the Yazoo, the Totopotomoy and the Chickahominy.

But the Bible and the Indian were far outnumbered in the Civil War landscape – in the American landscape – by the little names of little men who'd cleared little spaces for themselves in the wilderness. Every day the papers reported a battle or a skirmish at somebody's ford or somebody's mill, somebody's ville or burg or bluff, somebody's mountain or hill or fork in the road. Ball's Bluff, Carrick's Ford, Champion's Hill, Frayser's Farm, Harpers Ferry, Kernstown, Logan's Crossroads, Wilson's Creek, Bartlett's Mill, Clark's Mountain, and of course, Fredericksburg, Chancellorsville, Gettysburg and Vicksburg. I don't suppose Messrs. Frederick, Chancellor and Getty, Reverend Vick, or any of those fellows had any notion what immortality they were in for when they scratched their names in the woods or on the bluffs. They were just being American. Blaze the forest, clear your space, drive down stakes, raise the roof and notch your name. America was the only place you could do that, an Eden for the new Adams to name, and they did so like happy dogs, marking every bush and tree.

If you believe a young historian whose pamphlet is on my desk as I write in 1895, this makes a man more typically American than anything else. His name is Frederick Jackson Turner, from Wisconsin, and his pamphlet *The Significance of the Frontier in American History* takes its cue from the census of 1890 which noted that so much of the country is settled that nothing called a "frontier" any longer exists. When I was born, when a young Frenchman named de Tocqueville toured the young country, the frontier was in my mother's back yard along the Tonawanda and there was no such place as Turner's Wisconsin. I've lived from Tocqueville to Turner, and the frontier has followed the sun and vanished into the Pacific. The nineteenth century – my century – killed slavery, killed the Indians, opened the frontier, filled it, tilled it and shut it down.

At the end of May, 1863, the climactic forces of the war gathered east and west. In the east Lee was moving north again, in a sweep around the mountains that would soon converge his columns with Meade's in southern Pennsylvania. In the west, Grant was smashing towns and railroads in western Mississippi, cutting Vicksburg off, and wheeling to join Sherman in a stranglehold. The burgs of Mr. Getty and Reverend Vick trembled. And on a day in early June, 1863, as I stood in my dusty field at Tonawanda watching crows eat my new-sprouted corn, a uniformed rider pounded up to my fence waving a letter. My absence at the ball had been noted. After two years of waiting and patient petitioning, after two years of discreet and unsigned notes of hope from Quentin Winslow, I had a commission. I was to be a staff adjutant, whatever that was, ordered forthwith to join the army tightening on Vicksburg.

It was as Captain Parker that I traveled west to meet Grant again, first to Pittsburgh, then down the Ohio and Mississippi, closing in on Vicksburg by water while the rest of the army closed in by land. I don't know what I expected to see in the country at war, but it wasn't what I got. Maybe I expected blue troops standing elbow to elbow along the Ohio shores. Maybe the smoking wreckage of transports choking the passage. Burnt-out forests and festering cattle corpses. Sharpshooters in hidden ambuscades. There was none of that. Pittsburgh was unruffled, its Monongahela River untroubled by the possibility that Lee's army might now be drinking from its headwaters. War-bound supplies choked the docks at Cincinnati, and I amused myself wondering how many of the barrels contained salt from the Flagler works. But aside from the few signs of martial bustle the impression I got from the waterways was still of vast space rather than vast commerce. The country at war looked remarkably like the country at peace. History's bloodiest war was convulsing the continent and leaving barely a trace on the land.

After we swung south at Cairo, the steamer slowed, and the pilot kept well out from the shore. Missouri and Arkansas on the right bank and Kentucky and Tennessee on the left were still only semi-Union, and there was fear of snipers and floating mines. All went well until we reached Memphis, where, as we swung from midstream and made for the dock, the city suddenly exploded with shot and shell, rockets and gunfire setting the shoreline ablaze, sending smoke trails in great spirals skyward. Our pilot reversed engines, and we all lurched against the rail and held on. Had the rebels retaken the city? Had the arsenals been sabotaged? Eyes turned to me, a uniformed officer, for information, advice, or reassurance, but I had none. It wasn't until the cannonade slackened and we heard bands playing, trumpets and fifes and drums across the waters, that the pilot felt safe to land. As we docked people rushed down the wharves shouting up to the decks, "Vicksburg has fallen!"

The joyous news was redoubled with more news as we filed ashore. Just yesterday, July 3, Union troops under General Meade had thrown back Lee's final assault at Gettysburg, sent the Army of Northern Virginia reeling back toward Richmond, and were about to pursue Lee into surrender or annihilation. Two rebel armies, east and west, were on the brink of capture, and the end of the war seemed imminent. Even as I joined the celebration, coming providentially on the country's four score and seventh Independence Day, and even as I rejoiced in the war's end, I felt regret. Two years of obstruction and prejudice had kept me from the greatest passion of my generation, and I had missed it by days.

We made steam for Vicksburg, arriving on the seventh. By that time it was becoming clear that the country's hopes weren't to be realized, that Meade would let Lee escape across the Potomac, and that the war, in the east at any rate, would go on. In the west, though, Grant had captured all of Pemberton's army, the second army he'd swallowed whole in two years, and as Lincoln put it, from Minnesota to the Gulf the Father of Waters went unvexed to the sea.

John Rawlins met me on the Vicksburg dock. It took me three looks to recognize him with his new black beard and a few more to recognize the stripling who stood next to him. It was Fred Grant, now thirteen years old and grown about a foot since Galena. I snapped off a salute, which surprised Rawlins, but he returned it with all the formality he could muster. "*Colonel* Rawlins," I said, smiling. "*Captain* Parker," he said, and then we were shaking hands and clapping each other on the back.

"We're too busy to do much saluting out here," said Rawlins as I gathered my bag. "You remember young Fred, of course."

"How are you, Mr. Parker?" said Fred, sticking out his hand. I took it and grinned at him. Fred wore a uniform shirt with the sleeves rolled up and pants that barely reached his ankles.

"Come down to join the victory?" I asked him as we walked past the warehouses and shanties along the dock.

"Hell, no," said Fred. His adolescent voice cracked, and he cleared his throat. "I been here the whole time." He pointed out at the river. "Ever since Porter and the navy ran the guns. I was almost the first one into Jackson. Almost captured the flag on the Capitol."

I raised my eyebrows at Rawlins. "Oh, yes," he said. "Fred's in the army now. If Mrs. Grant had had her way, she and the other children would have ridden along too."

"You should have seen it, Ely, I mean, Captain Parker," enthused Fred, his voice cracking, wavering between soprano and baritone. "It was like the Fourth of July. Mother and father and all of us were on deck, and the navy dropped away down the river in front of us, dead slow, running silent. The suspense was awful! Then bam! The whole sky exploded! We could see Vicksburg lit up like a thunderstorm and Porter's guns answering back, boom boom! Mother and father sat there, holding hands through the whole thing, just like at a picnic. Then the guns were booming further off, but we couldn't see them any more, because the fleet had got round the bend. Or they'd sunk, we didn't know which. In the morning, father took off on a horse lickety-split and found the ships safe and sound down river."

Rawlins ruffled Fred's hair and the boy batted his hand away. We turned off the dock by the Washington Hotel, a corner of whose roof had been knocked in by the shelling, and walked uphill along Jackson Street. It was a steep climb, though the cobblestones gave easy purchase both to our boots and to the horse and mule drays that labored up and down alongside us. Glass crunched underfoot. The town had undergone a hellacious shelling, both by land and water, for upwards of two months. Yet most of the buildings were still standing. There were holes in roofs and walls, and sometimes the whole side of a house had been shorn away, showing the inside as in cross-section. Dirt and dust covered every surface, and there wasn't an intact pane of glass. The air reeked of smoke and gunpowder.

As we progressed uphill, we rose through caste levels as well, the shanties of the quayside giving way to shops, then frame houses, then mansions toward the summit. Vicksburg was barely a generation old, and the immigrants had brought their heritage with them, so the town was an architectural anthology of mid-century America. In a single block stood a New England saltbox, a lacy New Orleans balcony, a broad Charleston veranda, a columned Greek Revival manse and a brick four-story that would have looked fine on Lark Street in Albany. So steep were the streets that no two houses were on a level, and flights of stairs led at crazy angles between them. Citizens were sweeping out and making repairs, all of them gaunt and haggard, haunted about the eyes, and tired from a siege diet of dried peas and shellfire. At a sudden noise, the crash of a barrel hitting the sidewalk, everyone looked up startled, and a dog who had been watering a post ducked his tail and darted under some stairs. "Everyone's still spooked," I noted.

"Oh, yes," agreed Rawlins. "The silence is vast. My ears are still ringing from the shelling."

Fred threw a stone after the vanished dog. "Must be one of ours," he said.

"The shelling killed most of theirs?" I asked.

"Their owners killed 'em," grinned Fred. "Then they ate 'em." I looked down at him and he shrugged. "I tried some. It was tough. Not nearly's good as mule."

As we continued climbing, we passed ledges of bare earth, where citizens had dug caves to shelter from the bombing. They were not rude dwellings. One had a dining table in it, an easy chair, books, magazines, and an oil lamp. A man sat in the chair smoking his pipe while his wife swept the oriental carpet.

"Prairie Dog City," murmured Fred.

"That's what they call it," agreed Rawlins. At the top of the street, where Washington crossed Jackson, we reached the town square. The courthouse stood intact, a memorial to the haphazardness of long-range gunnery. Union artillerists had sighted on it, lobbed thousands of shells at it, and it withstood them all. Its four-faced clock showed the correct time all round, and only the stars and stripes fluttering from its flagpole conceded defeat. On wooden steps and hitching posts under the balconies, soldiers of both sides chatted in the noon sunlight. This was my first sight of Confederate soldiers, and I was interested to see that their supposed gray uniforms were more often butternut-brown.

"Prisoners?" I said, indicating the southern troops, who didn't look to be under guard.

"Oh, no," said Rawlins. "Just fraternizing. We couldn't spare the transports to take everybody prisoner. We captured the whole damn army, you know. Thirty thousand, near enough. We're disarming 'em, paroling 'em, and sending 'em home. They'll rejoin, some of them, but most not. The war in the west is over."

Fred left us and hovered around the edges of some blue and butternut troops in front of a general store. "Picking up lingo," smiled Rawlins. "He beat just about everyone into Jackson, you know. He and Mr. Dana from the War Department commandeered two big farm horses and just kept on riding. They would have captured the flag if the scouts hadn't got there first. Grant and Sherman burned the place to the ground. Chimneyville, they call it now."

I watched the troops chatting, more like opponents after a lacrosse match than people who, less than a week ago, had been trying to kill each other. We walked south along the crest of the hill toward the railroad station, where headquarters was set up. The crowds increased, soldiers standing around in the shade of the buildings, scratching themselves and spitting into the dust. "Grant's in there," said Rawlins when we reached the depot. I made to continue, but Rawlins held my sleeve and looked around to make sure we were unheard. He looked at me and his black eyes and his voice got soft. "I'm glad you're here, Ely," he said. "Grant needs men like us around him."

I frowned. "Us?"

Rawlins nodded. "Galena men. Men he knows, who he can get comfortable with. War is dangerous, and not all the danger comes from the enemy without. The enemy within can eat you away." He tapped his chest. "It's not so bad when we're close to home base, when Julia can be with him. Or when there's fighting, which keeps him active. But the siege ate away at him. There have been incidents. And there may be more if we're kept inactive over the summer."

I squinted at John. "Drinking?"

He pursed his lips and nodded grimly, so like a temperance minister I almost laughed. "He had a case of wine with him to celebrate the victory. I took it from him and broke every bottle."

"You didn't!" I said.

"I certainly did."

"French or American?" I shuddered to picture grim-visaged Rawlins tossing bottle after bottle of Bordeaux over the ramparts.

"Who cares?" Rawlins waved his arms. "The point is he wants to drink. Does drink when he gets away from me. He spent two days drunk on the Yazoo during the siege, commandeering riverboats and nearly breaking his neck riding too fast. A newspaper reporter saw him and so did Dana of the War Department. I managed to shut them up, but it was close."

"What do you want me to do about it?" I asked.

"Stay near him when you can. Keep an eye on him. Above all, don't drink with him."

I shifted my bag from hand to hand. In it I had two bottles of whiskey, one a present for Grant. Rawlins's gaze seemed to bore right through me. "I'm no baby-sitter, John," I told him. "I'm here to work."

Rawlins put his hand on my shoulder. "I know, Ely," he said. "But you and he liked to share a drop back in Galena." I shrugged, unable to deny it. Rawlins nodded. "Well, out here we have to make our own society. The only restraints are our own. So, a word to the wise, eh?" He raised a black eyebrow and ushered me through the station door.

Inside, all was bustle. The benches had been pushed aside. Boards were thrown over barrels for desks, and officers of all shapes and sizes and varying degrees of formality strode and lounged and pointed at things, brandishing papers. Rawlins led me to a room in the corner, entered without knocking, and there was Grant, his hands behind his back, his coat unbuttoned, cigar in his mouth, frowning at a map on the wall, a young officer with colonel's stripes and a shock of blond hair pointing things out to him.

"Captain Parker reporting, sir!" said Rawlins, and Grant turned. I snapped off a salute, which he returned, smiling with the cigar-less half of his mouth. I don't know what I expected. Some magic transformation into military genius, a foot taller, the frog become a prince. But it was just Grant, scruffy, unshaven, stoop-shouldered. Even the uniform didn't add much, the slouchy way he wore it.

"Glad to see you, Parker," said Grant. He stuck out his hand and I shook it and he nodded me up and down as if mulling something over. "Yes. Could have used you earlier."

"I tried to get here, General," I said. "Did the best I could."

"Sure," said Grant. "Could have used you this winter. Hell of a time for an engineer to show up, *after* a siege. Sixty thousand-man army, and how many engineer officers? Two. One of 'em's Wilson here."

I turned and met the young, blond officer, James Harrison Wilson, two years out of West Point and a picture of eastern self-assurance. "Only two engineers?" I asked him.

"The general's being modest," said Wilson smoothly. "He actually, by the end, had something like several thousand engineers. Every man in the ranks pitched in."

"It was quite a sight, Ely," said Rawlins, tapping the map on the wall. "Had to march the army through fifty miles of swamp, with the river at flood, to reach the crossing-point below town. Every low place had to be bridged, every road shored up. Pontoons, struts, everything built out of found materials. Swamp houses and shacks and fenceposts that we tore down."

"But these western soldiers are farm boys," chimed in Wilson, "if they didn't know how to build a bridge, they improvised. Time and again I'd be called out to throw a span across some bog and by the time I got there, the men had bridged it and gone across. Same with repairing caissons, digging fortifications. They've all built wagons and dug foundation holes. They just adapted and moved on. Quite a different attitude than the east."

"Wilson was under McClellan until Antietam," explained Rawlins.

After more chat, Rawlins and I left the office and plunged into the noise and bustle of the big station lobby. "Wilson says that an army becomes like its commander," he told me. "He says in the east, every man in the ranks is a McClellan. They all dress nice, parade beautifully, and wait and see what the other fellow's going to do. But Grant's army has become Grant. They see a problem, they fix it. They see an opportunity, they take it. They dress ragged, can't march in step or carry a tune, but they sure can get a job done. Look, there's Rowley. Up to his ears as usual."

Across the floor red-haired Will Rowley sat at a board-and barrel desk surrounded, it seemed, by the enemy. Some dozen officers in southern butternut stood around berating him, waving papers in the air. "See what you can do for him," said Rawlins, nudging me in Will's direction. "I'll catch you up later."

So, Grant soldier that I now was, I tightened my grip on my bag, lowered my shoulder and elbowed through the crowd until I stood in front of Will. "Captain Parker reporting, sir," I told him. "Colonel Rawlins' compliments and what the hell can I do for you, you little shit?"

Rowley snapped his head up, saw my smiling face and sarcastic salute, and hooted a welcome. He waved the crowd of southerners to make way for me and I edged around the desk to sit beside him. "God, Ely," he said, pumping my hand, "am I glad to see you! Look at this mess!"

The desk was littered with papers, some stacked up with rocks on top of them, others just scattered around, some tossed in boxes, others spilling onto the floor. They were little squares, uniform in size, but widely various in color and content. "What is it all?" I asked him.

"Paroles!" said Will. "That's what! Paroles, Ely!" He grabbed two fistfuls and shook them in my face like a mad alchemist. "They're driving me mad, do you hear me? Mad!" He let out a loud cackle and crossed his eyes.

"How long we gotta wait, Colonel?" drawled a secesh lieutenant. "I been standin' here all afternoon."

"And I been sitting here for three days!" barked Will. "Wait your turn, lieutenant."

"What's going on?" I asked Will.

Rowley ignored the pleading mob around the desk and explained. "It seemed like a good idea. We captured a whole army, thirty thousand men. What do we do with them? Send them to prison up north? That not only ties up our transport, it also means we have to house and feed them till war's end. So Grant paroles them. All they have to do is lay down their arms, promise not to fight any more, and go home. Hell, the war in the west is done, no fighting left for them. Except for a few hundred fire-bellies, they've had enough. They'll go home and stay there."

"So what's the problem?" I asked.

"The problem," said Will, the mad-actor look making his eyes spin again, "is that they have to promise *in writing*! In duplicate! Thirty thousand of them! Sixty thousand pieces of paper! And I'm in charge. There wasn't that amount of paper left unburnt in the whole town. The newspapers had been printing on old wallpaper rolls, and even that was gone by the end. Most of the printing presses were busted too." He laughed and waved helplessly at the papers that fluttered around the desk. "So that's how I celebrated the victory of Vicksburg, Mother, signing my name sixty thousand times."

I examined some of the paroles. They were printed on a remarkable variety of paper, from wallpaper to butcher paper to card stock to flimsy. The only thing uniform about them was they all said the same thing, that so-and-so promises to lay down his arms and not take them up again until properly exchanged, with the soldier's signature and a Union officer's signature, usually Rowley's or somebody named Bowers, at the bottom.

"Who's Bowers?" I asked.

"The question," said Will, grabbing a sheaf of paroles from an outstretched southern hand, "is *where* is Bowers. What he is is my co-worker, and he's supposed to be sitting right where you are. *Where* he is is usually someplace else." Will riffled through the paroles an officer had handed him, checked them against a regimental roster, wrote out a receipt, handed it to the officer, clipped the paroles together, and tossed them in a box. "Might as well join in, Ely. Your army initiation."

I was soon pitching in, signing my name to the first of thousands of official documents that the war would shove under my nose. I must have signed "Ely S. Parker, Capt. U.S.A." several hundred times that afternoon. It was a bureaucratic nightmare, but by day's end we had it well under control. Only then did the absent Bowers show up.

"And who might you be, Captain?" said a voice behind me.

I stood up automatically and found myself looking down at a small pepperpot of a colonel with flashing eyes and a bristling manner, but so short that his military bearing looked comical. He had close-cropped hair and a long black beard that hid his throat and made him look like you could pick off his head and find him filled with chocolates.

"This is Ely Parker, Joe," said Rowley without looking up. "Ely, Colonel Theodore Bowers, known, when we can find him, as Joe. Keep his chair. You've earned it."

I sat down again and Bowers hovered between us, chatting away. "Sorry, lads. I got caught in an emergency."

"As usual," said Will. I would learn that Bowers's way was always to set off on one mission, get diverted to another, then another, then another, until his first objective was quite forgot.

"It was genuine," said Bowers, looking hurt. "I found some of our boys digging in a widow's yard, looking for her silver. She wouldn't tell them where it was, so they pretty near dug up the whole yard. When I got there they'd just unearthed the coffin of her little girl who died during the siege. Well, the weeping and wailing, I tell you. So I had to get the provost marshal to take the men in hand. And then nothing would do but I had to fetch her a preacher and bury the child all over again. Mr. Dana was there. Here he is now."

I wiped my pen on my pants, shook my hand to get the cramps out, and signed my name again. A tall civilian with a beard even longer than

112

Bowers's and a dusty frock coat approached the table. He had a patrician look about him, a fine nose, and a general air of breeding.

"Mr. Charles Dana," said Will with mock pomposity. "Meet Ely Parker, secretary extraordinaire and muckamuck of the Seneca nation."

Dana looked at me quizzically as he shook my hand. "What's jumping on the Tonawanda?" he asked me.

"Many fish, as usual," I said, as naturally as could be, and stopped dead with my mouth open. Mr. Dana had asked and I had answered the question in Seneca. I stared at him.

"I'm from western New York," explained Mr. Dana, still in Seneca. "My uncle carried on trade with your people, and I learned the language from an early age."

"You do it very well," I told him. "Except you move your lower lip too much."

"I know," said Dana. "A true Seneca talks without your knowing where his voice comes from."

We both laughed and I saw Bowers and Rowley transfixed. "Wal, Jesus," said a southern lieutenant waiting by the table. "Ah knew you Yankees talked funny, but that beats all!"

With Bowers returned, the work went faster. But it wasn't until two weeks after the surrender that all the paroles were finished. They filled a box three feet long, two feet wide and two feet deep, which Rawlins took to Washington. Some years later I went looking for them and found them, still in their original box, unopened, untended, in a top-floor storeroom of Ford's Theater. The theater, haunted by John Booth's assassination of Lincoln, never saw another performance, but was instead taken over by the War Department's Records and Pensions Division, repository of paper after paper. On June 9, 1893, as a hearse carried John Booth's dead brother Edwin to the Little Church Around the Corner in New York, somebody put one paper too many into Ford's Theater, and the whole building collapsed, killing twenty-three people and burying forever the Vicksburg paroles.

We finally had the satisfaction of watching Pemberton's rag-tag army march out of town and disperse, as they were bound to do by their paroles and had to do in order to live. There was no food or forage left near Vicksburg. General Sherman, in an early rehearsal for his march to the sea seventeen months hence, had stripped and torched the land, leaving central Mississippi a wasteland.

Our own army, though better off than Pemberton's, was rag-tag enough. The only uniform thing about the uniforms was their lack of uniformity. The wagons and transport were miscellaneous – from fringe-top buggies to ox-drawn cotton wagons, to somber plumed hearses pressed into service. So skilled had the army got at improvising that they'd far outstripped a mere Indian. Despite my woodland birth and skills, despite my engineering title, I proved less apt than an ordinary Illinois farmboy at rough-and-ready road-building, stream-bridging, and axle-repair.

What proved in demand was, ironically, my office skills. I had spent years in official correspondence with Washington for my tribe and more years drawing orders and contracts for the canal company. I could dash off and docket an order quicker than most soldiers could write their names. So while the white men labored happily in the open air, the Indian was fettered to an office stool, on Grant's staff, where I stayed till war's end.

Chapter IX

GRANT'S DRUNK, AGAIN

Vicksburg 1863

FROM THE FALL OF VICKSBURG UNTIL THE END OF HIS LIFE General Grant was the most famous man in the world. Not Gladstone, not Disraeli, not Bismarck, not the third Napoleon, not the emperors of China and Japan eclipsed him. You'd think that Gettysburg, with Pickett's charge and the "high water mark of the Confederacy," would have produced a hero, but it didn't. The Army of the Potomac had seen so many generals come and go, and Meade had come in so late, that the victory was the army's, won almost in spite of whoever the general happened to be. But people knew instantly what Vicksburg meant, and now the name on everybody's lips was Grant, the "unpronounceable man" with the cigar in his teeth who kept cropping up farther and farther down in the Confederacy with the unsurprising news that victory was possible if you just kept grinding it out. Grant's fame was won at Vicksburg, and it never left him through all his peacetime failures, his presidency, his financial ruin, and his public death. For two of those years, from Vicksburg to Appomattox, the fame was utterly deserved, as he acted with ever-increasing sure-footedness, and just about as flawlessly as a military commander can act.

In the summer of 1863, however, the most famous man in the world was stuck for something to do, and the powers in Washington were stuck for something to do *with* him. It happened after all Grant's victories. The north sighed its relief, counted its dead and its lucky stars and let the enemy escape, ignoring the third tenet in the Grant canon: Find out where the enemy is, beat him, *and then move on*. Had they let him move on after

Donelson, he might have ended the war there, before anybody heard of Robert Lee. Or after Shiloh, when they were so appalled by the slaughter that they nearly cashiered him. Now they dawdled and ordered brigades here and there, disassembling the army that won Vicksburg.

There was one thing, though, that the most famous man in the world had to do, and that was to show himself. More than a war of armies, this was a war of people, and the people had to see the victors in order for the war to continue. The Mississippi was open from source to mouth? Very well, let the commanding general steam the river to prove it. So back and forth to Memphis Grant went, where toasts resounded and bands played, and where he sat and stewed and sweated in his dress uniform while Rawlins rationed him to water and said no to the sommeliers.

In late August, it was determined that the general should go down via Natchez to New Orleans, and for some reason neither Rawlins nor Bowers – the staff temperance men – was available to go.

"It's up to you, then," John Rawlins told me and Will Rowley sternly on the dock. "Keep an eye on him. Don't let the side down."

"Yes sir, General Rawlins, sir," Rowley and I piped in unison, honoring John's recent promotion to brigadier. Rawlins looked at us hard, undecided whether to grudge the mockery, then gave us a smile, a nod and strode up the wharf. Rowley and I watched him go, then wheeled to march up the gangplank.

"Don't let the side down," muttered Rowley. "I don't know about you, Parker, but I'm for the saloon as soon as we sail."

"I'm with you," I told him, casting a glance at Rawlins's erect and vanishing back. Shipping time found me and Rowley on the saloon deck, glasses in hand, leaning over the rail and watching Vicksburg slip away. The sun was in the sky, the breeze was in our hair, Grant was in his cabin, all was right with the world and it stayed right for some time. Grant, busy with paperwork, emerged only for meals, where we joined him and drank water. The rest of the time we were on our own and it was like slinging our jackets over our shoulders after church.

We elbowed Grant through the welcoming committee on the New Orleans dock and got him settled at the St. Charles Hotel. Though there was nothing scheduled that evening, our dinner in the hotel dining room became an impromptu reception, as people rose to applaud Grant's entrance and didn't stop until he got seated, uncomfortably, at a table smack in the center of the room. There, introductions and congratulations fell on him, and Rowley and I kept turning people away and explaining to the ladies that the general couldn't rise to greet each of them or he'd spend his meal like jack-in-the-box. Finally, Grant nudged Rowley, and Will rose to give the response Rawlins had prescribed. "General Grant never speaks in public, but he thanks you from the bottom of his heart for your kindness, your hospitality, and above all for your loyalty and devotion to the cause of liberty and union." Will sat down amid a clatter of applause and manly nods as the citizenry approved the hero's reticence.

There was finally a lull and we settled in to feed, but a band struck up in the lobby rotunda, and Grant, sighing in almost physical pain, muttered, "What are they playing?"

"It's called 'Kingdom Coming'," I said, surprised that the general hadn't heard it. It referred, after all, to the "Linkum gunboats" on the Mississippi that had driven the plantation "massas" away. I sang a little for him, but Will Rowley nudged me. Grant was shaking his head.

"I have no ear for music," he sighed. "To me it's all just noise."

"Come now, General," said Rowley. "You've said you know two tunes."

"Yes I do," Grant told me. "One of them's 'Yankee Doodle'."

"And the other?" I asked.

"Isn't."

He put his knife and fork down and closed his eyes against the headache the music brought. I excused myself, eased into the lobby, exchanged words and greenbacks with the band leader, and returned to find gratitude on Grant's face and nothing in my wineglass.

I was sure it was full when I left. I turned to say something, but Will tipped me a wink and Grant licked his lips and fell to his roast beef, a smile at the side of his mouth. So that's the way it was to be, eh? I filled my glass from the bottle and looked at Will, who dropped his fork on the carpet. As he bent to retrieve it, Grant's hand flashed out, grabbed Will's glass, drained it and replaced it faster than a frog snapping a fly. Will emerged from under the table, wiped his fork on the cloth, reached for the bottle, and refilled his glass as if nothing was wrong.

It was childish as hell but sort of fun once we got into it. Grant, a convivial if cautious drinker back in Galena, was now a public figure with a reputation as a drunk, and in order to escape the whispers he had either to abstain or drink on the sly, the first of which was an insult and the second a prescription for incontinence. Throughout the meal, Will and I kept finding opportunities to look away or leave the table, refill our glass on our return then absent ourselves again. By the time Grant had finished his pear tart and was spooning up the cream and calling for coffee, he had a nice glow and a happier smile than I'd seen in the two months since I'd joined the war.

Next morning General Banks came to call. I went out early to hire a carriage and a pair of horses for the two generals to tour the city, and I got the best pair the stable held, bay geldings so fine I told the stable owner it was a shame to harness them to a carriage. "These are a man's horses, to be ridden straight up," I told him as I looked them over, and he agreed, saying it was only the great demand for carriage horses that had obliged him to bend these two to the harness.

Grant gave a low whistle when he saw the two fine horses drawn up in front of the hotel, and General Banks too was pleased. As the generals were just driving around town, neither Rowley and I nor any of Banks's staff accompanied them, so nobody but the generals could give an account of what happened. All I know is that two hours later, when the rig clattered up to the hotel porch, with Grant still at the reins, the horses were lathered and foaming and Banks was sitting tight-lipped, arms folded firm across his chest, and had to be helped, trembling, from the carriage. He brushed his sleeves, stared at Grant, and headed for the bar, shaking his head and muttering to his staff about the "scariest hours of my life."

Grant descended jauntily, said "Fine horses, Parker. Absolutely splendid," and disappeared with Rowley into the hotel. I walked the bays around to cool them off and returned them to the stable where I had to listen to a quarter hour of complaints from the livery man about his horses "steaming like locomotives." I overpaid to mollify him. "General Grant likes to drive fast," I told him. "When he saw your pair, he had no choice but to give them their head." I walked slowly back to the hotel, wondering if last night's wine and this morning's mad ride were the worst of it or if they were preludes to some real disaster.

That evening General Banks threw a formal reception at his captured mansion out in the garden district, away from the heat of the port. Grant was on his best behavior for the four hours of public exhibition and the innumerable hands offered for his touch. It was politics plain and simple, and Grant knew it, a reception for the planter class whom Lincoln was wooing to forget the past and rejoin the Union.

Back at the St. Charles, however, enough was enough. Grant had his collar and sash undone before he was through the door, where he handed his sword to an orderly and headed, unvexed by Rowley and me, for the bar. There, in a quiet corner, he took several large breaths followed by several large whiskeys, and for a few pleasant hours it felt like the old days back in Galena. The bar was dark and woody, like bars everywhere, and the men, like men in bars everywhere, left the distinguished visitor alone and bent to their glasses and flagons, their pipes and cigars. There was no expectant hush, no gossip behind fans, no rustle of lace and crinoline, no music except the clink of glasses and the low hum of voices. Grant didn't talk much, and Rowley and I followed suit, the three of us just unwinding slowly and letting the evening pass.

We were up early the next morning for the grand review of the troops at Carrollton, a few miles upriver. First, though, there was the inevitable breakfast reception at the hotel, with Grant again at the center of the head table. The St. Charles management, with a winner on their hands, was wringing him for all he was worth. Breakfast was huge slabs of ham and giant griddle cakes with butter and syrup sliding off them, and as soon as the sweetness burst in my mouth I realized that last night's drinks had hit me hard and I was ravenous. Rowley and the general fell to with equal enthusiasm, and it wasn't long before we were calling for seconds and great quantities of coffee. A black waiter, spotting our hangovers, whisked fresh plates under our noses and followed them with thick crystal glasses of reddish-amber liquid topped by a cherry and a sprig of mint. Alert to scandal, Grant waved his away, but Rowley and I weren't on display, so we kept ours and raised them in silent and grateful toast.

The first whiff, as my nose passed the rim and nudged the greenery aside, was of bourbon and strong mint, with something smoky and mysterious beneath it. I sipped and smacked my lips, eying Rowley the while. Will matched me and took a second sip, and we both lowered our glasses in happy surprise. Unless my tongue deceived me our eye-openers were spiked with absinthe, and the licorice vapors caressed my headache with silken hands, rolled it into a puffball, and breathed it away. Life was good. I took another, larger sip and attacked my plate again.

Out of the corner of my eye I saw my glass disappear, heard a slurping, and saw it hit the table with a clank, empty. I looked up at Grant. His fingers were still on the glass and he was sitting bolt upright, lips pursed, beard bristling, cheeks flushed, eyes wide and shining, staring straight ahead as at a revelation. He looked like a man who'd just swallowed a porcupine – and liked it.

"Your glass is empty, Parker," he rasped. "I think you need another."

I don't know how much Grant drank for breakfast that morning. I do know that at least four of the magic elixirs made their way to Rowley's place and an equal number to mine, and that I couldn't swear to have drunk one of them entire. I also know that I was full of *bonhomie* and felt like singing as I pushed myself back from the table and wheezed toward the door. Rowley and I were bagged proper, and I wondered fleetingly, if those eye-openers could stagger us, what effect they might have on Grant, a stranger to drink for many weeks.

The general seemed placid enough as we embarked our carriages and clattered up the river road to Carrollton, another name I dimly added to my list of "American places named for obscure individuals." There we transferred to horses, and Grant's pace quickened as he strode toward the mount Banks had chosen for him, a muscled white charger of classic proportions. Grant barely broke stride as he fitted his boot in the stirrup, pulled himself upright and swung his leg over the saddle. It was as smooth and economical a mount as you could wish, putting the little man aboard so quickly he looked like he'd floated there. Rowley and I clambered atop our smaller mounts and lurched forward as Grant spurred ahead. Other generals and aides scrambled on board, and soon a whole cavalcade was strung out behind the commanding general like the tail of a kite. General Banks, determined not to be cowed like yesterday, muscled through the crowd of riders to the fore and was soon pounding along on Grant's flank.

It was a wild, hard ride, exhilarating once we forgot our fear and the full breakfast roiling inside us. All of us, including the New Orleans officers, had spent so much time cooped up in garrison duty, that it was a rare treat to gallop full out and feel the breeze streaming. Hats whipped in the air, riders screamed and howled, all rank forgotten as generals and colonels and their aides vied to catch Grant at the head of the pack. I chucked my normal reticence and let out a full-throated Indian whoop.

Rowley, behind me, echoed it, and the whole string of horsemen picked it up, and along we rode, the cream of the Union army, the sober symbol of federal authority, strung out along the river road, pounding like the apocalypse and howling like banshees. The citizenry who lined the path for the march-by of the troops, if they'd had any doubts about the wisdom of bowing to the federal yoke, must have had no second thoughts now. Surely, if they hadn't yielded, this screaming band of Mongols would have stolen their women's hats and eaten their babies for breakfast.

Up ahead, Banks shouted and pointed and Grant turned with him and reined in beneath a copse of trees where a reviewing stand was set up. The rest of us skidded to a dusty halt around them, dismounted, handed our reins to waiting liverymen, and whopped each other on the back, suddenly just a pack of boys, exulting over a wild ride we'd just taken for no other reason than it was summer, the sun was high, and we were young. And we *were* young! Grant was forty-one, I was thirty-five, and Rowley was younger than me. Around us were generals who were barely thirty. If one of us had torn off his clothes and jumped into the river the rest would have followed without a thought, Grant included, and skinny-dipped the day away.

But the tramp of marching feet called us back, and we straightened our clothes and our faces and stood to attention. First Banks's Nineteenth and then Ord's Thirteenth corps swung down the road in review. The sight of Ord's corps in particular must have brought a wince of pain and pride to Grant's throat. This was another unit from his victorious Vicksburg army, detached for service in a useless Texas expedition, another chipping away from the Union's main strength. Then it was boots and saddles again, and we sprang to our mounts, but now our pace was slower and more stately down the river to Mays's Landing, where a luncheon was spread out under the trees. I felt sober and somewhat washed out, and I hoped that Grant too had had his fill of high spirits, both liquid and otherwise.

The general was pensive at lunch, staring at middle distance and seeming not to hear much conversation. He found his wineglass full when he sat down, and when I moved to have it taken away, he stayed my hand, took a sip, nodded, and gestured to me that it was all right. I raised my eyebrows at Rowley, who shrugged. In the course of lunch, I'd bet Grant drank a full bottle's worth and seemed prepared to sit there all day. He was done sneaking drinks. Now he was just drinking, as if morose at the sight of Ord's departing corps. He'd gone in three days from a sip or two at lunch to a drink or two at night to a couple of stiff belts in the morning and now seemed settled in for a full-day's binge.

We tried to get him into his carriage after lunch, but he shook us off and strode for the white charger that stood pawing beneath a tree. Banks called for his own horse, and there was a scramble as other officers summoned their mounts. My horse had been completely unbridled and unsaddled, and as I saw Grant disappear down the road, I grabbed a bridle from one of Banks's aides and spurred to catch up.

I was twenty paces behind Grant when disaster struck. The railroad track bent close to the road we were riding, and at a curve up ahead, a locomotive suddenly rounded the bend and gave out a shrill whistle, seeming to bear directly down on Grant's horse. They were in no danger, but the horse didn't know that. He reared and pawed the air, and from behind they looked for a moment like an equestrian statue, posed and immobile. They hovered there for interminable seconds and seemed about to come down right. But though Grant tried his best to control him the horse lost purchase, scrabbled with his hind hoofs on the dirt road, and tumbled sideways like a tower going down. The general, his feet in the stirrups, went down with him, and the horse rolled over, legs and hooves pawing at nothing, Grant pinned under him. The horse righted himself and stood up, abruptly calm and riderless. He dropped his head as if in apology and nudged the fallen Grant, who lay in the road, not moving, suddenly a small and pitiful heap of rag and bone.

I reached him first, skidded out of the saddle before my horse stopped and crouched beside him. Grant's face was scraped bloody where it had met the road, and as I turned him over I saw pain contort his face and cloud his eyes, which went white as he slipped from consciousness. For a horrid moment I thought he was dead, until I felt for his heart and saw his pulse beat in his throat. Hands pulled me away and Banks's physician bent over him. I backed into the crowd that hovered anxiously around. The same thought was in everyone's mind. If Grant died the army died too. If he was crippled, so was the Union. It was pitiful to think that the fate of the north, with all its might, lay beside a Louisiana ditch, gritting his teeth against the pain, the only general who knew how to win suddenly tossed helpless by a noisy train, a frightened horse, and, as wider and wider rumors would insist, another bout with the bottle.

A wagon came to ease Grant back to town, followed by a solemn and scared-sober procession of subordinates. He was borne to his room at the St. Charles, where he slipped in and out of consciousness for twenty-four hours before he was fully awake. I dispatched a message to Rawlins and chewed my lip awaiting a reply. Failures at baby-sitting, Rowley and I expected the worst, from solitary confinement to shipment west. What we got was silence, which was even worse. Once Grant was out of danger our own jeopardy loomed larger and larger, and we spent morbid hours in the bar speculating on our punishment.

Grant recovered slowly, propped up with pillows, smoking cigars, receiving reports and dispatching orders from his sickbed. There were no broken bones, but his entire left side, which had hit the roadway and got pinned under the horse, was all bruises and abrasions. His hip was wrenched so badly he couldn't walk, and even after two weeks, when he was given leave to travel, he had to be carried to the steamboat on a litter and hoisted aboard for the slow upstream journey to Vicksburg.

Rawlins met us at the dock, far more solicitous of Grant than censorious of Rowley and me. We got him up over the hill to his headquarters at the Lum mansion and installed in an upstairs bedroom. Then Rawlins turned to us, white-lipped and trembling, fire in his black eyes, ordered me to wait in one room, Rowley in another, and he closed the door to closet himself with Grant.

My room next door was a lady's bedroom, with a lace-canopied bed, mirrored dressing-table, and tiger-maple armoire. I made myself as comfortable as possible in a delicate chair with carved arms and embroidered seat and watched the dirt from my boots cake the oriental carpet. After a while I began to hear voices and realized it was Rawlins talking in the next room. Curious, I hunched my chair closer to the wall, then closer and closer as the words became more distinct, until I had my ear right up against the light-blue silk wallpaper. A pretty picture I must have made, eavesdropping on the commanding general and his chief-of-staff from the comfort of a lady's boudoir, but once I started listening I couldn't tear myself away. I had never heard one man talk to another that way in my life.

"I hope you know what you've done," came Rawlins's voice.

"I've about broke my leg and torn off half my face," growled Grant. "That what you mean?"

"Of course not! Don't be a fool!" This was Rawlins, if you please, talking to the commanding general. I hunched my chair closer.

"Very well, John," said Grant calmly. "What have I done?"

"You've nearly killed yourself, for one thing," spat Rawlins. "It would have been better if you had, perhaps, rather than return to me in such disgrace. How could you do it?"

"There was a train," I heard Grant say softly. "The horse shied."

"And I suppose you hadn't been drinking," said Rawlins. "Try and tell me you hadn't."

"I had been drinking," said Grant. "But the horse hadn't."

"Don't be funny!" shouted Rawlins. His boots took quick steps on the floorboards. "You had been drinking and the whole army saw you drinking. Whether the horse shied or not, you had been drinking, and that is the operative fact, General!"

I heard the bed creak and a sigh from Grant. "Well?" said Rawlins.

"Well, what?" growled Grant. "Yes, John, I had been drinking. But the horse would have thrown me, drinking or no."

"I hope you know your reputation is gone," said Rawlins. "Gone! Pf-f-f-t! A puff of smoke. You'll never take the field again. They're already stripping your army away. Now they'll take the rest of it and leave you here to rot. Just like after Shiloh. All my work gone to hell."

"All *your* work?" said Grant. "It's my reputation. I live with it, you don't."

"I live with it too!" shouted Rawlins. "It's my curse to be surrounded by drunkards, I suppose. To keep pulling you out of the mud, hosing you off, and setting you upright again. It's because I'm weak, I know it. If I were stronger, you wouldn't do it. Are you testing me?"

"Don't be a fool, John," said Grant quietly.

"Oh," flared Rawlins. "A fool! Is that what I am. For protecting you, for jollying the newspapers, for shielding you from Washington. This is what I get? I'm a fool."

"I'm sorry, John," said the general.

"Apology my ass!" shouted Rawlins. I almost fell out of my chair. "I've wiped my ass with your apologies for two years. That's what they're worth! I should resign! In fact I do! I'll have Parker draft it and deliver it right now!"

Rawlins's boots strode toward the door. I pushed my chair away from

124

the wall, expecting him to appear in my room at any second.

"General Rawlins!" came Grant's voice.

"Go to hell!" shouted Rawlins. "You and General Rawlins and everything about you! Your wife will be here tomorrow, and I leave her to you. Let her play nursemaid. I prefer to work with men!"

"Julia's coming? So soon?" Grant's voice softened and sounded childishly eager.

"Yes!" spat Rawlins. "And I hope she breaks a bottle over your head!"

"Come here, John," said Grant softly. I heard nothing for a moment, then Rawlins's boots slowly creaked across to Grant's bedside. "I'm sorry, John," said Grant. "You know I'd cut off my arm rather than hurt you. Or lose you. You won't leave, will you?"

"I don't see what good I do," said Rawlins stiffly.

"You do more good than you'll ever know," said Grant softly. "Hit Rawlins in the head and you'll knock out Grant's brains. That's what they say, no?"

"They're wrong," said Rawlins.

"I know that and you know that," said Grant. "But we'll keep it our little secret, eh? You must stay, John. You're the only one who tells me the truth."

There was silence for a moment, then Rawlins's quiet voice, almost a whimper. "You mustn't hurt me like this. I depend on you. I put all my faith in you. You mustn't let me down."

"There, there, John," said Grant again, and I could almost see the scene. Grant lying back in his bed of pain and Rawlins at his bedside with his head bowed and hands clasped in prayer. "Promise me you'll never drink again," said Rawlins, his voice regaining its strength.

"John, John," sighed Grant. "I don't make promises I can't keep."

"So you don't," said Rawlins. "We all have our faults, General. It's my curse, I suppose, that yours is found at the bottom of a bottle."

There was more conversation, this time of an official nature, and I backed off from the wall and had myself seated in the middle of the room by the time my door opened and Rawlins came in.

I rose to attention and saluted, ready for punishment, but Rawlins ignored it, brushed past me, and to my astonishment, threw himself full-length on the canopied bed, his arm flung over his eyes. He lay there for awhile, breathing heavily and sighing until I let my salute melt away and eased across the carpet to his side. "General?" I said.

Rawlins took his arm from his face and turned to me, his eyes moist. "Oh, Ely, Ely, Ely," he said. "What am I to do? I'm in love."

For a wild moment I thought he was in love with Grant. Politics isn't the only thing that makes strange bedfellows.

"With who, John?" I asked.

"Her name is Emma Hurlbut," he said.

"Ah," I said, obscurely relieved. "And who is she?"

"Who isn't she?" sighed Rawlins. "She's everyone and everywhere, Ely. Why, this is her very bed I'm lying on. I've asked her to marry me, Ely. And she has accepted." He drew a letter from his breast pocket. "I've been carrying her letter close to my heart."

"My dear fellow!" I cried, a little too heartily. "But who is she? Where is she? How did it happen? When? You must tell me all about it." I drew my chair up to the bed, all ears and good fellowship, hoping to make Rawlins forget I was in the doghouse.

His head rolling back and forth on the pillow, his pale countenance flushed, his black eyes wet with passion, Rawlins spilled out the whole happy story. When Grant had moved into this house after the siege, one of the houseguests was Miss Emma Hurlbut of Danbury, Connecticut, a Union lass who had been visiting south when the conflict broke out, trapping her here. She had been gracious to the conquering troops, particularly to Rawlins, and staunch, upright, loyal John Rawlins had tumbled like a slobbering drunk.

"So there I am, Ely," sighed Rawlins. "Doomed once more to infect yet another pure soul with my foul presence."

That was an odd way to put it. Rawlins's wife Emily, a frail sylph during my years in Galena, had died of tuberculosis soon after Fort Sumter, leaving him to care for three children. But there was never any suggestion that John's "foul presence" had infected her. In fact, John's pale complexion and fits of fever made it more likely that it was the other way round.

"You speak as if love were infection," I said.

"Mine is," said John simply. "I have the drunkard's curse upon me." Again he flung his arm across his eyes. "You know my father was a drunkard."

126

Who in Galena didn't know of John's alcoholic father? He told the story often enough of how the drunken speculator had left John, still a boy, to care for his mother and seven siblings. "But what has that to do with you?" I said.

Rawlins beat his forehead with his fist. "The drunkard's curse! The sins of the fathers! Who knows when I may tumble and be lost? Look at that sot in there!" He flung his arm toward Grant's room. "Look at you, at Rowley, at half the army. Drunkards! And I walk among you daily! How can I hope to stay unblighted?"

"I'm hardly a drunkard, John," I said gently.

"No. But I would be if I dared take a sip," he said. He went on like this for some time, tossing his head on what he called "her dear pillow" and lamenting the torment he was about to inflict upon poor Emma Hurlbut by offering his foul hand in marriage.

Eventually he subsided and turned to me, his eyes hound-like. "You must help me, Ely," he said.

"Of course, John. How?"

"You must not drink. And you must never drink with *him* again."

So that's the way it was to be. The only way to save the Union was for all of us to stop drinking, keep Grant from drinking, and thus spare Rawlins the drunkard's curse that lay heavy on him and threatened to soil the pale bosom of Miss Emma Hurlbut of Danbury, Connecticut. With Grant sober and Rawlins saved the Union would be preserved and so would the union of Rawlins and Emma.

"That's quite a stretch, John," I told him.

"It's the only way, Ely. I'm convinced of it."

"The only way," I told him, "is to get us all off our asses and get this army moving. That's the only thing that makes us drink. Idleness! Tell Washington to let us fight instead of picking us apart, and we'll all be sobersides quick as you wish."

Rawlins shook his head sadly. "There's no chance of that now. Grant is finished. They'll destroy him. They'll destroy me. They'll destroy us all. We'll never fight again."

Rawlins was wrong. We did fight again, and much sooner than he could have hoped, though through no initiative of ours. Nor did it require our taking the veil and going sober for Emma Hurlbut. As usual, the south had to act before Washington would. While Grant mended and Washington dithered and the western army lazed and drank and dwindled, Confederate General Braxton Bragg wheeled on our General William Rosecrans in eastern Tennessee and drove a furious wedge through his lines along Chickamauga Creek, justifying its Cherokee name, "River of Blood." The Union Army of the Cumberland reeled and fled back to Chattanooga, bottled up as surely as Grant had stoppered Pemberton in Vicksburg four months ago.

Lincoln and Secretary of War Stanton wrung their hands, looked north, south, east, and finally west, where they remembered a scruffy little general laid up, disgraced and smoking, on his bed of pain at Vicksburg, and decided, as they would decide from now until the end of the war, that only Grant could save them. At noon on October 10 came a telegram, "It is the wish of the Secretary of War that as soon as General Grant is able to take the field he will come to Cairo and report by telegraph." Grant rose, walked and barked orders. By four the tents were struck. At sundown we untied from the Vicksburg dock and steamed north.

Chapter X

THE MULE ROAD TO THE CRACKER LINE

Chattanooga 1863

"GENERAL GRANT! I RECOGNIZE YOU FROM YOUR pictures!"

We'd been told that a man from the War Department would meet us at Indianapolis, and here he was. We recognized him from his pictures too, with his gray tangle of bushy beard, his improbably smooth, youthful cheeks and his piggy blue eyes winking from his ruddy face. He wasn't from the War Department, he *was* the War Department, Secretary Edwin Stanton himself, bustling along the platform at the Indianapolis station, hand outstretched to greet General Grant. Unfortunately the face he claimed to recognize and the hand he now seized wasn't Grant's but John Rawlins's, who, to be fair, had a much more imposing beard than the little man who now hobbled forward on his crutch and introduced himself to Stanton. The center of the war, where we were headed, had come out to meet us.

"We're consolidating, General," said "Old Man Mars" Stanton as he wheezed himself into a chair in Grant's parlor car. Grant winced as the train lurched forward. "Everything from the Alleghenies to the Mississippi is to be under one command, and the commander is you." Stanton raised three stubby fingers. "The divisions of the Ohio under Burnside, the Cumberland under Rosecrans, the Tennessee under Sherman, they're all yours now."

Grant nodded, and Rawlins, sitting next to him, rubbed his hands together as at a feast.

"Rosecrans is in a fix in Chattanooga," said Stanton, spreading out a map on the table. "The president says he's like a duck that's been hit on the head. Bragg has him boxed in, east, south, and west. There is a single-track road over the mountains from the north, not enough to supply or reinforce him. The first job is to blast your way in and open a supply route."

"Or blast our way out, if we can get in," murmured Grant, his finger tracing the Tennessee River on the map. "How many rations have they?"

Stanton pulled a piece of paper from a pocket and blinked his piggy eyes. "Two hundred four thousand four hundred and sixty-two," he said. "With ninety thousand to arrive tomorrow. So says Rosecrans yesterday."

I tried to divide the rations among the forty thousand men trapped in Chattanooga, but Grant, the ex-quartermaster, was ahead of me. "About five days," he said. "Are you stuck on Rosecrans?"

Stanton pulled more papers from his pocket. "I have two sets of orders," he said. "Identical except that one leaves Rosecrans in charge, and the other replaces him with Thomas. Which do you prefer?"

Like a magician's shill picking a card, Grant frowned, pursed his lips and selected a paper from Stanton's hand. "I know Rosecrans," he said. "I'll take Thomas."

"So be it," said Stanton, pocketing one of the papers. Rawlins's eyes flashed. At Chickamauga three weeks ago, Rosecrans had broken and fled, leaving General George Thomas to hold the field and eventually retire in the only good order of the day. "The Rock of Chickamauga," aide James Garfield had dubbed him. "We are concentrating our forces here." Stanton's stubby finger pointed to Bridgeport, Alabama, only thirty map miles southwest from Chattanooga, but with no access through the steep hills or along the Confederate-held river. "Hooker is there with two corps from the Potomac. Sherman is already moving east from Memphis. How soon can he get to Bridgeport?" He raised his eyes at Grant, who was lighting a cigar.

Grant blew smoke and traced the line of the railroad across map folds and state borders two hundred long miles west from Bridgeport, through Alabama and Mississippi to Memphis. "Sherman destroyed that line to impede the enemy, and now he must rebuild it as he goes," he growled through his cigar. "When Sherman destroys he means it to stay that way. We'll see how quick he can un-destroy." Grant squinted at the secretary. "A month, perhaps. Six weeks."

"That long?" Stanton frowned.

Grant's eyes turned hard. "That soon, Mr. Secretary," he said. "Any other general would take all winter."

Stanton, unused to such bluntness, stared. "I see," he said, lowering his eyes to the map. "So that's the sequence, is it?" He raised the three stubby fingers again. "Open a supply line. Wait for Sherman. Bust out."

Grant nodded, folded his arms and leaned back, wincing at the sudden pain to his injured hip. "Assuming, of course, that I can get in."

Assuming. Stanton detrained at Louisville for Washington, while the rest of us chugged through the night to Bridgeport, the closest railhead to the army encircled in Chattanooga. There we met up with the two corps detached from the Army of the Potomac and had our first look at the eastern generals we had heard so much about. First aboard the train to pay his respects was one-armed General Oliver Howard, whose right flank Hooker had left in the air for Stonewall Jackson to smash at Chancellorsville. Then a finely-dressed subaltern swung up the steps and announced that General Hooker would be "delighted" to receive Grant at his headquarters, to which Grant replied that if General Hooker had anything to say he'd better come and say it. Soon "Fighting Joe," the other big loser at Chancellorsville, came aboard.

"Yes, yes," said Hooker, when he got comfortably seated. "Only thirty miles to Chattanooga as the crow flies. But the crows aren't flying, so it's seventy-five miles in over Walden's Ridge. We're sending in as many mule-wagons of supplies as we can, but it's murder, both on men and mules. Maybe half make it in, maybe half that many make it back. The road is a litter of busted wagons and dead mules. Dead men too. The track is mud and rock, much of it washed away."

Grant raised his eyebrows at Hooker. "You've traversed it?"

"Not on your life," growled Hooker.

"You?" Grant glanced at Howard.

Howard touched the empty sleeve of his right arm, shot off on the Peninsula. "Many two-armed men haven't made it."

Grant grunted and looked around at us. "We'll go in tomorrow," he said, and though Rawlins protested that his bum leg would make it impossible, the set of Grant's jaw brooked no argument. He had his head-butting look on, and woe to any brick wall in the vicinity.

Next morning we set off in a rain so gray that dawn made no headway, a line of slow, clopping horses soon so wet and muddy as to be indistinguishable from the landscape. It was pitiful to see the once-nimble Grant, who could float atop a horse like a butterfly, lifted aboard by Rawlins like a swaddled baby and lashed secure with his crutch at his side and his cape over his head. Up front rode an army guide, then Grant and Rawlins, with me behind them and Rowley and Bowers in the rear. Strung-out and bent over by the wet and the gloom, the rag-tag band set out to rescue Chattanooga.

The next two days were the most horrible up to then, fit prelude to the slog and grind of the war's last year. It wasn't a ride over the mountains, it was a climb and a stumble, a slip and a slide, a lunge and a retreat, our horses losing two steps for every three they gained, sometimes sliding backwards with their haunches on the ground and hooves clawing for a purchase as the cliffside yawned beneath them. The road – a single rutted track – was a tumult of wagons and mules, some making dogged progress, sixteen mules to a harness with sixteen soldiers wielding whips, tugging and cursing them, some pulled to the side and heeled over with broken axles or shattered spokes, mules balking and braying, muleteers cursing and flogging them, mules immovable and insensible, as intractable as the rain and the road, refusing to budge no matter how hard the curses and the lash. Rain pelted us like gravel. Hours passed in a trance, a hypnosis of struggling ever forward, my eyes seeing only the laboring and steaming rear of Rawlins's horse, the damp drizzly November in my soul and out, as we squeezed past broken wagons and slogging soldiers and mules and mules and mules.

It's the rain and mules I remember most. Even today I hear in every rainstorm the hideous braying, not like the whinny and snuffle of horses, who even in pain and panic sound of home and the barn, but a raw, inhuman, other-worldly, feral hee-haw, as if to damn us all with the screech of a thousand fiends. There were as many dead as live ones, fallen by the road, legs stiff in the air, gray bellies upturned and bloated, eyes staring white as if littering the path to hell. Ahead we slogged, sleeping in the saddle, jarred awake as empty wagons slid around the mountain trail and bore down on us, nodding off again as if drugged, the rain spattering our hats and capes like buckshot. We camped for the night but got no rest, as freshets of muddy water coursed through our tents, and Grant twisted and writhed, unable to find a position that wasn't torture.

The second day, we made better progress. At what passed for dusk – a deepening of the already impenetrable dark – the road flattened and broadened, and we could ride two abreast instead of single file. After some miles of level ground we passed the tents and fires of the army camp, then clomped hollowly across a pontoon bridge and saw the lights of the town before us. Our guide pointed his gloved hand and we eased off the road into the yard of a white, columned house and dismounted, Rawlins helping Grant to the ground. He leaned against his horse while his crutch was unlimbered, then stumped up the porch ahead of us and through the front door.

Inside was a parlor with a roaring fireplace, toward which we stumbled like orphans of the storm and huddled round, insensible to whoever else might be there. Thawed, and hearing footsteps behind us, all of us but Grant turned one by one, to find a curious assemblage of officers watching us. They crowded uneasily through the door and hovered by the walls, all of them well-dressed, with pressed blues and gleaming brass. One captain, improbably, held a punch cup in his white-gloved hand. From the back of the house came the tinkle of music and laughter. We'd ridden two days over mud-and-mule-choked mountains to rescue a beleaguered, starving army and interrupted a party.

A burly officer with two stars on his shoulders and a full beard shouldered through. "General Grant?" he said, frowning and recoiling as he examined us one by one.

Grant turned round with some difficulty on his single crutch. "General Thomas," he said, and the two stood looking at each other, uncertain how to proceed.

"General Grant." Another officer elbowed forward, shorter than Thomas, with a white, hang-dog beard and mustache that gave him a schnauzer look.

"General Smith," said Grant, and "Baldy" Smith tentatively shook Grant's hand, as, now, did General Thomas.

Grant's hands started patting his pockets and found a bent and soggy cigar, which, frowning, he straightened with his delicate fingers and stuck in his mouth. The staffs of both armies watched him, absorbed, as if they'd never seen a man light a cigar and expected him to produce a rabbit next. Grant patted his pockets for a light, and the white-gloved captain unfroze, clattered his punch cup onto a table and hurried forward with a candle. Another officer produced chairs, only two of them, and Grant and Thomas sat down in front of the fire, Thomas patting his thigh and clearing his throat, Grant smoking and starting to steam and smell as the fire warmed his wet clothes. A puddle spread beneath him, and his coat drip-drip-dripped audibly on the bare floor like a clock counting the seconds. Rowley, Rawlins, Bowers and I kept as close to the fire as we could, huddling in our chimney corner while the finely-dressed staff of the besieged army wrinkled their noses. For a moment we were just the rustic Galena boys we had been a few years ago, just good old me and Grant and Rowley and Rawlins, plucked from Orvil Grant's stove and plunked down amid the drums and trumpets and flags and finery of Mr. Lincoln's army.

I don't know how long we sat there and would have sat there, silent, huddled, and dripping, had not our War Department friend Mr. Dana, who had been trapped in Chattanooga with the rest of them, entered to find the commanding general being treated like a beggar. "General Thomas!" said Dana without any preliminary. "General Grant has been riding two days in the rain. He's wet and tired and his baggage is well behind him. Haven't you dry clothes and decent food for him?"

That shifted the Rock of Chickamauga. Thomas remembered his manners and got Grant bustled off for dry clothes. The staffs unbent and crowded round us, pumping our hands. "They're not impolite, just embarrassed," explained Dana. "You caught them in the middle of their last party. Eat, drink, and be merry, for tomorrow we die."

A table was prepared, and we fell to our first hot food in three days and my first taste of siege rations. Boiled dried peas, potatoes that had been harvested from fields still within the lines, and a slab of grey meat that may have been mule, it was ornery enough. "Cattle's so skinny if it gets here at all," said a staff man, "they call it beef dried on the hoof."

When the table was cleared, Grant called for a map, lit another cigar, and we took a look at our fix. Chattanooga lies on the southeast bank of the Tennessee River, in a valley between the parallel heights of Missionary Ridge on the east and Lookout Mountain on the west, which sweep up out of the south like marching lines of infantry, shearing off when they meet the river and locking the city between them. The Confederates' occupation of these two heights and the valley between had bottled up Thomas's army. The Tennessee River, cutting serpentine from the east through the mountains, bends south at Chattanooga, then abruptly north again past the upper end of Lookout Mountain in a hairpin turn that forms the peninsula of Moccasin Point, directly across the river from the city.

Grant's finger traced the line of the river past Lookout Mountain. "Fortified?" he asked.

"Bristling," said Thomas.

"Longstreet," added Smith, and Grant looked up. "Old Pete" Longstreet, detached from Lee for service in the west, was the South's defensive genius. He'd been at West Point with the three generals at the table. He'd been best man at Grant's wedding. The war was getting clubby.

Grant's finger continued tracing the river as it snaked towards Bridgeport, Alabama, where supplies for the starving army lay. "Yes," said Smith, as Grant's finger passed Brown's Ferry on Moccasin Point, due west of town, where the river, still flowing north, went out of range of the Lookout Mountain guns. "There's a road straight across Moccasin Point to there. The opposite bank is lightly held."

Grant's cigar started puffing faster, as if it was on to something. From Brown's Ferry the river flowed north, then west and south again to form the larger peninsula of Raccoon Mountain, through which a gap led straight across to a place on the Tennessee called Kelly's Ferry. Smith's finger joined Grant's. "Yes," said Smith. "From Kelly's Ferry to Bridgeport the river is ours."

"I see it, General, I see it," said Grant, nodding and puffing vigorously. "So that's our cracker line, is it?"

Smith's mouth tightened in satisfaction. "It's a matter of seizing the crossing at Brown's and throwing a bridge across," he said. "I've got materials out there already on our side of the river. We need to drive away the enemy and establish a bridgehead on the other."

"It's Longstreet, remember," said Thomas.

Grant flashed Thomas a look as if he'd issued a challenge, stood up from the map, arched his back and spoke to us all. "We'll ride out tomorrow first thing."

First thing meant first thing, and I turned reluctantly early out of the first bed I'd slept in after days of trains and tents. As if to honor Grant's arrival, the weather cleared into a fine, crisp fall day, the sky blue with high, white clouds, and the ground firm underfoot as we rode out. We rode south of town first, to get a look at the heights that had us holed up.

"Do-ne-ho-ga-wa," said Secretary Dana, reining in beside me on the southern outskirts.

"Dats-ka-he," I called him in return, which means "hard talker," or diplomat.

He laughed and continued in Seneca, pointing out the features of the terrain, which didn't need much pointing out. Missionary Ridge rose like a wall on the left and Lookout Mountain paralleled it on the right, their tops plumed with campfire smoke. "Chattanooga means 'mountains looking at each other,'" said Dana.

"In Cherokee?" I asked him.

"Yes. We're at the ancestral center of the Cherokee nation. From creation until a few years back."

"I met John Ross in Washington," I told him. "Chattanooga is Ross's Landing."

"Indeed." Impressed, Dana pointed down Missionary Ridge, stretching south to the horizon. "His birthplace, Rossville, is behind the ridge, tucked in a little gap in the mountains."

I calculated. "He must be over seventy now. Out in Oklahoma. Ancestral lands or no, he's well out of this."

"Don't be so sure," said Dana. "They're having their own civil war out there. Tribe against tribe, slave factions against free. Just like us. Nice heritage we've brought them."

I looked down the valley and tried to imagine Indian villages instead of the billowing tents, remembering John Ross's description of the Trail of Tears, which began right where we were standing. Twenty thousand Cherokee, stripped of their property, farms, schools, printing presses. Five thousand dead before reaching Oklahoma. All so whites could have their land. I looked up at the tents and cannon sprouting on the mountain slopes. Fine use they'd made of the Cherokee lands. More than five times twenty thousand white soldiers now faced each other here, seventy thousand Confederates to the Union's forty thousand. If I knew Grant, more of them would die here than Cherokee on the Trail of Tears.

To my surprise Dana waved, as if saluting the mountains themselves.

"What's that for?" I asked.

Dana grinned through his bushy beard. "Just letting them know we see them," he said. Indeed, as my eyes adjusted to the distance I could see southern troops lounging beside the cannons. Other soldiers wandered among white tents that dotted the slopes, and the notes of a band playing drifted down.

"They don't do much," said Dana, still talking Seneca. "Don't have to. Just wait for us to starve and wave a white flag."

Grant rode slowly up to us, cigar in his mouth, staring up at the mountains. "A pretty fix, Mr. Dana."

"I've heard of worse," said Dana, trying to sound nonchalant.

"You have, have you?" said Grant. "Well, I haven't. Let's look at the back door." He bit his cigar and wheeled his horse back for town.

As we rode through town and the army camps, the army's precariousness revealed itself. Hasty fortifications used any materials at hand. Boards ripped from the city's dwellings were hammered into defense works, odd patches of gay wallpaper blossoming on the fences. Haggard, tattered men haunted the streets, many of them too weak to do anything but sit and stare at each other or into space. There was none of the ballplaying, drilling, and band-playing that filled most army time, nor any of the squabbling and fistfights that idleness encourages. No horses galloped importantly in and out, with men gathering around the messengers for news and gossip. There were no horses at all except for some dead ones that lay unburied behind the tents. All was listlessness and apathy, forty thousand men sinking into torpor.

We clattered across the bridge to Moccasin Point, left the river behind us, trotted across the neck of the peninsula, and soon saw the river again opening up in front of us. "Brown's Ferry," said Dana. "It's nine miles by river from Chattanooga to here. But only one by land."

As we reined up on the riverbank a sentry cried, "Turn out the guard – the commanding general!" and the guard snapped to attention. To our surprise there came an echoing cry from across the river. "Turn out the guard – General Grant!" and a gray line opposite presented arms and stood to mock attention. Grant lifted his hat to them and the Confederates broke formation, some of them hurling less polite epithets across the river. Though we were in musket range there were no shots.

"Gosh, Ely," said Will Rowley, riding beside me. "I knew it was a civil war, but not that civil."

"There's no keeping secrets in this army," said Dana, shaking his head. "The pickets are so close to each other and so bored that they make their own truces. Know how we heard Grant was here last night? I was out touring the lines and some pickets told us the Rebs had told them Grant was in camp."

We dismounted and Baldy Smith led Grant into the woods and showed him stacks of bridge-flooring under tarpaulins, concealed from rebel eyes. Standing on the shore and pointing here and there, he explained his plan to Grant, while rebel pickets, out of earshot on the other bank, leaned on their rifles and looked on. We then rode back toward town, but stopped before crossing the bridge and turned off onto a dirt track that led along the shore of Moccasin Bend. At the end was a hidden sawmill chuffing away, with the few able-bodied men I'd seen in Chattanooga working at it, hammering together odd-looking craft that looked like bathtubs.

"Pontoons!" I said, and since Smith's plan was now clear to me I explained it to a puzzled Rowley. "Load the pontoons with troops. Float them downstream under cover of darkness. Land on the opposite shore, drive away the pickets, and secure the bridgehead. Engineers lash the pontoons together like steppingstones across the river, cover them with planking, and troops waiting there cross the river in force."

Rowley frowned and nodded as I counted the pontoon-boats already completed and whistled low. "Fifty of them, Will. Fifty assault boats carrying – I don't know – twenty men in each . . ." I started counting in my head.

"There will be sixty boats," said a voice behind me. "And they will carry two dozen men each."

I wheeled and saw General Baldy Smith standing directly behind me, with Grant leaning on his crutch next to him. "Who is this officer?" asked Smith, waving his gloved hand at me as if at a fly.

"Captain Parker," growled Grant. "One of my adjutants."

Smith nodded, his blue Prussian eyes looking me up and down. "Adjutant, eh? He's wasted, General. You should make him an engineer."

Grant's eyes twinkled. "He's that, too, General. Out west we do a bit of everything."

Smith nodded and continued inspecting me. "Feel like a nighttime cruise, Parker? I'm short of engineers. That is, if you can spare him, General."

Grant shrugged. "Why not? You missed running the guns at Vicksburg, Parker. Here's your chance to make it up."

The two generals retired to inspect the sawmill. I turned to see Will Rowley step out from behind a tree, where he had smoothly disappeared while I got singled out. "Gotta keep your mouth shut, Ely," he grinned. "Start showin' off, you pretty soon get volunteered for something."

Chapter XI

THE CHARGE OF
THE MULE BRIGADE

Chattanooga 1863

"ALL RIGHT, MEN. LOAD IN. QUIET THERE," CAME GENERAL Hazen's muffled voice. The full moon had gone behind Lookout Mountain and fog lay low on the darkened river. It was three in the morning. As the order passed along the line I saw shapes start to move down the riverbank.

"Follow me, Chief," whispered Sergeant Avery, and my squad of twenty-four men from the 23rd Kentucky eased down the bank, stepped into our rectangular pontoon and sat with our backs against the sides. Four oarsmen took their places, two to a side, Colonel Foy hopped in and men on shore put their shoulders to the bow to shove us off. Upriver the dark shapes of the next two boats in line lurked out to join us, and that's as far as I could see. But behind our lead boat I knew there were fifty-nine more lumbering out from shore and turning slowly downriver with the current, squat, bulky, unseaworthy craft, but they only had to be seaworthy for nine miles of river bend. Then, their naval service over, they'd heave to and hunch their shoulders together as pontoons to support the bridging planks that would reunite the Union armies.

"Damn!" One of the oars clunked out of its lock and the oarsman swore softly.

"Quiet there!" hissed Colonel Foy. All of us had stripped to the bare necessities. No canteens, tin cups, bayonets, nothing to rattle and clank.

Each soldier had a new Spencer repeating carbine and an ammunition pouch, and six men carried axes, their blades now muffled in cloth, to cut down trees and make an abatis around the bridgehead. I had less than that, just a Colt revolver, ammunition belt and a length of rope coiled over my shoulder. I hoped the pistol would be just for show. My job was strictly to lash the lead boat once we hit shore.

"Like Indian-style, huh?" whispered Sergeant Avery, huddled next to me in the bow. I grunted and saw his grin flash in the dark.

"Indian-style," I whispered, "you'd be naked with a knife in your teeth."

"And my nuts frozen like minnie balls," he chuckled. I rubbed my arms. The night air easily pierced our thin blouses. I felt naked, cast off from shore and at the mercy of the current. Our oars were good only for steerage, not strong enough to muscle us back upriver. We were committed, the river sweeping us straight toward enemy guns. The rocking of the boat and the slight queasiness of being without anchor or gravity made the precariousness more acute.

"Row on the right!" rasped Colonel Foy, as we drifted too far from shore. We wanted to hug the trees of the northern bank, as far as possible from rebel ears and eyes. The outside oarsmen dug deep, twice, thrice, and pointed our nose obliquely at the tree-line. The following boat clung to our wake and almost ran up on us before it fell back. I heard a splash and muffled laughter, then swearing, and looking back I saw the next boat wallow motionless then lurch to the side before righting itself and continuing.

"Damn you, keep up!" hissed Foy. "What the hell happened?"

"Lieutenant Branscomb got knocked overboard by a branch," came a voice. "We had to stop for him." Men in both boats laughed.

"Quiet!" said Foy. "Next man in the water stays there to drown!"

We eased along in silence, huddled low, barely able to see above the gunwales, not a dashing posture for a conquering army. Down past the town we floated, what few lights there were of it, and out into no-man's-land. Indians indeed, I thought. If this were an Indian war party there would be only a few, just enough to leap silently ashore, slit the throats of the sentries and slip away leaving the dead men as a warning. Nothing in Indian tradition contemplated either the organization or the slaughter of which our small expedition was the vanguard.

"Dead still now," whispered Colonel Foy, the order hardly necessary. Across the river, menacingly close, gleamed the first campfires of the enemy pickets, and their low conversations drifted across the water.

"What kinda dawg, Hanson?"

"Hail, I dunno. He was jest a *dawg*, that's all." And laughter.

Further downriver we drifted into earshot of a guard corporal teaching his men harmony.

"Rock of ages, cleft for me, Let me hide myself in thee," came four men's voices.

"No, hang it. Jimmy, sing the tenor line alone with me. Lak this." The leader cleared his throat and sang, "'Rock-of-ages, cleft-for-me,'" his voice on a single, high line.

Jimmy sang along with him, getting it right. "Ah know, Fred," said Jimmy. "It's just having the others there that gits me all bollixed."

"Do it again," said the leader, and this time all four sang and I could hear Jimmy's voice holding the tenor line. "Hang it," said the leader, "now *you're* off, Elmer. Sing the bass harmony, not the melody an octave lower." They continued to work out the harmony as we eased downriver, water lap-lapping at our planks.

"What's that!" came a shout from across the river.

"Quiet now. Quiet," whispered Foy, and we hunkered down smaller in the boat.

"What?" said another sentry.

"There. Look there, Luke. You see something moving there?"

We waited, imagining Luke squinting into the dark at us. "I don't see nothin'," said Luke. "Where?"

"There, against the trees." Luke took his time before answering. I felt a giant tarpaulin peeling off the whole operation, leaving us naked. Sixty hulking scows, fifteen hundred men, lurching downriver with the current. How could they miss us? I had a wild thought to jump overboard and swim for safety. Surely their cannons were even now drawing a bead.

"Where?" said Luke.

"Right . . ." said the other man, grunting, ". . . there!" A stone he'd thrown splashed in the water.

"Shit," said Luke. "Ain't nothin' there. Mebbe a log."

"Mebbe a gator."

"You shit. Ain't no gators there."

"*You* shit. Take yer leg off soon as look at you." They fell to arguing about alligators as the sixty scows, a strung-out line a quarter mile long, drifted past them. I felt huge and obvious and squeezed tighter down in the boat. All they needed over there was one leftover Cherokee with good ears and night vision to blow us out of the water. At the bottom of the loop, the deepest we would go into enemy territory, I could feel the current tugging at our balky craft, trying to pull it on a tangent, straight out and across the river.

"Row on the right," hissed Colonel Foy. "Keep her close to the bank." Men on the inshore side reached up and grabbed branches to keep us from drifting out. Oarsmen grunted as they fought the current. Across the river, Lookout Mountain loomed end-on to us, rising straight up into the night sky, slumbering now, but I imagined a great eye about to shutter open in its darkened slopes and trap us in a beam of light. I felt a sharp pain as Sergeant Avery, who thought he was grabbing his own knee, sank his fingernails into mine instead.

Then we were around the bend and heading north, and ahead signal fires marked the ferry landing where the assault brigades waited. "Pull in, Colonel Foy," came General Hazen's voice from three boats back, and the sudden sound made us all jump. We eased toward shore and I could see the dark silhouettes of our own soldiers waiting for us.

"Well done, lads," said a voice.

"Where's Farragut?" said another.

"Mother, I'm seasick," whined Sergeant Avery, and there was laughter on the shore until the officers hissed everyone silent. I looked up, as if waking from a reverie, and saw the sky pale above us. The river, which had been just a dark sloshing against our planks, now gleamed black and glossy, and I could see all the way across it. Our landing point was just opposite, a little break in the trees from which a road led up between the mountains and across the peninsula.

It took a few minutes of grunting and muffled cursing to wrestle the boats into an assault line, but soon they swung round, sixty rough craft with their bows all pointed west, and the oarsmen held them there awaiting the order. General Hazen looked right and left, saw all in readiness, and gave the order to shove off.

"Go man! Race 'em!" shouted Sergeant Avery. The silence broke all along the line as the little craft strained forward, an assault line several hundred yards long, straining for the opposite shore.

"Don't fire till we land," Colonel Foy reminded everyone. His holster was unbuttoned and his revolver in his hand. I unholstered my pistol and Avery held his carbine across his chest. Halfway across, the pickets onshore opened up, first with a few tentative shots, then a concentrated wham-wham-wham of explosions spuming water up around us, then a "thunk-thunk" as they found the range and struck the boats' timbers.

"Hot damn!" shouted Avery to the oarsmen. "Row you bastards!" They needed little urging, exposed as they were, and the boat lurched ahead faster. Poking my head above the gunwale, I saw puffs of smoke in the trees, like chrysanthemums, and already a fog of smoke lay on the shore. But it was just single shots from scattered pickets, not sustained volleying. I saw an officer emerge from the trees waving a pistol and turn his back to us, issuing orders.

Then, still improbably far from shore, the boat ground into the gravelly bottom, throwing us all forward. "Now, men, now!" shouted Colonel Foy, and he leaped picturesquely off the bow into the shallows.

"See ya later, chief!" said Avery, leaping out to follow his commander, and all the others except me and the oarsmen went over the sides, firing their carbines as they landed and wading through knee-deep water toward shore. All along the line the other boats hit the shallows and dispensed their assault troops, who swept toward shore firing as they went. The fire from the new repeating rifles, borrowed from the cavalry for the assault, was immense, overwhelming the single shots from shore. "At Chickamauga the regiment fired 45,000 rounds from these babies in five hours," Avery had told me. "Some rebs we captured thought we was a whole division!" Now on the shore the fire from 1500 seven-shot carbines easily trebled the assault wave's fire-power. I sat for a moment watching with awe the first combat I'd seen.

"Where to, Captain?" asked one of the oarsmen, reminding me I had a job too. The boat, relieved of its troops, floated free. Up and down river, oarsmen in the other unladen scows turned for the far shore to ferry the rest of the brigade across.

"Straight in," I ordered, sounding much more authoritative than I felt, pointing my untrembling hand at the gap in the trees that led to the ferry road. The men leaned on the oars and we lurched forward. My job was to swing the boat broadside at the shoreline and anchor it as a benchmark, for the bridge-builders siting pontoons and laying planking from the other side to home in on as the floating bridge reached out from shore. The air hummed around me like bees and whit-whits sliced past my ears. Instinct told me to duck and dodge, but I realized the futility of it. How do you dodge something you can't see? So I stood, gaining confidence as more and more whit-whits missed. We glided past a wading soldier, who reached out one hand to guide us along. As he did so his arms flew up and he fell backwards into the water, his rifle splashing down beside him. A companion, wading behind him, grabbed the wounded man's collar and dragged him to shore, leaving him gasping there and holding his bleeding shoulder.

"Close enough, Captain?" grinned an oarsman as the boat grounded again, and I found I could step out of it onto dry land.

"Swing her around!" I ordered and looked around for a tree to lash my rope to. The first assault wave was onshore now, up and down the beach and sweeping into the woods. There was a lot of firing, but most of it seemed to be moving away from us. We were pushing them back and the whit-whits past my ears had stopped. Other assault boats were halfway back across the river and the rest of the brigade, eager for action, crowded down the far bank to jump in as soon as the boats reached them.

"There she is, Captain," said the oarsman. Our boat was now grounded broadside on the shore, and I stood and looked at it. It looked square to me, so I took two handkerchiefs out of my pockets and waved them at the opposite bank, where I saw another officer signal back.

"Here," I said to the oarsmen, handing them the handkerchiefs. "Fix these to the oars and stand 'em up in the boat."

Soon we had our little boat secure, anchored with banners a-flying for the bridge to aim at. I passed a length of rope through the bow and stern loops and found trees to lash them to. The firing had moved inland and soon tapered off entirely, replaced by the thunk-thunk of axes as trees were felled for barricades. As I finished lashing the rope to the first tree, Sergeant Avery came out of the woods grinning and mopping his face with his sleeve.

"Jesus," he said. "Can't believe it. There was nothin' here but a guard. Couple dozen men. We drove 'em out quick's that." He snapped his fingers. "Had to cease firin' cause all we had to shoot at was each other."

I grunted as I pulled the rope tight. "Better have a care. It's Longstreet out here, remember."

"Longstreet," spat Avery. "It was Stonewall himself, be too late now."

I moved to a tree on the other side of the landing space and passed my rope around it. The sky had lightened and the water glinted blue. The troops ferrying across the river looked like a regatta now, an unopposed crossing, and as men landed they spread out up and down river as well as inland, widening and deepening the bridgehead. Boats were landing farther and farther up and down river, around the curves and out of sight. Any counterattack would now have to be on a front almost a mile long. A few wounded men limped or were helped out of the woods and down the bank into a returning boat.

"I tell yuh, it was a fright at first," said Avery as I worked at my rope. "I looked back once and saw all them boats floating away, thought we was bein' left to die. Then I got busy crankin' and firin' and next time I looked, here they all was again, comin' back."

I nodded at him and grunted as I secured my rope. On the river, the number of boats diminished slowly, as one by one they pulled out of line and got recommissioned as pontoons, and the bridge started making progress toward me. Birds, taking heart from the lack of firing, started singing. Suddenly there came a crash of musketry and a high-pitched yelling up ahead, as if the whole woods was exploding and tumbling down upon us.

"Counterattack!" yelped Avery, jumping to his feet. He grabbed his carbine and trotted up the road, but in a minute or two he was back, and with him came a crowd of others, backing up and firing as they went. A gray battle line, elbow to elbow, emerged from the woods and descended toward us.

I dropped the rope and grabbed for my revolver, but in the overconfidence of our quick success I had closed the holster and had the damndest time unsnapping it. My fingers seemed fat and rubbery, and I felt and heard the whit-whit around my ears again, and then thunk-thunk as bullets slapped into the tree I was leaning against. Splinters spat my face. Then the gun was in my hand and cocked and as I looked up I saw a musket barrel aimed right at me and I swear I could see a minnie ball rattling down it towards me. I fired, and the musket wasn't there any more, then I pelted down the bank, jumped into the anchored boat, felt no safer there, and clambered over the other side into the water, joining others who had had the same thought. But even as we crouched there, and I fired my pistol until it was empty, men in blue uniforms converged down the bank from both sides, formed a four-deep line, stepped off, and strode steadily up the road, driving the rebels before them. The firing moved back into the woods and soon died out entirely.

I stood up and so did the rest of the refugees behind the boat, all of us soaked to the armpits and slightly sheepish, but alive. It hadn't been a big breakthrough, just a concentrated spearhead on the center of the line which had failed for lack of support. Avery was right. Longstreet, defensive genius, had neglected to cover the road from the ferry.

I took a few deep breaths and holstered my revolver, careful not to button it this time. The sun was up full now, and the rebel attack seemed fleeting, like the reprise of a nightmare before the dawn. Gingerly, keeping my head up, I picked my way through the water and up to the trees to check my ropes. A dead rebel soldier lay next to the first tree and I rolled him out of the way without really thinking. He flopped over on his back and I saw the lower half of his jaw shot away, just a hole left there under an extraordinary set of buck teeth and a pitted complexion. What an ugly youth he must have been a few minutes ago! I squatted with my hat dangling from my hand and tried to imagine him alive, but it wouldn't come. Maybe he'd been one of the boys who had jauntily saluted Grant from across the river a few mornings ago. Maybe he was Jimmy, who had worked so hard to learn the tenor line of "Rock of Ages." Whoever it was, the rock had cleft for him now and swallowed him. Maybe, even, he was somebody *I* had killed. But try as I might I couldn't put any life or history into his dead eyes. He was just somebody dead.

Across the way I found Sergeant Avery sitting against my other tree, his hat pushed back and a mocking grin on his face. "What the hell you grinning at?" I asked him as I squatted to check the rope. "Just because I ran and you didn't?"

He didn't answer and I nudged him with my elbow, not hard, but enough to tip him over sideways. I reached to catch him and watched him slide away, leaving his hat behind him, stuck to the tree by the blood and hair that a bullet had matted there as it took off the back of his head.

"Jesus!" said a voice behind me. I turned to see one of my oarsmen, his face white, cover his mouth with his hand and puke through his fingers. I quelled the bile that rose in my own throat and reached out to peel Avery's hat away from the tree. I knelt over his body, turned him so he faced the sky, looked at him, shook my head, and closed his eyes. As the Seneca say, he was now eating the strawberries that grow along the path to heaven. I hid the damage to his head as best I could, placed his hat beside him and stood up, removing my own hat for a moment. Here lies Avery of the 23rd Kentucky, I thought. I didn't even know his first name. Murmuring Melville's words from "Shiloh" – "What like a bullet can undeceive!" – I put my hat on and turned away.

The work on the bridge continued and so did the ferrying of troops across the river and the fortifying of the bridgehead. Avery's body got hauled away, as did the dead southerner's. About noon I inspected our new abatis and found it high enough to stand behind, zig-zagging through the woods, across the ferry road, and down to the river, its flanks on the bank at both ends. While an attack by a few regiments at dawn might have swept us into the river, by noon it would have taken a division or more. But there was no firing, and scouts and pickets, fanning further and further out from the bridgehead, uncovered no massing counterattack. The valley beyond and the road to Bridgeport were open, and the rebs had gone streaming back to Lookout Mountain. General Hazen, whose brigade had made the landing, went among the front lines telling them they'd "knocked the top off the cracker box." My oarsmen went scavenging and found far better rations in the dead rebels' haversacks than we had with us, so we had a lunch of bacon, beans, and hardtack, and then I lay down near the tree where Avery died and dozed on and off in the sunshine, watching the pontoon bridge stretch ever closer to me. By four o'clock the last plank was laid, and, my mission accomplished, I picked myself up, dusted myself off, and crossed with unmoistened foot to the other side.

Grant was standing there with Rawlins, smoking and watching the progress of men and supplies trundling across the new-planked bridge. "So far, so good," he said as I walked up.

I reported briefly and he nodded, chewing on the cigar.

"Only six dead and thirty-two wounded," said Rawlins cheerfully, and I reflected that my short-lived friend Avery was one of the "only six." Hell of an epitaph. "I can't believe Longstreet left the landing so ill-defended," Rawlins noted.

Grant nodded, eying the heights of Lookout Mountain, as if looking for Longstreet to be looking back at him. "Longstreet was at my wedding," he muttered. "He arrived late, but he stayed late too. He'll fight." Grant scratched his beard. "We have yet to hear from Hooker."

"He was off in good time this morning with two divisions," Rawlins told me. "Unless he's met opposition, he should be well down the valley by now." He pointed across the bridge to the road and the valley beyond, where the last linkup of the cracker line would be made. "Somebody should get down there and make contact."

Grant's eyes returned from the hills, settled on me, and turned thoughtful. "Ye-e-e-s," he said. "Feel like a ride, Parker?"

"Whatever you say, General," I told him. Within half an hour I was mounted and clattering back across the bridge with two troopers from Hazen's brigade as escort. We trotted up the ferry road to the crest of the hill, where the logs in the barricades were slid aside to let us pass, and rode out into Lookout Valley as the protecting barrier slid shut behind us. I felt naked again, riding out there in the afternoon sun with all our troops left behind and the dark mass of Lookout Mountain rising up to our left. There lay the massed guns of the Confederacy and General James Longstreet, smarting from the morning's repulse, contemplating revenge. If he fired now, I was the only one in range.

"Don't worry, Captain," said one of the troopers riding alongside me. "He can't hit you from there."

My escorts turned out to be Ohio boys, who had spent "the whole damn winter and the whole damn summer" waiting for General Rosecrans to do something, only to be stalled at Stones River, whipped at Chickamauga and driven to near starvation in Chattanooga.

"We coulda busted out, give us a chance," one of them said. "Didn't need no General Grant here to spoon-feed us."

"Thomas can fight and so can we," said the other. "Just nobody give us a chance. Now you-all's here and nobody never gonna know what we can do."

Eventually we saw a cloud of dust down the valley, and before nightfall we were among the advance of Hooker's army. My escorts gaped at the well-dressed, well-fed troops from the east marching along with full bellies and swinging steps, their knapsacks and commissary wagons bursting with bounty that the Army of the Cumberland had only dreamt of for more than six weeks. I got them fed and quartered and reported to General Hooker, who was in the lead with Howard's corps. I had last seen these two generals, I realized with a start, only a week ago today in Bridgeport, on the rainy morning we set out on the mule road over Walden's Ridge for Chattanooga. A week, but it felt like a lifetime. Since then, Grant had ridden in, fired his armies' engines, sailed by night past drowsing pickets, attacked at dawn, built a bridge, scattered the enemy, and reached out a hand for Hooker to clasp and unite east and west.

In his tent, Hooker rubbed his hands as I detailed the day's events. "Good, good!" he said over and over. He sent a courier back to Grant and sent me three miles further down the valley to the railroad junction at Wauhatchie to report to General Geary, who was bringing up the rear with the Twelfth Corps. I trotted on into the night past tent cities and campfires, marveling at the manpower and equipment the Union could put on the road if so moved. Troop after marching troop had fallen out by the road; following the last brigade was a wagon train several miles long, each wagon rosetted with its brigade's colors so the quartermasters could find them in the night.

I reported to General Geary and bunked down with the headquarters staff in a comfortable tent, with stars and moon above us and the dark bulk of Lookout Mountain looming to the east. The heights were less threatening now that I was surrounded by the might of the Union army, with lots of fresh, young bodies between the guns and me. My tentmate was Captain Collins, Geary's adjutant, and the only element that provoked grumbling was that we had bivouacked close to the wagon train, and two hundred mules were tethered in a nearby field, adding their voices and their fragrance to the beauties of the southern night.

In the rush of activity last night and today, my body had ignored that it had been awake for thirty-six hours, but as soon as I lay down everything caught up with me and I fell fast asleep. So I had no idea what time it was or how long I'd slept when a crash of musketry shattered the night. I bolted upright, and Captain Collins burst into the tent, grabbed his gunbelt, and strapped it on.

"What?" I gasped, rubbing my eyes.

"Longstreet," he said. "Attacking on the left. Come on."

I grabbed my pistol, stuffed bullets in my pockets, pulled on my boots and followed. General Geary, by the light of a campfire, was dispatching staff officers, trying to find out what was going on. Outside the circle cast by the campfire, all was black.

"Sounds like they're trying to cut the ferry road," said Geary. "MacMorris, get down there and make sure the angle is secured. Carter!"

"Yes, sir," said a young officer.

Geary handed him a piece of paper. "If you can get around their left, ride to Hooker and tell him we're under attack."

"Surely he can hear that, General," said Collins.

Geary nodded. "Yes, lad. But try anyway. Let him know we're still alive and could use help. Schultz!"

"Yes sir!"

"Why aren't the artillery firing? Aren't they sited?"

"Yes sir," said Schultz. "I'll go see."

As soon as Schultz took two steps, a roar came on the left from our artillery.

"Anything else, sir?" grinned Schultz. Geary put a fatherly hand on his shoulder. "Get down there anyway. Tell 'em we'll maintain our lines and not advance. If they keep their firing elevation, they'll fire over our heads and hit rebels. Got that?"

"Yes, sir!" Schultz saluted and disappeared.

"Collins," said Geary to my bunk mate, "and . . ."

"Parker," I reminded him.

"Stay near me. I'll need you by and by."

We clung to Geary's side, as safe a place as any that dark and confusing night. The full moon shone intermittently through the clouds, but gave little help at ground level. A layer of gunsmoke soon covered us and made the dark impenetrable. All we could see was the winking of hundreds of rebel muskets to our left and front, the only targets our gunners had. Our line was formed in an "L," the foot of it along the ferry road, the long leg stretched out to the right, perpendicular to the road, and the attack started at the angle and foot of the "L", trying to turn our left and cut us off from the rest of the army. Geary and the rest of us were situated on a slight rise down the leg of the "L", where, when the smoke allowed, we could gauge the shape of the attack by the musket flashes.

"They're extending to our right," said Geary, pointing his hand that way, "along the railroad track. Umm . . ."

"Parker," I said.

"Yes. Get down to the artillery. My compliments and could they swing at least one gun around to the right."

"Yes sir!" I said, turned on my heel, took a deep breath, and plunged out of the circle of light. Northeast, my instincts told me, and I tried to keep a bee-line as I stumbled through the night. The rocky ground was threaded with streams and ditches, and more than once I fell. But I kept going, aided not only by instinct but by the artillery, the only cannons we had, booming away dead ahead of me. Men huddled behind what barriers they could find and fired into the dark, reloaded and fired again, with no hope or knowledge of what they were firing at, just keeping up a steady rhythm and a carpet of fire. Thrown off course, I hit the front lines, where a Pennsylvania regiment was methodically loading and firing, loading and firing, keeping up a steady line of chatter like workers in a factory.

"Keep their heads down, boys" said an officer conversationally. "Don't let 'em draw a bead."

I heard our guns booming behind us and turned that way. By luck the attack came right at the place our one artillery battalion stood, so we were firing round after round dead-on into the rebel advance.

"Hit the artillerists!" came a rebel cry not far away. "Fire at the guns!"

"They've been shouting that all night," said a rifleman, calmly turning to me as he tamped a shot home. "Long's they shoot at the cannons, they leave us alone." He rattled the ramrod out, turned, fired and shrugged. "Mebbe killed a tree, hey?"

I scrambled away from the line and up the hill to where the cannons were booming. There were only four of them, but they fired so briskly that it seemed like many more. As I stood up on the rise bullets whit-whitted around my head much thicker than down on the firing line. Men were laboring, nine to a gun, servicing their machines like hostlers sponging and feeding a team of smoking horses.

"General Geary's compliments!" I shouted to the first officer I found. "Could you please angle over to cover his right!"

"I am doing so!" shouted the officer. "Tell father to keep his head down!"

A strange, familial way to greet one's commander, I thought, as I turned off the hill to plunge down into the underbrush and feel my way back to Geary. Later I learned the officer was Edward Geary, the general's son, and that he was killed by a bullet to the head shortly after we spoke. But though the war was killing families, it was creating a nation, as the Revolution hadn't, and it was doing so in hundreds of skirmishes just like that night's. Virginia boys and Pennsylvania and New York and Ohio boys were killing each other in the dark somewhere on the margins of Tennessee and Georgia. The hash such battles made of state and regional borders spoke nationhood better than any speeches.

I stumbled back to the headquarters tents through brush and brambles, gunsmoke clogging my eyes and nose, bullets spanging off rocks and thudding into trees. Though my conscious (call it white) mind told me a thousand times I was lost, my instincts (call them Indian) homed me in, and at length, blowing hard, I saw the fires of the headquarters camp.

"Thought we'd lost you," said Collins after I'd reported to General Geary. "Two couriers haven't come back."

"Just as likely lost as shot," I told him. "Can't see out there. Just head for the firing and hope you bump into ours before you bump into theirs."

I peered into the smoke and dark, trying to make sense of the battle. The only battles I'd seen, except this morning's skirmish, were drawn with neat arrows on newspaper maps, and they bore no relation to the chaos and smoke, the rattle and pop and winking lights of musketry all around me. I oriented myself east, facing the long side of our "L" where southern troops were pouring down off Lookout Mountain in what sounded like overwhelming numbers. The heaviest firing now seemed dead in front of us, as if the rebels, raked by the artillery down at the angle, had swung around to outrange it, concentrating on our right, feeling in the dark for the flank, which, as I now visualized it, seemed dangerously up in the air. There was brisk fire all along the line in front of us, New York and Pennsylvania regiments commingling, loading and firing at the winking targets which grew thicker as if drawn together by magnets.

"Good lads," spoke an officer's voice, remarkably calm. "Keep up the pace now. Keep it steady. Aim for the flashes. Aim for the flashes."

The firing, which I thought could get no louder, reached a further crescendo and sustained it impossibly long. Collins and I crouched behind a log, pistols ready, poking our heads up as if we could see something if only we squinted long and hard enough. The firing in front slackened a bit, the battle seeming to consume itself with its own energy, but then came a flurry of explosions on our left, closer than before, drawing closer by the second. I thought at first it was an acoustical illusion, but Collins didn't.

"Jesus Christ!" he rasped. "They're bending us back on top of ourselves."

He grabbed my collar and held my head up above the log, and I saw it too. On our left, which had been impenetrable black before, the winking lights of gunfire now appeared; if I could see the flashes, the muskets must be pointed toward us. Rebel rifles, steadily advancing. I heard crashing in the underbrush behind us, our own troops withdrawing steadily, keeping up a field of fire, but inexorably yielding ground. The two sides of the "L" were collapsing, squeezing us at the hinge like a nutcracker. We ducked down behind the log, but it became a question which side to hide on, as shots whit-whitted equally from both directions.

"Cartridges!" came shouts from in front of us. "More cartridges!"

"Cahhh-tridges!" came a high mocking cry from beyond the lines. "Yankee-boys' well run dry!" The firing increased.

"Cartridges!" came the cry up and down the line, and behind us too from the retreating troops, desperate to hold what little line they had left.

General Geary's voice whiplashed in the dark. He was standing on the log behind which Collins and I crouched, heedless of the shot that whizzed around him. "Fix bayonets!" he cried. All along the line the word passed. "Fix bayonets!" "Fix bayonets!" "Fix bayone-e-h-h-h-ts!"

Having no bayonet to fix nor any musket to fix it to, I rolled over, broke open the cylinder of my revolver, and felt for my shells. Six shots. I could down six before I fell. I didn't feel afraid, strangely enough. If anything I was relieved, looking forward to *doing* something after what seemed an eternity behind that log as the battle roiled around me. I could feel footfalls through the ground as both flanks collapsed toward us, retreating toward Geary, solid in the center, as if huddling toward the general's skirts. Now amid the pop and crash and whit-whit of musketry came the harsh sound of steel on steel as with a whoosh and a clank bayonets unsheathed and stoppered each rifle. As our firing dimmed, so did the rebels', bringing an odd hush in the night and smoke, as the battle drew in its breath for one all-scattering blow.

In the hush, I heard the sound.

It started as a low moan like wind in the pine trees, almost a lament, a slow, keening chorus. It rose to a hum as of many voices in urgent agreement, joined by more voices, then more and more, until it ascended the scale, slow and grinding like a siren. My scalp tingled as if giant fingers were ripping it, as the sound, soon a mad and scarlet scream, drew more voices to it. It became a mindless, directionless wail, springing from the earth all around us and scaling the heavens, a hideous soprano yodel drawing strength and terror from the voices all around it, redoubling upon itself, draining the marrow from my bones. Higher and higher it strained, an ululating shriek, echoing off the distant mountains and flinging itself back upon us as if to batter us into the earth where we crouched and trembled with our fists in our ears, clinging to our last shreds of sanity as the din rose like a demon chorus.

My bowels dissolving, my teeth chattering, my hair on end, I gripped my pistol with one hand and dug my nails into Collins's shoulder with the other. "The rebel yell!" I breathed.

"No," said Collins, shaking his head, his eyes showing white. "The mules."

I had forgot about the mules.

So had everyone else, it seemed, including their teamsters, who, as the southern line extended and brought them under fire, had abandoned their charges and fled rearward, leaving their tethered, terrified beasts as the only anchor to the right flank of the whole Union line.

I don't know what it must have been like to be a mule that night or what went through their mulish heads as fire and shot careened around them and their masters and protectors fled. Had I been a mule, I would have followed the teamsters, knowing that where they went, there lay food and safety. But I was not a mule and they were, and I had learned in those two days climbing Walden's Ridge that mules don't follow worldly standards. These two hundred mules, trapped between two lines of fire at Wauhatchie Junction, knew that rearward lay safety, but that rearward too lay the burdensome wagons they'd be hitched to come morning for another day's haul. But which of them could say what lay in front of them? That may have been what the hideous discussion was about, the screams and cries for recognition and points of order as they made their braying minds up. Security to the rear or freedom to the front? The vote came loudly and suddenly and unanimously in favor of freedom. Breaking their tethers and dragging their clanging trace chains, they bolted and fled toward the rebel lines. The earth quaked and trembled beneath their pounding feet, and between the mad tattoo of their hooves and the mad shrieking of their battle cry of freedom, they swept all before them as they headed for the hills.

Nor do I know what it must have been like to be a southern soldier that night, victory in my grasp, hearing the desperate cries for cartridges on the other side, the slacking of fire and the clatter of fixed bayonets. Perhaps I would have been just standing up, musket ready and drawing a bead for one last volley into the charging mass of blue, when suddenly the shriek from two hundred feral, frightened throats split the night, and eight hundred pounding hooves, dragging chains like Marley's ghost run mad, swarmed out of the night and thundered down upon me.

Straight across our front the mules stampeded, rolling up the rebel line and scattering it back to the hills in terror and disarray. The battle ended with as little warning as it had begun. "We thought it wuz the cavalry," said a prisoner later on. "But damn if we could figger out what the damn brayin' wuz about."

And as the stampede faded into the distance and the firing flickered down to a few pot-shots, dazed men stood up along our line and started cheering.

"Hurrah for the mule brigade!"

"Hee-haw! Heehaw!"

Then we heard the sound of marching feet, and from our left, in good order, came a full detachment Hooker had sent down to help us out. It may, in fact, have been the arrival of Hooker's men on their right, as much as the charge of the lop-eared irregulars on their left, that sent the rebs a-flying. But you couldn't tell that to history, which started its own version of the event on the spot, immortalizing the "lop-eared two hundred" of "The Mule Brigade," and promoting them to "honorary horses."

"Hey soldier boys, where ya been?" sang a mocking voice from our lines.

"Come to save your ass, son" growled a trooper from the line of march.

"Too late, slim," returned the other. "Our own asses done already saved us."

Chapter XII

YOU'RE *HOW* OLD, MISS SACKETT?

Virginia 1864

THE REST OF THE BATTLE OF CHATTANOOGA – THE OFFICIAL part – is well known. Sherman's arrival from Tennessee across the cracker line; Hooker's "Battle above the Clouds" on Lookout Mountain; Sherman's profane and blustering attempt to roll up the Rebel right, only to find mountains and rivers in his path; and the final, un-ordered "Miracle of Missionary Ridge," as Thomas's army ascended the ridge hand-over-hand and swept Bragg's army back to Atlanta.

On the final day I watched with Grant and the rest of the staff on a little rise called Orchard Knob as blue troops ascended the heights, routed the defenders then romped amid cannons and wagons and stores, throwing caps and haversacks in the air. Mr. Dana of the War Department was incredulous as the rest of us. "I thought that ridge was impregnable, General," he said to Grant.

Grant took his cigar out of his mouth, blinked at Dana and shrugged. "Well, it *was* impregnable," he said.

The Battle of Chattanooga drove the Confederacy out of Tennessee, certified Grant as a military genius, and shut down Union Army operations for the winter. Rawlins went to Connecticut to marry Emma Hurlbut and came back without his beard, I went to army headquarters at Nashville to push papers, and Grant went to Washington to be named the first Lieutenant General since Washington, given command of all the Union armies, and feted and feasted until he packed his valise and went back to the army in Virginia, telling Lincoln he was "tired of all the show business."

Come spring, the cast reassembled in the woods and fields around Culpepper and Brandy Station in Virginia for the final push to Richmond. Not Hannibal, not Caesar, not Napoleon ever had under his command the might that Grant now ruled as his demesne. On May 4, a week after Grant's forty-second birthday, 120,000 men crossed the Rapidan via Ely and Germanna Fords, their objective "Lee's army. Wherever Lee goes, there you will go also." With them went 3,500 wagons, 29,000 horses, 20,000 mules, herds of cattle, ten days' rations and ten days' fodder, in a train so long that though Sheridan's 13,000 cavalry splashed across the shallows first, before dawn on the fourth, the last wagon didn't cross until thirty-six hours later, at sunset on the fifth. Had the wagons made direct for Richmond and gone unimpeded, the first one would have rolled into Richmond's Capitol Square while the last one's rear wheels cleared the Rapidan sixty miles behind.

For forty days and forty nights this grand assemblage, brilliantly equipped, well-fed, ably generaled, slugged and fought through jungle and swamp, over river and stream, through mud and rain and hail and corpse-rotting sun, through choking dust and eye-ripping smoke, through woods set blazing by the fire from its own cannons, which burned and consumed the wounded where they lay, through blood-soaked, corpse-choked trenches using their own dead for foot-purchase, slugging and swearing and gripped in combat. The two armies locked fingers to each other's throats, knives to each other's bellies, unwilling, unable to let go, grappling and slip-sliding, teetering slowly clockwise, each with his back to his own capital, rocked but not falling, blowing hot, sour breath and baring yellowed teeth in each other's streaked faces and hanging on, hanging on, and slugging and tearing away.

Forty days, seventy-five miles, and a dozen spring-swollen, Indian-monikered rivers later, ripped and battered, torn and hollow-eyed, choked and wheezing, but in good order, missing arms and legs, unhinged jaws underslung with bloody bandages, unable either to take Richmond, whose church spires we could see through the battle-haze, or destroy Lee, whom we clubbed and battered daily only to see him slip his skin and ooze away like a snake. We fought every day of the forty days, in everything from a dust-up to a cavalry charge, from skirmishing to the conflagrations of the Wilderness, Spotsylvania, and Cold Harbor. We lost 8,000 killed, 40,000 wounded, 9,000 captured or missing, losses about equal to Lee's whole army. "O heavens, what scene is this?" moaned Walt Whitman, wound-dresser. "Is this indeed humanity, these butchers' shambles?" as wagon after wagon of wounded ground north through Fredericksburg and boarded hospital steamers for Washington.

Forty days of this were enough to break the spirit of any man whose body escaped intact. So intense and continuous was the fighting that not a day went by that I myself was not under fire and in direct danger of dismemberment or death.

They were the happiest forty days of my life.

We were at the center of the universe! The Civil War was history's main event, and we were the eye of it. All eyes were upon us, and we could get anything we wanted. The government, which earlier had seemed to conspire with the Confederacy to befuddle Grant, now marched in step with him. Fresh troops and supplies arrived daily, the supply line extending almost to infinity, fanning out through the loyal states to feed the might of the north into Grant's army and the few hundred square miles of Virginia that the world had come down to. We started out with 120,000 men, took 60,000 casualties, and still crossed the James with 120,000, so efficiently did the government scour the north, denude it of troops, hand them rifles, and send them south to join us.

The other thing was that I was so damn *busy*. All my grown-up life I had sought the center of the white man's world only to find the path choked with office work and to spend my best hours pushing papers. Except for the battle at Chattanooga, I spent the whole war before we crossed the Rapidan behind a desk. But once the army moved, my, how busy I became. Rarely did we spend two nights in the same place as we ground south. Rarely did I spend a single day in one place, as all of us were called upon for myriad tasks, from receipting orders to copying dispatches, to courier service, to scouting, to laying out entrenchments and siting batteries. Every man was employed to the hilt, and never have so many days passed when I've fallen to sleep exhausted, every fiber of my being and every iota of my capability squeezed to the sticking place.

We were always up and out early, the dew on the tents and on the grass, horses blowing smoke, the sky blue and bright, everyone moving crisply and with purpose, and the smell of bacon and coffee from the headquarters table that was one of the many pleasures of the life of violence we'd plunged into. "Headquarters in the saddle," came the joshing cry, as we swung aboard, our hindquarters and headquarters in the same place. So busy were the forty days that I can't separate one from another, and even the letters I then scribbled to Nic and Carrie, as I shuffle through them here before me on yet another desk in 1895, yield no sequence but only a cloud of impressions.

As the Wilderness exploded around us, Grant sat in a clearing, whittling a stick, smoking, nodding as reports came in, not doing much, letting the battle develop. One general came roaring into camp complaining to Meade about this and that and God-damning this and that to hell and points beyond, and when he was gone, Grant squinted up at Meade and suggested that an officer who swore so ought to be arrested. "Oh, no," said Meade. "That's just his way. He wasn't swearing. He was merely expressing his extreme vehemence on the subject matter." This so amused Grant that it became a staff watchword for the rest of the war. Rawlins, for instance, even at his brimstone best, never swore, just "expressed extreme vehemence on the subject matter."

The overlapping of staffs and proliferation of generals were a headache. Orders took time to filter down, reports to filter up, generals and their staffs argued about turf while their troops died for lack of support. "What's wrong with this army?" stormed Grant. "Oh, nothing," said Rawlins. "Nothing that can't be solved by giving Parker a gallon of whisky, a scalping knife, and sending him out to kill the first dozen generals he sees."

What tipped the balance was Grant. It happened simply enough. After two days in the Wilderness, both armies worn out and choking and the woods in flames, with no general on either side able to see anything he could call "victory" or "defeat," Grant stood up, wiped his knife on his pants, looked at the map, looked around the circle at us, and muttered, "We'll move by the left flank." Eyes snapped, jaws and fists clenched. The left flank pointed south.

It was that simple. Grant just declared victory and moved on. Even so, he almost lost it, not through any failure of design or strategy, but by one of those absurdities that history injects when the drama gets too big for itself. This particular moment proved that not only was it necessary for Grant to be there to win in the Wilderness, it was necessary for *me* to be there too.

We were picking our way through Hancock's Corps toward Todd's Tavern and Spotsylvania, the smoke thick, the woods on fire down to the road's edge. The staff made a long train, with Meade's crowd and ours intercombined and everybody bumping to get up closest to the generals. Rawlins, Bowers, Rowley and I got squeezed to the rear, where we rode with our heads down, kerchiefs over our noses against the smoke. I had gone into a sort of trance, half dozing and trusting my horse to follow the one before it, when something seized me by the back of the head and pulled me upright.

"What's going on?" I said to Rawlins, riding beside me.

"Hush," he said. "New road. Go to sleep."

New road? What was he talking about? My scalp froze and my hair stood on end. I looked ahead to see Grant and the lead horsemen veering off on a right fork, where the road was less clogged. "Short cut," came the word from up front.

"Hell it is," I said to Rawlins. Something was wrong. In the smoke and dark and woods I couldn't see stars or moon, but my skull was fit to burst as its compass spun and screamed that we weren't heading south any more, but west, directly at the enemy.

I grabbed Rawlins's sleeve. "Ride up, John! Ride to Grant! This isn't the road! We're heading west!"

"You sure?" he said. I didn't wait to argue but slapped his horse to make him spring forward.

I sweated and gasped for breath, less from fear and smoke than from disorientation. My compass was clanging inside my skull, pulling me left, left, you idiot, almost knocking me off my horse. It was like being blindfolded and led toward a cliff, being told all the time, "It's safe, it's safe," but feeling the updraft, sensing the void, and knowing with all my fluids that it *wasn't* safe.

"He says this is the road," said Rawlins, returning. "He's got a local guide. Says it veers south up ahead."

"Hell it does," I said and spurred forward, pushing horsemen off the road, clawing up through the ranks of aides until I squeezed my way to Grant. "General," I panted. "We're heading toward the enemy. South is that way." I flung my hand out to point across his chest and nearly knocked him out of the saddle.

Grant and Meade reined in. "Who is this man?" said Meade.

"Parker," said Grant, patting his horse on the flank to settle it. "Get back there. I won't turn around. I won't . . .." He peered at my face and frowned in sudden alarm. "Are you sure?"

"Absolutely," I said and saw him waver. This was the man who never backtracked, the boy who would go over hill and dale rather than retrace his steps. He looked over his shoulder, then at the road ahead, uncertain for the first time since he crossed the Rapidan.

"No . . ." he started to say, but hoofbeats came from up ahead as the guide pounded back around a curve.

"Back! Back!" he cried, waving at us. Through the smoke behind him we could see horsemen in gray sitting astride the road, looking in our direction.

Grant yanked the reins to turn his horse. "Back!" he shouted. "Parker, you lead." And, for perhaps the first time in his life, Grant retraced his steps, with me in the lead, panting and sweating, my head spinning until we regained the road and I pointed a trembling hand south. Grant patted my shoulder as he passed, and my head went clunk! as if its cogs had shifted back into place.

My other Indian faculty, that bee-line instinct, also helped. After we missed outflanking Lee at Spotsylvania we had to entrench, and I was detailed to lay out a line across a field. No problem. I could ride a straight line on my horse while men laid out fence rails behind me to mark it. Only problem was a farmhouse directly in the path, and as I sat and pondered whether to lay the line behind it and expose the house to fire or in front of it to protect it, a woman in a gray dress came bustling out and stood on the porch berating me.

"You'd better not harm this house!" she shouted.

"Ma'am," I told her. "You'd best ride on out of here. There's going to be a fight."

She folded her arms across her bosom and stood proud. "I'm safe right where I am," she announced, pointing to the tree-line opposite. "My husband's brigade is over yonder. He'll see that not a shot harms his house."

That settled it. "Lay the line behind the house," I told the men. "And site a battery in the yard. Woman here says we'll be safe as can be."

We entrenched behind the house, put cannon in the yard, and it wasn't until late in the day that the homeowner in the woods got tired of our firing on him unmolested and, cursing the while, ordered his artillery to destroy his house.

On and on the slugging toiled, slipping ever sideways by the left, never quite disengaging, slogging across river after river, all the cross-cutting streams Grant had warned about back there in Galena. The Rapidan, Wilderness Run, the Ni, the Po, the Ta, and the Mat, which flowed together into the Mattaponi. The North and South Annas, the Totopotomoy and the Pamunkey, and down toward the Chickahominy and the crossroads of Cold Harbor, where, the night before the assault, I saw men writing their names and home towns on pieces of paper and sewing them to their uniforms so they could be shipped home and buried after the slaughter. At Cold Harbor, Grant got, as every general got sometime in the war, the delusion that a frontal assault could take an entrenched position. It worked as well for him at Cold Harbor as it had for Burnside at Fredericksburg and Lee at Gettysburg. For three days afterwards, thousands of men lay wounded, then dying, then dead, under the Virginia sun, as Lee and Grant fought long-distance whether to call a truce, who was suing for it, and when *exactly* ambulances could collect the wounded. Two delirious and dehydrated men survived the days and nights of this officer correspondence.

Then it was hide fox and all after, up stakes and go, and Grant gobbled the last twenty-five miles to the James in one gulp, motioning a hundred thousand men to sneak behind his back while he stood eye to eye with Lee at Cold Harbor, sending them across a half-mile pontoon bridge, and sweeping them all the way around to Petersburg before Baldy Smith slammed against Beauregard's defenses, took too much time getting organized, and we all encamped for a nine-month siege that made Vicksburg look like dance class.

Unable to end the war quickly, chagrined that Grant's vow from Spotsylvania to "fight it out along this line if it takes all summer" now was amended to include fall and winter, we dug in at City Point, on the south side of the James, where we established the best-built, best-supplied headquarters of this or any other war. By fall we had built a company town, generals had their wives and families in camp, there were stage shows, band concerts, parties and reviews, and the war came to seem like a permanent but far-off thing that men commuted to, the only difference between this and other day jobs being that when they stayed late they didn't come home.

During the first few days on the banks of the James, though, routine wasn't well established, nor were demarcation lines, so there was a lot of unsupervised wandering. Men looking for their units and sightseeing civilians blundered into the headquarters encampment before sentries could shoo them away.

I was sitting under the fly of Grant's tent one day shortly after our arrival, a lazy June afternoon, the sun high and hot and glinting off the river, the sky blue and still, clouds grazing in it like sheep. The headquarters tents were on a hill, to catch the breeze, and the canvas rippled gently. There was the hum of insects in the air. Below me, boats churned up and down the river delivering supplies, their engines muted by distance, their stacks puffing white. From the docks came far-off cries of teamsters and mules, of navvies stacking crates and barrels. Jesse Grant's leather goods and Henry Flagler's salt pork, I mused. The war had gone on long enough for Henry's salt mines to make a killing up in Michigan, though not nearly as impressive as the killing we'd been doing down in Virginia.

"You there! Hey you!" At the shout, I raised my heavy lids and eased my eyes into short focus. Just below me, on the green slope, a lone, lanky civilian in a stovepipe hat was making long strides uphill, pursued by an anxious sentry.

"Yes, you!" shouted the sentry, as the civilian stopped, turned, and pointed to his chest. I looked on, bemused, as the civilian attempted some explanation, his long arms flapping, and I expected the sentry to take his elbow and escort him downhill. I was surprised, therefore, to see the sentry draw back, lower his musket, come to awestruck attention and salute. The tall, black-suited civilian laid a fatherly hand on the boy's shoulder, turned and continued his walk up through the grass toward me.

Some War Department muck-a-muck? I pushed back my chair, prepared to rise and receive him, and kept on rising as the man loomed closer and closer, ducked under the tent fly, his hand holding his hat brim and covering his face, then removed the hat and showed me a face I had seen in portraits and photographs, in newspapers and magazines, on thousands of posters over the last four years. I had even seen him in person, in Washington during the Mexican War and speaking in Illinois, before he had either his beard or his office, but never up this close.

"I'm looking for General Grant," he said, in a twangy voice. "He here?"

"Yessir, Mr. President," I stammered, erect now and trembling like the sentry had. I moved one hand then the other to my brow and down, momentarily forgetting which one to salute with, and decided instead to take off my hat, which I dropped on the ground and had to bend to retrieve. "He's right inside. I'll, um, I'll go get him. Please, um . . ." I waved at the chairs and stumbled into the tent, buttoning my jacket.

When I emerged with Grant and other reinforcements, Lincoln was sitting in a camp chair, legs crossed, squinting at the river and tapping his foot. Orville Babcock, one of the new staff, took charge, seating people and generally bustling about. Lincoln sat placidly through the introductions, nodding, registering each face, repeating names as Babcock said them. Grant, never shy about rank, sat in a chair next to the president. I got squeezed to the rear and hovered by a tent-pole as the conversation sputtered to start.

"I thought I'd hop a boat and come down, General," said Lincoln, practiced at ice-breaking. "Not that I can do much good. But it's a part of the country I haven't been permitted to visit, so I thought I'd take a look."

"Wish we could show you Richmond," said Grant. "I'd thought, by this time, we'd be able to."

Lincoln clucked his tongue and shook his head. "I've been told that by too many generals, General. If you'd promised me, I wouldn't have believed you."

"The president won't let me tell him my plans," Grant told us, looking around at the hovering staff. "Afraid of leaks."

"Be blunt, General," laughed Lincoln. "I was afraid *I'd* leak. I tend to blab." He scanned us with a smile and we all forced a chuckle.

"Have you no escort, Mr. President?" Babcock dared to ask. "You came by yourself?"

"Oh, I have a man with me," said Lincoln. He waved vaguely toward the dock. "Last I saw he was inquiring around the wharf for the headquarters tent. I left him there and set off on my own." He uncrossed and recrossed his legs and looked sideways down at Grant. Even sitting he was tall. "You're a hard man to find, General. You've eluded me for years."

More chuckles, still forced, and we fidgeted and waited for Lincoln to say more. He was balancing his stovepipe hat on his knee and seemed intent on seeing if it would stay there. We watched the hat for awhile.

"They're still giving me trouble about Vicksburg," Lincoln told Grant. "People are real upset about your paroling a whole army."

"You concurred, sir," said Grant, not sure if this was a rebuke. A blue jay squawked in a nearby tree. I swatted at a fly.

"Me?" Lincoln shrugged. "People think I'm a fool anyway. It's you they blame. But I've learned a way to fix it for you. I just tell them about Sykes's dog."

He looked around, eyebrows raised, for somebody to supply the feed. "Sykes's dog?" Rawlins finally asked.

"Yes, General Rawlins," nodded Lincoln. "Some congressmen came to me complaining about Grant's paroling the army, and I told them it was all right. Some parts of it might still fight, but it was useless *as an army* any more. They didn't get that, so I told them about my friend Bill Sykes." Lincoln put his hat on the ground and leaned forward, elbows on knees. "Sykes had a yellow dog that was the meanest cuss you ever saw. Chase you down the street, frighten the horses, kill the chickens, you name it. Not much anybody could do about it, 'cause Sykes himself was pretty mean, and he did love that dog. It was a fix." Lincoln shook his head. "Well, one day a bunch of the town boys decided to do something about it. They fixed up a cartridge with a long fuse, put the cartridge in a piece of meat, dropped the meat in front of Sykes's door, and sat on a fence opposite with the end of the fuse in their hands. They whistled for the dog. The dog comes out of Sykes's house sniffing the air," Lincoln screwed up his face so his nose seemed twice as long, "and pounced on the meat, gobbled it cartridge and all, the fuse hanging out his mouth. The boys touched off the fuse, held their ears, and pretty soon the dog exploded like a kettle of beans. All over the place. Old Sykes hears the explosion, comes out of his house and sees pieces of his dog raining down all about him. He picks up a portion of the back part, with a piece of the tail still wagging, and after looking it over, says, 'Well, I guess he'll never be much use again – *as a dog!*'"

We laughed as heartily as nephews at a favorite uncle's story, and with the laughter our skittishness vanished. Conversation became general and animated, the president no longer having to sustain the burden alone. Still, I could see the fix Lincoln was in. When he talked, even aside to Grant, everyone else shushed up and listened, so even his most banal utterance took on gravity. I got a quick flash of my younger self, standing in the White House with my hat in my sweating hand, our lands in peril, nodding gravely as Polk told us how good the beds were at Gadsby's Hotel.

Everything seemed to remind Lincoln of a story, and it wasn't long before eyes rolled skyward when he said, "that reminds me," and launched in. For the most part, though, the anecdotes were *a propos*, and it was better to hear folksy stories from a politician than the blather most of them spouted. Told that this army was the "same" one that had been defeated on the Peninsula in '62, Lincoln said, "That reminds me of the farmer who said he'd had the 'same' axe for ten years. He'd only had to replace the handle five times and the head twice."

There was some shuffling that summer in the Grant family. Will Rowley went home on a sick leave that turned permanent. Rawlins, who had coughed since Vicksburg, left for a couple months' recovery, leaving me the one Galena man among the brass that surrounded Grant. I felt like an old retainer, kept to remind him of his humble past, and the new men treated me almost like a pet. My rank advanced, though. I became Colonel Parker, Military Secretary, replacing Rowley. In real terms it meant no more courier riding, no more time in the field, no more laying entrenchments and free-lancing. Just a total concentration of my duties into the few square yards surrounding the headquarters tent and reams of correspondence. Good-bye to the sunshine and the mud, the rivers and the rain, hello to a new stripe on my sleeve and a new strain on my buttons as I sat and sat and grew fat. As Lincoln said the fellow said while being tarred and feathered, if it wasn't for the honor of the thing I'd just as soon have skipped it.

Visitors kept me amused. A Sanitary Commission delegate looking for Grant poked his head in one day, saw me and walked away muttering, "If that's Grant he's got all-fired sunburnt since last I saw him." Other visitors treated the place as a sort of tourist attraction, coming down on day trips to visit the war.

One regular visitor was a Reverend William Welsh of Philadelphia, an Episcopalian minister who busied himself with the spiritual and other moral needs of the troops. He looked into sanitary and educational arrangements, distributed books and bibles and fought vainly to rid the camp of pictures of naked women, which were the main output of the Mathew Brady studio, far more prevalent and lucrative than the war photos for which he later became famous. Welsh seemed harmless enough, a busybody who might accidentally do some good, though I later came to regret my underestimation. He was a pinch-faced fellow with a hawk nose and a white beard that encircled his chin, leaving his upper lip bare. His voice was high and reedy, squeezing like a pipe through pursed lips. He never paid me much mind, though now and then he eyed me curiously, as if confused by my provenance.

Family members came into camp seeking news of sons and brothers reported missing or captured. We had a regular system for getting such inquiries through the lines to Richmond, and Reverend Welsh set himself up as an offeror of safe passage, seeing families through the lines and back. Toward the end of August, Reverend Welsh brought a mother and daughter from Washington in search of their husband and father, missing since the forty days. Welsh bustled about, commandeering a carriage, sniffing around the tents, eventually driving off with the mother toward a checkpoint while the daughter, a young woman in her early twenties as I judged, waited at City Point. She waited, in fact, in the headquarters tent, where for reasons I forget I found myself alone with her, scratching at correspondence while she idled in a chair near the door.

"What's that you're writing, Colonel . . . ?" she asked.

I turned to her, surprised. People tended to treat me like furniture. "Parker," I said, the tilt of her question and her head indicating she wanted my name. "Just a routine report, Miss . . . ?" I imitated her tone and tilt.

"Sackett," she said. "Minnie Sackett."

I smiled. "Minnie Sackett. Sounds like an Indian name. Like Minnehaha."

She raised one eyebrow, which I found endearing because I couldn't do it. Her eyebrows were dark, but her hair, pulled back from her face, was cornsilk blonde. She wore a light-blue dress and black, high-buttoned traveling boots. A lone sunbeam found its way through the tent-flap and cast a glow on her. "Is that true?" she asked. "Minnehaha, I mean. I thought Longfellow made it up."

"No, it's true enough," I told her. I crooked my elbow over the back of my chair and waxed knowledgeable while my pen dangled in the air. "Minnehaha is a Sioux name. It means 'falling water.' Minne just means water, like Minnesota, Minneapolis."

Her big blue eyes absorbed my words. A wisp of hair blew across her face and she shooed it away. "So my name is water," she said. "One whose name was writ on water."

"Thou still unravished bride of quietness," I rejoined, matching her Keats for Keats.

"My, my," she said. "Serves me right. I have a *penchant* for unattributed quotations." She pronounced it "pongshong" like French. "Though whether I'm still unravished is none of your business. Are you a Sioux, Colonel Parker?"

"Um, ah, no, no," I told her, stumbling, aghast at her frankness. "They never would have left you alone with a nasty Sioux. I'm a Seneca. One of the Iroquois tribes." And, since she asked, I told her a little about the Iroquois Federation, about the six tribes, and, not incidentally, about my position as Grand Sachem, at which she was duly impressed.

"And what would my name be in Seneca?" she asked. "Minnie."

I frowned. "We have so many names for water," I told her. "River, lake, stream, spring, swamp."

"I don't think I should like to be named after a swamp," she said.

"Well, how about Ska-no-da-ri-o," I said. "It means Beautiful Lake, where your word Ontario comes from."

She tried the word a couple of times and wrinkled her nose, then laughed like falling waters. "I think I'll stick with Minnie," she said. "The vagaries of Indian nomenclature are dangerous shoals."

Quite a vocabulary. I liked the way she talked and felt a foolish grin on my face as I watched her. She said rahther for rather, cahn't for can't. "I'm keeping you from your work," she said, standing as if to leave, and I stood too, flustered. My staring had made her nervous.

"Not at all," I said. "Please. Sit down." I turned my chair around to face her, closed my log book and put my pen down. "There," I said. "It'll keep."

"Well, if you're sure," she said, settling back into the chair. She looked at her hands. "I must say this is fun. I hadn't expected to meet anyone so . . .." she looked shyly at me, "exotic."

My face got hot and I cleared my throat, glad my complexion didn't show blushes. "Well," I said heartily. "I hope your mother returns soon with good news of your father. It was kind of you to accompany her."

She looked at me strangely, as if I'd missed something, then shrugged slightly to dismiss it. "He's not really my father," she explained. "Oh, not that I don't hope he's all right. But my mother married him after my real father died. Come to that," she said, smiling, showing small, white teeth, "Anna's not my real mother, though she raised me since I was little. My mother died when I was born, so my father married her. Then he died and she married Colonel Sackett. It makes me an orphan, almost. Rather complicated, no?"

I smiled. *Rahther.* "It's not unusual," I told her. "My friend Henry Flagler, for instance." I tried to remember Flagler's genealogy. "He was a child of his father's third wife and grew up with half-brothers and -sisters from the other two, as well as a brother from his mother's first marriage. I think they all grew up calling each other cousin."

She smiled and cocked her head. "And you, Colonel Parker? Since we're getting so personal. How many parents have you had?"

"Just the two, oddly enough," I told her. "Both my parents died fairly recently, and they'd been married only to each other."

"Is that usual for Indians?" she asked, surprised. "I always assumed . . . um . . . ." She touched her lips with her fingers.

"What?" I asked. "That we were . . . indiscriminate in our affections?"

"Nicely put," she laughed. "But, being close to nature and all, I assumed Indians would be more like wild creatures." She smiled. "Free from the societal restraints that shackle the whites, let's say."

I laughed. " Free-lovers? Godwins and Shelleys, you mean?" She blushed and looked at her hands. "Not at all, Miss Sackett. We mate for life. Like Canada geese, African lions and some white people. We do have some slightly different traditions, though."

"Such as what?" She looked sideways up at me, slightly fearful, expecting what? An exegesis on the Indian wedding night?

I frowned, trying to explain. "For one thing, most of our marriages are arranged by our parents and elders."

"Oh, how terrible!" she said, hand to her chest. "But suppose two people are in love. Can't they just get married? Do they have to run away?"

I shook my head. "We don't really fall in love. Not the way you mean. I think love is an almost literary emotion. It has to be learned. Only the best-educated Indians have ever heard of it. Maybe they fall in love. But the rest don't."

"And how well-educated are you, Colonel Parker?" she asked, grinning.

I grinned right back at her. "Extremely, Miss Sackett," I told her. I was having more fun than I'd had in ages. We were straight-out flirting. The smell of canvas and leather in the tent began to feel musky.

She coughed and lowered her eyes. "So tell me more about Indian marriage customs."

"Well, for one thing," I told her, "we not only have six nations, we have clans within the nations. My father was a Turtle, for instance, and my mother a Wolf. That makes me a Wolf, along with my brother and sister, because the clan is inherited from the mother."

"How civilized," frowned Minnie, working it out. "It makes perfect sense, doesn't it? They're children of her body, so they should be children of her clan as well."

"There's more than that," I told her. "People can't marry within the clan, so the clans get dispersed among the six nations. And since we're forbidden to make war on anybody in our own clan, that makes war impossible."

"How clever!" She clapped her hands and held them to her breast, where I allowed my eyes to follow. The fabric strained prettily as she leaned forward to ask, "Is that your only 'impediment to marriage'?"

I cleared my throat, my loins stirring, and forced my eyes from her breast to her face. "That's the only formal prohibition," I said. "But there are customs as well. A young man usually marries an older woman, for instance. One who's been married before. So he's initiated by an, um . . . experienced partner." I crossed my legs and shifted in my chair.

She was fascinated, still leaning forward, hand to her chin. "And the woman," she asked. "How does she get her . . . experience?"

"The same way. A young woman marries an older man. One whose older wife has died. It's a continuing cycle. You marry an older partner, to gain experience, then you marry a younger one, to pass your knowledge on." I shrugged. "Almost scientific, you might say."

"Yes," she breathed, a little scandalized. "And so *calculating*. There seems little room for spontaneity."

"There's plenty of spontaneity in nature," I said grimly. "So much that Indians are threatened with extinction. We need rigid marriage customs to keep the tribe alive."

"I see." She swallowed, her hand flat against her chest. "But still. I can't imagine submitting myself so coldly. Being pawed over by some randy old Indian . . . ." She shook her head and shuddered, then folded her arms across her bosom and looked up at me. "And you, Colonel Parker," she said, her smile returning. "Which wife are you on at present? The old one or the young one?"

"Neither," I said. "I've never been married. When it was time for me to marry the old one, I was too busy making a living. Now, I suppose, I'm ready for the young one and waiting for the right one to come along." I gave her the least lascivious smile I could manage. "And you, Miss Sackett?" I asked.

"Me what?" she asked, still smiling.

"How is that you are still *Miss* Sackett?" I said gallantly. "Are you coy or choosy?"

She laughed uncertainly. "Whatever could you mean, Colonel?"

Was I not being clear? Was I speaking Seneca? "You're not married," I said straight out. "Why not?"

She blinked those blue eyes a couple of times and her mouth trembled as if to laugh. "Good heavens!" she said. "How old do you think I am, Colonel Parker?"

"I don't know." I waved my hand impatiently. "Twenty-one? Twenty-three? I can't tell white women's ages."

She tightened her lips and shook her head, trying to look serious, but her eyes were dancing. "I've only just turned fifteen," she said with a straight face, and as I shot out of my chair she burst into a shower of giggles. "Oh dear," she said, trying to hide her laugh behind her hand. "I am sorry, Colonel. You were being so gallant, condescending to flirt with me. I thought you knew. I had no idea I looked so . . ." she laughed some more. "So mature." Matoor, she said.

I sat down, picked up my pen, tossed it on the desk, and folded my arms across my chest. I had been discussing the sex life of the American Indian with a fifteen-year-old. "Kind of you to accompany your mother," I'd said. No wonder she'd eyed me strangely. She could either accompany her mother or stay with her nanny, I suppose.

Little Miss Sackett, whose curves I could now see as baby-fat, was as delighted and flattered as could be. Attempting to console me, she came over and put her hand on my shoulder. I could feel her warmth and smell her milky sweat. I looked up at her fifteen-year-old bosom, which still trembled with stifled laughter, and it was in that position, her hand on my shoulder and my randy old Indian eyes on her still unravished tits, that her mother and Reverend William Welsh found us when they came through the tent flap.

They both looked horror-struck, and we scurried apart. But it wasn't us that caused the mother's horror. "He's dead, Minnie," she said, and her daughter cried out, flew to her mother and put her arms around her.

Reverend Welsh, on the other hand, made directly for me, his face like the wrath of God. Before he could speak, however, other officers came in with condolences and consolations, fatherly pats on the women's shoulders and murmurs of concern. With a backward I'll-deal-with-you-later look, Reverend Welsh remembered his pastoral duties and joined the grieving women.

I was crowded to the rear again and didn't even say good-bye to Minnie Sackett as she and her mother made their slow way down the hill, their arms around each other's waist, Reverend Welsh urging them on protectively with many a backward glance at me.

Fifteen years old! I'd been romancing her like a Regency buck. She was more a playmate for Fred Grant than for me, and at the bottom of the hill it was indeed Fred, now fourteen and a strapping, uniformed youth, who offered Minnie his handkerchief and his arm, escorted her slowly down to the wharf, where she boarded a boat and, I figured, sailed out of my life forever.

I let the tent flap drop and returned to my work, unable to concentrate. That night, for the first time in a long time, I made my way to the sutler's compound downriver, drank too much whiskey, and, as if to remind myself of the difference between a woman and a child, availed myself of one of the "hookers" who kept shop there and who did more to immortalize their eponymous general's name than any of his military exploits. My favorite was a high-yellow, high-breasted gal with a gap in her front teeth, and after I rolled off and lay panting, spent but unsatisfied, my head on her breast, she stroked my hair and murmured, "My, my, Chief. You sure was busy. Bet it wasn't me you was thinkin' about," and she was right, damn her eyes.

Chapter XIII

IS THERE ANYONE
I CAN SURRENDER TO?

Virginia 1865

As 1864 GREW INTO 1865, THE WAR BECAME PERMANENT and so did our encampment on the James, transforming the sleepy ferry-landing into the world's largest seaport. The tent city became a real city, as log houses grew up to shelter us for the winter, the smoke from their chimneys making the place a vast Plymouth Colony in the snow. Even the local war, the closest trenches ten miles away, was remote, consisting largely of extending our line to the left, Lee extending his to meet it, then extending it farther, stretching him thin as taffy so the breakthrough, when it finally came, would cause us the least possible loss. But with Lincoln mindful of the November elections, and Grant mindful of the "Butcher Grant" handle he'd won, neither wanted a breakthrough just yet, reluctant to add to the casualties until sure that one push would end it. So, since it couldn't end, the war continued.

Grant winked in and out of camp like a comet. With rivers and railroads utterly at his disposal, he could pop up anyplace. A commander who didn't move fast enough might wake one morning to see the commanding general, cigar at the boil, stumping chin-first from the landing toward his tent. "That's Grant," men said. "I hate to see that old cuss. When he's around there's sure to be a fight." In September the little whirlwind hopped a dispatch boat, steamed down the James and up the Potomac, past Washington without even waving at the War Department, threaded through rivers and streams into upper Virginia, and yanked Sheridan's chain. By week's end, Sheridan attacked Winchester, and Grant was back at City Point, having even taken time to stop off to rent Julia a house in New Jersey and see the children off to school.

"I told Sheridan to whip him," he told us around the fire.

"I'm sure," said Babcock, stickler for protocol, "that you put it more correctly than that, General."

"No," said Grant. "I told him to whip him."

On November 16, Sherman burned Atlanta, cut the telegraph, and marched off the map into Georgia. For a month there was silence. "He's gone like a mole," Lincoln told Sherman's brother the senator. "I know the hole he went in at, but I can't tell you the hole he'll come out of." While we scanned anxious eyes south, as if willing to see the columns of smoke Sherman was raising, Grant looked west, where General George Thomas had turned from the Rock of Chickamauga into the Hard Place of Nashville, refusing to move out and attack Hood until he had more troops, the weather was right, the horses were fed, the ice was melted, the moon was fair, the entrails read positive . . . . Grant near tore his beard out and burned up the telegraph line screaming at Thomas to move, and finally moved himself. He packed a bag, shipped out, got to Washington on November 30 and was on his way to Nashville by river and rail when Thomas, perhaps hearing his footfall, attacked at Franklin and annihilated Hood's army. In December, Sherman surfaced at Savannah, offered the city to Lincoln as a Christmas gift, and the only strength the Confederacy had left was sitting in front of us at Richmond.

Come spring, the cast was in place for the last-act curtain to rise, and perhaps needing an audience, Grant wired Lincoln on March 20, "Can you not visit City Point for a day or two? I would like very much to see you and I think the rest would do you good." Lincoln, tickled, steamed on down. This time he brought the whole White House entourage, including young Tad and Mrs. Lincoln, and it was more like a fancy-dress ball than the just-us-boys days of last summer. But Lincoln was in good spirits and seemed happy to be back at the headquarters mess. Asked about his journey, he said, "The captain vacated his bunk and gave it to me, and since he's about a foot shorter than me I spent a pretty cramped night. When I told him the bed was a mite short, he gave it the weight of a state order. Had his carpenter spend the day making the bed wider and longer.

Next day he asked me how I'd slept, and I told him fine, except that I seemed to have shrunk about a foot all round." Lincoln slapped his knee. "Captain stared at me a good half minute before he got that."

Wednesday March 29, Grant started his final whirlwind. Sheridan moved west past our entrenchments to lure Lee out in the open. We dismantled our headquarters, leaving only Joe Bowers behind, and moved west, shadowing Sheridan. It was almost like leaving home. We had gone into camp there last June, sweated through the summer, built cabins in the fall, shivered through the winter. All of us had accumulated books, papers, pets. Last June Lincoln had been touched to see a new litter of kittens at headquarters. Now they were full-size commissary cats, two of them pregnant. General Rufus Ingalls, Grant's old friend from West Point and Mexico, now Quartermaster General, had acquired a spotted puppy in the fall. "Are you intending to take that dog to Richmond, General?" Grant had asked him. "Oh, sure," Ingalls replied. "They say it's a long-lived breed." The pup was now a dog and still hadn't seen Richmond.

Lincoln walked us to the train, about five minutes away, and it was like a father bidding us farewell, a tall drake ushering his brood. He shook all our hands and had a personal word for each of us. To me he said, "Perhaps now we can do something for your people," a nice enough thought from a man so preoccupied. Then we all got on board, lifted our hats, and Lincoln lifted his and waved it until we were around the bend and out of sight.

When we got seated there was a moment of silence. We'd all got so used to City Point, that there was some apprehension about the unknown territory ahead. Grant lit a cigar, blew smoke, and sat back. "You know," he said, "everyone who comes down here, civilians, politicians, soldiers, all of them ask me what my plans are. The only one who's never asked is right back there." He crooked his thumb over his shoulder. "President Lincoln."

The railroad, built since last June, took us south from the James, then curled west, skirting the Petersburg fortifications that had held us in stalemate so long. We could see men servicing cannons and hauling trench materials off to our right, then the fortifications disappeared and we chugged across the roads that radiated south, until we reached the end of the line and of our entrenchments, ten miles southwest of Petersburg and twenty miles from City Point. Somewhere in front of us, Sheridan was toiling west, probing for Lee's right flank. We detrained, mounted our horses, rode some ways down the Vaughan Road until we saw the advance guard and pulled off into a cornfield, where we pitched our tents by a narrow stream. The commissary had a fine dinner spread out, and we all turned in early for what might be the last good sleep for many days.

Toward midnight I was awakened by a crash and a pattering on the tent like gravel. I rolled over, squinted my eyes open, and saw Rawlins silhouetted at the flap, staring out. Lightning flashes illuminated not only him, but heavy raindrops spattering at his feet. "Hell and damnation!" fumed Rawlins. "Of all the hell-cursed luck! We've got the bastards by the balls, and now heaven rains piss! God damn, damn, damn, damn, damn them!" And to the homey hum of Black John's curses, I rolled over and fell asleep again.

I was up at dawn for a soggy breakfast and a soggy view of swamps for miles around. What last night had been cornfields were now shimmering sloughs. The stream by which we camped had got swallowed in the general inundation. Wagons sank to their axles, and teamsters lashed at balky mules, but the mules could find no purchase and got mired themselves. As I stood at my tent flap, grimacing at sour, cold coffee, I watched a mule absently paw the ground only to have it liquefy under him and swallow him to his belly, where he floundered till ropes rescued him. Rawlins was in Grant's tent, dour and downcast, urging the general to return to City Point and wait for better weather.

"At least call Sheridan back," Rawlins insisted. "We can't supply him in all this."

Grant raised his eyebrows and handed Rawlins a note, which I read over Rawlins's shoulder. "I feel now like ending the matter," he had written to Sheridan at the height of last night's rain. "I do not want you to cut loose." Rawlins and I both looked at Grant, saw the glint in his eyes and realized talking him out of it was like trying to talk an avalanche back up a mountain.

Couriers splashed into camp all day with reports of bogged-down units. Our greatest fear was for Sheridan, out beyond the flank with the cavalry. Any hope of supplying him by wagon or reinforcing him with infantry was washed out. By mid-afternoon, even Grant seemed to toy with calling him back. All of us began to yearn for the dry beds and solid walls of our camp along the James. We stood on planks around the fire, bemoaning this and that, when who comes riding up out of the gloom but Sheridan. Swimming up was more like it, for the road was now so awash that his horse sank to its knees with every step and looked more swamp walrus than steed. At first, in fact, we thought it was Rienzi, the famous black of "Sheridan's Ride" last summer, but when he got closer it proved to be a high-stepping Kentucky white, stained pitch-black from mud. In Sheridan himself undampened fury burned.

"You look like chickens on a roost!" he chortled, as we shifted from foot to foot on our planks near the fire. Stamping about and growling, he heard our gloomy prophecies. When Rawlins started detailing the difficulties of supplying him, Sheridan cut him short with a wave of his glove.

"I'll have Custer's division corduroy every road from here to Dinwiddie to get supplies out to us," he said. "Get me some infantry and I'll destroy Lee's right."

Impressed, we sent him in to talk to Grant, and he came out of the tent even more determined. He vaulted onto his horse, looked down at our bedraggled little group, and told us, "I tell you, I'm ready to strike out tomorrow and go to smashing things." We roused ourselves to a hearty and sniffling cheer as he wheeled his horse in the mud and plunged westward.

Saturday, April Fool's Day, was the first dry day since we left City Point. At 11 AM word came that infantry had reached Sheridan, and we strained our ears for the sounds of battle. Noon passed, no firing. Shadows lengthened, no news. Around four o'clock guns roared in the west and continued for several hours, but we could make no sense of them. Couriers we sent out for reports vanished like Noah's doves. Finally, at nightfall, a rider skidded into camp screaming of a great victory at Five Forks. Pickett's division was annihilated, and so elated was the courier that he actually grabbed Grant and pounded him on the back before he remembered who he was talking to. General Pickett, told by Lee to "hold Five Forks at all hazard," had instead gone off to a shad bake and was two miles away with his hands full of fish when Sheridan overran his lines. Poor old gold-ringleted, George Pickett enters the Civil War the eponym of his doomed charge at Gettysburg, loses his first division there, and survives to fight again only to exit aghast, white napkin under his chin, picking shad bones from his teeth while his last division streams past him in tatters at Five Forks.

That night Grant handed me papers for dispatch, ordering "an immediate assault all along the lines." At first light, 4:30 AM Sunday, artillery roared, every gun on the line, the sky winking light and dark for an hour like an aurora borealis. Then came an abrupt silence followed by the susurrus of musketry and the tramp of many feet, the whole Union army advancing for the first time since Cold Harbor, assaulting every inch of the lines that had resisted us for almost a year. Anxious hours passed, then reports started coming in. Wright had broken through. Parke had broken through. Ord had broken through. Humphrey had broken through. Lee was cut in half. Sheridan was coming from the left, rolling up the line as he went. The firing reached a climax, then abruptly ceased, and that was that.

Monday morning rose bright and sunny for our ride into Petersburg. It was curious to enter an actual town after a full year in the field. I expected devastation, ruined buildings, smoking hulks of warehouses. But this wasn't Vicksburg. The war had raged outside the city. Inside all was intact, though a thin film of dust ghosted things. Dogs barked. People who hadn't fled with the army stayed indoors, and though a few children played in the yards, their mothers called them to the door and held them to their skirts, staring wide-eyed and resentful as we passed. Forsythia and honeysuckle and lilacs bloomed. Negroes stared and started following us, first in ones and twos, then in a whole procession, bringing up the rear as I imagined them doing with Sherman's army in Georgia. We dismounted at a house on Market Street and Rawlins knocked on the door and asked permission to sit on the porch.

"Make yourself at home," said the old man, opening the outer door. "My name's Wallace. You're welcome to come inside if you like."

"Papa!" said a younger man behind him. "You're not going to let that man in here, are you?"

The old man grinned. "Well, son," he said. "I reckon a man with 50,000 troops can go wherever he likes."

Grant, hearing the colloquy, spoke diplomatically. "I'm smoking," he told the men. "I'll stay out here."

"Well that's fine," said the older Mr. Wallace, and, buttoning his undershirt and pulling up his suspenders, he came out to join us. A crowd gathered in the yard, most of them black, most of them staring as we stared back. I was leaning on the porch railing smoking a cigar, when a little Negro boy ran up to me, touched my boot, and ran back to his

companions, exhibiting his hand, like he had counted coup. I suppose he
didn't know what I was, somewhere between black and white. I smiled
and waved and they sucked their fingers and waved shyly back.

A group of horsemen turned the corner and came up the street,
and they proved to be President Lincoln, with Admiral Porter and the
president's two sons, Robert, who had graduated from Harvard and been
with the army since winter, and Tad, twelve years old tomorrow. Lincoln
dismounted, leaned over to open the gate, and eased through the silent
crowd to the porch steps, where Grant rose to greet him. Lincoln took
Grant's hand and held it for a long time, nodding, grinning, and staring
the general in the eyes.

"Do you know, General," said Lincoln. "I have had the sneaking idea
for some days that you intended something like this."

"Am I as transparent as that?" asked Grant.

"No, no," said Lincoln. He clapped Grant on the shoulder, selected
a peeling rocking chair, and sat down in it, stretching his long legs out. "I
thought you might wait for Sherman to come up and get in at the kill."

Grant shook his head, looking down at the seated president. "It would
have been fine symmetry, but no. Sherman and I agreed long ago that the
eastern army must win in the east." Something touched my sleeve and I
looked down to see that Tad had joined me leaning back against the rail,
imitating my posture, elbows hiked high up to hook the rail behind him. I
grinned and tousled his hair.

Lincoln was shaking his head. "Sounds like something I should have
thought of. Political matters, you know. But no. I didn't care how it got
finished. I just wanted it finished."

The general and the president sat and talked, and soon Tad grew
restless and turned around to look at the growing crowd on the lawn.

"Hey, Yank," one of the colored boys got up courage to say to him.

"Hey yourself," said Tad. It was the same boy who had run up and
touched my boot.

"That Mister Linkum?" the boy asked.

Tad nodded. "He's my father."

"Whoa!" The colored boy drew back and put his hand to his mouth.

The younger Mr. Wallace, deciding hospitality was the better part of
valor, appeared at the door with a plate of sandwiches, and Tad dashed
up and back in a flash, with one in each hand. As he sat on the porch

munching, looking out at the crowd, the colored boy again approached, almost hypnotized, chewing his fingers. Tad saw him, looked at the sandwich in his hand and offered it between the balusters. The colored boy wiped his hands on his pants, chewed his lip, finally reached out and grabbed it, jumping back as if Tad would bite him. He and Tad chewed in unison, eying each other.

Rawlins checked his watch, cleared his throat and shuffled his feet. Grant got the message and stood up. "I'd hoped to have Richmond for you today, Mr. President," he said. "Maybe that was too much to hope for."

The president stood up. "Well, since I have no place else to go for the moment, I reckon I'll stay here a spell," he said, and we all nodded and bowed and scraped our way down the path to our horses. It was always hard to know with how much ceremony or informality to treat the president, and most of us over- or underdid it. Only Grant got it right.

We rode west, following the Southside Railroad, where a rider overtook us and handed Grant a message. He read it, took off his hat, looked at the sky, and wiped his brow. "Richmond has fallen," he told us. We whooped and cavorted our horses dutifully about the road, but there was more relief than triumph.

"Parker," Grant told me. "You won't get lost. Take an escort, go back and find the president, and give him the news. You'll find us at Sutherland Station." He pointed vaguely down the road. I took two orderlies back to town, where, luckily, Lincoln was still on the porch, enjoying a quiet chat with old Mr. Wallace while both men's sons looked on. I dismounted and climbed the steps, passing Tad on my way, who was sitting there chatting easily with a group of Negro boys.

"Colonel Parker," said Lincoln. "You're lucky to find me still here. Mr. Wallace turns out to be an old Whig like myself, and we've been politicking. Seems I've got at least one constituent down here."

Old Wallace cackled.

"I wish I could offer more sandwiches," Lincoln continued, showing me the empty tray. "I'm afraid Tad gave them away."

"Mr. President," I said, saluting and unable to offer any banter in response. "General Grant's compliments, and Richmond fell this morning."

Lincoln brought his fist down on his knee. "Well, that about makes today perfect, doesn't it? Admiral Porter," he said, raising his eyes to his escort. "Care to accompany me to Richmond?"

"I'm not sure that's wise, sir." Porter stepped forward. "Maybe wait until it's secure."

"Nonsense," said Lincoln. "I'm going, and you're welcome to come along if you wish. How 'bout you, Mr. Wallace?"

Old Wallace threw his head back and cackled again, the president's captive. "Oh, I don't think so, sir. My neighbors'd probably burn my house while I was away!" He cackled some more.

"You, Colonel Parker?" the president asked me with a wink. "Got plans?"

"I'm sure General Grant has plans, sir," I told him. "In fact, I'd better go see if I can find him again."

"Yes," said the president, standing to leave. "You do that. Give him my heartiest thanks and good wishes."

He reached out his hand, and I shook it and went down the steps, past Tad and the colored boys, and out to my horse. As I rode away Lincoln was at the bottom of the steps, shaking hands with Negroes as they came timidly up to him. I wasn't around for the president's venture into Richmond on the morrow, where, escorted by a dozen of Porter's nervous marines, he was set upon by Negroes throwing themselves at his feet and kissing his boots, while the white citizenry hung silent and sullen from windows and trees and lampposts to get a look at him. He sat at Jefferson Davis's desk, toured the Capitol and Libbey Prison, and departed with the advice to the occupying troops to "Let 'em up easy. If I were in your place I'd let 'em up easy."

My escort and I picked our way west through the wreckage of two armies to catch Grant. The next days we toiled west along the railroad line from Petersburg, and Lee followed the southwest line from Richmond, somewhere over to our right, aiming for North Carolina. The lines crossed at Burkeville, and we raced him for that junction, where Jefferson Davis and the Confederate cabinet had passed through on Monday and Lee had rations waiting. Sheridan was also out there to the right, probing for Lee, and so was Meade with three divisions of infantry. Reports from the two generals were in continual conflict.

On Wednesday night Grant was as restless as I've ever seen him, stumping around the campfire, slamming his fist into his palm, smoking a storm, and muttering.

"Halt!" came a sudden bark in the darkness, and we heard the jingle of harness and the slap of hands on weapons. "Who goes there?"

"Message from General Sheridan!" came the reply, and Grant's head whipped round. He motioned me to see what was up.

By the perimeter, at the edge of the woods, the guards were holding a sweating horse by the bridle and poking their muskets in the face of its rider, who wore a tunic of Confederate gray. "Hands up, Johnny," said a guard. "Dismount easy."

The rider dropped his reins, put his hands in the air, slung a leg over the pommel, and slipped to the ground light as an acrobat.

"Hello, Campbell," I said, recognizing one of Sheridan's scouts.

"Parker! Thank God!" said Campbell. As he lowered his hands and reached for mine, a musket nudged his side.

"It's all right," I told the sentries. "He's ours." They eased back, muskets ready.

Campbell fingered his tunic as I led him up to Grant. "It was an even chance what to wear. There was more of them out there than there was us."

"You came cross-country?" I asked him.

"Direct from Sheridan," he said. "Left him not two hours ago."

Grant had his hands behind his back and his chin out. "Well?" he asked Campbell.

Campbell looked around at us and worked his jaw.

"Spit it out, man!" sputtered Rawlins. Campbell's eyes crinkled as a chewed-up cylinder of tin-foil emerged between his front teeth. He looked at Rawlins, spat it into his hand, unrolled it carefully, and handed a crumpled piece of flimsy to Grant.

"Lucky you didn't swallow it," I growled. "We'd have had to gut you for it."

Grant cleared his throat. "Sheridan has Lee trapped," he said. He looked in Campbell's face. "Can you lead me to him?"

Campbell nodded vigorously, and Grant turned on his heel and went into his tent. I read the message over Rawlins's shoulder. "I wish you were here yourself," it said. "I feel confident of capturing the Army of Northern Virginia if we exert ourselves. I see no escape for Lee."

Grant emerged from his tent buckling on a sidearm. "Lead me to him." he told Campbell. "The rest of you can come along."

"The rest of us" consisted of me, Rawlins, Babcock, and one or two others, and we looked at each other in wild surmise as Grant ordered his horse brought up.

"You can't do it," protested Rawlins. "We don't know the road. The enemy's all over the place."

Grant thrust his chin at Sheridan's scout. "He knows the way. Don't you, Campbell?"

Campbell shuffled his feet. "More or less . . ." he said, and Grant cut him off.

"There. You see?" he said. "Mount up."

"But, General," said Rawlins, going so far as to lay his hand on Grant's sleeve. "There's no order out there. You could be shot by anybody. Your own troops. At least wait till morning."

Grant shook his head, and he and Rawlins spent some time in a standoff. Babcock, seeing how the wind was blowing, ordered our own horses saddled and even rounded up a cavalry escort, a dozen bewildered riders whom he herded into the headquarters clearing.

"There, you see, John?" said Grant as the cavalry arrived. "An escort. There's nothing to fear. Parker's got a good sense of direction."

Some escort, I thought as I swung aboard my horse. Even traveling in broad daylight, a commanding general had to have several men along who knew the way, in case one of them got lost or shot. We had only one, and he, presumably, had ridden to us through byways and detours he had no certainty of finding again, and which may now be in enemy hands. As for my vaunted sense of direction, I could ride straight and I could find north, but whether Sheridan was either straight ahead or due north was anybody's guess. At least, I supposed, if we started riding in a circle, I could stop us.

We plunged into the night and the woods and the brambles, Campbell out front, me behind him, Rawlins and Porter on either side of Grant, Babcock behind. The cavalry distributed itself around us, keeping Grant in the center of a diamond, putting as many bodies between him and danger as they could. It was mostly open country, so we could ride bunched up that way, and bright moonlight illuminated the path. Illuminated us as well, for anybody who was looking. But with fields to our right and woods to our left we were screened and in shadow. After about an hour of riding due north Campbell called a halt.

"What?" I asked, catching up to him.

He pointed at some fenceposts. "There were rails on that fence when I came through. Cavalry's been here since."

"Not ours," I said.

He nodded and eased us into the woods that edged the field, where we had to string out single file for several miles, leaving the whole line vulnerable. When we could ride side by side again, Rawlins rode up beside me.

"You're sure of this man, Parker?" His voice was hard and his black eyes flashed.

"I'd stake my life on him," I said.

"That's exactly what you're doing," he said, and eased forward to ride with the scout. A little later, we saw campfires across the field.

"Lee," whispered the scout, and the single word made us rein in and look with awe, as if by straining our eyes we could actually see the southern host crouched in front of us. Lee's army was out of its entrenchments for the first time in a year, on the move and vulnerable, campfires winking for perhaps the last time in its long, stubborn life.

"Move along there," growled Grant, and we chucked our horses again. Presently we saw more campfires up ahead, which Campbell seemed sure were our own.

"Ride behind me," Rawlins ordered the scout. It was senseless to risk his Confederate disguise with more nervous pickets. Rawlins looked back to assure that Grant was buried deep within his escort and waved us forward.

"Halt! Who's there!" came a cry.

We halted and put our hands in view. "My name is General Rawlins," said Rawlins loud and clear. "From the commanding general's staff." He was careful not to say "Grant," lest we'd blundered into southern lines. "Come out and let me see you."

Seven nervous young soldiers with muskets ready moved across our path. I sat back in my saddle as I saw they were dressed in blue, but there were still some shaky moments to get through. We knew who they were, all right, but would they believe we were who we said we were? "Get down!" said a voice. "Keep your hands where I can see 'em."

Rawlins dismounted, as did Campbell and I, and approached the guard corporal. "Who's he?" said the corporal, pointing at Campbell and his gray tunic. "Prisoner?"

"One of General Sheridan's scouts," explained Rawlins. "He's . . ."

"You saw me pass earlier," said Campbell.

"Oh, yeah," said the corporal, squinting at him, his rifle still up. "Who's that behind you? Don't try nothin'. I've sent for reinforcements."

"We're escorting General Grant to General Sheridan," said Rawlins, as importantly as he could.

"The hell," said the corporal, his jaw working for a minute. "Let me see him."

Rawlins allowed himself a smile. "You'd recognize him?"

The corporal, still chewing, slowly shook his head. It occurred to me that very few men in the army, very few people in the country, would recognize General Grant in broad daylight, let alone in a dark field at night. They'd recognize Lee, all right. They'd recognize Sheridan, with his Mongol face. They'd recognize Sherman, with his craggy jaw and blazing blue eyes. But Grant? Even people who'd met him two or three times had trouble picking him out.

We soon found ourselves seated at a campfire with a delighted Phil Sheridan, who couldn't sit still but kept leaping up and smashing his fist into his palm, staring close at Grant's face to make sure he was real. Thirty-two years old, Philip Sheridan had a bullet head and slashing eyebrows. He was what Lincoln called "one of those long-armed fellows with short legs that can scratch his shins without having to stoop over."

"You said you wished I was here, General," said Grant. "Here I am. Any other wishes?"

"I wish," said Sheridan, "that it was daylight right now. We'd have Lee's whole army like *that!*" He shook his fist in Grant's face.

"Daylight will come soon enough," said Grant, sounding weary. "We'll grab him then."

For once, Grant was slow and wrong. Daylight came, but not soon enough, and when Sheridan grabbed for Lee all he got was air. Advancing skirmishers found Lee's rifle pits empty, dummy rifles and cannons propped up in them. His camps were abandoned, nobody left but some wounded. Riders from the north reported Lee's whole column on the march around Sheridan's left, where nobody had figured him to go. The fox had stolen another march, this time on Sheridan. It was as if Lee, finding another hot general opposing him, had to show even this most quicksilver of Union foes that there was still a general faster off the marks.

Lee might as well have skipped it and saved a few thousand lives, for the upshot of his nighttime escape was to make Sheridan very, very angry. He stormed around the breakfast fire kicking coals, harrying cooks and orderlies, damning the sluggish Army of the Potomac through the circles of hell, and generally "expressing his extreme vehemence on the subject matter." Then he got his cavalry into the saddle, his infantry onto the road, ordered the wagons and caissons to catch up as best they could, and set out to catch Lee, make him stand and fight, and write the day into the calendar as the "Black Thursday of the Confederacy."

The Battle of Sayler's Creek, for that was where Sheridan grabbed Lee's collar and almost unhorsed him, was three battles in one, as units of Sheridan's army caught pieces of Lee's column and fought them where they stood. Sheridan was all over the field on his huge black horse Rienzi. With him rode only one orderly with a battle flag, and nobody knew where the bullet-headed little pug would pop up next, waving his hat, windmilling his arms to sweep the blue wave forward, his face black and eyes flashing, shouting "Smash 'em up, boys, smash 'em up! I'll show you the way!" By the time they finished the battle every man was convinced that Sheridan had been beside him the whole time. A soldier actually beside him got shot right through the throat, his blood spurting all over the general. "I'm gone!" cried the man, falling. "Nonsense," Sheridan told him. "You're barely scratched. Pick up your rifle." And damned if the man didn't blink at Sheridan, pick up his rifle, and advance ten yards before falling dead.

Even though he'd destroyed a third of Lee's army, Sheridan was still not satisfied. "We can't hold onto him all at once," he said of Lee, who even in defeat had slipped off west again. "He's turned from a big fish into many little fish."

That night we waited on the porch of a brick hotel in the little town of Farmville while the wrecked bridge was rebuilt. When the bridge was ready, there came the tramp of marching feet, as the head of Wright's 6th Corps came through town on its way down to the river. Seeing Grant, they raised a cheer and hullabaloo, struck up their bands, and marched with quickened feet and burning torches. It seemed to take forever for the army to pass, and Grant squinted intently, almost as if counting them, surprised at how many there were. As the bands and tramping feet faded up the road and a film of dust settled on the little town, as dogs came out and started to bark and smoke rose from chimneys, Grant said, "Hm!" He stared at me.

"I have a good mind to ask Lee to surrender," he said, as if surprised by the idea. He stumped into the hotel with me behind him and there, at a table in the lobby, sketched out a note, which I copied for dispatch:

> General Lee: The result of the last week must convince you of the hopelessness of further resistance on the part of the Army of Northern Virginia in this struggle. I feel that it is so, and regard it as my duty to shift from myself the responsibility of any further effusion of blood, by asking of you the surrender of that portion of the C.S. Army known as the Army of Northern Virginia.

Seth Williams, a staff member who had been Lee's adjutant at West Point, volunteered to get the message through the lines, and we all retired for the night in beds Lee's staff had used the night before. At daybreak Williams returned with an equivocal answer from Lee. "Though not entertaining the opinion you express of the hopelessness of further resistance on the part of the Army," Lee nonetheless requested "the terms you will offer on condition of its surrender."

Rawlins, the lawyer, frowned as he studied the paper. "It's not responsive," he concluded. "He's playing for time. He's in no position to ask for terms."

"Nonetheless," said Grant, "he's talking to me. That's more than I thought he'd do."

"And what of Unconditional Surrender Grant?" parried Rawlins.

Grant looked at his subordinate with tired, kindly eyes. "Times change, John. There's no harm in spelling it out for him." He grabbed pencil and paper and wrote a response, which I transcribed and handed to Seth Williams for a second venture through the lines.

> There is but one condition I would insist upon – namely, that the men and officers surrendered shall be disqualified for taking up arms against the Government of the United States until properly exchanged.

After Williams left we all went out to the porch and found a Confederate officer leaning against a column and squinting up at the front of the hotel. "Excuse me, gentlemen," he said, coming to vague attention. "Is there anyone here I can surrender to?"

We looked at each other, and Grant stepped forward. "I'm General Grant," he said.

The officer blew out a breath and smiled. "Well, I guess you'll do, won't you?" he said. "My names Nokes, General. I'm proprietor of this hotel. Was, at any rate. Haven't seen it in three years. But we seemed to be coming in this direction, so I figured I'd just fall out and come home. Are there, um, formalities?"

Grant examined the man's stripes. "Where's your regiment, Colonel?" he asked.

Nokes gave a dry laugh. "That's just it. My regiment's all from around these parts. When I woke up this morning they'd all gone home. Fact is, I'm my regiment, General, and I hereby surrender it."

Grant reached out and touched the man's shoulder. "Just hang up that uniform, Colonel. That's all. You won't need it any more." And with a friendly pat, he directed Mr. Nokes through his own front door. "If Lee's army's come down to one-man regiments," he remarked to us, "we should have no trouble today."

We set out across the Appomattox from Farmville on a strangely peaceful Saturday, the sun shining brightly and most guns silent, so we heard birds for the first time all week. Every hour we expected a reply from General Lee. But the morning passed and then noon, and by midafternoon Lee's silence combined with the wreckage of his army to make us silent and morose. The thought of yet another fight against a foe so shredded depressed us. Could Lee mean for us to slaughter them all rather than surrender?

By evening Grant had fallen silent. He kept raising his hand to squeeze his forehead and pinch his eyes and at nightfall told Rawlins he had a splitting headache and could ride no further. We halted at a farmhouse with room enough for both Grant's and Meade's staffs in the rooms, on the porch, and in several outbuildings. I slept on the floor on a folded-up oriental carpet of surprising quality, and I remember little of the other furnishings except for a piano in the parlor, which Meade's crowd insisted on pounding well into the night. Nobody had the heart to quell their high spirits, and it was hell on the little tone-deaf man upstairs, his head in his hands, assailed not only by a shrieking migraine but by a cacophony he couldn't decipher.

Toward midnight, Rawlins nudged me awake and beckoned me upstairs. The piano was still tinkling, but the mood had turned sentimental, and it was to "Lorena" that we mounted the broad staircase. A family painting with the name "Clifton" under it hung over a washstand in the hallway. Rawlins knocked softly at a door, and Grant grunted, "Come in."

So pitiful a sight I never saw. The commanding general of all the armies was sitting in a chair, barefoot, his pantlegs rolled up over his skinny shanks, his feet in a basin of mustard-water. His shirt was open, showing his bony chest. His head was thrown back and to his forehead he held a brown rag, so reeking of mustard we might have been in a *wursthaus*. As we entered, Grant lolled his head toward us, his mouth open and his eyes red.

"How's the headache, General?" asked Rawlins quietly.

Grant closed his eyes. "What do you want?" he asked faintly.

"There's a message from Sheridan," said Rawlins.

"Not from Lee?" It was almost a whimper.

"No sir," said Rawlins. "But there will be soon, I'm sure. It's just had trouble finding us."

"What from Sheridan?" groaned Grant.

As Rawlins reported, Grant eased his feet from the basin, rose unsteadily from the chair, and, holding the cloth to his forehead, staggered across the room, leaving sad footprints on the floorboards, and flopped on a couch, breathing heavily. Sheridan, with Custer in the lead, had reached Appomattox Station, captured Lee's ration train, corralled a dozen cannon in a nighttime fight, and was dug in across the Lynchburg road.

"He's got there, General," said Rawlins, fighting to keep his voice low. "He's in front of Lee."

"With cavalry only," said Grant quietly. He lowered the mustard-rag and let it dangle from his hand.

Rawlins squatted down next to him, his boots creaking. "Infantry will be there soon enough. He's trapped."

There was a knock on the door, and Rawlins nodded me to open it. It was, at long last, Seth Williams, mud-spattered and breathless. "From Lee," he said. The piano downstairs stopped. But Lee's message was hedged, not nearly the surrender Grant wanted. We spent some time discussing it, Rawlins insisting on clarification, Grant inclined to meet Lee no matter what, promising "If once I get Lee face to face, I won't let him go till he surrenders." Finally, worn out, Grant held his pleading hand up, and Rawlins subsided. "Parker," said Grant to me. "I won't need you. I won't write anything tonight. Let's get some sleep. We'll discuss it further in the morning."

I was up early, but Grant was up earlier, his head bursting, walking up and down in the yard with his mustard-rag around his head and shoulders like a prayer-shawl. We forced some breakfast down him, which made him feel a little better. "Well," he growled. "Let's try once more to get it right." He sent another message out to Lee, then, just as I had put my feet up on the porch rail to await a reply, the door banged open and Grant came out pulling on his gloves.

"What's up?" I said to Rawlins, right behind him.

"Change of base," said Rawlins. "Don't ask me where."

I scrambled to my feet and followed them down the steps and into the saddle, Grant as pale and red-eyed as death. We rode west from the Clifton farm, Grant wincing with pain every step, toward the sound of distant guns that began to shiver the morning calm.

"Explain," I told Rawlins. "How's anybody going to find us?"

Rawlins shrugged. "Magic, I suppose. You know him. He wants to be unencumbered." And very calmly, leaving scant word, we rode off the map and into the trackless limbo between the two armies.

I saw dimly then, but didn't grasp fully until we were in the McLean house how unerring Grant's instinct was in riding out alone that morning. He did things solo. He didn't want Lee to find him till he was ready, and he wanted the minimum people around him: Rawlins, me, Babcock, a few others, a small cavalry escort, the same crowd that had ridden to find Sheridan a few nights ago. We hadn't changed our clothes since, and Grant wanted to shed other baggage as well. If Lee's last message that morning had reached him in the midst of the Army of the Potomac, there would have been another staff to consult, protocol to deal with, officers diving into their tents for swords and braids and fresh collars. On the open road Grant had nobody to consult but himself. He could meet Lee as he chose.

With only the sound of the guns as a guide, we rode overland through fields and farms and woodlands, the river on our left, the guns in front of us, and, we hoped, the Confederate army off to the right. At one point, as we rode single-file, fending off tree branches with our forearms, the cavalry escort up ahead halted, looked, and doubled back to us, ushering us quietly to retreat. "Gray stragglers," they whispered. "They've lit a campfire up ahead."

Grant wheeled about, retracing his steps for only the second time since the Wilderness. "That'd be cool," muttered Rawlins, following him. "Captured on the brink of victory."

"Maybe we should go ask them where the front is," I suggested.

Grant decided to cross the river and follow its south bank, keeping it between us and them. After an hour or so, the sun high and getting hot and Grant pinching his forehead and reeling in the saddle, we halted by the riverside, where a small pile of logs was burning. We dismounted, lit cigars, stretched our backs and legs, and abruptly heard pounding hoofs. A lone blue horseman was galloping to overtake us, and as he neared we recognized Lieutenant Pease of Meade's staff.

Pease reined in, saluted, and handed an envelope to Rawlins. He, frowning at Pease's poker face, tore it open, shook out the letter and read it. He glanced at Pease and read it again. He turned it over and looked at the back, then handed it to Grant, who studied it with equal solemnity, nodding as he did so, and handed it back to Rawlins.

"You'd better read it aloud, General," he said. His voice was raspy and he cleared his throat.

So did Rawlins. Then he read, the letter trembling in his hands,

> General: I received your note of this morning on the picket-line, whither I had come to meet you and ascertain definitely what terms were embraced in your proposal of yesterday with reference to the surrender of this army. I now request an interview in accordance with the offer contained in your letter of yesterday for that purpose. Very respectfully, your obedient servant, R.E. Lee.

Rawlins let the letter dangle and looked at our faces. There was a whoosh like air leaving a balloon as we all sighed, shook our heads and looked at the ground. Babcock whirled his hat in the air and cheered, but when the rest of us didn't join he subsided. I noticed for the first time that Babcock's uniform was fresh, as if he'd carried a spare along with him for the occasion.

Grant, cigar in his teeth, took the letter from Rawlins's limp hand and flicked it with his fingers. "Will that do, John?" he asked, his eyes suddenly blue and bright.

"Yes," said John, and as he nodded more and more vigorously, a grin split his face and tears lit his eyes. "I think *that* will do!"

Grant called me to the riverbank, where he sat and wrote a note. I copied it and handed it to Babcock, who mounted and pranced back down the road with Pease in search of the truce lines. We pressed ahead, watching the stream diminish to a trickle, then splashed across the shallows to the little town of Appomattox Court House. As we rode up the main street, the adjacent valley revealed the picture that had led to Lee's surrender. A line of gray infantry was strung out across the valley floor, cannons deployed and ready, battle flags flying, putting on a brave show to the end. Opposite them, occupying the heights from hill to hill, lapping both ends of their line and more, was the Union army, twice as wide and five times as deep as Lee's remnant. I could almost see our cannoneers' hands on the lanyards. With an order to fire, Lee's army would vanish.

At the edge of town we met a group of dismounted officers, Sheridan among them and pacing about, slamming his fist into his palm.

"How are you, Sheridan?" said Grant.

Sheridan smiled, his eyes afire as if he'd just eaten raw meat. "First rate, thank you," he said and patted the nose of Grant's horse.

"Is Lee up there?" asked Grant, nodding up the street.

"Yes he is," said Sheridan. He pointed out McLean's brick house.

"Very well," said Grant. "Let's go up." He chucked his horse forward. He had greeted none of the other officers by name, and it was clear that the invitation included only Sheridan, who mounted up and followed.

"How's your headache, General?" Rawlins asked.

Grant put his hand to his forehead and blinked, surprised. "You know, John," he said. "It seems to have vanished."

In front of the McLean house, we dismounted, and Grant was about to walk up the path when the pounding of hooves coming up the street stopped us. To our great surprise, it was Joe Bowers. The little man with the big beard, whom we had left behind to man things at City Point, had been able to stand the suspense no longer. He'd put himself on the road, pressed on to follow Grant, reached Farmville last night, got news this morning that things were ending, and ridden like hell to get in on the finale.

"Well, hello, Joe," said Grant.

"Made it," panted Bowers, out of breath. "Just made it, General." He dismounted and joined us as we made our way up the path, me in the rear, suddenly disgruntled. With Bowers ranking me, he'd be doing the secretarial honors, leaving me a wallflower for the last dance. Little did I know the favor he'd done me. Out of breath, hands trembling, sweat streaming down his face, little Joe would spill the ink, blot the paper, push back his chair in despair, and let me write my own footnote into history.

In late afternoon, with Lee gone, we stood in the yard of the McLean house wondering where to go next. Officers, blue and gray, mingled in the street and sat on fences talking. From the distance came the roar of cannons saluting the victory, and Grant sent a rider off to make them stop. A commissary man rode up and told us the headquarters baggage had arrived, so we mounted up and followed him down into the valley to find our tents set up and waiting. Quite a string of people followed Grant now, not only staff and officers, but civilians and newspaper reporters, all awaiting the great man's great words after his great victory. But Grant was silent, just nodding here and there as people greeted him.

He dismounted and called me to follow him into the tent. We had work to do. There were prisoners to be exchanged, rations to be sent over to Lee's army, arrangements to be made for the formal surrender and stacking of arms tomorrow. We'd started the work at the McLean house, but the relic-hounds had driven us out. Now Grant sat down at his camp desk, which he hadn't seen in a few days, and rubbed his hands absently over its surface. A stack of dispatches was there waiting for him, and he thumbed through them, then coughed abruptly, took the cigar out of his mouth, shook his head and smiled.

"More of Grant's luck," he said.

When Grant went outside the tent, later on, a crowd of people still lingered, still curious what the general would say. Reporters licked their pencils and hovered close. Spotting General Rufus Ingalls sitting on a log, Grant walked over to him. Ingalls, a classmate of Grant's at West

Point and fellow-soldier in Mexico, had self-effacingly refused field command in the current army to fill in as quartermaster, for which Grant was undyingly grateful.

"Hey, Rufe," said Grant, sitting down next to him and picking up a twig. "Remember that old white mule in Mexico?" Reporters looked puzzled at each other and wrote it down.

Ingalls frowned and shook his head. "White mule? Remind me."

"You know, Rufe," said Grant, nudging him with an elbow. "Up on Popocatepetl. The white mule with all the baggage. The one that fell off the mountain."

Ingalls smiled and remembered. "Oh yes. That mule. You know, Grant, I always suspected that mule was part cat. Had enough lives in him anyway."

The victorious general sat on a log and talked about an old mule in Mexico, while the reporters scribbled in their notebooks and frowned. How commonplace the man was! Grant had just won the biggest war in history, and now he was talking about some dumb mule. He was either the coolest customer they'd ever seen, or else, as more and more of them would begin to suspect as the war faded, he had no idea what he'd just done, had blundered to victory by accident, and was just plain stupid.

But I knew. I was leaning against an apple tree listening, and Grant' story about the mule took me back. Five years back. Grant was no victorious general, but a broken little ex-soldier in a ragged vest, sitting across from me at a table in the DeSoto House in Galena, slowly twirling a whisky glass between two fingers while he told me about a white mule back in Mexico. It had fallen off a cliff, he said. They'd given it up for lost, they'd forgot all about it. But late that night, who wandered into camp, bruised and bewildered, but still unbroken? The white mule. And next day, when everybody got snowblind and couldn't find their way, who had taken the bit in his teeth and led them all with practiced foot down the mountain to safety? The white mule.

And who was now the country's white mule? Grant puffed on his cigar, took out his whittling knife, wiped it on his pants, and nodded quietly to himself.

Chapter XIV

MINNIESACKETT,
YOU LITTLE
COPPERHEAD!

Washington 1865

"SURELY IT'S *GENERAL* PARKER BY NOW?"

The woman's voice was familiar, and I turned to see her standing in the street, corn-silk hair and meadow-blue eyes. At a sudden May breeze she lifted her hand to her white straw hat.

"Miss Sackett," I said, pleased and surprised, recognizing Minnie Sackett from City Point last summer, where I had preened and flirted for a half hour before she told me she was fifteen.

"Or is it *Mrs.* somebody by now?"

She laughed. "Still Miss. Though I'm sixteen now." She raised an eyebrow, which I'd found fetching last summer. I stepped back, looked at the rest of her and she struck a pose. Her face and waist had thinned and her bust and hips widened, a big girl now. Throats cleared behind me. Rawlins, Bowers, Wilson – now Generals all – and other officers were descending from the White House reviewing stand, some of them eyeing Minnie.

"Go on, boys. I'll catch up to you later," I told them grandly, but they lingered within earshot, talking behind their hands. Up on the platform Grant and Sherman were still seated, making stiff conversation with President Johnson. We were standing in the middle of Pennsylvania

Avenue, cleared of traffic for the Grand Review of the troops. Two hundred thousand men had marched for two days from the Capitol to the White House in endless rows, flags and bunting waving from every balcony and rooftop, replacing the mourning crape that had hung for Lincoln for six weeks. In the afternoon sun, soldiers mingled with civilians and hoisted children onto their shoulders.

"You didn't answer my question," said Minnie Sackett.

"I'm sorry. What?" I asked.

"*Are* you a general yet?" she asked. "Everybody else seems to be." Behind her a group of girls, in white gowns and white gloves like Minnie's, stood with their hands over their smiles, as if they'd dared her to speak to me.

"Why yes," I told her. "Brevet Brigadier General. But don't be impressed. I'm still just a secretary." Everyone was a general now, swept up in postwar promotions.

"Secretary indeed," said Minnie Sackett. "Grant's Indian, the papers call you. Faithful companion and chief scribe. I saw you preening on the platform. You looked in your element."

I cocked my head. "Following my career? They have to print something." I was pleased of course. Appomattox might have been another lifetime, so quickly had peace and spring taken hold. My scribbling at Appomattox was now indelible, and the footlights reached me as I bowed in the second rank behind Grant and the other generals in the war's curtain call. For the last two days I had basked in official attention as, from the White House reviewing stand, I had watched with the president, with Grant, Meade and Sherman, as the victorious armies marched by and rank on rank snapped salutes at us.

Minnie's friends were still whispering behind her, and, behind me, Rawlins, Bowers and Wilson were twisting their mustaches.

"Let's give them something to talk about," I told her, offering my arm.

She wrinkled her freckled nose, and curtseyed slightly. "Honored, sir," she said, and, with the white man's blue-eyed daughter on my arm I swept past the goggling generals, Minnie's schoolmates squealing like strangled geese.

"Oh, Parker," said John Rawlins, trotting to catch up.

"General Rawlins," I said.

Grant's chief of staff touched his cap to Minnie. "Emma and I are having a reception later on, remember. I hope you can join us." His eyes included Minnie.

"Perhaps, John" I told him, flicking dust from his lapel. "But my regrets to Emma if we're detained." We strolled off, leaving him standing in the sunny street, coughing into his fist.

"Well done, General Parker," murmured Minnie, hugging my arm tighter, her breast against my elbow. Sixteen years old? I was twice her age plus five.

I cleared my throat. "Well, what now? May a soldier buy you an ice cream?"

"An ice cream indeed," she said, sliding her eyes up at me. "Nasty old uncle. But a cold drink would be nice."

We found a place outdoors at the Ebbitt House, where a black waiter cleared a table under a sycamore tree. Minnie frowned at the menu and ordered "A lemonade and a *mille feuille*," lipping the diphthong so deliciously I didn't dare follow but simply ordered "the same."

"So," I asked her. "The Grand Review. Did you enjoy it?"

"It was thrilling!" she said. "Especially today."

"How so?" Yesterday the Army of the Potomac had marched past with other eastern troops. Today had featured Sherman and the armies of the west.

"Well, I've seen parades in Washington for the past four years," Minnie said. "Almost since I can remember. They're all the same. Ranks of men with new mustaches and new blue uniforms. Tramp, tramp, tramp. Yesterday there were just more of them, is all, like row on row of tomatoes." Tom*ah*toes, she said.

Our drinks and pastry arrived and she took a big mouthful. "There was that one officer, though," she said, sugar on her upper lip. "The one on the horse with the golden curls. Not the horse, the officer."

"Custer," I said.

"Oh, yes," she said, chewing and nodding, her straw hat bobbing. "Custard, my friend June Healy called him, because that's what she said he turned her heart to. Warm custard."

I smiled. "He's married."

"Girls can dream," she said, raising an eyebrow. She touched her mouth with her napkin and drank lemonade. "Anyway, I loved the way he

198

suddenly spurred forward and galloped past the reviewing stand. Even the president, old stone-face, looked impressed."

"That's Custer," I said. "Claimed he lost control of his horse."

"Well, if he did, I'm glad. It provided some excitement. The rest of the march seemed so . . . controlled. War is so wild, yet here are thousands of men, mincing by in perfect order. You'd think they had no emotions. Then they go and die with the same straight faces."

"And what of today?" I asked her.

She flopped back in her chair. "Now *that* was thrilling. Almost terrifying."

"How so?"

"Well, first, they weren't so well-dressed. The uniforms were faded and ragged, with holes. Their ankles poked out as if they'd outgrown them. They looked like they'd *fought*."

"The western army was never so well-supplied as the east," I told her. "They wore whatever they could find. Ate whatever they could find too."

"Yes, that's the other thing," she said, leaning forward, eyes wide. People strolled past, idly assessing the unusual pair of us. "They seemed taller, thinner than the other army. Not gaunt or unhealthy, just big, tall, raw-boned men who'd been chewing dried beef. And walking all the time too. They had, I don't know," she twisted her shoulders, "a *swing*. They step right out, arms swinging way up and back, like they'd walked here clear from the Mississippi."

"A lot of them did," I told her. "That's the army that took Vicksburg, stormed Missionary Ridge, took Atlanta and marched through Georgia. If the sea hadn't stopped them they'd be marching yet."

"Are they as wild as they look?" she asked in an excited whisper. "What will they be like when they get home?"

I smiled. "They're just men and boys like any others," I told her. "They'll go back to their farms and shops and live with their memories. Oh, the marching?" I waxed technical. "It's an actual military pace. The regulation step is twenty-two inches. Sherman increased it to twenty-four to cover ground faster. That's what gives the swagger."

Minnie looked at her plate. "Leave it to you to take the drama out of it," she said. "I'd rather thought it was all instinctive, just raw passion expressed stride by stride." R*ah*ther, she said. She laughed and ate more pastry. "The other thing, of course, was the whole side-show."

"Side-show?"

"The wagons and Negroes and dogs and pigs and chickens!" She laughed. "It was a sketch." Sherman's army, unable to rid themselves of the Negro horde that had followed them from Georgia, and unwilling to part with their captured wagons, pigs and dogs and milk cows, their bloody ambulances and cackling roosters, had put them in the parade, each unit trailing a clanking motley. "But it was also frightening, don't you think?" said Minnie.

"How so?"

"Well, that's the country too, isn't it? Big, scary men with ragged coats and slouch hats and hard eyes, and troops and troops of Negroes. I'd never seen them before, except the tame ones in the city. Everybody I know is white and civilized and English. Suddenly there seem to be whole hordes of other people clamoring to get in. It's very confusing."

"They're already in," I told her, eating pastry. "Like it or not. I'm in, for instance. I've been in for some time."

"Oh, you," she said dismissively.

"Me what?"

"You're as white as the rest of us."

I grinned at her, somewhere between insulted and flattered. It was nice to be considered one of "the rest of us," but it would be nice too to be able to rouse the flame of risk and danger that the men of the west lit in her eyes.

"Strangers," she said. "It's so hard to get used to that man being president, for instance." Her mouth was a straight line.

"Johnson," I said. "You liked Lincoln."

"Not really," she said lightly. "I'd just got so used to his being there, is all. I'd see him, summers, riding almost alone to the White House in the morning. He seemed so solitary. Like he was the only one who cared what was going on, while the rest of us were going to school and teas and dances. He was president most of my grown-up life."

I raised my eyebrows over my lemonade glass. "Your grown-up life?"

"Oh, pooh," she said, batting a white-gloved hand at me. "You know. Ever since I became aware of anything. I was only twelve when he came to town and the war started."

I slowly lowered my glass. Twelve. When the war started I was thirty-three. That day in the spring of '61, when I met with Secretary of State Seward at his office just down the street, this girl was twelve. Maybe she'd been rolling a hoop down the cobblestones right outside. I cleared my throat and shifted in my chair.

"What?" she said.

"Oh, nothing," I said. "I just keep forgetting you're . . . . Never mind. But it's an odd way to put it. Lincoln came to town and the war started, as if cause and effect."

"Well that's the way it seemed," she said. "The other presidents were nice old men that everybody knew. Buchanan and so on. Then came this strange man Lincoln from out west, and suddenly there was a war and everybody's father and brother were dying."

"And, soon enough, so was Lincoln," I said.

We looked at each other. "Where were you . . . ?" we asked simultaneously.

"The question everyone asks," I said. "You first."

Minnie's eyes grew wide. "I was there!" she breathed.

"Where?"

"In the theatre. Ford's. We'd gone to see the last night of Laura Keene. We didn't know the president would be there until suddenly they stopped in the first act and the band played 'Hail to the Chief'. Then there he was, up in a box to the right of the stage, a bearded man with him, and I thought it was Grant."

"Grant was on a train to Philadelphia," I told her.

"Yes. I found out later," said Minnie. "Anyway the president bowed, waved to the actors, sort of apologizing, and they went on with it. Nobody could see into the president's box, right by the stage, so after awhile I forgot he was there. Mother and I were in back under the balcony. We're not rich, you know, we just act it. Then the second act was on, and I was yawning because it was late. I think my eyes were even closed, because I heard a loud 'thump' that woke me up."

"The shot?"

"I didn't know. Nobody did. First I thought maybe a flash-box had gone off backstage. It wasn't part of the action. There was only one actor onstage, the 'American cousin' character, Harry Hawk playing him, and he stopped stock still and stared up. Then there was smoke drifting down, and suddenly a man on the rail of the president's box with a knife in his hand. He sort of half-jumped, half-fell onto the stage, waving the knife around, and said something."

"*Sic semper tyrannis.*"

She shrugged. "That's what they say. I couldn't tell. The thing of it was, when he stood up, we all saw it was John Booth, so we thought it was part of the act."

"What do you mean?"

"John Booth, the actor. We'd seen him many times. At Ford's even, in March, doing 'The Apostate'. Other times too, Richard III, Hamlet, Merchant of Venice, Romeo. He was wonderful! A little wild, but thrilling. He'd been to our house!"

"Your house?"

"We give Sunday lunches. Of course he was there. Everyone's there at one time or another. Mostly he ate a lot and flirted, like all the actors." She returned to the night. "Anyway, we expected him to say something else. So did Harry Hawk, the actor onstage, I think. He stared at him, like 'What's Johnny Booth doing here?' Then Booth was gone, and Hawk was gone. People were standing up all over the theatre There was a scream, Mrs. Lincoln, and the bearded man I thought was Grant came to the rail and said, 'He has shot the president.' Two men got up in front of us and spread their coats like bats, to protect us I guess, though how a coat could stop a bullet I don't know. Then everyone was shouting, and we nearly got trampled getting out of the theatre, even though we were in back."

"What did you do?" My mouth was dry. I had talked to nobody who was there that night.

"We just stood in the street and waited. People were saying all sorts of things. The southern army is back, Lee's at the gates. They're killing the whole government. Jeff Davis is behind it. But nothing happened. We were outside nearly an hour. Then the doors opened and a soldier came out with his sword drawn. They were bringing Lincoln out, and he needed a pathway across the street. He waved his sword and called us all sorts of names, but we couldn't budge. There was too huge a crush of people."

"How did they get him through?"

Minnie raised a finger and swallowed lemonade. "Sorry," she gasped. "It's got me excited all over again." She put her hand on her chest and took a breath. "Well, the doors opened again, and Laura Keene came out. She was still in her costume, but there was blood all over it. She'd been holding the president's head, the show-off. People gasped and moved back like parting the waters, and Laura Keene – she looks older close up – just swept across the street like Niobe-all-tears and soldiers came behind her carrying Lincoln. They went into that boarding house, and that was it. Everyone was saying he was dead, but he didn't die till morning. Not that he knew the difference, poor man. Then other rumors started. Seward had been attacked, so had Grant, Johnson and Sumner and all sorts of people."

"Just Seward," I said, staring into my lemonade.

"That's what we found out later," said Minnie. "But it sounded so dangerous that mother said we should go home. We were so scared that we didn't go to bed till dawn. By that time it was all over." She drank lemonade, sniffed and used her handkerchief on her eyes and nose. "I'm sorry," she said, brushing a stray hair from her eyes. "I didn't know it still affected me so." She blinked a few times and tried to smile. "And you?"

"I was at Willard's Hotel," I told her. I had been in the bar at Willard's, muddy and picturesque in my Appomattox uniform, letting civilians buy me drinks and making plans for a night with a tobacco-shop girl. "Somebody came rushing in saying the president was shot. My first thought was don't be ridiculous. I'd just seen the president that morning. I'd gone with Grant to the White House, and Lincoln shook my hand. He couldn't be shot. He'd looked fine."

I shook my head and looked at the crumbs on my plate. Minnie touched my hand. "Never mind, if you don't want to."

"It's all right," I said, raising my head. "It's just that I'd met Lincoln so often. He'd been in camp with us. Almost one of the lads. That night, though, as soon as enough people came in to make it sound true, I went outside Willard's. Everybody was running toward the theatre, but I went the other way, to army headquarters. It's just over there." I gestured up the street. "My first thought was for Grant. He was on a train for Philadelphia. Joe Bowers, the other secretary, was already there and said they'd just got a telegram off to him. Grant got back Saturday morning, and by that time Lincoln was dead and Johnson was president. It was like the war again – no time to think, just act. We had to make sure there was no conspiracy, no rebel attack, no reprisals from the armies in the field. Rebel troops were still at Appomattox waiting for parole and we had to make sure they got off safe. It was just like Wauhatchie and the mule brigade."

"Wauhatchie?"

"Surprise attack," I said. "I'll tell you about it some time. One minute everything was fine, next minute everyone running for cover and pulling out their guns." I drank lemonade and sat back, shaking my head. "It was just luck, the assassination, the residue of a conspiracy that fizzled. All sorts of coincidences had to happen to make it work for Booth."

"Coincidences," said Minnie. "I'll tell you a coincidence. Lucy Hale, the senator's daughter? She was secretly engaged to John Booth, the fat little flirt. That night she went from dinner with John Booth to the White House. She was in Robert Lincoln's bedroom when his father got shot by her fiancée."

I shook my head, trying to take this in. "What? Who? What are you talking about? Who else knows this?"

"Just us girls," said Minnie, self-satisfied. "Don't tell. Know what else?"

"What?"

"June Healy came over on the Sunday morning," said Minnie softly. "Know what she said? 'Any word from the tomb?'" She smiled. I didn't smile back. "You get it, don't you?" she said. "The tomb? Easter Sunday?"

"I get it," I told her. "Not very funny."

"No," she said lightly. "Not funny, just bizarre. The coincidences. Lee surrenders on Palm Sunday, Lincoln re-enters Washington like Jesus to Jerusalem. He's shot on Good Friday. What else to expect on Sunday?"

"He was my friend," I told her. "He was the president."

"Well, I know that," said Minnie softly. "But when it comes to that, he was just a man."

I frowned. "What do you mean?"

"Just that," she shrugged. "For heaven's sake, Ely . . ." She put her hand over her mouth. "General Parker, I mean."

"Ely will do," I said, still frowning. "What do you mean, just a man?"

"Just that." She toyed with her fork. "Half a million men were killed in the war. My stepfather. June Healy's brother. Everybody knows somebody who was killed. Lincoln was just one more. Poetic justice, sort of."

"You're not serious," I said.

"Perfectly serious," she countered. "Lincoln came here, the war began. The war ended, Lincoln left. That's all."

I moved my plate aside and put both palms on the tabletop. "Miss Sackett. Minnie. May I call you Minnie?"

"Please do," she said, narrowing her eyes, not sure what was coming.

"Minnie," I said. "The war was fought for a reason. It wasn't fought to kill people, though people died. It was fought for an idea, and nobody understood that idea better than Mr. Lincoln."

"I'm not so sure," said Minnie easily. "I began to think only Mr. Lincoln thought it was for an idea. Everybody else was fighting it because they wanted to shoot guns and be manly and kill each other. When there was almost nobody left to kill, they stopped. That's what men like to do, isn't it?"

My face was hot. "My dear little girl," I said. "There were ideas involved. There was the question of what sort of government we're going to have."

"Yes," said Minnie, cool, blotting crumbs with her finger. "That's what they said. But I don't see that it matters much what sort of government people have. It's certainly not worth half a million men's lives. We get born, we live, we fall in love, we have babies, we live some more, we think a little, we eat a lot, we die. What does government matter?"

I hunched myself forward and stared at her. "The war freed the slaves, Minnie. It put the Union back together. You're not too young to understand that."

"Don't patronize me, General," she said, her cheeks coloring. "I read the Gettysburg speech. Fourscore and blah-blah-blah. But as to the Negroes, surely you don't think people are actually going to let them vote and go to school and own property and run businesses, do you? They're free, but free to do what? They were better off slaves."

I opened my mouth but she raised her gloved hand. "As to the Union, what does it matter? Why do we have to be one big country? Europe's smaller than us, and they have dozens of countries. Surely it wasn't worth all the dying."

I couldn't help smiling at her. "Why, you little Copperhead," I told her. "Are you in the debating society at school?"

She raised her chin. "I think what I choose. It's somewhere in that Constitution you all were waving at each other between the bullets."

"You're very pretty when you're angry," I told her. Before she could spit a reply I patted my hand at her. "Just baiting you, dear. But look here, Minnie. The war was fought to save representative government, and we did it. Yes, there will be trouble. But soon the Negro will be able to vote like everyone else."

"Like who everyone else? I can't."

"Can't what?"

"Vote."

"Well, of course you can't," I said, smiling. "You're just a . . . "

She folded her arms and raised that eyebrow. "Yes? Just a what? Little girl? Woman? Which is it that keeps me out of your lovely little democracy?"

I rubbed a finger on the table. "These things take time," I murmured.

"And how about you?" asked Minnie, still huffy.

"What about me?"

"Can you vote?" She cocked her head and half-smiled.

"Well, no," I admitted. "But. . ."

"But, but, but," she said. "Everybody can vote. But women. But Indians. But Negroes. But anybody they don't like." She put her hands in her lap and shrugged. "Anyway, it doesn't matter. Suppose we could vote, who is there to vote for? I see all these senators and congressmen. They come to lunch. All they do is blow hard and take money under the table. Could I have some more lemonade?"

I ordered us each another glass and sat silent and frowning, bested in an argument I hadn't started. Minnie, the cold-eyed adolescent, sipped her drink, looking brightly around, perhaps for her abandoned friends. Sixteen? When I was sixty she'd still be under forty. Nice comfort for an old man.

Minnie pushed her chair back and stood up. "You're preoccupied," she said. "I shan't bother you . . ."

"Where are you going?" I asked sharply.

"I don't know," she said. "I thought I'd just . . ." She waved her hand in the air.

"Sit down," I said.

She blinked at me and bit her lip. "I don't think . . ."

"Sit down!" I said, too loud, and she dropped into her chair and froze like a scared puppy. People at other tables looked at us and whispered. I moved my chair around to sit next to her and put my hand on her forearm, which I wouldn't let her pull away. "Now you listen to me, Minniesackett," I said, my face close to hers, my voice low. "You're right, blast your little eyes. I wasn't in the war to free the slaves or to save democracy or anything like that. I was in it because I wanted to be where the action was. I wanted to do something heroic, and I did. There. Are you satisfied?"

She nodded nervously, her eyes wide. I didn't smile and neither did she. But I saw vindication in her eyes and she started to say something.

"But," I cut her off and put my finger on her nose. "If you ever tell anybody I told you that, I know Indian tortures you've never dreamed of."

She grinned, her eyes glistening. "You big old bear," she said, and she grabbed my hand and nipped the tip of my finger.

"Now," I said, my voice still low and my face close to hers. I took her hand. Her shoulders were shaking and she was fighting to keep her face straight. "There is a reception at Mr. and Mrs. Rawlins's. I'd like you to accompany me. Will you?"

"Yes," she said. Her voice was a squeak and she pursed her lips and tried to look serious.

I put my arm on the back of her chair. "But you must promise me one thing."

She nodded again. "What?"

"While we are there, you will be polite. You will talk about dresses and flowers and balls and plays. Whatever nice girls talk about. You will compliment the officers on their uniforms and swoon at their tales of bravery." She nodded solemnly. "But if you mention one word of politics or government, I'll put you over my knee and spank you. Is that clear?"

She put her head back and laughed so gaily her hat nearly fell off. "For you, General, I'll be a giddy goose." As I was about to rise and pull her chair back, she put her hand on my cheek and kissed me quickly, hiding us with her hat. "To seal the bargain," she whispered.

So at the end of a lovely spring day, through sun-dappled Lafayette Park the big Indian sauntered, the white man's flaxen-haired daughter on his arm, her sixteen-year old breast pressed to his elbow, as mothers clutched their children to their skirts and their soldier husbands thought dark thoughts and fingered their weapons.

Chapter XV

LEND ME $1,000, PARKER

Bellevue, Ohio 1865

EYES ROLLED MY WAY NEXT MORNING AS I STROLLED IN the headquarters door and skimmed my hat at a hall rack. Joe Bowers, bustling across the floor with papers in his hands and a pencil in his teeth, paused to look me up and down and ask, "What's Seneca for robbing the cradle?"

Grant and I and the rest of the staff worked, not at the War Department building next to the White House, but at army headquarters, a two-story town house at Seventeenth and F Streets. It was appropriate for Grant. In the war, visitors to the front were surprised to find him, not in a planter's mansion, but in a plain tent or log hut, eating beans, bacon, and cucumbers with vinegar. Now the most famous man in the world worked in a converted parlor upstairs in a brownstone. Anybody wanting to see him – lots of people did – had to hike a few blocks from official Washington, wipe their feet on the mat, ascend a rickety staircase and knock on the door.

Old army comrades working there kept the family atmosphere. I bantered some remarks before ascending the stairs to my cubicle outside Grant's office, where Rawlins sat at the other desk. "Well, well, Parker," he said. "You should have heard the tongues wag after you left."

"Made an impression, did she?" I asked.

"Did you both," said Rawlins. "The citizenry's worried about Negroes stealing their women. Little did they know Indians were on the dance card." He tried to laugh but coughed instead, holding his hand to his mouth.

"It's the uniform, John," I assured him, busying myself with papers.

Rawlins quelled his cough and sat on the edge of my desk. "What does her mother think?"

I looked up at him. "She's profoundly disappointed, of course." I had seen Minnie home after the reception and reintroduced myself to her mother, who was gracious as could be.

"Disappointed, is that all?" Rawlins laughed and coughed. "Scandalized, more like."

"No," I said lightly, initialing a piece of correspondence. "Disappointed. She's closer to my age and chagrined at not spotting me first."

"Dog." Rawlins hopped off my desk and returned to his. "Well, Emma says she's welcome any time. She's good company for the other children."

I balled up a paper and threw it, grazing his shoulder, and he had picked it up to return fire when Grant emerged from his office, looked back and forth at us, and handed me some papers. "Travel plans," he muttered. "John, I need you," and Rawlins followed him into the office, making threatening gestures behind his back.

Travel plans. Summer 1865 was devoted to trips north, south, east, and west, showing the flag and the victors to the newly-united land, much the way Grant had sailed the Mississippi after Vicksburg. There was a cachet to sitting on bunting-draped platforms, nodding at pretty admirers, introduced as "General Parker. You know, Grant's Indian." We were binding the country together by showing them who had done it. To a storekeeper in Bangor, Maine, the war was remote, except for the young men who came home wounded or maimed or not at all. But General Grant on the town green brought the war home, where farmer and tradesman, housewife and publican could see that the men of the hour were flesh and blood like them.

Soon such traveling circuses will fade. In 1895 we have the telephone, voice recordings, we even just got something called the Vitaphone, which projects moving images on a screen. Imagine if there had been a Vitaphone camera at Appomattox! There would have been no need for Grant to visit hamlets from Maine to Iowa. He could have sent a moving picture on national tour and stayed home.

In June we went to New York, to the Astor House and Cooper Union, where Grant, with customary reticence, spoke almost as briefly as he had done on public occasions in the war. "I rise only to say I do not intend to say anything. [Laughter] I thank you for your kind words and your hearty welcome.[Applause]." July took us north through New England, west to Albany and Saratoga, to Buffalo, Cleveland, Chicago and a sentimental journey home to Galena. I dropped out for a few days to visit Tonawanda, where I was feted, feasted and sent on my way with the assurance that everyone was doing fine without me and I could do them far more good as a national hero than as a local notable. My farm, which I had fruitlessly tilled while wangling my way into the army, was rented out and proved far more fertile in other hands than mine.

Galena was another homecoming. Though Grant had lived there for only a year before the war, he discovered now that he had more friends than he knew existed. In the anxious days of last summer, with the war a sun-baked stalemate, people had approached Grant to run for president. "My only political ambition is to be mayor of Galena," he told a newspaperman. "I'd build a sidewalk from my house to the harness store and then resign." Now it was built, and a banner in front of the DeSoto House proclaimed, "General, here's your sidewalk!"

In August the road show swung through Ohio and the sites of Grant's boyhood, to Cincinnati, Columbus, and Cleveland, then back via Pittsburgh. I found time to detach myself and loop around to Bellevue, Ohio to visit my old friend Henry Flagler. Throughout the war, until the last year when we'd both got too busy to write, he'd crow in his letters from Saginaw, Michigan about his salt mines' making money so fast it was "criminal." Henry had moved back to Bellevue after the war's end shrank the salt market, and I was looking forward to seeing him again, with the vague hope of recouping some of my thousand-dollar "investment."

I detrained on a sunny September afternoon, consulted the new return address on Henry's latest letter, got directions at the station and hiked into town to register at the Mansion House. Bellevue was still a perfect American village, with white clapboard houses, white fences, green lawns, children and dogs frolicking in the dusty streets. A streetcar clanged down Main Street, drawn by six horses. I watched the houses pass by, including the Gingerbread House, where Henry had lived before the war. The neighborhoods deteriorated, and still Henry's house number failed to appear. Finally there it was, and I rang the car bell and descended, sure there must be some mistake. The house was a gray and narrow two-story affair, with weeds instead of a lawn, rickety and unpainted porch steps, ragged curtains in the windows.

A face peered through the dirty glass, a stranger, who frowned at my copper face. When I held up the letter and pointed to Henry's return address the man squinted and opened the door. He wore a long-sleeved undershirt under his suspenders, and as he took in my uniform he made a show of buttoning it.

"I'm sorry," I said, "I'm looking for the Flagler house."

"Oh, this is it," he said with a wry smile. "Half of it, anyway. They seem to grow into more of it day by day. Come in, come in."

I waited in the vestibule at the foot of a narrow staircase, while the man scampered up shouting, "Henry! Henry!" I heard him knocking on a door. The house was dark, with gummy-looking wood wainscoting halfway up the walls, and dark, stained wallpaper up to the flaking ceiling. Spilling out behind the staircase were the odds and ends of packing boxes. The air smelled of crumbling plaster and boiled rice. Nothing of it breathed Flagler's former wealth. My thousand dollars faded into the faded wallpaper.

"General Parker, by God!" said a voice from the top of the stairs, and down bounded Henry Flagler. He grabbed my hand and shook it, and we looked each other up and down. I was the one to look at, in my no-nonsense blue uniform with modest campaign medals and brass buttons. Henry looked seedy and down-at-heel. He had, in fact, no heels at all, but a pair of worn carpet slippers on his feet. His white shirt, open at the throat, was clean, but had a frayed neck and no collar, and he wore a pair of maroon velvet trousers, which would have been impressive had not the fabric worn away to show bare patches.

"Oh, Sam," said Henry, turning to the other man, who followed him down the stairs. "Ely, this is our landlord, Sam Kingsley." He winked at "landlord," as if at a shared joke.

Kingsley took my hand. "Pleased," he said.

"Pleased!" cried Henry, his lavender eyes snapping. "You're honored, Sam. This is Grant's Indian from Appomattox. The hand you're shaking wrote out Lee's surrender."

"Well, by God," said Sam Kingsley, and he shook my hand until I had to pull it away.

"We'll use the parlor, if you don't mind," said Henry, ushering me into the front room.

"Not at all, not at all," said Kingsley, following us into the room as if to join the parley.

"Just close the door, would you Sam?" said Henry smoothly. "We don't want to disturb you. Or have the girls overhearing. Mum's the word, eh?"

"Oh sure, sure," said Kingsley, nodding conspiratorially. Inferring that weighty matters were at hand, he put his finger to his lips and softly closed the door.

Henry turned to me and smiled. "Likes to be in on things, does Sam. Good fellow, though, letting us camp here." He waved at the room and rubbed his hands together. "Sit! Sit!"

I selected a red mohair chair with soiled antimacassars in the corner near the windows, where heavy maroon drapes blocked out the sun. Henry sat on a matching sofa, which creaked under him, and crossed one shabby-elegant leg over the other. The pictures on the wall were faded, tilting mezzotints of ancient ruins. "I have you to thank for all this, you know," said Flagler, with his habitual half-smile. "You and your damned General Grant."

"How so?" I said. "What's happened, Henry?"

"I've gone bust, that's what," he said. "Flat as a skillet. Even had to borrow $50,000 to pay everybody off. At ten percent, mind you. Holed up here with my tail between my legs looking for work. Proud of yourself, Parker?"

"How is it my fault?"

"Not you, I suppose," grinned Henry. "You weren't important enough. It was Grant, plain and simple."

"What did he do?"

"He ended the war, that's what!" cried Henry, slapping his breast in mock-pain. "Did me dirt. Up and ended the war just as I geared up for another season of boom. Left me with thousands of barrels of salt and no army to sell it to. I was lucky to escape with my shirt." He fingered his worn cuffs. "Nice shirt it once was, too."

"But surely you saw it coming, Henry," I said.

Henry flung his arms in the air. "Of course I saw it coming," he said. "But I saw it coming a year early. In '64, when you made that big push for Richmond? I figured that was it, so I started scaling down. Then when you didn't make it and the war went on, I had to scramble to catch up. Hadn't even the inventory to fill the demand. Had to *refuse orders!*" He shuddered, as if refusing orders was a mortal sin.

"So?" I said. "You were scaled down when the end came."

"I was not," said Flagler. "I scaled right back up. I wasn't going to let Grant catch me napping again. I prepared for the war to go on forever. I was at fuller production than ever when the spring campaign started." He raised two accusatory fingers at me. "Two weeks! Two weeks, Parker! That's what it took that bastard to end the war, leaving me enough product to resalinate the Atlantic." Henry slapped his knee, as if bested by an adversary he couldn't help admiring. "The bottom was out of the market. A dollar fifty a barrel, if you can believe it, less than it took to produce it. Sold out for half what things were worth and lucky to get it. Fifty thousand dollars in the hole. One more good year of war and I'd be in clover."

"I'm sorry, Henry," I said. "Had I only known, I would have told him to drag it out."

Henry waved his hand at me. "Nothing you could have done. Not your fault. And look at you, will you? War hero and all. Are people bombarding you with offers?"

"Offers?"

"Directorships, railroads, meat-packing. Everybody wants a war hero on his board."

I shook my head slowly. "I'm staying in the army, Henry. I'm staying with Grant."

Henry frowned and leaned forward, looking closely at me, as if probing for a secret. "But you can't make money in the army, Parker. You'll never be more famous than you are now. This is the time to capitalize. If you wait, you'll be like me, with a huge inventory and no place to peddle it. Unless, of course, you're waiting for . . ." Henry's eyebrows shot up. He nodded, smiled knowingly and sat back. "Of course. That's it, isn't it?"

"What?" I said.

"Grant's going to be president, isn't he?" nodded Henry. "As soon as they dump Johnson. Very clever, Parker. Ver-ry clever. Hitch your wagon to a star."

"What are you talking about?"

"You, of course." Henry's eyes were rich with schemes. "Stay with Grant. Let him become president. Then make your move. You'll be the closest one to the federal tree when the plums fall. Oh, Parker, you're cannier than I thought."

"I'm not . . . " I started, offended. But I let him have his way. This was Henry Flagler. If I told him I felt loyal to Grant, that I was at the center of the white man's orbit and wanted to stay there, that being inside was better than money and power, he'd just laugh. "And you, Henry?" My eyes roamed around the shabby room. "Surely this isn't the end of the road."

Henry's fingernails rasped his chin. There was stubble on his cheeks and red in his eyes, his chiseled good looks gone seedy. "For the moment," he sighed, "this is it." He shrugged, looked at the door, and spoke quietly. "I've even taken a job selling yard-goods downtown."

I nodded and winked, sharing his secret.

"I have plans, of course," he said, brightening a little.

"Something's bound to turn up," I said cheerily.

"Things don't turn up," said Henry. "You turn them up. Remember John Rockefeller?"

I frowned, trying to place the name. "Cleveland. The grain dealer."

Flagler nodded. "Got it in one, Parker. Well, young John is all of twenty-six years old now, cashing in his grain business, and heading for the oil fields."

"You said there was no future in oil," I objected, remembering Flagler pooh-poohing petroleum before the war.

"Wasn't then. Is now," said Flagler. "Rockefeller's showing the way. Invested in a refinery in Cleveland, did young John, and sputtered along for a few years during the war. Now he's easing out of the grain business and into oil. Cleaning up, too."

"How?"

Flagler frowned. "I've been studying it some. The supply of petroleum is immense and growing daily, far outstripping demand. Far outstripping refining capacity. So the ribbon goes to the man who can refine and sell cheapest. That's what Rockefeller's doing. Bypassing middlemen, buying crude direct from the fields, doing his own hauling and coopering. Most of the oil men are just oil men. Rockefeller's a businessman and giving them quite a run." Henry started to glow, as he always did when talking about success.

"Has he asked you to join him?" I asked.

"One thing at a time, Parker," said Flagler. "I've barely begun wooing."

"And what," I asked wryly, "will you bring as a dowry, Henry?" I looked at the peeling wallpaper and wiped a finger on the dusty tabletop.

"Don't get cute, Parker," frowned Henry. "There are more important things than money."

I pointed a trembling finger at the figure on the couch. "Who are you?" I demanded. "What have you done with Henry Flagler? Who gave you leave to use his body?"

Henry laughed. "All right. Not many things. But I have ideas. And ideas make money."

"What ideas?"

Henry pursed his lips. "They're ill-formed, of course. But I'll give you a notion." He got comfortable on the couch, flinging his arm across the back of it, and waxed visionary, the Henry Flagler of old. "First you get control. Rockefeller's on his way to that. Deal direct with suppliers, own your own freight cars and warehouses. Control the inflow of crude, the refining process and the outflow of kerosene. That way you undersell the competition. The second thing is volume and transportation. Kerosene must be shipped by rail to New York for the European market. You ship in such volume that you get a special rate from the roads. A rebate. A concession." Flagler rolled his hand around and looked at the ceiling, testing the words.

"Or else what?"

"Or else you withhold your product," said Flagler with a smile. "You just make sure you have enough capital to survive the battle. But it shouldn't come to that. We'll have such volume, you see, that they'll have to meet our price or travel empty. It's a market they won't be able to give up, however low the profit per shipment. What they lose in the short run they make up in the long. Volume, you see?" He leapt from the couch and started pacing the room. Flagler's grasp of business was numbing, as was his capacity for fantasy. He and John Rockefeller had become "we" in minutes. Henry turned to me, white spittle gathering at the corners of his mouth.

"That's quite a leap, Henry," I said, trying to calm him.

He waved his arms. "Well, I'm talking far into the future, of course. One step at a time, eh, Parker? Still, it's good to know where you're going when you start out. If you haven't a vision, you just walk in a circle."

"And what does Rockefeller think of your scheme?" I asked.

"Rockefeller?" said Flagler, momentarily derailed.

"Your partner," I said.

Flagler stared at me. "I haven't spoken with John Rockefeller in four years," he said.

"Ah."

"But that doesn't affect the scheme," Henry hastened to add. "You buy it, don't you?"

I shrugged. "You lost me back there among the volumes and rebates," I said. "But I don't count. The question is, will Rockefeller buy? You haven't seen him in four years. He may not even remember you."

Henry looked doused. "Not remember me?" he murmured. He made a fist and looked at it. "He must," he whispered harshly, as if to himself. "He simply must."

There was an awkward pause, Henry looking at his fist and his dreams, me trying not to look at him as his jaw clenched and unclenched, fever burning in his eyes. Was he ill?

"Well," I said, recrossing my legs, hoping to the change the subject. "It's a lovely pipe dream, Henry. Meantime, though, you have to make a living like the rest of us." I was ashamed how pleased I was at Henry's comeuppance.

"It's no pipe dream," he said, standing over me and looking down quizzically. "It's a cut-and-dried business process. I'm no visionary, Parker."

"Of course you're not," I laughed. "And how will you get Mr. Rockefeller to buy your scheme, Henry? You say people listen only when money talks."

Henry looked at the door, looked at me and sat down on the end of the couch nearest my chair. He put his elbows on his knees, leaned toward me, and spoke softly. "I have money."

"You do?" Henry nodded and laid a finger beside his nose. "Then why . . . ?" I asked, waving at the shabby room.

"Sh-sh-sh," ordered Henry. "I'll tell you. You're familiar with Senator Sherman?"

"The general's brother?" Henry nodded. "What of him?"

"The tax act of 1862," said Henry.

"Ye-es," I said slowly, frowning. "Remind me."

"Sherman was on the Senate Finance Committee," said Flagler, lips barely moving, eyes flicking toward the door. "In charge of the act. They were debating a provision to tax whiskey."

"So."

"So," said Henry, his eyes holding mine. "We were still in the whiskey business here. My half-brother Stephen was running it while I was in Michigan. We had made, um, contributions to Sherman in the past."

"I see."

The corners of Henry's mouth tightened. "Sherman came to us. Told Stephen the liquor tax was going to pass, whiskey prices would soar, and a word to the wise, you see. In the six months warning Sherman gave him Stephen poured every cent and all we could borrow into buying and making whiskey and stamping it before the tax passed. Extended us to the limit. Stephen owns a bank in Monroeville. Looted not only our savings but every other depositor's."

"But that's . . ." I objected.

Henry's eyebrows went up. "Risky?"

"I was going to say illegal."

Henry waved it away. "Only if we'd failed. But we didn't. Made it by a whisker. When the tax passed, we had warehouses of pre-tax liquor for sale at post-tax prices. Two dollars a gallon profit, Parker." His voice was a low growl. "We made three hundred thousand dollars. Still have two hundred thousand. That's Rockefeller's dowry." He patted my knee and sat back.

"What happened to the other hundred thousand?"

Henry flicked dust from the arm of the sofa. "We gave it to Sherman, of course."

"Bribery," I said.

Henry looked shocked, his neck rising high from his shirt. "It certainly was not. What do you take me for, Parker? If anything, it was extortion.

Sherman came to us, selling the information. If we hadn't bought it, someone else would have. Others probably did, in fact. Sherman would have been a fool to depend on us alone."

I shook my head. Here on the end of the sofa sat American business, seedy and half-mad, preening as if he'd swallowed a canary. Bribe a senator, loot a bank, flood the market with cheap booze. Use the profits to invest in a scheme to monopolize oil and squeeze freight companies. If it turns out to be illegal, buy some senators to pass new laws. This dark and shabby room with its peeling wallpaper and lumpy horsehair furniture seemed just the place to hatch such schemes. I would have feared for the future had I any notion that Flagler was serious.

I touched his knee. "May I take you and Mary to dinner?"

"Hm?" he said, off in some reverie. "Oh. Why certainly, Parker. Mary isn't well, I'm afraid. As usual. But let me just see."

He bounded out of the room and up the stairs. His fantasy and resilience were remarkable. Rockefeller, whom he hadn't seen in four years, was part of "we." His half-brother Stephen, who had made whiskey while Henry was spilling salt, was part of "we." I heard a clattering on the stairs as Henry tore down them, pulling on a black frock coat. "Mary regrets, as I suspected," he said. "So it's bachelor night. Where to, Chief?"

I took him to the Mansion House, where he devoured a double portion of beef, talking all the while, gulping claret, and spinning webs of dreams and profit. So grateful did he seem that I invited him back for breakfast next morning. When I came down, bag in hand to catch the train, he was already at the table with relays of waiters rushing trays back and forth.

"Again, apologies from Mary," he said, wiping his mouth. "Just can't shake this, I don't know, whatever it is."

I knew what she couldn't shake, her husband and his cloud-visions. A moment's peace was the best present I could give her. During breakfast, though, Henry was quiet and had trouble meeting my eyes. As I paid my bill he hovered and even grabbed my bag, insisting on walking me to the station, holding the hotel door open for me like a porter. On the platform, he rocked on his heels, humming, glancing at me out of the corner of his eye.

"What is it, Henry?" I finally asked him.

He laughed. "Oh. Obvious, am I?"

"You're a lousy poker player, Henry," I told him. "Out with it."

He looked around. "Here, let's sit," he said, and we sat on a bench. He checked both ways, but I was the only one waiting for the train. "I've got a proposition for you, Ely."

I put my hand on my heart. "No," I said. "You? A proposition?"

"I'm serious," he said, putting his arm behind me leaning close, Iago to Othello. "Here's the thing, Ely. I'd hate for you to miss out."

"On what?" I asked him.

"Why, Flagler & Rockefeller, of course," said Henry, his face perfectly serious.

"Ah." I looked up the track for my train.

"I don't expect to be taking investors for some time, of course," he said. "We must build slowly. But I'd make an exception for you."

"How big an exception?" I asked, recalling the last thousand-dollar exception he'd made for me.

He blinked. "Well, you're straightforward, aren't you?" He leaned closer. "I promise you, Ely, I haven't forgotten your thousand-dollar investment in salt. Well, here's your chance to double it. If you have another thousand dollars to spare, you couldn't do better than put it in this hand right here." He poked a finger into his palm. "It will pay you back many times."

"In how long?" I asked him. I heard a whistle down the track. "As long as my first thousand?"

"Don't ask me that," said Henry, talking faster and hunching closer to me, bacon and onions on his breath. "It will take time, of course. But you'll be one of the original stockholders, you see. Before stock is even issued. In ten years' time, there's no telling how much today's thousand will be worth. That, plus re-investing your first thousand."

It will be worth exactly nothing, I told myself, just like the first thousand. But it was so pathetic that I found my heart again going out to Henry Flagler, who was, simply, in his own way, asking for another loan of a thousand dollars. A gift, more likely, for how, working at a dry-goods store and trying to pay off his fifty-thousand dollar debt, would he ever pay me back? But for him to put it as a business venture was so perfectly Henry Flagler, that I couldn't resist.

"I have some money," I said. "Army pay is low, but so are army expenses. My farm at Tonawanda is paying now that I'm not running it. I could spare another thousand." And, as the Cleveland train chugged in and blew and wheezed, I once again took out my note case, wrote Henry a draft for a thousand dollars, blew the ink dry and handed it over.

Henry looked at it as if it were manna and looked at me gratefully. "Thank you, Ely," he said, his lavender eyes never more honest and clear. "You have no idea what this will do. My dearest friend." He folded the draft, put it in his pocket, carried my bag to the train and hoisted it aboard. "You won't regret this," he said, wringing my hand adieu.

I patted him on the shoulder and climbed the steps. "I don't regret it already," I told him, and I stood in the doorway waving to him, and he waved at me till the train was around the bend. Two thousand dollars down the Flagler drain. Would I never learn?

Chapter XVI

A GIRL'S ONLY PROPOSAL SHOULDN'T BE SO OBLIQUE

Washington 1867

1866, THE COUNTRY'S FIRST FULL YEAR OF PEACE, witnessed momentous events. The 13th amendment to the Constitution abolished slavery and the 14th would, in theory, guarantee citizenship to everyone born here, including Negroes but excepting Indians. The Union Pacific and Central Pacific Railroads drew a long bead on each other and started laying track, from Nebraska west and California east. The Atchison, Topeka and Santa Fe inched west from Kansas City. On western buttes and bluffs, Plains Indians watched and muttered.

The country's industrial and manufacturing plant, fueled by war, roared happily into peace. Power-driven sewing machines, created to make uniforms and military shoes, started making dresses and high-topped boots. Blast furnaces boomed, and the country's rails, ravaged, rebuilt, and ravaged again by war, clanged with new locomotives and rolling stock. George Pullman's sleeping cars began to appear. Bessemer steel rails proved more durable than iron, and a new steel industry took root in Pittsburgh and on the Great Lakes. Petroleum flowed through the first pipeline from Pithole, Pa. Henry Flagler wrote from a new address in Cleveland that "With the great news from Pithole, Rockefeller has abandoned all other holdings and gone completely into oil." He failed to mention my two-thousand-dollar "investment."

Closer to home, the Grant official family suffered an ironic loss. Joe Bowers, my fellow secretary in the war, was always late for things. "I'll finish up here, fellows, and be right along," was his refrain. He almost missed Appomattox, catching up with Grant on the doorstep of the McLean house, so out of breath he couldn't write the surrender document. "Parker, you'll have to do this," he muttered, and I wrote my name into history. In March, 1866, Joe Bowers was late one last time. Departing West Point with Grant after a visit to Grant's son Fred, Joe fiddled too long on the platform, saw the train pulling out, leapt for the car and fell to his death under the wheels. Grant, tears in his beard, sat in his car writing orders for the funeral.

Aside from Joe's death, it was an easy year for me. I spent my days in the army office, my nights at my boarding house in Georgetown, and evenings and weekends being expansive and expanding at hearthsides and groaning boards around town. I was still "Grant's Indian from Appomattox," and invitations were plenty. Almost every Sunday found me lunching at the Sacketts' and watching Minnie grow. She would be eighteen next year.

Sunday lunch was an institution at the Sacketts', and I a habitué, joining high and low officials around a bowl of punch, a joint of lamb, platters of salads and sweets, discoursing on weighty matters and flirting. Badminton and croquet flourished on the grass. Though Minnie had her choice of boys her age and of the younger officers, she was at my side more often than not. I couldn't tell what I was to her – exotic stranger, adopted uncle, large pet – but it was my arm that she clung to as we walked the lawns and parlors, little, blossoming white girl and her dusky old forest swain.

She was an uncanny combination of girl and woman, able to draw from me feelings I'd never put into words. In the fall of 1865, for instance, I went to Fort Smith Arkansas, part of a commission to sign treaties with the tribes the U.S. had dumped there, and who had divided north and south, free and slave, in a mini-Civil War of their own. It was unsatisfactory, of course. As with all Indian treaties, the government's main interest was to grab land.

When I returned it felt like I had never left. I had departed on a Sunday in August, leaving the Sackett lunch and the lawn games in progress. I returned on a Sunday in October, just in time for lunch, and except for the turning of the leaves, it might as well have been the same lunch, going on uninterrupted, while I made a loop in time and space. Croquet balls thocked on the lower terrace. A shuttlecock game dissolved in merriment.

I sat on the porch rail with my back against a post and Minnie sitting rapt on a stool in front of me.

"Speak, pensive Hamlet," she said.

I grimaced and threw the dregs of my punch onto the grass. "It was a land-grab," I told her. "In the end, it meant give us your land before we take it."

"Did anybody win?" she asked.

She handed me a piece of cake, which I dutifully chewed. "The Choctaw and Chickasaw will do all right for awhile." I laughed. "They even got the commission to promise that the U.S. would try to remain united and not cause the Indians such trouble ever again. But they'll all lose in the end."

I poured more punch from a crystal pitcher. Through the long windows I could see into the Sacketts' parlor, where a soldier was playing the piano, a girl in a blue dress turning pages for him. On an October Sunday, it was hard to summon any pity for the distant Indians. They were far away, and the little, sun-warm white girl was close at hand. "What do you think?" she asked, frowning prettily.

"About what?"

"About the Indians. You're an Indian. What should they do? Fight on, though doomed to lose?"

I looked at my punch cup and drained it. What would I do if I were a Chickasaw? What had I done already? I banged the punch cup down on the porch railing harder than I meant to, making Minnie jump. "I think they should give it up!" I exploded. "I think they should be like me! Educate and assimilate. The old ways are dead, and the sooner they give them up the better. If I was a young Choctaw, I'd learn English. I'd go to St. Louis or New Orleans and learn a trade. I'd stop being an Indian and be an American. That's what everybody else does. What's so special about Indians?"

"Just that they were here first," said Minnie quietly.

I shook my head. "That doesn't work for the current generation. Maybe once America owed them something special, but no longer. An Indian boy should be no more special than a German boy or a French boy born here. They've got an equal chance and they should take it."

"Is that possible? For Indians, I mean?"

"Possible," I said. "Even desirable. I've done it. But they're so damned stubborn. Half of them can't speak English, and they don't teach their children English. What are they hanging on to? Pretty soon the whole country will look like this!" I swept my hand at the green, sloping lawn, the hedges and gardens, the young Americans at play. "There will be no Indian Territory left."

I laughed, remembering. "They should do what Dolley Madison said. Sell their lands and move to town."

"Dolley Madison?" asked Minnie.

"Yes," I said. "Didn't I tell you? I talked with her once."

Minnie rose, her hand to her chest. "You? Dolley Madison? When?"

I shrugged. "Eighteen forty-six, forty-seven. She was very old. She and Mrs. Polk were in a carriage. They gave me a lift."

Minnie's mouth dropped open. "Dolley Madison was alive in 1846? And you were old enough to talk with her?" She shook her head. "I wasn't even born!"

"Mm," I said.

"I'm a child," she wailed.

Her bosom heaved. "Less and less," I said.

Christmas 1866 brought changes.

"Wake up, Parker," said John Rawlins roughly one day. "Take a look at this." He coughed and shoved a telegram under my nose.

I blinked myself awake. It was the morning after Christmas, and I had been dozing, feet up, at my desk, sleek, fat, and slightly hung over from dinner at the Sacketts'. The telegram Rawlins handed me was from a Colonel Carrington, at Fort Phil Kearney, Wyoming Territory:

> Send reinforcements forthwith. I have had today a fight unexampled in Indian warfare. My loss is eighty-one killed, led by Captain Fetterman. Nearly three thousand Indians involved. I need reinforcement and Spencer repeating arms. I need officers. I need men. I have, at best, one hundred nineteen left at the post. Our killed show that any remissness will result in mutilation and butchery beyond precedent. This post will be held so long as a round or a man is left. The Indians desperate, and they spare none.

I banged my chair down. It wasn't the first time Indians had killed soldiers out west. Usually, however, the numbers were smaller and far outweighed by the Indians killed in response. A massacre of over three score soldiers was new. I read the date again. December twenty-first, five days ago. "This just arrived?" I asked Rawlins. "Where's Fort Phil Kearney?"

"That's what we're looking at." Rawlins motioned me into Grant's office. "Far north in Wyoming Territory." Grant and the rest of the staff were bent over a map, Grant's cigar at full boil. Rawlins's pale finger traced west from Omaha, along the Platte River and the Oregon Trail. Where the river forked in western Nebraska, John's finger followed the north fork into the wilderness almost to its source until it tapped twice on Fort Laramie. There his finger left the Oregon Trail and traced a thin secondary line into the Powder River country between the Big Horn Mountains and the Black Hills, the Bozeman Trail, connecting to the newly discovered gold fields of Montana. It threaded its way through a tangle of streams that drained into the Missouri, streams with names like Rosebud and Crazy Woman Creek, the Tongue and the Powder, the Yellowstone, and the Big and Little Bighorn.

"Fort Phil Kearney is on the Bozeman," said Rawlins. "Two hundred-forty miles north of Fort Laramie."

"Yes, yes, yes," said Grant, waving smoke away, frowning at the sketchy map. "The massacre occurred on the twenty-first. Why are we just hearing about it now?"

"Closest telegraph to Fort Phil Kearney is Fort Laramie," said Rawlins, his finger tracing due south again. "Somebody had to get there through two hundred miles of snow and ice. Twenty-five below zero yesterday at Laramie."

I shivered, wondering about this "somebody" who fought through the ice and snow from Phil Kearney to Laramie. The telegram was dated Christmas day, just yesterday. While I was tipsy and eloquent at the Sackett mantelpiece, "somebody" was blundering half-dead into Fort Laramie to report the men at Fort Phil Kearney massacred and besieged, their wives and children widowed and orphaned. My snug, smug Christmas palled.

"Hysterical," growled Grant, snatching Carrington's telegram. "Give me men, give me arms, give me Spencers. How did the attack occur? He doesn't say. How many Indians killed? He doesn't say. Do they have guns or just bows and arrows? He doesn't say. The fort will be held as long as a round or a man is left. Bravado. Three thousand Indians. Is that possible?"

He looked at me, as close to an Indian expert as he had. "That's a lot of Indians," I said, "if he means three thousand warriors." I calculated. "It means something like twenty thousand Indians camped up there. That's more than the whole Cherokee nation in Oklahoma. I doubt it."

Grant grunted. "Carrington's to be relieved?" he asked Rawlins.

"As soon as the snow stops and the reinforcements get through."

"Good," said Grant. "Let's get him where we can talk to him. Somebody's made bad mistakes here."

As the days progressed and the glow of Christmas chilled, the cross-country telegraph hummed and the late lights burned at army headquarters. There was no further news from Fort Phil Kearney. The whole country west of Omaha was being whipped by blizzards. For all we knew the Indians had followed up what was now being called the Fetterman massacre by wiping out the entire garrison. Our only hope was that the blizzards keeping reinforcements from leaving Fort Laramie were bottling up the Sioux as well.

The frontier bristled. Generals who hadn't smelt gunpowder since Appomattox sniffed the air like Dalmatians. From General Sherman at St. Louis came an offer to "act with vindictive earnestness against the Sioux, even to their extermination, men, women, and children." Hancock, at Fort Leavenworth, swore to march up the Arkansas as soon as the snow cleared and assure that no such mayhem as the Fetterman massacre occur among "his" Indians. "Pursue and punish," raved Sherman. Grant calmed his lieutenants and paced the office demanding news.

Dispatches from western forts filled in some blanks and, examining our files, we discovered clues we might, had we paid attention, have seen as portents. In June a treaty was signed at Fort Laramie by two chiefs of the Teton Sioux, Spotted Tail of the Brulé and Red Cloud of the Oglala, that guaranteed safe passage for whites along the Bozeman Trail, along with the construction of forts, including Phil Kearney. At least that's what *we* thought the treaty meant. Red Cloud apparently thought different, and his Oglala were harassing the forts and killing immigrants. Reports showed at least thirty deaths on the road in summer and more in the fall. Scarcely a wagon train got through without a fight and some losses, for a total of sixteen soldiers and fifty-six civilians killed from July to November. On December 6, twenty-one men guarding a wood-cutting train had been killed at Fort Phil Kearney. Yet it wasn't until Fetterman's disaster that the western command connected the dots and discovered a full-scale Indian war in their hills.

A relief column left Fort Laramie January 3. On January 12 a further communication from Fort Phil Kearney reported

> Severe cold and drifting snows, with mercury at twenty-two degrees below zero. Fetterman's detachment was several miles from the wood train they were sent to relieve, and pushed over Lodge Trail Ridge in order of pursuit, after orders three times given not to cross that ridge. I found Lieutenant Grummond's body; also Fetterman and Brown – evidently they shot each other.

Grant shrugged. "At least the fort's still there. No further attacks."

We scoured our maps but had nothing in sufficient detail to show "Lodge Trail Ridge" or any other landmarks. "I can't see it," growled Grant, banging his fist on the map. "I just can't *see* it." Grant, who could read in his head the map of the entire Civil War, stared blind at the western maps as if willing them to speak.

In February, Grant moved, and what he moved was me. "Got a commission for you," he said to me. "You're going west." He handed me a paper, which contained honor and burden in equal measure. I was to join a delegation in Omaha on February 23 and travel thence westward through Nebraska and Wyoming, taking testimony among the various tribes and forts. "The great object," said the orders, "is to prevent a general Indian war." In pursuance of this we were directed to find out which of the Indian bands in the Powder River country around Fort Phil Kearney were friendly and which not, which band had committed the massacre, to separate the friendly from the hostile Indians by establishing the friendlies on reservations and to determine the root of the conflict.

"Problems?" asked Grant, as I read the paper.

"What? Oh, no. No," I said, folding it. "Well, one. Why leave so soon? The Overland Trail will be snowbound till April. All we'll do is sit in Omaha for a month at government expense. Might as well sit here."

Grant raised the corner of his mouth that was cigarless. "The people want action."

"This isn't action," I said, waving the paper. "It's just motion."

Grant grunted. "Very neat, Parker," he said. "But motion itself is better than standing still. Anyway, president's orders."

I nodded slowly, scanning the orders. "How long will it take?"

Grant shrugged. "As long as it takes. Four months. Six. Till summer anyway. Big distances out there. Anything else?"

"No sir," I said, though my stomach tightened. "Be a nice change from city life."

Grant squinted at me and blew smoke. "Very well," he said. "Dismissed."

There *was* something else, and as I sat at my desk and stared at the orders, I let it in. I now had Joe Bowers's old desk and his old position as chief aide-de-camp. Aside from Bowers's death, and John Rawlins's continuing cough, the Grant family was chuffing along. Grant was now general-in-chief of the army, and I'd been getting comfortable in his service and in Washington. I'd also got fat and lazy. A change of scene and a frontier assignment would be good. So what was the problem? I chuckled. Years later, in his *Memoirs*, Grant described how, as a young army officer near St. Louis, he'd taken to hanging around Miss Julia Dent. "We would often take walks, or go on horseback to visit the neighbors," he said, "until I became quite well acquainted in that vicinity." In fact, he says, had not he been ordered away to the Mexican War, "this life might have continued for some years without my finding out that there was anything serious the matter with me."

The anything serious the matter with me was Minniesackett. I had first treated her like a schoolgirl. But as successive summers turned to autumns and she from a girl of sixteen to a woman of eighteen, our chats in the den grew more serious, her playing and my singing at the piano more passionate, our hellos more thoughtful, and our farewells slower. The touch of her hand or a peck on the cheek became links in a chain of affection. "She loved me for the dangers I had seen." To me and my fellows I may have been a dusty scrivener, but to her I was a warrior,

"Grant's Indian from Appomattox," who quested forth to bring peace to a troubled land.

But I had never been gone long. Excursions with Grant and the president to bask in public esteem. Fort Smith for a month. Inspection tours of a few weeks. Now, with the prospect of a six-months' absence, I pondered my situation anew. I was becoming "quite well acquainted in the vicinity" of Minnie Sackett and had no desire to leave it without getting a few things settled. The victors were marrying the spoils up and down the east coast. Rawlins had married his Emma, Harry Wilson had just married a Baltimore nubility of seventeen. But those young men were at least within hallooing age of their brides. They were also white. Would old unreconstructed Washington yield its blossoming daughter to a forty-year-old Indian? Would the daughter herself? Was I anything to her than a friendly bear?

"Six months!" gasped Minnie, rising from the couch. We were alone in the den after Sunday lunch. From the music room came the tinkle of the piano and punch cups and laughter.

"Yes," I said. "That was my reaction too. When Grant told me." It wasn't exactly my reaction. I didn't, as Minnie now did to me, turn to Grant with my hand to my breast and my eyes aflutter.

"But that's . . ." Minnie counted. "September!" I nodded and put my coffee cup on the end table. She turned her back to me and moved to the window, her blonde hair gleaming, head bowed, fingers idling at the maroon drapes. She moved to the bookcase and started pulling out volumes, putting them back and rubbing her fingers. "Martha really should dust these," she murmured. Her voice caught. "Yes, they're very dusty. Out of order too. I really should . . ."

"Minnie," I said.

"Yes, Ely," she said, her back still to me.

"Come back here." I patted the couch.

She came back and sat down, sniffling, her eyes wet. She pulled a handkerchief from her sleeve. "Dust," she explained, blowing her nose.

"It might not be as long as six months," I said. "But I have to be prepared for that."

"We'll miss you," she said, her eyes downcast. "Mother and I, that is. Whoever will carve the lamb?"

I smiled. "Woodland skills."

We were silent for awhile. Minnie continued to sniffle, and her chin was trembling. She tried to hide it with her handkerchief, but I pulled her hand away and held it. "Minnie," I said.

She cleared her throat and tilted her chin. "Yes, General?"

I groped forward. "I want you to do me a favor."

Her forehead wrinkled. "Of course."

I examined her palm, deciding the best way to put it. "While I'm away," I said slowly, "if anybody should chance to ask you to marry him, I wonder if you would do me a great honor?"

"An honor?" she said, puzzled. "What honor?"

"Would you," I took a breath and plunged ahead, "do me the favor of at least saying no? Until I return, that is?" That sounded about right. I looked hopefully at her face.

She frowned, her lips moving as if translating. "Why, what an odd thing to say, Ely," she finally said when she'd teased it out.

"I- I'm sorry," I stammered. Heat flooded my face and I let go her hand. She was upset. "I didn't mean to insult you."

She put her hand under my chin and made me look into her eyes. "Did I just miss something? You spoke so elliptically. Did you just ask me to marry you?" Her face was stern.

"Why no," I said, laughing. "No. Of course not." Poor little thing, she'd got it wrong. "It's just that I realize you're getting older and, you know, marriage is the next step." I waved a hand. "I'd hate to come back and find you engaged to somebody else, is all. Without my having a chance to speak up myself." I waved the other hand. "That is, having a chance to hear you say yes or no if I asked. You see?" Why were my hands waving? I forced them down between my thighs.

She examined my face, shaking her head. "*Do* you want me to marry you?" she asked.

I laughed. Too loud. "Not at all," I hastened to assure her. "Not right now, I mean. There's the trip and everything. Who knows what could happen? I just don't want you to marry anyone else, you see. Until I return and we have time to . . . . You know." My hands started waving again. I stared at them, unsure where they belonged.

Minnie narrowed her eyes at me, stood up and took a couple of thoughtful steps away, before rounding on me with her hands on her hips, suddenly looking very tall. "Let me understand, Ely. You don't want to marry me."

"No," I said, slapping my knee, glad she'd got that right. With her standing over me like that, I felt myself growing smaller, shrinking back into the couch.

"But you don't want anybody else to either."

"That's not exactly what I meant," I said. She was getting it bollixed up. "I mean . . ."

"What you mean," she said, interrupting, "is you want to have your cake and not eat it. You don't want me to marry anybody else and you're not ready to ask me yourself. But you do want me to marry you. Some day. Is that it?"

I thought about it. That, in fact, was it, though I hadn't worked it out to myself quite that way. The room felt close, and so did she. I was sweating and short of breath. My collar felt tight. I looked up at her, quite mature all of a sudden, with her hands on her hips waiting for a reply. I realized that, planning this scene, I'd omitted her part entirely. I shrugged and moved my mouth. A strangled "I guess so," emerged.

"You guess so," she said. "Why don't you come right out and say it?"

"I- I didn't want to insult you," I said. "I was afraid of what you might say."

Minnie shook her head as at a bad child. "Well, I must say," she said. "You have an odd way of not insulting me. You don't even propose, you just offer a treacly little maybe. Jennie Majors is six months younger than me and she gets proposed to full-out once a week." She looked at the floor. "It's very disappointing, Ely," she said quietly. "A girl's only proposal shouldn't be so oblique."

"I didn't want to presume," I said and stopped. What had she said? "What do you mean, your only proposal? Lots of men are going to . . . . Oh." She could hold her face no longer. A smile blossomed and her shoulders shook. "Oh," I said, beginning to understand. "I'm –"

"I'll tell you what you are!" she said, throwing herself onto my lap and putting her arms around my neck. "You're a big old Indian prude, is what you are!" She kissed me on the cheek and snuggled into my shoulder. "It's my only proposal because I'll accept no other, you fool." I looked quickly toward the door, lest her mother come in and find my lap full of her daughter. I had a strange impulse to bounce her up and down as if dandling a child, but her breast against mine stifled that thought and stirred deeper ones. I put my arms around her.

231

"Does that mean yes?" I asked her, surrendering to a proposal I'd had no plans to make.

She laughed and snuggled closer. "Yes," she said softly. "To whatever you ask. I'll say no to every pimply-faced little boy who comes along. And," she raised her head to look me in the face. "When you return from the wild west, I don't want some pregnant little squaw trailing behind you. I'll also then expect a full and honest proposal. No hedging. I mean on your knees, General. With flowers."

I hugged her and hugged her and for a thrilling moment she was all breasts and thighs. She let her body yield, then pried my hands off her and stood up straightening her hair. "If I'm to wait, so are you," she said, breathing hard. "It's cold outside. Let's go there. I want to walk miles and miles with you."

The next few weeks before my departure I spent as much time with her as I could, talking in the den, singing at the piano, taking long walks in the darkened streets. We kept our arrangement secret, but the bend of her body toward me when I slipped my arm around her to say goodnight, the way she took my hand under the table at dinner, the way her daughterly pecks softened to real, lingering kisses told me she was mine. More likely, I was hers.

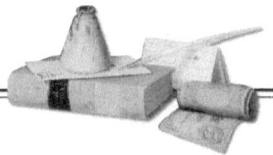

Chapter XVII

HIS NAME IS, UM, CRAZY HORSE

Nebraska 1867

OMAHA IN MARCH, 1867 WAS REPUTED TO BE A BUSTLING place, the eastern terminus of the new Union Pacific Railroad to California. Its population had doubled to twenty thousand since the war, as workers flocked to the railroad. End-of-track was now at mile 291, over several distant horizons. Dockworkers and brickmakers shouldered through the streets and saloons, logging teams scoured and denuded the Platte and Missouri valleys, shipping ties and timbers to the ever-stretching road. Shop buildings and sawmills sprang up, a brick roundhouse boasted ten locomotive pits, and dwellings for the workers and their families grew into an adjunct city that dwarfed the original town. Steamers groaned up the Missouri, vomited their stores onto the wharves and dropped down river for more. Farnham Street, leading inland from the docks, was muddy and brawling, with mule teams lurching its length and the profane cries of teamsters exciting the *Weekly Herald* to weekly howls about the ruin of civilization. Land speculators and lawyers worked from nail-keg chairs and flour-barrel desks. One reporter counted "127 saloons, 25 temples of vice, 10 full-fledged gambling establishments, to a mere six places of worship." The swelling population even managed to create an underclass, as the paper pleaded for donations to help the "indigent poor."

That's what they said, anyway. I couldn't swear to any of it, because it snowed the whole time we were there, making what surely must have been a vivid landscape a blur of white. For the whole of our two week stay, the commissioners shuffled stoop-shouldered from our rooms at the Cozzens Hotel to army headquarters and back, our faces swaddled in scarves against the blizzard, unable to see anything but the few yards before us.

We weren't there to see the sights, however, but to investigate the Fetterman massacre and interview Colonel Henry Carrington, commander at Fort Phil Kearney at the time. A small and scholarly officer, former lawyer, nervous and fidgety, with pince-nez spectacles that he polished with his handkerchief more than he needed, he had the look of the desk about him (a look I knew well), an unlikely sort to command a remote and dangerous post.

"I was sent there to build forts," said Carrington in a high, clipped voice, sitting across the council table from us. "There was no indication that the Indians were hostile. They signed a treaty last June allowing the forts and guaranteeing safe passage through the Powder River country. I have a fair copy of the treaty right here." Carrington licked his thumb, peeled a document from the stack he had arranged before him and handed it across the table.

Our commission was small, with General Alfred Sully joining me as the military representatives and a western type named George Beauvais as the lead civilian commissioner. Beauvais took the treaty from Carrington and sat back to read it. Beauvais had come to Omaha from the west and looked it. He owned what he called a "ranch" near Fort Laramie and made a good living trading with the Indians, traveling the wagon routes in and out of Wyoming with some regularity. My vision of an Indian trader came from magazine pictures of Kit Carson, and Beauvais didn't disappoint. He wore a fringed leather jacket, a jaunty neckerchief, and a broad-brimmed hat, which he threw back to hang from a string around his neck, revealing long untrimmed blond hair. He read the treaty with his boot up and jiggling against the edge of the table, then threw it down with a snort.

"Red Cloud signed this?" he asked.

"He did indeed," said Carrington. "Made his mark, at any rate."

"How the hell did that happen?" asked Beauvais. "Red Cloud would never sign this thing if he understood it."

"What he understood is moot, isn't it?" said Carrington with a tight smile. "It was explained to him and he signed. 'Touched the pen,' as the

Indians say." Carrington smiled nervously at me. "His subsequent actions are therefore illegal." He rapped the table with his knuckle.

"Illegal and deadly," growled Beauvais.

The treaty passed from hand to hand. General Sully had some questions. "Perhaps you'd better explain to us how this treaty came about," he said. "Since it seems to be at the root of the problem." With his droopy black mustache and beard and his watery hang-dog eyes, Sully was one of those men who come to resemble their names. "Sullen," would be the word to describe him.

Carrington folded his hands and hunched forward, blinking. "Well, I wasn't there, so this is hearsay, of course." Sully waved him to continue and, as Carrington spoke, took notes on a pad of paper. "Yes," said Carrington. "Well, the Nebraska Indian Superintendent, Taylor, engineered the whole thing. Got Spotted Tail and the Brulé into Fort Laramie last spring, and enticed Red Cloud and the Oglala to come down to meet them there. Swift Bear, Big Mouth, Man-Afraid-of-His-Horses, they were all there. Taylor herded them into the telegraph office at Fort Laramie and let them listen to the 'singing wire' click out the terms of the treaty." Carrington smiled a tight, condescending smile. "The savages were so impressed and terrified they would have agreed to anything. They thought the telegraph was the voice of the Great Father himself." Again, he looked at me, seeming to apologize.

"So they signed," said Sully.

"As you see," said Carrington.

I had read the treaty by now. It did, indeed, promise that the Sioux would leave emigrant trains alone on the Bozeman and would let the army build the three forts, including Phil Kearney, that were now under siege. "Let me get this straight," I told Carrington. He blinked at me as if surprised I could speak, let alone speak English. "The terms of the treaty first reached the Indians' ears as telegraph blips?"

"Yes," nodded Carrington.

"The people at the fort then translated the blips into English and wrote them down."

Carrington nodded again.

"Then they translated them orally into Sioux and asked the Indians to put their names to the English version. Is that the sequence?"

"That's it exactly," nodded Carrington, as at a bright pupil.

Sully, still writing on his pad, said without looking up, "So there's no assurance that the Sioux had any idea what they were signing."

"I have heard from other Indians," put in Beauvais, "from Big Mouth. He's the chief of what we call the Laramie Loafers, the tame ones that hang around the fort. He says all Red Cloud thought he was signing was a promise to come back after consulting his tribe. When they started building the forts, he decided not to come back but went on the warpath instead."

"That's possible," said Carrington. "Nonetheless the treaty . . ."

"The treaty," said General Sully with some finality, frowning at what he'd written on the pad, "was clearly understood differently by the whites and the Indians. And since it was the Indians who were to give concessions, and they didn't, I think we can conjecture that it was imperfectly explained to them. I have statements from officers at Fort Laramie that agent Taylor was strutting around boasting . . . . Where is it?" Sully rustled among his papers. "Yes," he said, reading from one. "He was sent by the government to make a treaty, and he would accomplish it if it was made with but two Indians. That," Sully put the paper down, "seems to be about what he did. His treaty was the triumph of hope over facts."

"But –" sputtered Carrington.

Sully waved him quiet. "Colonel," he explained. "You're off the hook. You went to occupy territory you thought the Sioux had ceded. They thought differently and we now see why. Let's leave it at that."

I could see Carrington the lawyer fighting with Carrington the colonel. The lawyer thought the treaty technically valid. But the soldier saw it was to his advantage to have it fraudulent and himself sent into danger unaware. "I see," he said.

"Let's move on," said Sully, and we drew from Carrington the tale of the massacre.

"That very morning, the twenty-first," said Carrington, "while Fetterman and his command were out guarding the wood train, several mounted Indians appeared on the crest of the ridge opposite the fort. Clearly they were gauging our strength and vigilance. I fired a cannon at them and they dispersed."

"Just to be precise," murmured Sully, continuing to write. "You *ordered* a cannon fired at them, correct?"

"I am precise," said Carrington. "I fired the cannon. I was the only officer in the fort trained in ordnance."

"But that's preposterous," I said. "Suppose you were hurt or killed. Why did you hold no training sessions?"

Carrington blew out his cheeks, exasperated. "I had no time, General," he said tightly. "My instructions were to build a fort and supply it for the winter. I didn't know I would have to do so in the face of enemy fire. All my energies were devoted to building and fortifying our shelter. I had no time for parade-ground niceties such as drill and ordnance instruction."

I was about to continue, but Sully put a hand on my arm. "Yes, yes," he said. "Let's return to the twenty-first."

Carrington crossed his legs and adjusted his glasses. Blasts of wind and snow shook the windows as he continued. Sully went back to his writing, now vigorously crossing things out.

"About noon I heard the sound of musketry," said Carrington. "Not, as I'd expected, from the direction where Fetterman had led the wood party, but from Lodge Trail Ridge, much farther away. It started as single shots then became volleys, like alternate ranks loading and firing, diminishing again rapidly to single, random shots. I detached Captain Ten Eyck with cavalry, infantry, and two wagons to aid Fetterman, but it was over when he got there. All he saw were Indians, who fled at his approach after pillaging and despoiling the bodies. Eighty-one men dead, shot through with arrows, stripped naked, scalped." Carrington paused and took off his glasses, but not to clean them. They dangled from his limp hand as he pinched the bridge of his nose.

There was silence, except for the blizzard howling outside, as all of us looked at the table, the only sound the scrape of Sully's pencil.

"How long was it, Colonel Carrington," asked Sully, "from the first shot until the last?"

Carrington frowned and shook his head. "It was very brief. I'm sure no man could have gotten off more than two shots." He sighed.

"The Indians had no rifles?" I asked. "Just bows and arrows?"

"That's correct," said Carrington. "Of all the men killed, only Fetterman and Brown had gunshot wounds, one each to the left temple, with powder burns all around. I conclude they shot each other rather than be taken. Almost serves them right," he muttered as if to himself.

"Serves them right?" asked Sully.

Carrington cleared his throat. "Not to speak ill of the dead," he said. "Fetterman and his friend Lieutenant Grummond were headstrong. Men overheard them laying bets as to which would take an Indian scalp first. The most likely explanation is that, contrary to orders, they double-dared each other away from wood-gathering and into the fatal pursuit. The Indians got lucky, pounced on them and ran away."

After a few more questions we adjourned, and I passed behind General Sully as he was gathering up his papers. On top of the stack lay not notes of the interview, but a vivid line drawing of Colonel Carrington, accurate even to his ribboned pince-nez, with one hand raised to adjust it. Sully looked up and saw me.

"West Point," he muttered. "We all had to draw."

I had seen the serviceable battlefield sketches Grant and others could rip off. "Not as well as this," I said, looking more closely at the portrait. In the background Sully had sketched in a frosted window with snow building up on the outside sill.

"My father was a painter," said Sully, brushing the sketch with his hand as if to dismiss it. "This is as far as I go."

I learned in my travels with laconic General Sully that his father was Thomas Sully, a Philadelphia society painter, and that Sully had chose a military life in rebellion. He spent much of the Civil War in Minnesota fighting Indians – the same Sioux we would encounter in Wyoming. A man of few words and no airs, in the months we were to spend together he amassed a considerable book of sketches which, when I admired them, he dismissed as automata.

In subsequent days, we interviewed other Fort Phil Kearney survivors, including Mrs. Fetterman and the young, spunky, pregnant widow of Lieutenant Grummond. Their testimony corroborated Carrington's, so it was with his view of the massacre that we left Omaha and headed west. The Indians signed a treaty they didn't mean to. Forts started arising in their territory. The Indians harassed the forts without attacking. Then two headstrong officers double-dared each other and led their men into a lucky ambush. The Indians, surprised and elated, had despoiled the corpses and run off to dance around their campfires, too ignorant to press their advantage and attack the fort *en masse*. A combination of white stupidity and Indian luck had led to the greatest massacre in the west since the Alamo.

A poster in Omaha's Cozzens Hotel announced:

THE SHORTEST AND QUICKEST ROUTE
between the
MOUNTAINS AND THE EAST
is via the
UNION PACIFIC RAILROAD
now open from
OMAHA TO NORTH PLATTE
300 miles west of the Missouri and 200 miles nearer Denver than any
other railroad line
direct connection via Chicago and Northwestern from
CHICAGO TO OMAHA
with one change of train 600 miles directly west of Chicago
PULLMAN'S PALACE SLEEPING CARS
equipment new, road in perfect order.
Good eating houses at convenient points on line

Well . . . .

As government commissioners we were given the best the railroad had, which exposed a system with a few flies still on it. Our locomotive was the *General Sherman* and our carriage the famous Lincoln Car, built for the president, but finished only in time to carry his body back to Springfield. It was luxuriously appointed and centrally-heated, and a good thing too. The trip, touted as fifteen hours, took many times that, with constant stops to shovel snow off the tracks, shore up jerry-built trestles, ease over sections that hasty grading had crinkled into washboards. The "convenient eating places" existed only in the writer's dreams, and by the second day we were scouring our hampers for crumbs and rationing firewood. Still, we covered twenty miles in an hour, which would have taken a coach or wagon a full day.

At the end of the line we swung off the train at the "Hell on Wheels" town of North Platte, which had no reason at all for being there except it's where the road had got to when winter closed in. "Started as about two hundred tents," said George Beauvais, the Indian trader. "Now look at it. Streets, saloons, whorehouses, stables. The UP travels with its own knock-down village. Put 'er up, tear 'er down. Come spring, when end-of-track moves on, this'll all be desert again. Biggest settlement between Omaha and Salt Lake. Glance away this spring, and it'll vanish."

"Don't blink," I told him. "You'll miss American history."

We hitched a buckboard out to Fort McPherson, constructed from the neighborhood's red cedar and looking prim next to wild North Platte. Built to protect the stage and telegraph lines from the Indians, it was ending its usefulness as the railroad bore down on it. The rounders, roustabouts and railroad men of North Platte outmanned and outgunned the fort a hundred-fold, and they had more subtle weapons against the Indians too, as any Indian that ventured into town to complain soon got too drunk to remember what he'd rode in for. North Platte had, in short, everything but civilization and, except for the domesticated Pawnees, Indians. We had sent messages from Omaha to the Sioux tribes to meet us at Fort McPherson, and though we now dispatched riders onto the prairie, all returned empty-handed. The coldest, snowiest winter on record slowly yielded to a spring with the greatest rainstorms since the Flood. We daily scanned the horizon for blue skies and Indian visitors, but none came, and messengers that slogged their way back in early April reported wearily that the tribes, fearing reprisals for the Fetterman fight, wouldn't meet us at McPherson or at any fort at all and demanded neutral space.

"Well, hell," said Beauvais. "Why not my big ranch? It's halfway from here to Laramie."

So we sent more messengers out into the rain and mud, and by mid-April reports came in. Yes, said the Indians, Beauvais's ranch was fine, so we mounted horses and followed the trader up the North Platte.

Our party was now augmented by one, a translator we picked up at Fort McPherson. Charles Sylvester, from Quincy, Illinois, had lived the adventures that many eastern boys dreamed of. Captured by the Sioux as a youngster, his family scattered, he had lived among the Indians for seven years and found, on his rescue by the whites, that he had no inclination to seek his lost family or even to live civilized. He wore moccasins and leather breeches, rode his pony bareback, squatted on his haunches when we made rest stops, chewed grasshoppers and other wildlife, and eyed Beauvais's dog as if measuring him for stew. To his delight, we nicknamed him "Indian Charlie." He was fourteen years old.

The route we traveled was the famous Oregon Trail, paved and grooved by the passage of innumerable wagons, following the North Platte and packed down solid as rock many miles wide. "It's deserted now," said Beauvais. "Wagons don't leave Missouri till the grass is four inches high. Middle of May, usually. Then you'll see such a sight! Wagons billowing like sails as far as you can see. From May to September I've sat and counted as many as a hundred wagons a day. They're never out of sight, and they bring their trash with them."

We stopped along the way at several ranches. "Ranch" in those days had not today's connotation, when a ranch is something like the Spanish *hacienda*. These were rude huts with sod roofs, barely distinguishable from the surrounding landscape, spaced along the road every ten or fifteen miles – about a day's stagecoach journey apart – where they served as way stations, hotels, and the "good eating houses" promised in the UP posters. A dollar and fifty cents, which in Washington would buy a night at the Willard, here rented two square yards of dirt floor to spread out a bedroll. Another dollar fifty bought dinner of buffalo or antelope meat, with bread, butter and coffee, cooked over a fire of perforated, honeycombed gray buffalo chips.

We reached Beauvais's ranch on April 19, at the California Crossing of the North Platte, where wagons crossed to the north side for the trip to Fort Laramie and the west. This was a more substantial structure than the way stations, a solid log house with a big chimney and warehouses and outbuildings spread out behind. The ranch hands spent a day clearing out a warehouse to use as a council hall, and the next morning at dawn Indian Charlie rushed in shouting that Indians were in sight.

We piled out of the ranchhouse and stood in the clearing to watch. The weather had cleared, a pale blue, almost white sky replacing the gray we had seen thus far. Over a bluff we saw dust, which resolved itself into a column of horsemen, advancing single file, cresting the bluff one by one until a whole arrow of them pointed at us from the horizon. As the column advanced the sun, perhaps thinking it proper, shot its rays down the river, jumped onto the land and illuminated the column, where spears and ornaments began to glitter.

About a half mile from us the leader stopped, and others moved alternately up on either side of him, as neat a move from column to line as you'd find in the Army of the Potomac. Then, about forty abreast they advanced slowly upon us. At a signal I couldn't discern a low, moaning sound arose among them, which sounded like the wind at first but soon rose above it, a chant-like wail that they soon pierced with single whoops, sharp cascading cadenzas that broke away from the main chant, ululating across the prairie, then returning to join the choir while another solo departed.

"Impressive, ain't it," muttered Beauvais. I felt naked and glanced at my fellow commissioners and the ranch hands, the few of us standing alone and windswept in front of the ranch house. Though we represented the power of the federal government we looked feeble in the face of the ancient civilization advancing upon us. Soon I could make out paint on their faces, feathers braided into their hair, and not only bows and arrows, but repeating carbines slung on their backs. About fifty yards distant they stopped, ended their song with a unison whoop and stood waiting for us. They looked at us, and we looked at them. Then Beauvais and Sully took the lead and advanced on foot across the dusty plain to the horsemen, the rest of us following. Not until we reached their rank did the horsemen unbend and raise their hands in salute, some of them even smiling. But not until we reached up to shake hands with each of them did the party dismount and, leading their horses, join us to walk back to the ranch house.

"It's important' said Beauvais to me, "for them to maintain their superiority as long as they can. They know they have to submit, but they'll do it dignified."

The rest of the day other groups rode in with similar ceremony until there was a village of about fifty tepees by the river, complete with women, children, dogs and cooking fires. I wandered among them, my first sight of wild Indians in their native habitat. These Sioux were unlike the tame and civilized Seneca I grew up with or the equally tame Civilized Tribes of Oklahoma, who owned farms and barns and raised crops. These Sioux were literally from the Stone Age. Forty years ago a Sioux was born into a society that had never seen a white man, knew nothing of writing, and had never heard of the wheel. Now they were camped on the edge of a river that was the route for the greatest wheel-driven machine man could devise, the "iron horse" that they had been shooting futile arrows at as it drove them across Nebraska. A Sioux born in a wheel-less, money-less civilization could, by age thirty, buy a ticket on the transcontinental railroad.

Next morning we assembled in Beauvais's vacant warehouse, and again the Indians showed off their strength. Not until the commissioners had taken our places at the table, with Indian Charlie in the center next to me, did the Sioux chiefs appear, and they did so *ensemble*, treading in the door single file, standing, swathed in buckskins and blankets, staring at us until all had entered, then sitting down as one on the buffalo robes we had spread for them. Only the giggling squaws and children, peeping in the door, running away, and pressing their noses against the windows, marred the dignity of the entrance. A pipe was lit and passed among the seated Indians, but not offered to us. "It's not a treaty meeting," Beauvais explained. "Otherwise we'd all smoke. They're just here to receive our orders, so they smoke for their own solidarity."

When the pipe had passed, Sully looked at me. We had decided it would be politic for our one Indian to speak first. I rose, and Indian Charlie stood next to me translating. "Brothers," I began, looking at the circle of impassive faces. "You know that in early winter a large number of white men were killed by Sioux on the Powder River road, whose cries have reached the Great Father in Washington. He is gathering troops to wreak vengeance. When the weather clears and the roads dry they will come. Perhaps, if you put your ear to the ground, you can already hear their hoofbeats."

There were frowns and whispers among the Indians. "We, however," I continued, "do not come to punish. Our mission is peaceful, to separate those Indians who are peacefully disposed from those who are not and to ensure their protection from all enemies, both red and white. By your presence here, in response to our message, you indicate that you are peaceful. What we want you tell us is this: How many of you are there who will pledge to remain at peace? What section of the country would you like us to set aside for you so that you will not be harmed by the war that is coming?"

The Indians stared straight at me. "Your Great Father wants his red children to live," I told them. "When the war is done and the bad Indians are punished, he wants to work with you to find a permanent home where you may live in peace as good neighbors to the white man. We ask you to speak your minds freely on this question and also on other questions you may have."

I sat down and spread my arms. "That is what we have come for," I concluded. "We await your answer."

Again a pipe was lit, the Indians conferring among themselves as we waited. Sully was frowning at his pad of paper, his head cocked, scribbling, I assumed, not notes but sketches of the Indian chiefs. Finally one chief separated himself from the group and came forward, shook hands with each of us then stepped back and spoke. He was perhaps my age, no tribal elder, with long black hair parted in the middle. He wore large hoop earrings, traded or captured from whites, and a yellow cavalry neckerchief, but from there down he was pure Sioux, from his fringed shirt and bead necklace to his buffalo slippers. Indian Charlie stood to translate, but it turned out to be unnecessary.

"I am Spotted Tail, chief of the Brulé," he said in English. "I know you like things short. I spent a year in your prison at Fort Leavenworth, and you barely let me speak before you locked me up. I will tell you one other thing I learned at Fort Leavenworth. There are more white men than there are of us. Every day, from my stockade, I saw trains of wagons heading west with oxen, a line so long it never stopped from sunup to sundown. When I returned to the plains I told Red Cloud of the Oglala of this and he laughed. He said the white man did it to fool me, that he rolled the same few wagons past me day after day, that there could never be as many white men as I say. But Red Cloud is wrong."

General Sully interrupted to ask, "Will Red Cloud meet us here, do you think? Or at Fort Laramie?"

Spotted Tail looked at the ground and shook his head. "I have no control over Red Cloud and his Oglala, but I say no. He's full of himself after the Fetterman fight. He thinks he can keep you from the Powder River country."

"And what do you think?" asked Sully.

Spotted Tail raised his arm to point out the window toward the river and the plains beyond. "It seems such a big country. There should be room for all. But the white man is like the buffalo. Though you don't see him, you feel his rumble on the earth. Though you don't see him on the land, the land lies in wait for him. The white man needs the land and he will take it. He's like a buffalo herd with brains and guns and the iron horse. If we do not yield today, we'll yield tomorrow. I say, why not today. My people agree."

Indian Charlie was translating into Sioux for the Indians who sat on the ground behind Spotted Tail. Many nodded, while others stared forward, stoic but compliant. Sully cleared his throat. "How many are you?" he asked. "The Indians, the Brulé, whom you control."

"About twenty-five hundred," said Spotted Tail.

Sully raised his eyebrows. "And you will voluntarily separate from Red Cloud and the Oglala? You will go where we tell you?"

Spotted Tail lifted his shoulders. "As you say. But I will tell you where we want to go."

"And where is that?" asked Sully.

"The grass is up," said Spotted Tail. "Our ponies can eat and travel far. We want to go south of the Platte, to join our brothers the Cheyenne in the spring buffalo hunt."

Beauvais had a map, and we all looked at it. Spotted Tail was offering to take his entire band south not only of the Platte but of the railroad line, cutting himself off entirely from Red Cloud.

Sully looked up. "That is satisfactory. Will you stay there after the buffalo hunt, to live in peace with your Cheyenne brothers and with the Great Father?"

"If your soldiers leave us alone," said Spotted Tail, "that is our desire."

Sully rose and extended his hand. "That's very generous of you. Tomorrow we'll touch the pen and give you presents for your journey."

Spotted Tail looked at Sully's hand. "Presents are one thing. Guns and powder are another. The buffalo grow fewer and so do our ponies. There is not enough grass to feed the buffalo, the white man's horses and our ponies. We can no longer hunt close up, on horses, with the bow. We must shoot him from afar, like cowards, with the rifle. Will you give us rifles?"

Sully looked to me. As Grant's representative I had discretion to grant this request or no. Rifles could kill not only buffalo, but soldiers and settlers. I knew Spotted Tail's history. If any Sioux could be trusted, it was he. I nodded slowly.

Sully turned to Spotted Tail, his hand still out. "Yes," he said.

The Sioux shook Sully's hand. The other Indians rose and crowded round us, shaking hands, grunting in Sioux, chattering faster than Indian Charlie, his face glistening with sweat, could translate.

That night there was resigned feasting and singing at the Indian camp, in which we gingerly joined. The Indians, though not happy at the journey before them, were glad to get out of the line of fire. We commissioners, though we had accomplished part of our task, still had a long road ahead. Red Cloud was still hostile and defiant on the Powder River, and we had, as yet, not heard the Indian side of the Fetterman massacre.

I was sitting by a campfire, momentarily alone, when Indian Charlie eased out of the dark to squat beside me. "Got a minute?" he said quietly, flicking twigs into the fire.

"What for?" Something in his voice made my skin prickle.

Indian Charlie looked around to see that we were alone. "There's more Indians," he said, his lips barely moving. "Across the river."

I sat up. "Hostile?"

Charlie shook his head. "No. They're afraid you are. Or might be, once you find out."

"Find out what," I frowned at him.

Charlie still had his head down, flicking twigs. "They're Oglala. They were in the Fetterman fight," he murmured. "They want to talk to you."

I rose to my knees, looking around for the other commissioners. "Where's Sully?" I asked him.

"S-s-s-t!" hissed Charlie, motioning me back down. "No quick moves. I told them there was an Indian officer here. They want to see you alone."

Charlie had two horses with him, which we rode quietly across the ford of the darkened river. When we reached the other bank, someone stepped out of the trees and took our bridles. Charlie had a whispered conversation, then we dismounted and were led behind some rocks, where a low campfire showed about twoscore braves huddled around it. I squatted down before the fire so they could see my face, at which grunts of wonder arose. Hands reached out to touch me, as if to see if I was real.

"I hear you know about the Fetterman fight," I said without preliminary.

Charlie translated. The Indians sucked in their breath and looked at each other, each apparently unwilling to speak first. They sat silent for some minutes.

"We weren't there," one of them finally said. "None of us. We only heard from friends who heard from warriors who were there. We know what was said around the fires, that's all."

I looked at Indian Charlie, who shook his head imperceptibly. "We too have heard tales," I said. "I'll tell you what we've heard if you tell me in return." I raised my eyes to the Indians and saw brief nods. "Indians attacked the wood train," I said, "as they'd done before. But this time only a few Indians attacked. Why was that? Was it only the brave Indians who dared attack, while the others waited behind?"

The braves stared at me stone-faced. I stared back and shrugged. "As soon as the soldiers guarding the wood train gave chase, the Indians got scared and ran away. They retreated behind Lodge Trail Ridge, where they knew the soldiers wouldn't follow. But the soldiers did follow, and the Indians became more frightened."

A voice spoke from among the squatting braves. "Who told you this?" Indian Charlie translated, looking for the source of the question.

"Who spoke?" I asked. Nobody moved, but I saw Charlie's eyes on the front row. "You?" I asked a young brave with two eagle feathers in his hair.

The young brave looked around and reluctantly stood. "My name is Two Moons," he said. "I want to know who told you this."

"Carrington," I said. "The commander of the fort."

"Carrington lies," said Two Moons.

"Were you there?" I asked him.

"Carrington lies," Two Moons repeated, sitting down. "What else does he say?"

I told them more, altering Carrington's story to make the Indians seem stupider and luckier than either I or Carrington thought. I kept one eye on Two Moons, whose face stayed steady, but whose body leaned more and more forward, eyes flashing at Indian Charlie's translation. "When the Indians got to Lodge Trail Ridge," I said, "the soldiers were so close the Indians threw down their weapons to run faster. Then the soldiers pursued further than they were ordered, and the thousand Indians who were too afraid to attack the wood train finally came up to defend their friends. Only when the soldiers caught up to them did the Indians turn and fight. They killed all the soldiers, surprised at their luck, then fled to the Powder River, where they trembled in fear lest the other soldiers come and kill them."

Two Moons was frowning darker and darker. When Charlie translated "thousand," he almost leapt from his blanket. He stared at me hard, then looked at other braves around him, from whom he seemed to receive a silent signal.

"There were far less than a thousand warriors," he said. "With bows and arrows and spears. Some had rifles, but no powder. The soldiers were killed with the weapons we've used since time began."

"Were you there?" I asked him quietly.

"I'll tell you how it happened," said Two Moons, avoiding a direct answer, "and you judge for yourself." He looked around at the other braves, who nodded at him.

Two Moons swallowed. "The massacre was no accident. Fetterman may have been stupid and unlucky, but he was made so because we were smart. We planned this raid for three months. Tasunke Witco drew pictures of it in the sand. We rehearsed it many times, once even drawing the soldiers all the way to Lodge Trail Ridge before letting them escape."

I gestured him to continue. This was new.

Two Moons nodded. "We feasted and held ceremonies over Tasunke Witco's plan. Our augurers told us we would succeed, that we would kill one hundred soldiers. The date was chosen with care. The shortest day, when night would close fast and prevent pursuit." Suddenly, Two Moons raised his voice in anger and shook his fist. "Do you think we are fools? Savages? We don't need your almanacs to read the sky. We don't need your glass rod to tell it's cold. We don't need books to teach us strategy. We have it up here." He touched his brow. "And here." He touched his heart.

"You say 'we' now. Two Moons was there," I said.

Two Moons shrugged. "On the day of the attack," he said, "it was Tasunke Witco who led the decoys, who lured Fetterman to his doom. It was he who was the bravest and the loudest, who rode closest to the soldiers, taunting them, defying them, baring his breast to challenge their bullets."

A brave behind Two Moons said something, lifting his hands as if tossing something in the air. "What did he say?" I asked Indian Charlie.

Charlie smirked. "Says Tasunke Witco touches himself and his pony with mole-dirt, from a mole-burrow. Makes his enemies blind as moles. Makes him like he's burrowing under ground."

Two Moons nodded. "Other braves followed Tasunke Witco near the soldiers and rode breastwise past them. We were hiding in the culvert past Lodge Trail Ridge and didn't see them, but we heard them. Tasunke Witco had forbidden us to raise our heads from the rocks until the last soldiers were in the culvert." He touched the small mirror that hung around his neck. "From the hills, other braves were making signals with glass to mark the soldiers' progress."

"How did you get them into the culvert?" I asked him. "They were forbidden to go there."

Two Moons smiled. "That was the great task. Every other time, the soldiers stopped before the ridge and went back to the fort, even though Tasunke Witco taught the decoys things to say."

I frowned. "What things?"

Suddenly, in unaccented English, Two Moons shouted, "Soldier son-of-a-bitch!"

"You coward bastard!" shouted another brave.

"Dumb cock-sucker!" shouted a third.

The Indians fell silent, looking at us for a reaction.

"Do you know what those words mean?" I asked.

Two Moons shrugged. "I only know they make the soldiers mad. But never mad enough to take the bait. So this time Tasunke Witco taught us new words. We had spies, you see. Some pretended to be friendly and got into the fort to trade. Others crept up at night and listened through the walls. Some knew the white man's tongue and pretended not to. We found out who of the soldiers had wives there, and we used it."

"How?" I asked.

"There was a cavalryman, Grummond, his wife was there. So Tasunke Witco shouted, 'Grummond, I fuck your wife in the ahss-hoole!'"

He said it so perfectly he might have been a New York tough.

"Other Indians picked it up," said Two Moons. "Soon all were shouting the words Tasunke Witco had taught them."

"I fuck Mrs. Fetterman!" shouted another brave.

"Fetterman, you wife's a whoore!"

"Grummond, I lick you wife's pussy!"

"Missus Grummond suck my cock!"

Two Moons smiled. "Grummond, the cavalryman, charged first, past the ridge and between the rocks. Tasunke Witco rode in front of him, laughing, letting Grummond almost catch him. The other cavalry followed. When they were all in the culvert, some of us behind the rocks wanted to rise up, but our discipline held. Tasunke Witco told us to wait until the foot soldiers came in, so we could bag them all. And that's what happened. The foot soldiers came in, we all rose up and fired our arrows. It was over faster than you could eat dinner."

Two Moons sat down and smirked. I shook my head, half in admiration. It was a trick the Muslims used against the crusaders. Insult a white man's woman and his head goes hot and empty.

"The two officers, Fetterman and Grummond," I asked. "How did they die?"

"It was very funny," grinned Two Moons. "They were behind some rocks high on the ledge, and we were climbing up toward them, clubbing other soldiers as we went. The soldiers had no time to load the long guns, so they were swinging them like clubs. But close up, a tomahawk is more effective than a rifle, so we chopped them down. But Grummond and Fetterman had revolvers. We let them shoot for awhile, and while we waited for the sixth shot we looked up and they just stood there, looked at each other, and held the revolvers to each other's temples. Then they went 'Hut, hut, hut,' and pulled the triggers. It was cowardly and comical."

"Who is this Tasunke Witco?" I asked Two Moons. "We've never heard of him. Is he greater than Red Cloud?"

Two Moons frowned. "He's different. Red Cloud is a great chief and wise in council. Tasunke Witco is a great warrior. A pure individual whose medicine is very strong."

"He takes no part in ceremonies," said another brave. "He thinks tactics win battles."

"Never shoots from horseback," said a third. "Says it's a waste of arrows."

Phrases bubbled up from the Indians, which Indian Charlie translated as fast as he could, his face sweating not only with the effort but from the portrait that emerged. "Seldom speaks, always listens . . . paints himself with hail spots and streaked lightning . . . wears red-hawk feathers . . . a pebble around his neck prevents him from being wounded . . . doesn't take scalps . . . the purest warrior ever born on the plains."

"Charlie," I asked our translator. "What does the name mean, Tasunke Witco?"

Charlie looked at the sky, squinted, and mumbled, "Something about he saw a horse in a vision, a trance . . ." He looked at me and shrugged. "I guess, maybe, um, Crazy Horse."

Crazy Horse.

Chapter XVIII

A BLACK ROBE
AMONG THE SIOUX

Missouri River 1867

THE NEXT MORNING INDIAN CHARLIE REPORTED THE Indians vanished from the other side of the river. I reported my meeting with them to Sully and Beauvais. "We've got three versions of the Fetterman fight now," said Sully, "the telegraph version of isolated, wanton slaughter, the Carrington version of bravado and bad luck, and the Indian version of a well-laid and executed plan. Which are we inclined to believe?"

"The Indian version," said Beauvais. "It's the only one that explains all the facts. It's also the scariest. We should believe it and hope it isn't true." If it was true, Red Cloud's Oglala were angry and organized, strong, on home turf and learning strategy under a new, young chief named Crazy Horse.

"Still," said Sully, "we've accomplished two-thirds of our mission – find the truth about Fetterman, get Spotted Tail and the Brulé disposed. All that remains is to bring Red Cloud in."

This "all" proved elusive. We spent a few more days at Beauvais's ranch, distributing presents, feasting, watching the Brulé dance for a successful buffalo hunt and picking up more about Red Cloud's war on the Bozeman Trail. Then we saw the Brulé off to the south, where we hoped they'd stay. Sully surprised me by distributing to them the portraits he'd done, which filled them with awe and gratitude. Indian Charlie rode off with them. We then mounted our horses for Fort Laramie, where we hoped finally to meet up with Red Cloud and his Oglala.

We passed the celebrated milestones of the Oregon Trail, Courthouse and Chimney Rocks and Scott's Bluff, and reached Fort Laramie on May 4th. There we sat and waited for Red Cloud, but the only Indians we met were the "Laramie Loafers," seven hundred tame Sioux who huddled in the skirts of the fort. They taught me why Red Cloud and Crazy Horse wanted nothing to do with the white man and his forts. In addition to the smallpox and cholera the white man had brought to the Plains Indians, he was also bringing a subtler plague of lassitude and dependence that settled like a cloud over the Laramie Loafers.

In their encampment I felt like a fat, rich relative poking around his slum origins. The entire population was women, children, old men and cripples. Those who weren't drunk shuffled around hollow-eyed, drained of hope and incentive. "Where are your young men?" I asked Big Mouth, their leader.

He waved his flabby arm north toward the Bighorn Mountains and the Black Hills. "Joined the wild ones. There's nothing for them here."

"You should be planting things," I told him. "Where are your rakes and hoes, the seeds the government sends you?"

"Rusted away," said Big Mouth. "The soil is too hard and the people too lazy. We throw away the seeds and use the sacks for clothing."

"Spotted Tail is gone south to join the Cheyenne," I said. "Wouldn't you be better off joining him? Fresh air, the hunt, self-sufficiency."

Big Mouth looked at me with red-rimmed eyes and lifted a whiskey jug to his lips. "We have all we need here," he said sadly. "My people no longer want freedom. They wouldn't know what to do with it."

Finally, as Red Cloud stayed aloof, orders came for General Sully and me to return to Omaha, thence north along the Missouri to Dakota Territory, to report to Washington on the northern tribes. Beauvais joined us for the ride back to the railhead. We crossed the north branch of the Platte and headed south to intersect the railroad, which, with spring, had stretched further and further west. We had no idea yet how far it had progressed from its winter terminus at North Platte. Hill rolled after hill, strange outcroppings of rock loomed on the horizon and hovered there, seeming to draw no closer as our horses plodded along. Distances were impossible to calculate. A rocky hummock, that seemed a few miles distant at sunrise, seemed equally distant at sunset, as if we walked a treadmill in the unchanging wilderness. After several days' ride in open country we started to meet logging and hunting parties who waved us southward. Then one afternoon we crested a rise and saw the line of track creeping like a lengthening serpent across the plains, attended by swarms of tiny men and machines.

"Don't look like much from a distance, does it?" said Beauvais. From end-of-track, which we could see about a mile off, a line of stakes led over the horizon, followed by hundreds of men throwing earth up to make a level grade. An engine sat chuffing, and hooked behind it was what looked like a whole Main Street on wheels, mobile warehouses, dormitories, and workshops, looking less like railroad cars than houses perched on flatbeds. Many of them sprouted chimneys, others were like blockhouses, with cargo winches angling outward. Mule teams hauled covered wagons alongside, and near end-of-track eight-horse wagons unloaded piles of wooden ties. On both sides of the track, detachments of soldiers lounged in the shade of their wagons, and Pawnee scouts rode about raising whoops and clouds of dust. There were over four thousand men on the plains – graders, trackmen, trainmen, masons, bridge-builders, surveyors, tie-cutters, lumberjacks, cooks, and laborers – and we could see many of them from our hilltop. In two months the serpent had crept a hundred miles from North Platte, more than a mile and a half a day. Yet how insignificant it seemed, how fragile the line of track in the vastness of the plain! The thousands of workers were like a few lone swimmers, bobbing in the sea, the railroad a thin lifeline thrown out to them. But that thin line had divided the buffalo, broken apart whole nations of Indians and promised to exterminate both.

We had barely made camp at the rear of the railroad assemblage, near the telegraph tent, when we heard a whoop, and several Pawnee scouts rode in, pointing to a dust cloud on the horizon. "Sioux!" they shouted.

Detachments of soldiers trotted down the line, followed by several batteries of mountain howitzers. Work ceased, as graders and rail-carriers made for the shelter of the work-train.

"What the hell Sioux could that be?" said Beauvais.

"Too much dust for a raiding party," said Sully.

We mounted and rode forward until we were just behind the troops, drawn up in a double rank across the track line, the flanks anchored by the howitzers. More Pawnee scouts crested the rise and rode down toward us. When they got close enough, we could see they were laughing.

"Spotted Tail and all his squaws," laughed one. "Wandering like lost rabbits."

Beauvais, Sully and I urged our horses forward. The troops stood relaxed, and as we rode through them, I heard someone mutter, "Damn, I wuz spilin' for a fight."

A little ways out the Sioux started coming over the ridge, Spotted Tail in front with some warriors, and Indian Charlie alongside. Strung out behind them were the entire band of twenty-five hundred Brulé that had gone with Spotted Tail to join the Cheyenne and hunt buffalo. Horses and dogs pulled travois made of lodge-poles, while the women and children walked alongside, and the men rode dispirited horses. All eyes, including the horses' and the dogs', saw only the ground in front of them as they trudged along, covered with sweat and streaked with grime. A cloud of dust and flies hovered over the column.

"Spotted Tail," I said, reining in and turning to ride alongside him. "What happened?"

Spotted Tail looked at me with red-rimmed eyes, shook his head, and nudged Indian Charlie to speak. "Hancock got there before us," said the boy.

"Hancock?" frowned Sully. "General Hancock?"

"Yes," said Charlie. "Old Man of the Thunder and his henchman, Iron Backsides Custer. He rode with his men out of St. Louis as soon as the snow stopped. When we reached the Republican River, we met Cheyenne coming the other way. Hancock had burned their village, destroyed all but their ponies and blankets and sent the Cheyenne fleeing. There will be no buffalo hunt this season. How can we hunt when the soldiers burn the grass, burn our weapons and chase us from our homes?"

Spotted Tail, too tired to summon his limited English, exploded in a torrent of Sioux, which Indian Charlie, in tears, translated. "What kind of men are you? At Beauvais's ranch you tell us to go south. Down south, Hancock makes us go north. Do you condemn us to wander till we die? Every direction we go we are attacked by soldiers, who stand between us and our homes, the homes you promised us. Where shall we go now? Tell us, please."

"This blasted army!" Sully shook his fist. "Too many damn generals!"

We found a place for Spotted Tail and his bedraggled group to make camp far enough from the railroad, the soldiers, and the Pawnee. There we left them, erecting tepees and building cooking fires, while we took Spotted Tail and Indian Charlie to the telegraph tent. Messages flashed all afternoon between us, Omaha, St. Louis, and Washington, trying to straighten out what General Hancock had done and why, and what we were supposed to do with Spotted Tail.

Replies trickled in. Acting on his own Hancock had ridden forth to let the Cheyenne know there would be no Fetterman massacre on *his* turf. The Cheyenne ran from Hancock's advance, abandoning their villages, which Hancock burned. Now the Cheyenne were scattered across the prairie, mad as hell, raiding ranches and stage depots, disrupting the railroad, and causing the havoc Hancock had sought to prevent. Spotted Tail and his Brulé, caught in the middle and determined to stay peaceful, now wandered the plain like vagabonds.

"What shall we do with Spotted Tail now?" we telegraphed to Washington, and while waiting a reply, sat around the tent bewailing our Indian policy.

"Hancock was blind!" groused Sully. "He thinks that Indians fight like a white army. He figgered that destroying the Indians' supplies would destroy their fighting ability. But all he destroyed was the food for the women and children. Warriors live off the land, and now they're angry and doing just that."

"On the contrary," came a clipped voice from the tent entrance. "Hancock was superb. So was Custer. I've never seen warriors act with such decorum and humanity."

A young man with a dark mustache stood at the tent flap, pulling off a pair of long cavalry gloves. He had a blue felt hat pushed back atop his wavy black hair, a dusty blue cape thrown over one shoulder and cavalry trousers stuffed into the tops of rawhide boots. His accent was English, and he looked like a refugee from a theatrical troupe.

"Who the devil are you?" barked Sully.

"Stanley," said the newcomer briskly, coming forward and shaking our reluctant hands. "Missouri *Democrat*. Also New York *Times* and *Herald*, Chicago *Republican* and a few others. I was with Hancock and Custer. I saw the whole thing."

"Hancock's two hundred miles south!" sputtered Sully. "How did you get here?"

Stanley shrugged. "Followed the Indians. I figured they'd head toward the railroad. I needed the telegraph. To file my stories. May I?"

He moved toward the key operator, but Sully grabbed his elbow. "Not so fast, youngster. You followed the Indians? Two hundred miles across the plain? Alone?"

"Of course." Stanley drew back, peeling Sully's hand away. "Most direct route, eh? I kept well back, out of sight. Ate what I could carry." He patted his stomach. "Got dicey the last few days. Your mess set up?"

Sully pushed the reporter onto a canvas stool and stood over him. "You'll eat when I tell you. And you'll tell your story to your papers only after I hear it!"

Stanley brushed his sleeves and straightened his clothes, muttering "I say" and looking to the rest of us for aid. Finding none, he told his story straightforwardly enough. He'd marched out with Hancock on assignment from his papers, hovered around headquarters taking notes, interviewed settlers who had suffered Indian depredations, witnessed a parley where the Cheyenne chiefs had proved "damned hostile," and watched tepees go up in smoke and flame, "like signal beams at sea."

"Hancock had cannons," Stanley concluded, tossing one leg over the other. "He could have wiped them out. Nits breed lice, as General Sherman says. Instead he decided on a simple demonstration of power. It was a superb gesture of restraint."

Sully, after listening with his arms folded and eyes smoldering, pointed a finger in the reporter's face. "Hancock's superb *gesture*," he growled through clenched teeth, "has turned a peaceful tribe into migrants. He has undone in one day what it took us four months to accomplish." He gave Stanley chapter and verse about our commission's charter and our success with Spotted Tail and told him to write it down. "Now where do they go?" he demanded. "They can't go south, because Hancock's there. They can't go north, because Red Cloud's there. All we can do is find them some poor corner of land in between, devoid of game, empty because nobody else wants it. And there they'll sit, unable to hunt because the plains are at war, dependent on the government for handouts, growing demoralized and despondent. Your 'superb' Hancock produced a nation of beggars."

The newspaperman dutifully took notes, then tapped his lips with a finger, frowning and nodding. "I see," he said quietly. "This business may be more complicated than I thought." It was the watchword for everyone who stepped into Indian affairs.

Eventually we let Stanley use the telegraph to report to his papers. Over the next few days the government gave Spotted Tail a chunk of territory south of the Platte, away from the line of the railroad, to wander and hunt until a "definite and satisfactory arrangement" could be found. Stanley followed Sully around like a puppy, his allegiance transferred from the "superb" Hancock to the less glamorous veteran of the plains.

Then Beauvais left for his ranch, and Stanley accompanied us back along the railroad line to catch the eastbound train for Omaha. With the good weather and the track shored up, the trip was now the advertised fifteen hours, enlivened by an incessant stream of chatter from Stanley, who, for all his youth, claimed vast travels. Oh, yes, he said, the Indians were barbarians, begging my pardon of course, but they couldn't hold a candle to the Turks, who buggered and butchered their captives, paring them away a limb at a time. Oh, yes, he'd spent time in a Turkish prison, and damned if he wouldn't like to go back and bugger a few of the black buggers who'd buggered him.

He gave a vivid description of Wild Bill Hickock, who had ridden out with Hancock, and, when asked about his own background, poured a torrent of hair-raising blarney that, if only half-true, would have filled a lifetime for a man twice his age. He was "born a bastard" in Wales, raised in a Welsh workhouse, shipped as a deck hand from Liverpool to New Orleans, bummed and traded up and down the Mississippi, joined the Confederate army, got wounded and captured at Shiloh, joined the Union army, got sick, got discharged, took a ship back to Liverpool. Got shipwrecked off Barcelona and swam ashore, shipped back to the U.S., where he joined the Union Navy, fought at Fort Fisher, deserted at Baltimore, and made his way to New Orleans, where he joined a theatrical troupe bound for Omaha and Denver. From Denver he hopped to the California gold fields, came up empty, hiked over the Rockies, floated a barge down the Platte back to Omaha, joined an expedition to Turkey, where he got "jailed and jiggered within an inch of my life," escaped, sold his story to a newspaper and finally joined the Hancock expedition as a roving reporter. "Look," he said, showing us the buttons on his navy vest, which showed the Ottoman crescent and star.

At Omaha we pried loose from chattering Stanley and boarded a ferry across the river to Council Bluffs, where we would meet the third member of our commission, about whom Sully had been enigmatic, pocketing the telegram that named him and grinning mysteriously whenever I asked. Off the gangplank, we threaded past workers hoisting cargo, Indians selling blankets and pottery, Negro families standing bewildered amidst their few belongings, dockside lawyers and land sharks with barrels and chairs as their offices. At the edge of the crowd stood a black-robed priest, a squat and powerful-looking old man with his arms folded across a massive chest, squinting at the debarking crowd. When he spotted us, he gave a whoop of joy, threw his arms wide, and rushed straight at us, enfolding Sully in a bear-hug, lifting him from the ground and jouncing him like a sack of grain.

"Easy there, Father. Easy," protested Sully, prying at the enfolding hands, mindful both of his dignity and of his ribs, which the robust priest bade fair to crack.

Releasing Sully, the black robe assessed me, as if calculating whether he could hoist me too, but decided against it, instead extending his hand. "I am Pierre-Jean de Smet," he said. My hand, which I had extended, went limp at the name, so when the little priest grabbed it he came near wrenching my arm from its socket. "F-father de Smet," I stammered. "I'm Ely Parker."

"Of course you are!" exulted the priest, continuing to pump my arm and examining my face with clear blue eyes. "Your fame precedes you! Do-ne-ho-ga-wa, General Grant's own private Indian!"

"My fame," I scoffed. "I'm a scribe. But what Indian hasn't heard of Black Robe?" At his sobriquet the priest crinkled his wrinkled face and pumped my hand until my teeth rattled and I put my hand on his shoulder to stop him. He stood back, hands folded, and nodded as if welcoming a pair of lost nephews.

"Come," he said. "The tavern. Drinks for the travelers." And if we hadn't forestalled him by diving for our luggage, Father de Smet would have hoisted all our bags and hauled them along the quay himself.

Black Robe! I marveled as de Smet and Sully chatted along ahead of me. Father Pierre-Jean de Smet, at least as old as the century, was revered among the Indians. Born in Belgium, he was already hard at work in this country when I was a boy, traveling alone through Indian country. By 1840 he had established a mission here at Council Bluffs, then a rough outpost of Potawatomie Indians and French traders. He traveled west by wagon train before anybody had heard of the Oregon Trail, preaching among the Flathead in western Wyoming, returning to St. Louis via the Yellowstone and Missouri Rivers, a circle of nearly five thousand miles that soon became for him a seasonal jaunt. He had gone round Cape Horn to Oregon Territory, founding missions on the Willamette and Columbia Rivers and wintering as far north as Ft. Edmonton on the Saskatchewan River. He had crossed the plains a score of times, ascending and descending the Missouri as if it were his backyard creek. Settlers and soldiers arriving in Wyoming and Montana, in Washington and Oregon, were amazed to find the local Indians speaking rudimentary English and chanting the Latin mass – thanks to Father de Smet.

During the Sioux uprising of the mid-sixties in Minnesota and the Dakotas, Father de Smet was the only white man who could walk into an Indian camp, smoke with the leaders and argue for peace. The Indians we were about to visit on the upper Missouri were those who had most recently heard the spells and wisdom of Black Robe.

At a waterfront tavern we ordered wine, and Father de Smet fumbled into the folds of his cassock, from which he produced various pieces of paper. "I tell you, my friends," he said. "How this country has shrunk!" He raised two fingers. "Two days ago – two! – I was in St. Louis. I take the night train to Chicago, and I'm there in fourteen hours! I arrive there yesterday morning. At noon yesterday I leave Chicago. Today, here I am, one day later, on what used to be the rim of the world!" He shook his head and chuckled. "First time I came here, 1838, I walked most of the way from St. Louis, *pedibus apostolorum*, staff in hand. Thirty days it took me. Now it's thirty hours. Our days have become hours, and our hours minutes. But our wisdom?" He tapped his head. "It is still a slow and plodding thing, eh? Let's not be deceived. We have no quick work ahead of us." Father de Smet unrolled a map he produced from his cassock, anchoring the corners with wineglasses.

"Two days ago," said Sully, "we were in Colorado. Halfway between Denver and Fort Laramie. That's where the railroad's reached now. When it's done, Laramie will be a one-day trip from here."

De Smet shook his head. "We used to be lucky to reach Laramie in two months." He looked at us with those bright blue eyes. "Ah well, the east-west route may have shrunk, but where we're going, up the Missouri, not much has changed. Rivers don't yield as easily as the land." He pointed a finger at the map and traced the line of the Missouri. The priest's hand, like his arms and chest, was broad and thick and powerful. When he stabbed at landmarks the table shook.

"The Sioux agency at Yankton," said de Smet. "Just above Sioux City. That's our first landfall. From there we go overland *pedibus equorum et asinorum*, to meet the river again at Fort Rice, which is the farthest point upriver that may be said to be at peace. Beyond there are the Sioux, who have formed a coalition that is growing every day. All hatchets are raised against the whites and the peaceful tribes. Hundreds of scalps flutter from their lances. Eagle feathers are in great demand throughout the northern Dakotas. Their horses' manes and tails are covered with them – each plume denoting a scalp taken from the enemy. We go overland to Fort Rice slowly, so the Sioux may slowly rally to our approach."

Next day we boarded the sternwheel steamer *Guidon* for the trip upriver to the Yankton agency. I had never seen a vessel so crowded, an emigrant boat, with families and merchandise bound for the new territories of Montana and Idaho. Every inch of deck space held cargo and passengers, bales of cotton and cloth, farm and mining implements, crates of picks and shovels and drilling equipment.

"Gold," sniffed Father de Smet, settling on a clear space near the rail, waving his hand at the crowded deck. "This is what's causing Red Cloud his trouble in the Powder River country. Montana gold. It drove the Cherokee from Georgia, the Modoc from California, now it's driving the Sioux from the only place left." He shook his head in disgust and put his hand on my arm. "I discovered that gold twenty-five years ago," he said, winking and putting his finger beside his nose. "Oh, yes, my friend. Way up at the Three Forks of the Missouri, right where all these people are heading. I was up there at my St. Mary's mission – it's gone now – and I could see the gold shimmering in the water. I knew these people would come for it some day, but not by my doing. So I kept quiet. Didn't pick up a single nugget. Twenty years later, somebody did, and you see the result. The hills are on fire."

During the week it took us to steam up to the Yankton agency, two hundred fifty river miles from Council Bluffs, Sully and de Smet pointed out landmarks. "Look here," said de Smet, pointing at a mound of earth

overlooking the bank. "Here is the grave of Blackbird, the Omaha chief."
A few miles later, on the opposite side, he pointed to a high bluff. "There
is buried Sergeant Charles Floyd, who died on the Lewis and Clark
expedition. Two graves, my friend, of men who died at the same time,
but in two different epochs. Blackbird probably never saw a white man,
and Floyd had seen few Indians. Now Blackbird's few remaining Omaha
are confined to a reservation, and white men like Floyd have named a city
after them."

At Yankton we were met by a group of Yankton Indians who would
be our guides and translators for the overland trip to Fort Rice. They had
gathered wagons, mules and saddle horses for the journey, but my count
of the creatures and equipment came up a little short.

"Do not worry, my friend," said de Smet. "I have my own little wagon
and traveling companions. They should be arriving soon."

Father de Smet had shipped his wagon, two mules and a saddle
horse aboard the *Bighorn*, which hove into view the next day. Hearing the
steamboat's whistle, de Smet bustled down to the dock, robe and hands
a-flutter, as nervous as an expectant father. "You must forgive me," he
laughed, seeing my amusement. "They are my children."

It didn't take him long after the *Bighorn* docked to clap eyes on his
darlings. The first passengers off the boat, to the delight both of those on
board and on shore, were the two mules and the horse. Full of purpose, they
clattered down the ramp, and, ignoring de Smet's welcoming cries, made
straight for a grassy bank, where they hurled themselves on the ground
and rolled over and over, as if to attach themselves permanently to *terra
firma*. The first to regain his feet, the little horse capered about, tossing
his mane and whinnying, nipping at the hindquarters of the mules to make
them kick. The mules obliged by chasing the horse in a circle, then the
horse wheeled and chased the mules, then all three of them chased their
tails in a circle, whinnying and hee-hawing and drawing a happy crowd.

Father de Smet doubled over with laughter, clapping his hands on
his knees. "Like landlubbers returned to shore, are they not?" he gasped.
"Come here, my pretties."

The animals at length acknowledged his presence and trotted over
to accept onions and carrots from his hands. But the food reminded them
that they were not only free, but hungry, and they were soon back on the
grassy bank, tearing out green tufts and chewing and swallowing as if

they'd never eat again, rolling their eyes and nodding at each other. When, reluctantly, they let Father de Smet corral them for the night, each beast had a belly like a drum, and their tickled master was calling them "my darling haybags."

On the first of June, we set out overland for Fort Rice. Besides Sully, de Smet, and me, we had a few Yankton Indians, among them Black Eagle and a comical, round little chief with the unpronounceable name of Pananniapapi. We followed Father de Smet in calling him Pani. Black Eagle and Pani each gathered a small retinue, making a party of about a dozen, with three small mule-driven wagons carrying our supplies and gifts for the Indians.

The land behind the small settlement of Yankton rises slightly away from the river, then descends into gentle hills. The first time I turned in my saddle and looked back, I could still see the town and the river, but a few miles later when I looked, town and river were gone, and we were alone on a sea of grass. Between us and the gold fields of Montana lay only a few forts, a few trading posts, and some isolated farms, mostly abandoned now in the face of the Sioux threat, then miles and miles of grass and hills. I was seeing the country as it must have appeared to the Sioux when they first saw it a millennium ago.

And what country it was! Spring was in full bloom, grasslands reaching to the horizon, dotted with wildflowers winking like phosphorus on the waves. Like lone swimmers we made no impression on the landscape. The grasses closed to cover our tracks as we passed. Pheasants, grouse and prairie chickens, startled from their thickets, fluttered aloft with a whisper of beating wings. Deer and antelope spied us from the heights and scampered off. No wonder the white man wanted this country; no wonder the Indians wanted to keep it.

Round little Chief Pani rode between me and de Smet, as chatty and voluble as tall Black Eagle was austere. Seeing my Indian face, which had drawn only a shrug from Black Eagle, he'd got it fixed in his mind that I was a tame Sioux who would understand the Yankton tongue. So he chattered to de Smet in broken English, pointing out features of the landscape, then turned to me and repeated himself in Siouan. When I shook my head, he slowed down, speaking every word loudly and slowly, like an Englishman instructing a Hottentot. I soon started answering him in Seneca, which puzzled him at first. Siouan and Seneca share nothing but a certain chantiness, but Pani, reluctant to admit ignorance, answered in his own tongue, I responded in mine, and soon we two Indians were chatting uncomprehendingly to each other, laughing and nodding, so tickling Father de Smet that he nearly fell off his horse.

We camped at night in a grove of trees by a brook, and the Indians, riding out for game, returned not only with rabbits and pheasants but with a few more Indians. Though the visitors raised Sully's and my eyebrows, they seemed business as usual to Father de Smet and the Yanktons. They blended right in, cutting willow and cottonwood branches and bundling them up to make beds, filling the kettles and coffee pots, stripping the game and roasting it on sticks. They chatted with the other Indians and with us, passed the pipe, rolled up and went to sleep, same as we did, as soon as it was dark, and when we rose at dawn they were gone.

"Wilderness telegraph," explained Father de Smet. "The word will spread that Black Robe is here. Many lodges will meet us at Fort Rice. That is why we travel overland, to let the word spread."

Every night the pattern repeated, strange Indians riding softly into camp, bringing food, eating, smoking and chatting with us, then rolling up to sleep and disappearing before dawn. After awhile, some of the strangers rode along with us, then more, and a few more the next day. We were sweeping a great arm across the prairie, gathering in the tribes. By the time I felt the ground slope downwards and sensed that we were approaching the river again, our band had trebled, and when the river and Fort Rice came into view at the end of two weeks' journey, over a hundred lodges were gathered around the walls of the fort.

The fort's main structure, a cottonwood-log stockade four hundred feet square, enclosed agency buildings and storehouses of impressive size, clearly visible as we rode down the grassy slope to the fort and the river beyond. It was a peaceful and bucolic sight, with a few soldiers and civilians going about their business inside the stockade, herds of cattle and horses grazing on the perimeter, the white tepees of the Indians with the white smoke from their fires drifting into the blue sky, and beyond, the Missouri rolling gently southward. It took a leap of imagination to remind myself that the whites and the Indians were but a few angry words from each other's throats, that the blue sky of the Dakotas could turn suddenly black with storm, and that the gently rolling Missouri concealed shoals and sandbars that could sink a huge steamboat without a trace.

From inside the fort, looking out from the top of the blockhouse, we could see the Indian lodges and the horizon dotted with horsemen and horse-led travois kicking up plumes of dust as they descended to the council grounds around the fort.

"Who's here?" I asked the priest.

Father de Smet pointed out the different lodges, all of which looked the same to me. "Many Sioux tribes – Blackfeet, Brulé, Sans Arc, Minneconjou, even some Oglala. This is good, General. If some of the Sioux bands desire peace, that leaves fewer on the warpath."

The precarious state of the peace was evident as soon as we sat down with the Indians. The protocol of the meeting was what I had got used to at Beauvais's ranch – we sat in chairs while the Indians spread buffalo robes and squatted thereon, giving the unfortunate impression of submissive savages sitting at the feet of their uniformed masters. That this was illusory was evident from the first words of the Brulé chief Iron Lance to Father de Smet.

"What are you doing here?" he demanded. "You, Black Robe, we know you. You bring good medicine. You sprinkle us with water and say holy words. But these others? Why bring more generals among us? You know what we need. They know what we need. Give us what we need and leave us alone."

Father de Smet shifted in his chair. "Yes, I know," he said. "That is the white man's way. You talk until your face turns blue, and he nods, writes something in his book, promises to take care of it, and next year another white man comes and asks you the same thing." The Indians nodded and muttered to each other.

"But this time," said Father de Smet, "I bring you two men of great influence, sent direct from the Great Father. You know General Sully. Three times he has come into the territory to make war on the Sioux. Now, at the Great Father's request, he comes to make peace. And with him he has sent a great warrior and a great peacemaker." De Smet put his hand on my arm. "General Parker is Do-ne-ho-ga-wa of the great eastern tribe of the Iroquois Seneca, a tribe that very early felt the white man's lash. He is here to tell you how his tribe survived, and how they now prosper though surrounded by whites. They till the soil, they build barns and houses, they go to school. They speak English as well as their own tongue."

"Well, now, what of that?" interrupted Iron Lance. "For five years, since the Crow Creek Agency was built, the white man has come among us and told us to learn English. For five years we have asked for an English teacher. For five years the white man has nodded, written 'send English teacher' in his book, and gone away. And for five years, no English teacher arrives. I speak English, and a few others do. But our children? How can they go to schools that don't exist? How can they learn English without a teacher?"

Father de Smet shook his head. "This is a great tragedy," he said. "The Indian is hard to change. He is born with a cosmology in his brain, and anything that deviates is 'new medicine.' You tell him that the world is round, that it revolves around the sun, that men are descended from apes, he'll frown and nod and call it 'strange medicine.' Or he'll laugh. But he won't believe it. So when a tribe of Indians decide they want to learn the new medicine of English the time to teach them is *now*, before the impulse passes. But five years have passed, and nothing is done."

As the days continued we met more and more Indians in council, among them Iron Eyes, White Hawk, Hunting Bear, White Bear, Ghost, Yellow Hawk, and a quartet that told a story with their names: Dispersed-the-Bears, Killed-the-First, Took-the-Enemy and Served-as-Shield. They were angry but resigned. They knew, like their western Brulé cousins who rode with Spotted Tail, that resistance was useless. But they complained bitterly of broken promises.

"Only send us what you've promised," pleaded Iron Lance, "and our young braves will no longer flee to join the wild ones."

Just when I thought I could take no more tales of woe, a storm arose one night from the west with such speed and raining with such fury that I was sure we should all be washed away. The morning found the fort still high and dry, but, ascending the blockhouse to assess the damage among the Indian lodges, I was appalled to see many of the tepees lying flat on the ground, their owners scurrying about in agitation.

I found Father de Smet at the foot of the blockhouse stairs. "The Indian camp is destroyed," I said. "The storm has left them flat."

The priest's blue eyes twinkled, and he couldn't suppress a laugh. "Ah, no, my friend," he said, reaching up to clap me on the shoulder. "The storm caused no damage at all. The Indians are disassembling their own lodges and moving west."

"But the council. . .?" I sputtered.

"If we want further talks, we must go with them," he said. "Something else arrived in the night along with the storm. Scouts came back with word that *pte* has arrived in the west, a day, maybe two days' ride away. Too close to resist." The priest's eyes sparkled with excitement.

"*Pte?*" I said, not sure if I'd heard properly.

"Yes, yes," said the priest, tugging at my sleeve. "Come, we shall join them. *Pte* is Oglala for Uncle. That's what they call him."

"Call who?" I said, unsure what sort of medicine man could cause such excitement.

"Why the buffalo, of course," cried Father de Smet. "Come, child of the Tonawanda, you're going on a buffalo hunt!"

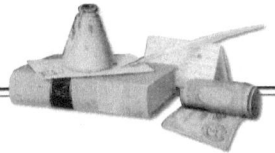

Chapter XIX

MEET THE BUFFALO!
MEET ROCKEFELLER!

Dakota and Cleveland 1867

IN BARELY THE TIME IT TOOK TO SADDLE MY HORSE, THE
Indian village was flattened, packed up and moving west, the lodgepoles
dragging behind the dogs and horses, becoming the legs of travois. It was
like the fall of 1863 when Grant at Vicksburg was ordered to Chattanooga.
At noon the orders arrived. By two the tents were struck and lay white and
flat on the fields. By nightfall, we were untying from Vicksburg dock and
steaming north. I had then thought Grant a whirlwind, but he was nothing
to the Sioux nation.

"But what of the council?" I protested to Father de Smet as we rode
west near the head of the column.

"The council is over," said the priest. He was riding along extremely
relaxed, one knee crooked over the pommel of his Spanish saddle,
showing a sturdy high-heeled boot under his black robe. "The buffalo
hunt sweeps everything before it." He laughed and shook his head.
"I was at Fort Laramie in 1851, where, after months of labor, we had
gathered the western tribes to sign a treaty protecting the Oregon Trail.
A thousand lodges! Ten thousand Indians from a dozen nations! Biggest
gathering of Indians ever on the plains. For two weeks we wrangled, until
all tribes signed the treaty and a good thing too. The next day, buffalo
were sighted three days south, and ten thousand Indians vanished like
the dew."

"They couldn't wait?" I protested. I waved my hand at the procession of Indians in our wake. "These can't wait? Certainly the buffalo can wait?"

Father de Smet shook his head. "The buffalo are magic. Though the herds are diminished, there are still millions. But to find them?" He shrugged. "You'll go to sleep one night at the edge of a valley, with nothing but grass from rim to rim. When you wake up in the morning, the valley is all buffalo, calmly grazing, snouts to the wind, as if God had snapped his fingers and *voila!* Buffalo! They appear like manna and are as fragile. You must pluck them quickly before they vanish again."

"Oh, come," I said skeptically. "They can't be so elusive. Surely they have seasonal migration patterns. Surely they seek out watering holes and streams. Why not just go where you found them last year and wait?"

The priest shook his head. "No, no, no. You'd think so, but no. The plains, you will find them criss-crossed with buffalo trails, some cut six feet into the earth. But do they lead anyplace? No. You could sit by a trail all summer and not see a single one, because this year they went someplace else. You could sit by a watering hole all summer, and see none. The buffalo is like the camel, he has a big hump. He never gets thirsty."

"But seasonal migrations," I frowned. "They must have patterns, like birds."

The priest shrugged. "After a fashion, but nothing reliable. He drifts south in summer, north in winter. But he migrates up and down as well. Upslope in summer, downslope in winter. He goes where the grass is. He's perfectly designed for the prairie and the plains." The priest laughed. "But not for the rivers. Every year he tries to swim and he drowns. At the great falls of the Missouri I have seen grizzly bears, year after year, sitting at the bottom of the falls, waiting for the buffalo to tumble down to them."

The train of Indians spread half a mile across the plains. In front rode Iron Lance and the other chiefs, heads of sometimes warring bands united in the hunt. Around them capered younger braves on their ponies, darting in and out of the column, riding across the plain to the horizon, then wheeling to return and urge the others on. To the rear stretched the caravan, dogs and horses with poles on either flank, dragging whole villages behind them. Women rode the horses or walked alongside them, while children rode, walked, scampered about, sometimes hitching a ride on the swinging travois. Also on the travois rode the elders and squaws who were pregnant or too fat to walk. One old dame lounged on her back as the travois glided along, painting her face in a bit of mirror, holding court like Cleopatra.

"Won't the buffalo hear us coming?" I asked de Smet, smiling at the gypsy caravan that rollicked about us. "Or at least see the dust?"

"It's not as disorganized as it looks," said the priest. "We make no bee-line, eh? We wander with the wind." He pointed at the chiefs in the van. "They keep the wind in their faces and lead the column as the wind shifts. We stay downwind of the buffalo, so no dust nor scent enters his big nose." As I so often found, the seeming chaos of the Indians had method in it.

We made night camp along a stream, parties of young braves riding in to assure us that "Uncle" was still out there, perhaps three hours' ride away. Though we had little to eat, munching dried meat and parched corn, the affair had a festal atmosphere. The Indians, solemn and sedate in council, literally let down their hair, braiding feathers into their locks, painting their faces, building bonfires and singing and dancing into the night.

How did I, an Indian in name if no longer in spirit, react to these festivities? Did I feel an atavistic surge of identity with my red brethren? Did my blood boil with ancestral longing for the tribe, the hunt, the dance and the slaughter? Did I leap up, tear off the white man's uniform and hurl myself, howling, into the fray that flickered and chanted and leapt around the campfire?

No. I sat cross-legged with Sully and de Smet, smoking the pipes that were passed to me, nodding, smiling and watching like a white hunter on safari, disturbed at how closely the natives resemble him. It won't do you any good, I wanted to tell them, to dance and yell and paint yourselves till dawn. The buffalo will be there or not, and you'll kill them or not, regardless of how you dance tonight. And why *this* dance, which you've danced for centuries, never varying a step? Why dance and chant in endless circles, kicking up the dust? I sat nodding and smiling, pretending to enjoy it, but there was one Indian there that night who wanted nothing more than to be back east, in white tie and white gloves, whirling around a ballroom with a little white girl named Minniesackett.

In the morning, covering all bets, the Indians put on clothes, stripped their paint, braided their hair and sat reverently while Father de Smet said mass, baptized those who asked and gave communion from a silver chalice. "The Indians say that any medicine is good medicine, and the more medicine the better," smiled the priest. "I'm not sure they understand the mass, but God understands their hearts."

Only the hunting party rode out that morning, a hundred or so braves and chiefs along with Sully, de Smet and me. The others kept busy in the camp, the women erecting racks for drying the meat. It reminded me of an army on the day of battle, the infantry marching out to the front, the staffs and support troops remaining behind, the supply wagons protected, the surgeons preparing their instruments. We rode for about an hour, the hunting party far less festive today. They held to their reins and stared straight ahead, silent and determined. The scouts, instead of riding out together, with whoops and thundering hooves, advanced singly and silently, and when they returned it was with a quick and muttered message, their ponies' feet whispering on the prairie floor.

I slapped a mosquito, loud enough to turn heads toward me. I slapped at another, and another and found Father de Smet smiling at me. "Here," he said, handing me a cloth. "Put this over your head." It was a wide-mesh burlap sack, which I felt foolish donning until I saw the Indians pulling on similar hoods. Father de Smet had one too, and the sight of the black-robed priest with a burlap sack on his head set me giddy.

"Have you read Washington Irving?" I asked him. "You're the headless horseman."

"Sh-h-h!" said the priest, raising his finger to his swathed lips. "It's buffalo sign," he whispered, riding close to me. "They draw the mosquitoes. And look there." He pointed at the horizon, two miles distant, where the air was dark and alive. "Birds," he said. "They're just above the herd. The buffalo draws the bugs, the bugs draw the birds and they all draw the Indian. Food chain, eh? Like gulls flapping over schools of fish."

The air now became full, not only of mosquitoes, but of something like feathers or milkweed pods, a fluffy substance that made the air palpable, and, along with the mosquitoes, set the horses to snuffling and blowing, shaking their ears and manes.

"Buffalo shed," said Father de Smet. "They are losing their winter coats. When you see them, they will not be the shaggy buffalo of song and story, but mangy and tattered, patches of hair clinging to them like the sails of a derelict ship."

We marched blindly on. "Stop, my friend. Dismount." Father de Smet's gentle voice and gentle hand on my reins halted me. Around me about half the braves were dismounting and hefting rifles, shooing their ponies back. The mounted half was dividing in two, trotting away from each other in two arcs that would take them to opposite horizons. I had still not seen a buffalo.

"Come here," said Father de Smet, motioning to Sully and me. We ascended a small rise, and there they were.

We lay belly-down, overlooking a sloping valley, like a dish scooped out of the earth, surrounded by low hills. It measured several miles across, every inch covered with buffalo, of all shapes and sizes. There were huge bulls on the slopes, as if in a protective perimeter, and the middle of the valley was alive with cows and calves. The calves frolicked, butting each other and kicking up dirt, but the rest were eating, snouts to the earth, pulling out grass, chewing, swallowing, thinking about it and going back for more. Now and then I'd see what looked like a puff of smoke.

"What's that?" I asked Father de Smet.

The priest pulled off his burlap hood and shaded his eyes, and so did I. The mosquitoes were either less intense or, having Uncle to feed on, considered us poor seconds. "Wallowing," he said. "That's what he does when he's not eating. He throws himself on the ground and kicks up dust."

Left and right from where we lay on the lee of the slope, fifty or so Indian riflemen deployed at regular intervals, in a pretty-near regulation firing line. I felt for my revolver, wondering if, when the time came, I'd have the heart to try my skill.

"Pssst! Pah! Get on with you!" said Father de Smet's whispered voice. A buffalo calf had wandered up the slope and was staring wide-eyed at us. At the sight of us, the youngster's mouth dropped open in shock.

De Smet waved his burlap hood at the animal. "Go away, you! Hssst! *Va t'en!*"

The calf, frowning, his wide-set eyes showing white, backed down the slope a step at a time, and when he reached level ground frisked away to a nearby bush, into which he thrust his head and stood rock-still, haunches trembling.

"Like the ostrich, no?" laughed de Smet. "What buffalo? I see no buffalo. Do you see a buffalo?" I took my hand from my revolver. I would shoot no buffalo today. I might hit that calf's mother. Across the valley, the two lines of horsemen, mirroring each other, circled slowly to converge on the horizon. The operation was much more businesslike than I'd imagined. After last night's debauch, I had imagined the hopped-up Indians cresting the rise and riding down on the grazing herd, shooting wildly. Instead the game was as deliberate as chess.

"See how he grazes," said de Smet, pointing. "Nose to the wind. The wind moves, he moves." The buffalo moved slightly, thousands of them shifting in chorus, adjusting to a slight change in the breeze, their noses moving from west to west-southwest.

"Give 'em shifting wind," said Sully, "they'll box the compass in an hour." He rose to his knees. "Here it comes!"

The slight shift in the wind was enough to bring the scent of the horsemen into the buffaloes' snouts. Thousands of shaggy heads rose, thousands of tails stood at attention.

"Ride for it!" urged Sully, and as if they heard him the Indian riders spurred their ponies and galloped to close the circle on the far side of the valley.

"The surround," de Smet, rising to his knees, explained. "Less exciting than the chase, but more efficient." He pointed to where the ring of horsemen were converging. "The buffalo has the horses' scent now, but he cannot flee west, because the circle is closed. He must charge directly toward us."

At that moment, the circle of horsemen converged across the way, and with whoops and cries spurred forward toward the herd. The buffalo, suddenly making up their minds where to go, wheeled and made straight for the slope where we lay. Along the crest, flanking us, fifty rifles waited. The ground trembled as the herd got closer and closer. Chin to the dirt, eyes front, I watched them close on us. Now the lead bulls were at the bottom of the slope, barely fifty yards away, and just as I feared that whoever was supposed to see the whites of their eyes had gone blind, a command set fifty guns ablaze.

The effect was instant. Buffs fell dead or wounded, but the riflemen were not shooting to kill, but to panic. The lead bulls reared and turned, braking with stiff front legs and swinging their butts in the air, pivoting at full speed and hurling themselves back on the horde behind them. The second rank managed to turn as well, and the third and the fourth, retreating down the slope. But the main body, still fleeing from the yipping horsemen at their rear, continued their headlong advance, unaware of the retreating horde falling back upon them. The ranks met like advancing and ebbing waves crashing into each other, colliding so hard that some got tossed in the air, clambering over the each other's backs and pawing for solid ground.

The horsemen closed on the rear ranks, firing arrows. Each horseman, steering with his knees, gripped a dozen arrows in his bow hand and fired, notching a second arrow even before the first had hit home. But even at such speed the firing was not random. I saw one brave at full gallop place an arrow just behind and below one cow's shoulder following it instantly with a second arrow, which hit an inch from the first. The cow tumbled on its head, digging a trench in the soil, and lay still, while the brave calmly notched another arrow, selected a second target, and hit it in the same spot. I looked for the calf in the bush, but he was gone.

The dust was swirling, choking us. Father de Smet, holding his burlap hood to his mouth, continued his muffled shouting in my ear. "They want them to fall where they're shot!" He pointed at Indian riders closing on their quarry. "They don't want to have to ride all over the plain for the butchering! Those that escape, they let them go."

It was hard, in the tumult and dust, the baying and screaming of the buffalo, the volleys of rifle fire and the pounding of hooves, to recognize *method* in this chaos. Then again, in the war, it was hard to remember, watching the slaughters at the Wilderness or Cold Harbor, men screaming and pinwheeling in the air, arms and legs flying, intestines ribboning out and festooning the shrubbery, that these slaughters too were being done by the book. The Indians killed the buffalo as the whites killed each other – methodically, with no celebration or wasted motion.

The thing was over in half an hour. A signal must have passed among the shooters, for in the space of a few minutes, the rifle fire tapered off and stopped, the riders slowed their horses, and those buffalo that remained alive fled west. When the dust cleared and I stood up, my revolver unfired in my hand, I was amazed at the concentration of the slaughter. In a space less than a mile square, over a hundred buffalo lay on the ground, most still, some heaving in their death throes. In the distance I was amazed to see the rest of the herd, their danger past, grazing again as if it had all been a bad dream.

"Look," said Father de Smet. "Here come the butchers."

A dust cloud on the horizon soon resolved itself into horses pulling empty travois, accompanied by many of the tribe's women. Without even a pause at the top of the rise to admire their men's handiwork, they descended into the valley. Most of the buffalo had died upright, noses to the dirt and humps to the sky, as if they'd had their legs cut out from under them and skidded to a stop. This proved convenient for the squaws. Close to me, the old fat Cleopatra I'd seen relaxing in her travois yesterday attacked a dead cow with her knife. With one stroke she opened it from collar to tail. Then, clamping the bloody knife in her mouth, she took hold of one side of the skin with both hands and ripped it downwards, exposing the hump and ribs. She did the same on the other side, then with a few deft knife strokes, hacked the hump meat away in a couple of bushel-sized hunks and tossed them onto the waiting travois. She then went to the front of the buffalo, yanked its snout up, operated in its mouth for a moment, and came away with the huge tongue, which she likewise tossed on the travois. That was it. Having carved perhaps twenty-five pounds from a thousand-pound buffalo, Cleopatra wiped her bloody knife on her skirt and moved on to the next cow, which she dissected in like fashion.

"They don't save the skins?" I asked.

"Maybe a few," said Father de Smet. "For tepees and such. But these are no good for robes. Most of their fur is shed. No, my friend, this hunt was for meat."

I frowned at Father de Smet. "That seems wasteful," I said. "Back east we speak of the Plains Indians as great conservators, who use every part of the buffalo."

Father de Smet spread his hands. "Eventually, they do," he said. "But not every part of every buffalo. They take what they need at the moment, keep what they can carry and leave the rest. In the fall hunt, when the fur is full, they strip the carcass, keep the robe and leave the meat. Today they leave the robe and take the meat. When the buffalo were more plentiful, they might kill a hundred and take only the tongues. It depends on what they need. The Indian doesn't think far ahead."

On the return journey, the chiefs and braves were in the lead again, blood-spattered and light-hearted, different from the grim-faced warriors who marched out this morning. They romped and capered about each other, their horses wheeling and bucking as their masters relived their morning's triumphs. Iron Lance leapt from his own horse to others, clinging behind five riders in succession before regaining his own galloping mount.

I turned in my saddle to look back to where the killing-ground was now hidden by the rim of the valley. "They killed over a hundred buffalo in less than an hour. Is that about average?"

Father de Smet nodded. "They will have another surround tomorrow, and the next day and the next. They will keep at it until either they or the buffalo grow tired and leave. By that time they should have enough meat to last until the fall hunt."

"In sixty-three," said Sully, riding alongside us, "after I beat the Sioux at White Stone, I burned five hundred thousand pounds of their buffalo meat. Dried meat. I pegged it at the time as the fruit of five thousand buffalo. At a pound and a half per person per day, that was a seventy-day food supply for four hundred lodges."

Seeing them in a quantifying mood, I asked de Smet, "How many buffalo do you suppose there are?"

The priest laughed. "How do you count the blades of grass? Sometimes people count them by the hour – how long it takes a migrating herd to pass a given point. I waited three days once between Fort Benton and the Milk River for a herd to pass. When I crossed the trail, it was trampled eighteen miles wide."

"So how many buffalo was that?" I persisted.

"I don't know," said de Smet. "But I will tell you one thing. However many millions there are now, they are much diminished from what they once were, when the country, as the Indians say, was one robe from coast to coast."

I frowned, remembering. "My grandfather spoke of seeing buffalo along the Niagara."

De Smet smiled. "I doubt it. But *his* grandfather might have. They were certainly in Pennsylvania, in all the eastern states. Now they are only between the Mississippi and the mountains. They are further divided north and south by the emigrant trails and the railroad. The Indians sense the diminishing, but I think they don't know how serious it is. If they did, they would strip those carcasses clean, instead of leaving such waste. Pah!"

There was another, greater feast that evening, a potluck, the lodges vying with each other to produce the most succulent dish. At evening's end, we lay with Iron Lance by a fire on the open ground, the prairie breezes drifting over us and a million stars above. Iron Lance amused himself by flinging bits of fatback into the fire, shooting up spurts of flame.

"This is how a man should live," he told us. "Upright on his horse, killing the buffalo and riding the plains, not bent over like a woman and scratching the soil." He turned over, resting on his elbow, and pointed a finger at us. "Here's what you tell your Great Father. To establish peace, he must send his soldiers out of the country, close up the emigrant roads through the Black Hills and stop the fireboats from coming up the Missouri. He can keep his land, while we keep ours. As long as there are buffalo, we need nothing from the white man."

"How long do you think there will be buffalo?" I asked him. Sully and de Smet's calculations had led me to some of my own.

Iron Lance rolled onto his back, rubbing his belly. "For as long as the grasses grow and the rivers run. The buffalo are as numerous as the million, million stars I see now."

I looked up at the star-splashed sky, where I was sure there were less than a "million-million." "How many buffalo do you suppose there are now?" I asked Father de Smet.

"Maybe four million," said the priest.

"Yes," said Iron Lance. "However many the white man kills, he can never kill them all."

"Don't be so sure," I said. The ragged Indian firing line of this afternoon, fifty rifles blasting at the milling herd, had put me in mind of the firepower I'd seen at Chattanooga, Spotsylvania and Cold Harbor. Suppose the Indians had mortars, canister, howitzers. Suppose a regiment had blasted away for half an hour, how many buffalo would have escaped? How many buffalo would have escaped the artillery duel at Gettysburg or Pickett's Charge? How many would have escaped the Crater at Petersburg, where we set off four tons of gunpowder?

"The white man," I told Iron Lance, "just had a war. In four years he killed half a million of his brothers. And his brothers had weapons; they could fire back at him. How long do you think it would take the white man to kill four million unarmed buffalo?"

Iron Lance rose on his elbow and stared at me, and for a moment his confident eyes wavered. Then he waved a hand and rolled onto his back, stroking his stomach. "Tales to frighten children," he said. "It will never happen."

But it did. Four million buffalo died between 1870 and 1880, most of them dispatched by the one-shot-a-minute ministry of the Sharps "Big 50" buffalo gun with telescopic sight. Some of the hides went for robes, for upholstery, wall coverings, and shoes, the meat for homes and restaurants, the bones for fertilizer. But the greatest consumer of the buffalo was the Industrial Revolution. The factories of the east needed leather belts to drive machinery, and belts needed constant replacing. The four million buffalo supplied the factories' demand, whipping power from drive to pulley from Lowell to Shreveport. In 1876, when Custer passed this way, perhaps trotting over this very ground, he didn't see a buffalo between the Missouri and his final stop on the Little Bighorn.

In 1884, a lonely buffalo bull attached himself to a herd of cattle near Brush, Colorado. When the townsfolk heard of it, they drove out to look at him, which they did for about an hour. Then they shot him. As I write now, in 1895, the Interior Department counts less than a hundred buffalo on the plains.

Two months after we'd left, our steamboat crawled back down the Missouri to Omaha. Sully and I bade farewell at wharfside to Father de Smet, who was returning to St. Louis. Sully delighted the priest with a sketch he'd done of him giving communion to the Indians, a buffalo herd in the background. When Sully himself left for the east to present our report to Washington, he gave me a fanciful sketch of me at a campfire, my army uniform on, but feathers in my hair, seeming to watch with interest the Indians' buffalo dance. Behind me, a buffalo calf peeks out from a bush. The picture hangs on my wall at 300 Mulberry Street, next to the Red Jacket medal and the Appomattox surrender copy that Grant signed for me.

I waited in Omaha for a few days for train connections to Cleveland, where I would hook up with Henry Flagler. In letters that had accumulated at the hotel, Henry was cryptic as usual but urged me to visit, promising "big doings." On the day of my departure I was at the hotel desk settling my bill, when a noise from one of the large wing-chairs spun me round. Somebody had coughed, a common enough sound, but this cough was familiar. Was it possible to recognize a man by his cough? I had begun hearing this cough at Chattanooga in '63, heard it through the Wilderness, Spotsylvania, and the Forty Days, heard it all summer and winter at City Point, even heard it stifled at Appomattox while Grant and Lee ended the war. I had heard it daily in Army Headquarters on F Street, but I had not heard it since I left there last winter. What was John Rawlins's cough doing in the lobby of the Hamilton House Hotel in Omaha, Nebraska?

It turned out to be attached to John Rawlins. I poked my head around the wing of the chair, and there was "Black John" himself, staring at a newspaper and coughing his face red. "John!" I said.

Rawlins crumpled the paper into his lap and stared up at me, his black eyes bright. "Well, my God," he said. "Parker. Ely. How are you?" And he was on his feet, pumping my hand, clapping me on the back, then embracing me like a brother. I was shocked, as I clasped him to me, at how frail he was. He had shrunk since winter, his cheekbones hollow above his black beard, his uniform hanging off him like a scarecrow. While Rawlins dismissed his cough as "this damn bug," we at headquarters had begun to whisper "consumption."

Though his frame was ravaged, his spirit was undiminished. "I've been ordered west," he told me, settling back into his chair. "For my health. I'm taking the train clear to Wyoming to breathe the mountain air. Grant's orders, by the almighty, and I feel better already. Between you and me, I think his damn cigars were doing it."

"You look superb," I lied, sitting down across from him. Eager as ever, Rawlins listened to the recital of my months among the Indians. "And how goes civilization?" I asked him.

Rawlins shook the newspaper, and I took it from him. "Grant's gone crazy," he said. "He was just waiting to get rid of me, so he could do *this*." He pointed a thin finger and I frowned at the paper's lead. President Johnson had fired Secretary of War Stanton, darling of the Radical Republicans, and Grant had accepted an interim appointment in his stead. Grant, the blunt, straightforward soldier, was suddenly in politics.

"Why interim?" I asked.

Rawlins looked at me. "Yes, you *have* been away, haven't you? Congress passed a Tenure of Office Act, forbidding appointees who have been confirmed by the Congress – *viz.* Stanton – from being removed without consent of same."

"Presumably unconstitutional," I said.

"Presumably," said Rawlins, the lawyer. "But not unless the Supreme Court says so. They can't rule on a hypothetical, only on a test case. And our general is now just that, knee-deep between Congress and the president. If I had been there, I might have prevented it, but as it is . . ." Rawlins flipped his hand. "I'm just as glad to be out of the line of fire."

We talked into the afternoon, catching up on each other, then Rawlins walked me to my train. "I may not be back in Washington until winter," he said, as I slung my bags aboard. "Get there soon, Ely. He needs his old friends more than ever."

He, as always to Rawlins, was Grant, over whom Rawlins took a proprietary interest as the general struggled with peacetime soldiering. In the war, the enemy was always clear, across the way and shooting at you. But in peacetime, you often didn't find out till after the fact who your enemy was. With Bowers dead and Rawlins gone, Grant had few old retainers left. I didn't flatter myself that he needed me much, but I promised Rawlins to give wings to my heels.

Accordingly, I was only able to spend one day with Henry Flagler in Cleveland, but the day was eye-opening enough. I had no affection for Cleveland and had never visited it. It existed in my memory from my grandfather So-se-ha-wa Jimmy Johnson's recitation at my parents' fireside. "In the white man's year 1796, General Moses Cleveland of the Connecticut Land Company met some Seneca chiefs at the Cuyahoga. He bought from them the land all round for five hundred New York pounds, two beef cattle and one hundred gallons of whiskey. No Seneca can visit the Cleveland settlement without tears."

I felt tears in my eyes as I detrained at Cleveland, not from sentiment but sediment, a sulfurous smoke that filled the air and thickened as I walked toward the river and Lake Erie, following the directions Henry had given me for his office. It proved to be on the fourth floor of the Case Block, a fortress-like building on Superior Street, just east of Public Square, and the name on the door was one of the surprises Henry had in store: Rockefeller & Flagler.

Henry bounded to the door as I entered, looking fully recovered from the seediness of my last visit two years ago. He wore a checked suit and a new mustache, a brown brush that he kept stroking with his finger, as if still getting used to it. "Welcome to prosperity!" he crowed as he shook my hand, then ushered me to a seat at an unoccupied desk. Two desks, in fact, were all that the office held, except for a few file cabinets and some charts tacked to the wall. Through the window I saw chimneys belching smoke.

Henry stood smiling down at me as if proud of a new acquisition. "Look at you," he said. "Same old Chief. I expected paint and feathers after your months on the plains."

"And I see just what I expected," I retorted. "On your feet again, Henry. You always bounce back. Rockefeller, eh?"

"That's his chair you're sitting in," said Henry proudly. "We work back-to-back. Even live back-to-back and walk to work together down Euclid Avenue." Henry flopped down in the desk chair opposite.

"So Rockefeller accepted your dowry?" I asked, recalling Henry's whiskey money.

"You remember," said Flagler, impressed. "Yes, young John and I encountered each other just as he needed money for expansion. He had the plant, I had the money, now we have each other. Look here." He lifted from the floor a large metal container with wooden handles, painted red and white, with a distinctive oval on the side containing the letters "S/O". "Eye-catching, no? It's an idea we've hit upon. Five gallon cans of kerosene for home consumption, each with our colors and our name on it. Standard Oil, you see? Simple and direct. We're the standard – everyone else follows."

I hefted the can, imagining them accumulating in kitchens and barns throughout America. "We ship them all over the world. More to Europe than to anyplace else. But soon, oil for the lamps of China!" It was a distinctive container, like a brand that would imprint the Rockefeller & Flagler name on the public mind.

Flagler raised a finger and winked at me. "The next step is incorporation."

"Ah," I said, replacing the can on the floor.

"Yes," nodded Henry. "That's the big one." His mouth turned sour. "Wish I'd done it in salt."

"Why?"

Henry shrugged, a cloud on his brow. "A partnership, like I had, like Rockefeller and I now have, is responsible for its debts. In salt, we got all the profits, of course, and they were tremendous for awhile. But when the debts came due, we were responsible for them too and went bust. But a corporation!" Flagler warmed to the possibilities. "A corporation is both immortal and irresponsible. It dwarfs and survives the people who comprise it. And if it goes bust, nobody has to pay. It's like being God without the bother of ethics."

"Charming," I said.

"Ever the Puritan, Parker," laughed Flagler. "Admire the construction without judging it. I've had time to study this, and incorporation is the way to go. With certain embellishments, of course." He brushed his mustache.

"And they are?"

Henry raised three fingers, one at a time. "Know your major shareholders. Keep half the stock plus one share for yourself, a voting majority. Print more shares and use them instead of money to buy up the competition and control prices."

"How?" I asked, already lost.

"Anybody builds a refinery, you buy him out. John's already doing that, with cash. But when we're incorporated, we buy them out with shares in Rockefeller & Flagler. We keep our fifty percent plus one, but meanwhile we're spreading stock thin on the ground so the competition's part of our organization."

"Monopoly," I said.

"Exactly," said Flagler. "And more." He hopped to his feet, pacing the room and jingling coins in his pocket. "A monopoly that leaps state boundaries. Oil is interstate. We get crude from Pennsylvania, refine it here, ship it to New York. We incorporate in every state where we do business. Ohio, Pennsylvania, New Jersey, New York. Everyplace from the source to the shipping docks." He made a fist. "The whole eastern part of the country will be in our hands. Then we interlock the corporations at the top into an interstate trusteeship, so we're not beholden to the laws in individual states. We move operations, on paper of course, from state to state as regulations catch up with us. We'll be bigger than any state, you see, yet smaller than the federal government. It's an area where no government entity has yet found jurisdiction, so we write our own rules. It will be years before the government ferrets us out and by that time it'll be too late."

I couldn't help laughing. We were sitting in a small room with two desks, overlooking smokestacks on the lake shore, and Flagler was spinning tales out of the Arabian nights. Before I could talk him down to earth, the door opened and a young man entered, saw us in conference, and started to duck out again. An office boy, I assumed. Flagler hurried to the door. "John!" he said. "Come in! Come in! Nothing private!" He ushered the young man over to me. "General Ely Parker, meet John Rockefeller."

The young man shook my hand and nodded his head briefly. "Pleased," he said, and I realized I was occupying his chair and stood up. Rockefeller moved to stand at the desk and seemed to check that I hadn't stolen anything. "How did things go with Stone?" he asked Flagler without turning around.

"Fine, fine," said Flagler, winking at me. "I'll tell you about it later."

"Tell me now," said Rockefeller. "More or less than thirty percent?"

"Thirty-six," said Flagler.

Rockefeller turned, smiled for the first time, did a little jump in the air and clapped his hands. "Splendid," he said. Rockefeller was plain enough for an entrepreneur whom Flagler so idolized. I was nearly forty, with Flagler two years behind, but Rockefeller couldn't be more than thirty. He had thin blond hair combed smooth over his scalp, a bushy blond mustache and a worried expression that never seemed to leave him. "Have you showed the General the refinery?" he asked Flagler.

"How could he miss it?" said Flagler.

"Refinery?" I asked.

"It's what you've been smelling," said Flagler.

Rockefeller led me over to the window, where now I could see, at the riverside, a stretch of buildings and machinery, with pipelines leading here and there. Barges were pulled up to the dock, and a rail spur traveled out of sight beyond the river bend. "The center," murmured Rockefeller. "Crude oil from pipelines from Pennsylvania, refined here, shipped east by barge and rail. Then to Europe and beyond." He sniffed the air. "I don't know how it works, of course, but it does. That's the smell of money."

Flagler joined us at the window, which had a film of oil on the outside. The whole refinery area was covered with the same film. Rockefeller looked my uniform up and down. "You should sign him up, Henry" he said. "Never hurts to have a general on the board."

Leaving Rockefeller to contemplate his wealth, Henry took me to lunch at the Union Club, then to the station. "You might consider it," he said. "The board of directors. When we incorporate."

"I expect I'll still be in government service," I said. "Conflict of interest."

"Conflict of interest," Flagler laughed, "is the whole point of government service. Oh, Parker," he said, his voice slightly troubled. "Your two thousand dollars?"

"No rush," I said, happy that he hadn't forgotten.

He patted me on the shoulder. "Good man," he said. "Need it a bit longer."

"But you seem so flush!"

Flagler chuckled. "On paper and in kerosene cans. But every time we get a cent we buy more – refineries, wells, equipment. When we print stock, money will free up. You won't be sorry, Parker."

"I'll wait," I said. "What was that Rockefeller asked about Stone?"

Henry frowned, looked around for listeners, took my lapel and whispered. "Head of the Lake Shore and Michigan Central Railroad," he said. "I met him this morning and negotiated a rebate for shipping all our kerosene on his line. Thirty-six percent below the published rate."

"That's what made Rockefeller clap his hands?"

Flagler laughed. "Usually he's dour as a mole. But make a good business deal and he claps his hands and jumps in the air."

Chapter XX

I MISSED MY
WEDDING NIGHT

Washington 1867

I HAVE BEFORE ME ON MY DESK A CIGAR BOX FULL OF yellowing newspaper clippings from 1867 that are the next signposts on my road to being a white man. The first one:

> Mrs. Anna Sackett, widow of the late Lt. Colonel William H. Sackett of the Ninth New York Cavalry, announces the engagement of her daughter Minnie to Brigadier General Ely S. Parker, aide-de-camp to General Ulysses Grant and Grand Sachem of the Iroquois Federation. The wedding will take place Tuesday, December 17 at the Church of the Epiphany. General Grant will give the bride away.

In my six month trip, Minnie's letters reached me at way-stations throughout the west, and mine, dispatched with equal frequency, tumbled back to Washington where I imagined her tearing them open and clutching them to her breast. Even at my first stop in Omaha, letters awaited me, and as we waited out the blizzard there, she kept me informed of parties and politics at home. When we moved west to Forts McPherson and Laramie, her letters reached me there. A packet greeted me at my next return to Omaha in June, and she even found me up the wild Missouri. As I stood on the plains outside Fort Rice, the rim of the world, watching a herd of wild horses milling and bucking, a blue and scented missive was slipped into my hand. When I returned to Washington in September, our reunion was more of two old and faithful friends than two anxious lovers, and her mother, who was much closer to my age than Minnie, gritted her teeth and put the announcement in the paper.

As the wedding day approached I ohh-ed and ahh-ed with Minnie over the swag that cluttered her mother's house. I walked with Minnie through Washington, picking out china and wallpaper for our new house in Georgetown. I submitted myself to drinks and joshing and backslapping from the headquarters staff. The closer the day loomed, however, the more thoughtful I became. A cloud seemed to gather above my head that no girlish laughter or nightly tussles on the sofa could dispel. Minnie bit her lip and pouted, the boys tried to jolly me out of it, even Grant tried to brighten my mood by lending me a red sash to wear for the event. While trying on the sash, along with my other groom's accoutrements, in my room at the Willard the night before the wedding, my worries and doubts gathered sufficient force to break through.

The Willard had been special to me since my first trip to Washington in '46. I stayed there with John Blacksmith and Isaac Shanks while negotiating with President Polk, and I remained there for the entire congressional session that followed and every trip thereafter. I had seen my first landfall in Washington grow from a middling roadhouse to a palace. It was in the Willard bar that I heard the news of Lincoln's assassination and there that friends and colleagues had stood me to drinks on all my returns to town. Now I had rented a spacious suite for our wedding night and claimed an extra night just for me.

As I sat there, feeling proud of myself, vanity nudged me to try on my wedding duds. I slid into my boiled shirt, wormed the pearl studs into place, tucked it into striped trousers and snapped braces over my shoulders. I folded a gray silk cravat around my throat, wound Grant's red military sash around my ample waist, eased my starched sleeves into a pearl cutaway, popped the tall beaver hat onto my head, gave it a tap, shot my cuffs and looked at myself in the full-length mirror.

I rubbed my eyes and looked again. I turned sideways and sucked in my gut. I straightened my hat, I smiled, I frowned, but nothing would disguise the truth. I looked ridiculous. I looked like a savage from the bush wandering town in clothes he'd murdered a white man for, a minstrel in blackface strutting for the white folks. I don't know why it struck me so strongly. I had been wearing an army uniform for five years without a qualm. But others around me were uniformed too, and the uniform subsumed race, age, everything but rank. For five years I had been neither an Indian nor a white man, but a soldier. Now, alone in my wedding clothes, I looked like an imposter. Who did I think I was? Dressing myself up to enter not only the white man's world but his daughter as well. Had I lost myself entirely? For the first time since I left Tonawanda for Vicksburg the absurdity of my dual citizenship flooded upon me. I was no white man. Nor was I an Indian. I didn't know who I was. I tore off the coat, unwound the crimson sash and sat on the end of the bed with my head in my hands.

When I looked up, the mirror was blurred by my tears, and I was sure I saw, hovering at my shoulders, the old chiefs John Blacksmith and Isaac Shanks, in the buckskins they had worn in Washington and everywhere else, muttering to me in Seneca, the only language they knew.

"You're marrying out of the tribe, Ha-sa-no-an-da," said John Blacksmith. "Your child will be not yours but theirs."

"You've sold us out, Do-ne-ho-ga-wa," said Isaac Shanks. "You are the last of your line. The whites have gathered you in and made you disappear."

"The child belongs to its mother's clan," said John Blacksmith. "However red your children are, they will be white inside. Our tribe will not accept them. Nor will theirs."

On the table by the mirror was a bottle of whiskey, compliments of the management. I uncorked it, sloshed some into a glass and drained it. I did it again, and again, and again, trying to steady myself, but the effect was the reverse. Feelings I thought I had banished clamored inside my skull. They weren't, as I'd thought, gone, they were just dammed up inside me, and now they overflowed, spurting through one crack, then another, until all the nails creaked and let go, the boards burst away and I was swept downstream with the flood.

The room was stifling. The hiss of the gas lamps, the closed windows, the drawn drapes, the heavy furniture, the coal fire in the grate all closed in on me. The walls themselves, with their heavy damask wallpaper, loomed and tilted in upon me. I tore the cravat from my throat, felt the collar buttons pop and gasped for breath. I needed air. Whiskey bottle in hand, I ripped open the door. A couple in evening dress, she in a peach-colored gown, were strolling down the hall toward the dining room. They shrunk to the wall as I bulled past them and plunged down the back stairs into the street.

I staggered down an alley and onto the sidewalk. Pennsylvania Avenue was crowded with traffic, but I dove into the maelstrom. Cabs clanged their bells and swerved to avoid me and horses reared and screamed and pawed the air. I reached the other side and clung to a streetlamp, which cast no warmth or glow and seemed to stand above me like an unforgiving sentinel. The traffic was a blur, the clank of wheels, the clop of hooves, the jingle of harness, the clang of omnibus bells a cacophony in the ears of a poor Indian boy from the woods. I had to get away from the city.

I lurched across to the Mall, where mud squelched beneath my feet, ruining my fancy shoes and spats. In front of me loomed the unfinished pile of the Washington Monument, and I scrambled toward it, stumbling over bricks, masonry and scaffolding. A dog barked. A watchman cried, "Hey! Hey you! Where you going?"

I plunged into underbrush, blundering toward the river, where long ago I had walked with John Blacksmith and Isaac Shanks, as they unfolded for me the mysteries of white man's politics. Where were the two wise chiefs, whom I had treated like fossils from a dead age, where were they now that I needed them?

"John Blacksmith!" I cried as, whiskey bottle in hand, I stumbled down the towpath. Branches and brambles grabbed for me, tearing my shirt and pantlegs, but I kept going, my inner compass beelining on what I was looking for.

There it was, the flat rock where Isaac and John and I had sat more than twenty years ago, them easy in their buckskins, me sweating in my frock coat. The black, oily Potomac lapped at its sides. I sprawled face-down on the soothing slab and clung to it as to an old friend. Though Washington had grown so big, here along the Potomac there was still wilderness, no city lights or buildings or night patrols. I drank long from the whiskey bottle, coughed, caught my breath and stared into the watery darkness.

"Isaac Shanks!" I shouted. Not even an echo answered, my words swallowed in the river depths. I drank some more.

That long, chilly night, I reverted to savagery and sympathetic magic, as I called out the names of all my ancestors, summoning them to help me. "Ga-ont-gwut-twus!" I called, my dead mother's name, whose clan I belonged to and would forsake tomorrow when I married the white man's daughter. "Jo-no-es-sto-wa!" I yelled to the oblivious dark, my father's name, who had died as I prepared to follow Grant into the Wilderness. "Ga-ha-no!" I cried, my sister Carrie's name, and Nic's name and all my other relatives, live and dead, back to Red Jacket and Cornplanter and Handsome Lake and Ha-yo-wen-ta. Nobody answered.

"Ha-sa-no-an-da!" I cried, my boyhood name, looking for the boy I was, to demand of him what idiocy set me on this journey, what made him think I could be a white man. "Do-ne-ho-ga-wa!" I sobbed despairingly, bidding farewell to the name my tribe had given me, trusting me to look out for them. How had I honored their trust? By marrying the pale, blonde girl of the transparent skin who would bear white babies, who would point at their father and laugh and call him ape. I looked at the dark water flowing past the rock and wanted to die.

I didn't die. I had more mourning to do. I drank more whiskey. "Squanto!" I cried, for the foolish Wampanoag who had walked into the settlement at Plymouth and taught them to survive. "Pocahontas! Powhatan!" I cried to the Indians who had spared the Jamestown Englishmen. "What have you done to me!"

The names of Indian tribes long dead rolled from my grieving tongue. I wept for the Montauk, the Pequot, the Narragansett, the Mohican, for the Potomac, whose stream rolled at my feet, for the Chickahominy and the Rapahannock and all the other tribes whose natal streams our armies had bloodied without a thought for the bones that lay beneath them. "Appomattox!" I cried, to the Indian queen who gave her name to the stream and the place that now lived only as the place of victory for hundreds of thousands of white men and one lone Indian who now lay face down on the bank of one last Indian river sobbing and soused and pathetic.

"John Ross!" I cried for the Cherokee chief, and while I was at it I cried the names of other Indians I had met in the west. The Creek, Seminole, Chickasaw and Choctaw, uprooted from the land that was promised them "as long as the eagle flies and the rivers run." The white man was killing the eagle and damming the rivers. That was the catch.

I wept for the Indians I had met on the plains. For Spotted Tail and the Brulé Sioux, wandering the Platte Valley looking for the homes the government promised them. For Red Cloud and the Oglala, holding out along the Powder River but doomed to destruction. For the Yankton of the Missouri, trying to farm as the white man told them, but finding their plows and hoes missing, their seed rotten, their supplies stolen by crooked Indian agents. I wept for the young Oglala Sioux Tasunke Witco, the pure warrior named Crazy Horse, who painted himself with hail spots and lightning, who dusted himself with mole-earth to hide him from his enemies. I wept for him and all his dying breed.

I don't know how long I sat and lay there, crying out lost names and weeping. At one point I gazed deep into the water beneath my feet and decided to end it all. With a war cry and a leap, I hurled myself into the black water, to find it came only to my knees, and I stood like a foolish fisherman looking for trout. I hauled myself out and sprawled flat on the rock, praying for death. It was dawn when I awoke, bone-chilled, lying flat on my Potomac rock, my whiskey bottle almost empty, a squirrel looking at me. It was my wedding day. I hoisted the bottle in a toast to the groom, drained it, then flung it out into the river. Unlike Washington's silver dollar it didn't reach the other side but splashed feebly a few yards out and was swept with the rest of the white man's detritus downriver to the sea. I staggered down the bank of the river to town.

I awoke in a cheap boarding house in Arlington. My mouth was dry as leaves, my clothes in a sodden heap in the corner. The landlord told me I had staggered in, thrown money about and demanded a room. It was now dark. My wedding day was over. With barely a thought for what must be going on in the world, with barely a shrug for the searchers that must be looking for me, with just a fleeting tug at my heart for the little girl I'd abandoned, I turned over and went back to sleep. She was, they all were, better off without me.

"General Parker!" said the astonished hall porter the next morning at the Willard. I had sneaked in the back way, still in the torn, muddy remnants of my wedding costume, and had almost made it to my room undetected.

"Yes," I growled, turning to stare at him.

One look at my red eyes and ravaged face told him not to ask too many questions. "Um," he said. "I'm glad to see you, sir. They were looking for you all yesterday."

"Is that today's?" I pointed at the newspaper in his hand.

"Yes sir," he said and handed it to me.

I fumbled in my pocket for coins, but he waved it away, took the key from my numb hand and opened the door to the room. Many messages had been slipped under the door, and as I stooped to pick them up I staggered, and the solicitous porter helped me to the bed. "I'm not here," I told him.

"I understand, sir," he said. "Can I get you some coffee?"

"Yes. No," I said. "I don't know." I buried my face in my hands and felt tears trickle through my fingers.

"I'll get you some coffee," he said quietly, closing the door as he left.

I flopped back on the bed and tried to breathe and stop trembling. Whether I was sick from exposure or still drunk or in a state of nervous collapse I had no idea. The coffee the porter brought helped. At least it warmed me. Unfortunately it also kept me awake, so I had to face what I had done. I flipped numbly through the messages. They were from Minnie, her mother, Rawlins, even Grant. Their tone early in the day was merely curious, as Rawlins came to call for me and found me absent. Toward noon, they grew more urgent, as the hour of the wedding approached and passed, and by nightfall they turned venomous. "If I don't see you by midnight," was Minnie's final note, "I never want to see you again."

Page one of the newspaper painted the picture. I clipped it from that very newspaper and hold it, yellowed and crumbling, in my hand this instant. I don't know if the stain on it is whiskey, sweat or tears.

SENSATION IN HIGH LIFE
WEDDING UNEXPECTEDLY
POSTPONED

The *haut monde* is startled today with conflicting rumors regarding the disappearance of Gen. ELY PARKER, of Gen. GRANT's staff, who was to have been married yesterday to Miss MINNIE

SACKETT, of this city. Gen. Parker had made every preparation for yesterday's event, invitations had gone out, and reception cards had even been issued for his friends in New York at the Metropolitan Hotel, and at his residence in Washington after his return from the bridal tour. He had purchased his wedding suit and on Monday evening borrowed from Gen. GRANT one of the General's military sashes to wear at the wedding, since which time he has not been seen.

At the appointed hour the bride's mother, Gen. GRANT and staff, and a large number of friends and distinguished guests were assembled at the church. The bride was in readiness. The church itself, however, stared blankly upon the throng of ladies and gentlemen who, in full dress, collected about its doors and wondered why they were closed. The wedding, it was announced, was deferred, in consequence of the groomsman's having failed to make his appearance.

Messengers were quickly dispatched to the usual resorts of the missing one, and when the report came that all search was in vain, the invited guests dispersed and retired, with many a heartfelt prayer for a lady so cruelly deserted. General Grant lit a cigar to soothe his ruffled feelings, and made his way to the War Department. All search today has proved fruitless, and no tidings of Gen. PARKER have been received. The most unpleasant conjectures are afloat. He was seen in Baltimore this morning; his body has been found submerged in the

Potomac; he was married to another person in Buffalo this day.

Miss SACKETT is, as may be imagined, terribly affected by the event, but her friends are doing everything to console her. Meanwhile the sympathy of the entire community is enlisted in the lady's behalf, and the confidence that, in the words of Mr. Dickens at his lecture here last week, something is bound to turn up.

I groaned and lay back on the bed, the paper over my face. I was a laughingstock. Grant would never speak to me again. *Minnie* would never speak to me again. I might as well be floating in the Potomac, as the reports had me, rather than lying here in wretched pain, having poisoned all those around me. My throat ached, my head ached, my entire being, down to my soul, ached. I sat up, wiped my eyes and winced through the rest of the newspaper story. Minnie was "Nineteen, pure blonde, with brilliant eyes, one of the most beautiful ladies in the capital." My own biography was drawn in hideous detail. I was "well-known throughout the country, of the Seneca tribe, the last descendant of the great chief and warrior Red Jacket," a devotee of "intellectual culture, unlike the aborigines, who love the excitement of the chase and the bloody attractions of the war path," an engineer, a veteran, a war hero, with "a dark complexion, piercing black eye, and coarse black hair," a scholar and orator, possessing "that eloquence of diction and figure which history has recorded as the qualities of the great chiefs of the powerful Indian nations of the early days." It was like reading my obituary.

There was nothing for it. I had a shred of honor left. There was no telephone then, as there is on my desk now, to make a quick and easy apologetic call. No, I had to do it face to face. The great scholar and orator had to go call on his bereft lady, make what excuses I could, explain why I couldn't marry her, apologize for the inconvenience I'd caused and then . . . And then what? Lose myself in the wilderness? You had to travel mighty far to find wilderness these days. Crawl back to the reservation? What use was I there? Hurl myself from a cliff? I'd tried that yesterday and just got my pants wet. In the same newspaper I read that the reporter we'd seen on the plains, Henry Stanley, proposed to set out for Africa to "find Dr. Livingstone," a Scots doctor who'd disappeared into the bush. Maybe I'd find Stanley and join him. A bastard Welshman and an orphaned Indian in the African jungle. We'd be eaten in a week.

I splashed water on my face, made what toilet my shaking hands allowed, pulled on my army overcoat, plastered my hair down and trudged down the Willard's back stairs. I hunched across Lafayette Square, lurked past army headquarters and hiked out to the Sackett house. So many times I had walked there with a glad heart and a spring in my step. Now it seemed dark and foreboding, a Poe house of gloom and despair. I paused at the front steps, turned around and went up the path to the kitchen entrance. It seemed fitting to show up shabby at the tradesmen's door rather than foul the parlor.

Martha, the black cook, answered my knock and frowned me up and down.

"Mr. Ely," she said. "Where the hell you been? You got everybody worried sick."

"Can I come in, Martha?" I asked.

She screwed up her mouth. "I'm not sure as I should."

"I'll just be a minute," I said. "Is Miss Minnie here?"

Martha held the door for me. "All right," she said. "I suppose so. 'Course Miss Minnie's here. Where else would she be? Cryin' her eyes out, poor lamb."

I stood in the middle of the kitchen, my hat in my hand. "Could you tell her I'm here, Martha? I won't be long."

"Well, I guess I could," said Martha, bustling toward the door. "But if she wants to see you I couldn't say."

The door flapped shut behind her. On the kitchen table were bunches of herbs that Martha was chopping and mixing in a wooden bowl. I wondered what happened to the food for the wedding reception. It was to be a catered affair, right here in the house. I imagined the caterers, white and starched, standing in the foyer ready to take people's coats, trays of hors d'oeuvres and Champagne at port arms, and only Minnie's and her mother's solitary carriage clopping up the drive. A whispered conversation, discreet exchange of cash and receipts and the caterers bowing themselves quickly out the back door. Or had they held the reception anyway? Thrift, thrift. The wedding baked meats coldly furnished forth the funeral tables.

"Yes, Ely?" Minnie stood at the kitchen door, which swung shut behind her. "What do you want of me?"

She had her back to the door, hands clasped in front of her. Her dress was gray and severe, buttoned high at her throat, her hair pulled back from her face in a bun. She looked at me with level eyes, uncommonly grown-up since I saw her last. Nothing like grief to age a girl.

I had not until then known what I would do or say. Scenes from romantic novels had flitted through my mind. Stiff upper lip: "I'm going to Africa to find Livingstone." Byronic: "I shall live alone in a castle by the sea." Noble: "My people need me, I belong among them."

Instead, within an instant of viewing her sweet, sad face, while the door was still swinging behind her, I was on my knees in front of her, hands clasped around her waist, face buried in her skirts. "Oh, Minnie. Minnie my love. Forgive me," I sobbed, crying uncontrollably. "I don't know what came over me."

She tensed as I grabbed her but didn't push me away. I felt her hands on my ears, gently pulling my face up, asking me to look at her. I wiped my eyes on my sleeve and sobbed. "But whatever happened to you, Ely?" she asked. "I was so worried."

"Worried?" I sniffed, looking up at her, her face a blur through my tears.

"Why of course," she said. Her fingers toyed with my hair. "At first, of course, I was angry. Then terribly embarrassed. We sent messages to your room. We got the manager to open it. He said it was a shambles."

"I threw things around," I said. My cheek was against her stomach and I could feel her breathing. It calmed me, and I began to breathe easier. "I was drinking."

She nodded down at me, giving her a double chin and making her look indulgent. "I thought you might be. But whatever for?"

"I was afraid," I sniffled.

"Of me?"

"Oh no! Well, yes," I said. "Afraid of . . . of what I was becoming." Her fingers in my hair were soothing. I seized her hand and kissed the palm and held it to my cheek. "Oh, I'm so mixed up," I said. I sat back on my haunches, put my face in my hands and sobbed some more.

"Ely, Ely," she said softly. She knelt down beside me and lifted my chin. She dabbed my cheeks with a handkerchief. "Tell me, please tell me what you're thinking."

I poured it all out to her. I was a deserter from my tribe, forsaking my heritage, mingling the races was a sin in tribal doctrine, our children would be outcasts, considered white by the Indians and savages by the whites, I didn't know who I was any more, years of trying to live white had caught up with me. "I'm nobody," I said. "I can't come to you like this. I'm an orphan. I have no idea who I am."

Kneeling in front of me, Minnie cupped my chin in her hand, looked deep into my eyes, shook her head slowly then pulled me to her and clasped my head to her bosom. "Oh, Ely, Ely," she said softly, and I felt her voice vibrate in her chest. "Is that all?"

"All?" I sniffed, my face between her breasts.

"Yes, all," she said, rocking me, holding me close. "I'm an orphan too, you know."

I looked up at her. "You?"

"Of course," she said. "I have no father, no mother. You know Anna's not my real mother. I have no tribe even, no relatives. I'm just me. That's all that's left."

"But you have . . ." I waved my hand at the well-stocked, warm-smelling kitchen.

"I have nobody," she said, putting both hands on my cheeks and holding my eyes with hers. "What I have is you. What I want is you. I come to you unencumbered and dowerless. That you come to me the same is no shame."

I buried my face in her bosom again. "How did you become so wise?" I asked.

I felt a sigh in her chest. "I've grown up some in the past twenty-four hours," she said, with an edge in her voice. "I saw my fairy tale wedding ignite, but I rose from the ashes feeling very clean and, for the first time in my life, free. Do you know what Dr. Hall told me about the wedding vows? Yesterday, while I still thought I was getting married?"

"What?" I sniffed.

"Let me sit back," she said. She sat with her back against the door jamb and eased my head down into her lap. Her cool hands smoothed my hair and sweating brow. "He said did I know what 'forsaking all others' means. I said of course, it means no more boyfriends, but he shook his

295

head. No, he said, it means *all* others. All other friends, all other family, all other connections, all other commitments. It means forsaking your tribe and mine. It means we *are* our family, we *are* our tribe, we two must be our own society. Whatever else our families or our societies want us to do, we needn't do, because we've put them aside and have only each other to be responsible to. I found that very frightening, but as I thought about it, very liberating too. All I had to do was say 'I do' to you, and we could say to hell with everybody else."

I lay with my head in her lap, breathing easily, no longer crying. I began to think that everything might be all right if only I could just stay there on the floor, not moving, and feel her warmth and softness breathing under me.

"Ely," she said softly.

"Yes," I said.

"Do you still want to marry me?"

"Yes," I said, without hesitation.

She thought a minute. "Will you make me one promise?"

I snuggled closer into her lap. "Anything," I said.

She stroked my hair. "Promise me you'll never drink whiskey again."

I looked up at her and sniffed. "I promise," I croaked. It wasn't hard to do with such a hangover.

"Are you sure?" she said.

"Yes," I sniffed. Then, for an escape clause, I asked. "What about wine?"

She smiled and put her hands on my cheeks. "Nothing but the best, my dear. And all the Champagne we want for as long as we live!"

I snuggled down in her lap again. After awhile I felt her body make a decision. "Martha!" she called sharply. There was no reply. "Martha!" she called again. "I know you're listening. Just open the door."

The door paused, then opened slightly, and I saw Martha's eyes, big as saucers, peering in. "Yes, Miss," she said. "I was just . . ."

"Martha," said Minnie. "Please take the rest of the afternoon off. Go see Jason. Go to a play. Anything. Don't come back until tonight."

"But your momma . . ." said Martha.

"I'll deal with mother," said Minnie. "Please go!"

Martha hesitated, holding the door, then shook her head and let it close. After a few minutes we heard the front door open and close and saw Martha bustle past the windows and down the drive.

"There," said Minnie, standing up and straightening her skirt. She held out her hand to me. "Come with me, please."

I hauled myself to my feet and took her hand. She led me out of the kitchen and, like a docile chimp, up the back stairs to the second floor. I shuffled dutifully along the landing behind her and into a sun-splashed room with pale blue wallpaper and a canopy bed. Her bedroom.

"Minnie," I said. "You don't have to . . ."

"Sh-h-h," she said, turning and holding my hands. "My wedding night was supposed to be last night, remember? You've kept me waiting far too long, Ely."

She gave me a little push toward the bed, then went to the windows and drew the drapes, giving us twilight. She came to me, put her hands on my shoulders and nuzzled into my throat. "I don't know how to do this," she murmured with a nervous giggle. "The novels are maddeningly unspecific. They get you to the bedroom door then back away."

"What should I do?" I asked dumbly, washed out from booze and tears.

She giggled again, leaning against me. "I'm counting on you to know, dear. You can start by getting into bed. I'll be along in a minute."

She whisked out a side door into what I assumed was a dressing room. I looked around her bedroom, thought briefly of escape, sighed and yielded. Fate was fate. I fumbled out of my clothes, hung them on a chair and slipped naked between the cool, soap-smelling sheets. I heard the dressing-room door open and bare feet pit-pat across the floor.

"There," she said, breathless, trembling and snuggling naked against me. "My all-untutored body awaits your command."

Well. All-untutored she may have been, but beware instinct! Once she got over her shock at how invasive the procedure was, once her wide eyes melted and turned dreamy, and she stopped saying "Oh!" every ten seconds, she clung to me and pounded lustily along as if bred for nothing else. I showed her how to hike her legs around my waist, slipped my hands beneath her buttocks, and just as she gasped, "How do we know when we're finished?" her body answered and sent her into grand convulsions as she grabbed my hair and I huffed and puffed and pawed her breasts and finished with her. We spent a few minutes locked together, breathing hard, our faces buried in each other's throats, then I rolled off her and looked at her face. She was staring at the ceiling, her hand on her stomach, stunned.

"My," she said, her mouth open and her eyes wide. "It leaves nothing to the imagination, does it?" Her hand moved to her chest. "I feel like I haven't a secret left in the world!"

I chuckled. "Women always have secrets."

"I suppose I'll have to discover some new ones," she murmured. "For the moment I'm a wide open oyster."

I stroked her stomach and felt each of her breasts, as she watched my hand with curiosity. "It feels so natural, your doing that," she said. "Why on earth do we keep ourselves so buttoned up?"

"For the mystery," I said. "If everyone admitted what fun it was, we'd never do anything else."

She stretched her arms and rolled to me, putting her head on my shoulder. "But now that there's no mystery left, what's to attract you?"

I stroked her flank. "The mystery of why it's so new every time."

We lay with my arm around her and her curled up beside me. "Forsaking all others," she had said, and now it seemed possible that just this little room could encompass a whole world. If only we could just stay here, with only each other, drawing the curtains, shutting them all out. I felt at peace. Was it possible that an hour ago I was seriously thinking of going to Africa? I was a creature of civilization. My lady's boudoir was where I belonged.

"Ely?" she said into my shoulder.

"Yes?"

"Um." Her finger drew a circle on my chest. "I think I have the hang of it. Do you think we could do that again?"

"Afraid you'll forget how it goes?"

"Not at all," she said, wriggling her head into the pillows. "I miss you inside me, that's all. I feel unfilled."

In short order we had her filled again and were on our way, when the downstairs door opened and closed with a jangle of Christmas bells. We froze.

"Martha?" I whispered.

Minnie's hands were on my shoulders. "Sh-h-h. I don't know."

Doors were opening downstairs. "Martha!" came a voice from the kitchen. Her mother. A door closed, and we heard footsteps on the stairs.

I made to roll off her. Flight was all I could think of. The closet. The dressing room. The window. The porch roof right outside. How long a drop could it be? I saw myself hopping through the streets of Washington, my pants around my ankles, dogs chasing me.

"Don't move!" whispered Minnie, holding me on top of her with strong hands and thighs.

The footsteps were outside the door. "Minnie!" her mother called. "Minnie are you in there?" There was a rap on the door.

Minnie put a finger to her lips. "Yes, mother, I'm here," she called. "Don't come in. Ely's here with me."

No sound came from the hallway. I imagined Anna out there, hand raised to knock, frozen in mid-air, her mouth open in shock.

"Mother," called Minnie. "Go away. I'll talk to you later."

Again, silence. Then I heard a sigh, a sort of collapse, and her mother's footsteps retreated, clipped down the hall, and, after pausing a full minute to decide, clunked slowly down the stairs.

My breath, which I had been holding, escaped in a rush, and my head dropped down on Minnie's shoulder. Minnie's thighs, apparently expecting to pick up where we left off, started moving under me, sensed an absence, paused, searched, and seemed puzzled. "Where did it go?" she asked, then "Where are you going?" as I rolled off her and onto my back, pulled the sheet up and flopped my arm over my eyes.

"Ely?" she asked. I peeked an eye under my arm and saw her propped on an elbow, frowning. I lifted the sheet and showed her. What moments ago held her skewered and wriggling like a trout had shrunk to a glistening suggestion.

"Oh dear," she said.

"Fear," I said.

She reached down to touch it. It jumped and her hand jumped back.

"Not dead," I said, "just resting."

"But how endearing," she said, holding the sheet up and staring, fascinated. "It's like it has a life of its own."

"It does now," I said, letting the sheet drop and holding her close. "And so do I."

She cuddled there and fell asleep. I stared at the ceiling and pondered the wonders of life. Although white people fancy Indians as children of nature, the Tonawanda of my youth was puritanical, but I got plenty of education when I early entered the white world. I had girls in Washington tobacco shops, Galena lighthouses, at Mollie Bunche's waterfront palace in Vicksburg and other places along the path of war and diplomacy. But as I lay with my wife in my arms, listening to her purr and watching her eyelids twitch, I realized she was the first white girl I hadn't paid for.

Within days, new wedding announcements hit the papers, society re-buzzed with rumor, and wedding finery was aired out for a second go. A week after the disaster, the day before Christmas, the crowd assembled at the church again, its numbers swelled by onlookers, curious to see the on-again off-again couple who had turned Washington inside-out. An outraged clipping tells the tale.

THE PARKER-SACKETT NUPTIALS
Washington Gossips Badly Sold
Ludicrous and Exciting Scene

The public were badly sold again today about the Parker-Sackett nuptials. The affair was fixed to come off at noon, and this morning the vicinity of the church was crowded with a promiscuous and silly looking assemblage of both sexes, of all ages and conditions, from misses in their teens and youths with downy mustaches to petrified old maidenhood and grave and reverend masculinity.

The church opened at eleven o'clock, and the ladies, all rosy and smiling, jostled the gentlemen, and a regular scramble for the nearest place to the altar rails followed. In the wings a great deal of evergreen ornamentation was going on, and boys and sacristans were moving to and fro, giving the impression that a huge matrimonial affair was indeed about to come off. But one of the artists in evergreen, finding his operations impeded, informed several of those assembled that the decoration was intended for the Christmas celebration, and that the marriage expected was a thing of the past, having been performed privately last evening.

The disappointment to the ladies cannot be described. A repetition of the grand matrimonial and spectacular drama of "Pocahontas" with the sexes reversed, or Do-ne-ho-ga-wa, alias Ely Parker, with his warrior's sash, plume, and tribal trappings, leading his fair Caucasian bride to the altar, was a picture so seldom presented in these prosaic days that no wonder if sentimental fair ones of Washington flocked to witness the romantic event. No wonder if their ideal expectations were cruelly wounded by the substitution of an April joke.

The nuptials actually occurred about twelve hours before. About six o'clock last evening several carriages containing the wedding party drove up to the residence of the Rev. Dr. Hall, alighted and entered the little parlor of the parsonage. The bride and bridegroom took their places, the bridesmaids and groomsmen assumed their proper positions, General GRANT acted as the parent of the fair lady, giving her away to the bridegroom, the knot was tied, the benediction was pronounced and the nuptials were consummated.

"Little did they know," murmured Minnie, reading the paper with me on the train to New York, "that the nuptials were consummated several days before."

"Sh-h-h," I told her, looking around the crowded railroad car as it rocked its way north. "Don't talk dirty."

Minnie snuggled closer. The fur collar of her traveling suit brushed my chin as we read the rest.

> The party had come to the house as quietly as possible and left just as mysteriously. There was no ostentation, no display, no pomp such as might have been expected at the nuptials of the descendant of the great Red Jacket, Chief of the Six Nations.
>
> This morning the red man Do-ne-ho-ga-wa, and his Caucasian bride made their appearance at the residence of the former, receiving congratulations, after which they departed on their delayed wedding trip to New York. The reason given for the private marriage was the couple's desire to avoid public gaze after the *fiasco* of last week.

"Any regrets?" I asked her.

"None," she sighed. "Being notorious is rather exciting." She kissed me on the cheek and snuggled close to me on the jiggling train seat. "Forsaking all others," she murmured happily, as our wedding express rumbled north to Manhattan.

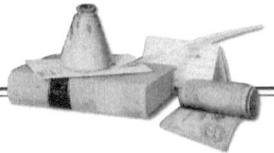

Chapter XXI

IF YOU EVER MENTION MY WIFE AGAIN I'LL SCALP YOU!

Washington 1869

T HE BIG EVENTS OF 1868 WERE THE IMPEACHMENT OF President Johnson and the election of President Grant, in both of which Grant figured prominently and in neither of which he distinguished himself. As the war faded, Grant grew less sure-footed, his timing off and his steps tentative. Politics lacks maps, and Grant, who could bridge real rivers and divert genuine streams with a wave of his cigar, found the way puzzling and the enemy unclear.

Take impeachment, which Grant got into and out of through the back door. By the Tenure of Office Act, providing that anyone appointed with the consent of the Senate could be removed only with consent of same, Congress wanted to keep South-hating Stanton as secretary of war. So, instead of firing Stanton, Johnson suspended him, appointing Grant secretary of war *ad interim*. When Congress revoked Grant's appointment, invited Stanton back and ordered Grant to surrender "the office," Grant did the most literal thing. He bolted the front door of the secretary of war's office from the inside, left by the back door and gave the key to a janitor. Then he left the building, strolled up the street to army headquarters, walked past me into his old office, sat down behind his old desk and lit a cigar. Fifteen minutes later, Stanton arrived at the

War Department, found the office locked, retrieved the key and resumed "the office" Grant had vacated.

It was as Grant as you could get, but Congress got mad at him, the president got mad at him, and the country began to wonder if he was the man on the white horse after all. In the spring, he regained ground by staying out of the impeachment circus. It wasn't so much that Grant rose as that everyone else fell. The president was holed up in the White House, Stanton in the War Department, the Senate and House were in an uproar, and the trial dirtied everyone who touched it. It was public spectacle unmatched since the Grand Review, and Inauguration-style crowds thronged the city, gawking on the streets and clamoring for tickets.

My well-connected wife wrangled admission almost every day and reported breathlessly every night. Congressman Ben Butler of Massachusetts, the chief prosecutor, was "about the slimiest thing not crawling on its belly, the cock-eyed old reprobate. Parading around in white tie and tails as if at a ball, sputtering and spuming all over his mustache. He says the president's a drunken, besotted, traitorous heathen who got his office by clambering over Lincoln's dead body. He's a perfidious, bloody, bawdy villain, brim-full of treachery and turpitude." Senator Ben Wade of Ohio, president *pro tempore* of the Senate, who would succeed as president if Johnson was removed, was "lurking like a cat under a canary's cage, sharpening his claws and waiting for the floor to drop."

I sighed and shook my head. "We've come a long way from Webster, Clay, and Calhoun. In my day, real statesmen prowled the Senate."

She laughed and plunked down in a pink wing-chair. "Oh pooh. Your day, indeed, old-timer. Daniel Webster was an amateur, Clay was a dreamer, 'Liberty and Union' my foot. Wade and Ben Butler would eat them for breakfast."

The impeachment trial dragged through March and April to mid-May, and public sentiment, at first against the president, swung toward him. Americans like an underdog, and as Bens Butler and Wade piled it on, the stolid man from Tennessee took on a lonely dignity. When Johnson escaped conviction by one vote, jubilation spilled into the streets. Torchlight parades serpentined, Johnson opened the White House doors and threw a party, the Marine Band played on the lawn, and Congress slunk out of town. But Grant, not Johnson, emerged triumphant. Within a week of the acquittal, the Republican convention in Chicago washed its hands of Johnson and nominated Grant for president.

It wasn't much of a campaign. Grant made only one swing around the country, which was touted as non-political. He and Sheridan and Sherman toured the west, three simple soldiers examining the Indian problem. Then Grant holed up in Galena, saying little. When asked for a statement, he'd retire to his study, smoke and issue a bland page, ending with his slogan, "Let Us Have Peace." So often did Grant refuse to speak, pleading fatigue or diffidence, that "Let us have peace" began to sound like "Leave me alone."

He got elected by far fewer votes than expected, and his first days as president dashed further hopes. His cabinet nominees landed with a thud. "Who?" the senators asked, shaking their heads at the list of unknowns and neophytes, so mismatched to their offices they might have been chosen by lot. "Darwin is disproved," announced Henry Adams from the Senate gallery. "The evolution from President Washington to President Grant is evidence enough."

Only two nominations gained wide approval: General John A. Rawlins to be secretary of war. And . . . General Ely S. Parker to be commissioner of Indian affairs, the first Indian to hold that office.

Rawlins's story doesn't last much longer. Though just thirty-eight years old, known to the public only as Grant's chief of staff and a creature of Grant's sole devising, Rawlins had proved so steadfast both in the war and after that no peep of "cronyism" greeted this most cronyistic appointment. Rawlins was so forthright that Grant's harshest critics admitted that a man who could choose Rawlins as his chief subordinate couldn't be totally stupid. "Hit Rawlins on the head, and Grant's brains will fall out," they said in the war, and it began to seem more so in peacetime. Unable now to let victories in the field do his talking, Grant relied increasingly on Rawlins as mouthpiece, and John did it so well folks questioned who was the ventriloquist and who the dummy.

But Rawlins was sick, with a cough that started in the rain at Chattanooga in '63 and never stopped. It persisted through the war, and though he and Emma and all of us prayed that only exposure and camp life prolonged it, peace brought no relief. He went west for dry air and exercise for the last half of '67, and though he wrote from Wyoming of "feeling better than ever," "breathing right down to the bottom," and "dining *al fresco* on antelope, buffalo, bear and strong coffee," he returned for my wedding more wasted than ever, his black eyes bright with fever. He opened his shirt to show me his sunken chest, blistered and scarred where he had bared it daily to the sun to burn the contagion away. Rawlins, Wyoming later got named for him, for all the good it did.

"He's going to die," Quentin Winslow told me shortly after the inauguration. "That's the word. Everybody should stay put until he does."

Quentin was still hidden by the thicket of storage cabinets in his corner at the State Department. Every time I visited the office, Quentin seemed more dug in and sealed from view, until I suspected I was the only one who knew he was there.

"I've survived," he told me. "Others haven't." He nodded at the two desks that flanked the secretary's door, where two disconsolate clerks were packing their belongings, making way for their replacements. "Stay low and survive."

Quentin had changed little over the years. His wispy blond hair had receded some, as had his chin. His eyes were redder and had bags under them, and his skin showed a convict's pallor. I was there to ask him either to move with me to the Interior Department, where Indian Affairs was housed or, failing that, to join Rawlins at the War Department.

He turned me down with a quick two shakes of his head. "You've become visible, Parker. Too big for me. I'd wither in the sunshine."

But as to Rawlins, "It's just a move down the street, Quentin," I told him. "You could even have the same corner down there." I was fresh from a visit to Rawlins's office and had seen his anteroom crowded with job-seekers. "Somebody needs to protect him from the crowds. He can't do his job."

Quentin moved his head from side to side. "I'd have to yield my space," he said quietly. "In civil service physical space matters, not anything abstract like title. If I move down there, I'd have to start all over again. Then Mr. Rawlins will die and I'll be adrift. Who will help me then?"

"I will," I said. "The president will."

Quentin shuddered. "No, no," he said, his lips tight. "I can't get noticed that way. I've won my spot and I'll keep it, thank you." He looked around me to see that nobody was listening. "I'll tell you what I will do, though."

"What?"

"I'll pass the word. I'll see that Mr. Rawlins is left in peace."

I raised my eyebrows. "You'll stick your neck out that far, Quentin? For me?"

Quentin's lips twisted into what he probably thought was a smile. "No. For me. These quadrennial office circuses do us no good. People see crowds in secretaries' offices and start crying for civil service reform. The day that comes, where will I be?"

"I see," I said.

"And, General," added Quentin. "I'm sorry I can't join you. But I shall, as always, keep you informed."

"As you've done since Polk's days," I said.

"*Eheu fugaces, Postume, Postume*," he surprisingly quoted Horace, "*anni labuntur.*"

Within a few days, the crowds at Rawlins's office dried up. But Rawlins's lungs didn't. He labored through the Washington spring rains and summer heat. By August he stopped going to the office and accepted quarantine at home. On one of my last visits I found Rawlins propped up in bed, thinner and paler than ever, but chipper. His house was on the heights, and breezes wafted through the windows. Emma stood by the door, coughing slightly into a handkerchief, as I pulled up a chair to John's side. He'd rigged a mass of pillows and a lap desk and was fussing with papers.

"What's this?" I asked.

John laughed weakly and started coughing, deep and hollow, as if he had no lungs at all. He put a handkerchief to his mouth and examined it when the coughing ceased. "No blood today," he muttered and slipped the cloth behind his pillow.

I lifted a blueprint from his lap desk and frowned at it. "A bridge," I noted.

He nodded. "The long-awaited Brooklyn Bridge."

"And what has the secretary of war to do with that?"

John winked darkly. "National security, Parker. I have my mitts in everything. A bridge across the East River must be tall enough for our tallest warship to pass under at high water."

"And is it?" I paged through various renderings of the bridge, a low-slung and graceful structure for so long a span, with cross-hatching suspension wires that looked delicate as a cobweb. The bridge leapt the water like a dolphin.

John shrugged his thin shoulders, bones poking through his pajamas. "Who knows? The bridge company wants the height minimized so as to have the shallowest possible grade. They claim one hundred-thirty feet above spring flood is the highest they can go."

"And the shipping interests?"

Rawlins shuffled papers and picked one up. "One hundred-forty feet, they claim, is the minimum. Anything lower, their masts won't clear, and the commerce of the port is wrecked." He waved another paper. "The bridge builders – the Roeblings – claim that raising the bridge ten feet will cost $600,000 and add thirty-two feet to the span."

"So what do you do?" I asked. "Commission your own engineering study?"

"Not at all," smiled Rawlins. "The safest thing is to assume both are exaggerating. I expect I'll compromise at one hundred thirty-five feet and make them eat it."

"At one stroke," I told him, "wrecking both the grade of the bridge and the commerce of the port."

John laughed, coughed and held up his hand, trying to catch his breath. Emma, by the door, looked stricken. "No doubt," he rasped, fighting for air. "But that's politics. If they asked us for ten commandments, we'd offer them five and settle on seven-and-a-half." He laughed and coughed, until I was afraid he'd shake to pieces. I felt Emma's hand on my elbow, saw the look in her eyes and shortly left. By early September, John Rawlins was dead.

Maybe I attribute too much to John Rawlins. Maybe he was not so much a rudder to Grant as I think. Maybe even Rawlins would have been unable to keep Grant steady in the storms that followed. But it certainly is no coincidence that less than a month after Rawlins's death the first of the Grant scandals started. In New York, speculators named Jay Gould and Jim Fisk tried to corner the gold market and enlisted a financier named Abel Corbin, who was married to Grant's sister Jennie. Taking advantage of this pipeline to the president, and with the probable connivance of others in the White House, they drove gold up to $160 and were about to rake their profit when Grant heard of the scheme, flooded the market with government gold and sent the price plummeting. Gould and Fisk got out, but thousands were ruined, banks and brokerages failed. "Black Friday," September 24, reverberated around world markets and shook the government. Grant's administration, naïve at best and crooked at worst, started on the downward spiral that makes it proverbial for negligence and corruption.

I was not untouched.

It came as no surprise to me, although it did to many others, that Grant, in his inaugural address, promised to "favor any course which tends to the civilization and ultimate citizenship of the original occupants of this land." This was the beginning of Grant's Peace Policy. He was the first president to have an Indian policy at all, let alone a Peace Policy.

Before Indian Affairs became one of the Grant scandals it was one of the rare Grant successes. When my appointment as commissioner of Indian affairs was announced, the question "Who is Ely Parker?" burned the wires from government office to army post to Indian agency, and details of my biography, both factual and fanciful, flashed abroad. Depending on your point of view, I was Grant's Indian from Appomattox, trusty scribe, straight-and-narrow aide who kept his head when others were losing theirs. I was a classical scholar, university graduate, hobnobber with the great from Polk to Palmerston, lawyer, engineer, leader of the Six Nations, heir to a great fortune, speaker of seven languages and consort of one of the belles of Washington. Or, I was a Grant crony and drinking pal, one generation from barbarity, a leach on the public treasury, architect of useless, pork-barrel projects, a lurker in the shadow of fame, debaucher of white women and conniver in the mingling of the races. In fact, I was a Negro.

I tried to let none of this bother me as I awaited confirmation. The senators, at first confused whether I was a citizen or not, decided it didn't matter and confirmed me with a shrug. Before the scandal hit we managed actually to implement some of the Peace Policy.

Although I was nominally under Interior Secretary Jacob Cox, Grant's policy called for a great deal of autonomy for the commissioner, so that I could directly purchase supplies and supervise agents without the middlemen that raked off the profit and poorly supplied the reservations. I also got permission to sack the mostly corrupt agents, whom I replaced with army men or Quakers. One of my great pleasures was that General Alfred Sully accepted the superintendentship in Montana. In November 1868, Red Cloud and the Oglala had signed a treaty, paving the way for their coming in to a reservation in exchange for our destroying the Powder

River forts and keeping whites out of their hunting grounds there. George Beauvais, from his ranch in Wyoming, was in contact with Sully, agreeing to serve as conduit for the many supplies the Sioux would soon require. Both Sully and Beauvais volunteered to assume their posts even before their official appointments arrived.

My office, appropriate to the inventive policy we anticipated, was in the Patent Office Building that occupied the entire blocks between Seventh and Ninth Streets on Avenues F and G, a sprawling structure, completed in 1856, huge enough to house and display the thousands of models of inventions that applying patentees were required to submit. Before the war it was a well-organized tourist attraction, its east and west wings full of everything from the minutely practical (corset-tightener, dentist's chair, egg-beater) to the fantastic (a plow with cannons for handles in case of Indian attack) to the astonishing (a machine for making B-shaped crackers named for Mr. Bretzel; a flatboat with air chambers for lifting it over shoals submitted by "A. Lincoln" in 1846). The war, however, had increased patent applications by hundreds, so the so-called galleries now had stuff piled every which way, an adjustable wig on a sculpted head surmounted by a metal army helmet; a sewing machine atop a sliding buggy-bench. And, of course, innumerable kinds of weaponry. Also during the war, part of the huge place was used as a hospital. Patent Office clerk Clara Barton tended the wounded here as did Walt Whitman of "The Wound Dresser."

Although the Interior Department occupied a small suite of offices in the building, and my department a small office therein, it was still heady to walk through those galleries on my way to work, a continual reminder of American brainpower and firepower. Though my office itself was small – about forty clerks plus myself – it was the center of an empire that stretched from the Abenaki in Maine to the Montauk at the tip of Long Island, to the Mohawk on the St. Lawrence, to the Sioux in Montana, to the Nez Perce in Oregon, Apache in the southwest, to the few remnants of the Seminole still occupying enclaves in Florida. About a hundred tribes, comprising three hundred thousand Indians in all, "fewer than the white men we killed in the war," Grant noted. There were seventy agents in the field, with fifteen superintendents above them. What with other agency employees – teachers, interpreters, doctors, millers, carpenters and, of course, more clerks and secretaries – the bureau had about 600 people in its employ and many millions of dollars at its disposal.

As a result of the Peace Policy, Congress had conferred on me more power – also more responsibility – than previous commissioners. In particular, all financial transactions, including the vital orders for supplies, went directly through my office. But Congress giveth and Congress taketh away. Congress had no sooner granted these extraordinary powers than it got an attack of what my wife calls *l'esprit de l'escalier* – thoughts on the staircase – and sent someone to look after me in the form of a Board of Indian Commissioners. The name itself was designed to invite confusion, as if I was only one commissioner in a board of ten. The Board that Congress appointed, however, was not part of the Bureau but a separate civilian commission of trustworthy businessmen and clergy, whose job was to prevent repetition of the abuses of the past.

Some bureaucratic sniffing gave me advance warning of the commissioners' names, one of whom was Reverend William Welsh, whom I dimly remembered from City Point in the war.

Minnie remembered him better. "Reverend Welsh? Old sourpuss? He was with me and mother at City Point, when we came looking for my father."

"Ah," I said. I also now recalled a scene in Grant's tent, young Minnie Sackett with her hand on my shoulder, the tent flap opening and a shocked ministerial face staring at us, then continuing to stare back at me as he escorted the white women away. William Welsh.

"Welsh?" said Quentin Winslow when I mentioned the name to him. "Hs-s-s-t! Not here." He motioned me outside his office, where we sat on a bench in a windowless corridor.

"Yes," he murmured. "The implacable Reverend Welsh. Friend of those who have no friends."

"Such as?"

"Indians," said Quentin, "but only in the abstract."

"I'm an Indian."

"Yes." Quentin allowed himself a small smile. "But you're far from abstract. People like Reverend Welsh want to help the Indians as an idea. Confronted, however, with real Indians, they get confused."

"Religious groups visited City Point," I recalled. "Quakers and Episcopalians, making sure the camp was sanitary, the prisoners well-treated, the trenches full of Bibles and free of bad language. Welsh came down there offering passage through the lines for anxious relatives."

"And found you fondling a white girl," added Quentin.

I sat up straight. "You know that?"

"H-s-s-s-t!" he said, looking anxiously around. "I know much, but I don't tell."

"That's it?" I asked. "The white girl? My wife? But that was years ago!"

"Not to Reverend Welsh, I expect. You, Parker, you're not supposed to be educated, famous, wearing a uniform, marrying white girls. You're supposed to be sitting in a schoolroom reading Mr. Welsh's schoolbooks and thanking the distant white father. Or on the plains, romantic and unapproachable, the noble savage, untainted by graft and greed. Either way, keeping your distance."

I thought about it. "Surely he can cause me no trouble now," I said.

"People like Reverend Welsh are always trouble," said Quentin. "Keep your eyes open, Parker, and your powder dry."

My first meeting with the Board of Commissioners was in a conference room at the Interior Department, my turf. Providentially, the date was May 11. On May 10, news flashed around the world from Promontory, Utah that the two tendrils of the intercontinental railroad had met, with a ceremonial spike planted between the facing cowcatchers of two locomotives, under the eyes of government dignitaries, Chinese and Irish workers, tavernkeepers, roustabouts and a few watchful Indians. The journey from Omaha to San Francisco, four months or more by wagon train, would soon take four days in coach cars with crystal glasses. The new line across the country also drew a line in history, determining the fate of the Plains Indians more surely than any decisions we would make in Washington.

Though I was prepared to suffer William Welsh as one of the ten commissioners, I was shocked to enter the room that bright May day and see him seated at the head of the table as chairman. He was as I remembered him – rail thin, hawk nose, and a short, white beard that circled his face, leaving his pursed lips bare.

"Come in, come in, Commissioner Parker," said Welsh as heartily as he could in his cackly voice. Nine other heads turned toward me.

"Good morning, gentlemen," I said, hiding my chagrin, and took the seat Welsh waved me to at the end of the table. It was a bright room with windows overlooking Eighth Street and restful landscapes on the walls, mostly Hudson River scenes, with peaceful Indians gazing from the woodlands. Sitting down I could just see Ford's Theater through the window down the block, not an encouraging omen. Welsh introduced the other commission members, including George H. Stuart and Felix Brunot, businessmen philanthropists from Pennsylvania, and William E. Dodge, of similar ilk, from New York. The commissioners, I realized, knew each other already, at least by reputation. As Welsh introduced each and gave a few references, smiles, nods and rumbles passed among the bearded white men, like Indian chiefs grunting at each other. I saw the pattern – rich businessmen, philanthropists and pillars of the church from the northeast. No military. Nobody from the south. Most unfortunately, nobody from the west.

"Perhaps we should start, Commissioner," said Welsh, standing, as if calling the meeting to order, "by telling you what we expect of you."

"Absolutely," I agreed, keeping my seat and grinning around the table. "And then I'll tell you what I expect of you." A few of the commissioners chuckled. They were all looking at me, curious. I don't think any but Welsh had ever laid eyes on me before, and I wanted to show them a relaxed, well-spoken, unruffled executive.

Welsh glanced around the room, gauging their reaction. "To be sure," he said, smiling as much as he was capable of. "Now we know that President Grant has announced what he calls a Peace Policy, which seems designed to bring savages off the plains and into business within a generation." He waved his hand at his colleagues' surprised reaction. "Forgive my blunt speaking," he said. "My disagreement with this policy is well known. But I shall not let it interfere with the performance of my duties. Now I gather, Commissioner Parker, that you think the key to this policy is the quick and honest delivery of supplies to the reservations. For that reason, you have arrogated to yourself the sole duty for approving all orders for and dispatching of supplies."

"Almost," I said. "Congress gave it to me. I just decided to take it."

Some men chuckled, but Welsh rode through it. "Would you care to explain this unprecedented arrogation of power?"

Staying calm despite his hostile tone, I did so, making eye contact with each commissioner in turn. I explained about the role of supplies in helping Indians make the transition from plains to reservation, how keeping Indians on the reservation by means of adequate supplies was the prerequisite to everything that would follow. "As you know, Mr. Welsh," I said, "the great problems have been speed and corruption. The Indians like to say an agent arrives at a reservation with a carpetbag and leaves with two boatloads of goods. I believe we've solved the corruption by stripping the agencies of all superintendents and agents with any temptation to profit, replacing them with army men and Quakers, each of whom has his own higher power to answer to. That relieves my office of the necessity of enforcement."

"So you say," said Welsh dryly. "And how does your being at the head of the supply line solve the speed problem?"

"By cutting out middlemen," I said promptly. I leaned forward and addressed the men on both sides of the table. "You are all businessmen. You did not get where you are today by entrusting your business to others, particularly your inventory and the quality of your goods. Speed and quality are my main assets. By taking personal responsibility both for the quality of the supplies and the speed of their delivery I cut out both the delays and the dilution of quality that can be caused by middlemen." I saw nods of agreement around the table.

"Yes, I see," said Welsh. "But aren't you leaving out something?"

"What's that?" I asked.

"Your own potential for corruption," said Welsh, still smiling sourly.

He ruffled me but I didn't let it show. Instead, George Stuart, Welsh's Pennsylvania colleague, snapped his head back like he'd been slapped. "Now see here, Welsh . . ." he stammered.

I patted a hand at Stuart. "Corruption?" I asked mildly.

"Well," admitted Welsh, seeing the consternation around the table, "forgive me again for speaking bluntly. But let's face it, Parker. You are an Indian. You have negotiated with Indians. You have negotiated with this government on behalf of Indians. You know how to play both sides." He was making my dual identity, my main strength, seem a liability.

"You have already," Welsh lifted two papers and waved them at me, "appointed two of your cronies to lucrative posts in the west. I refer to Alfred Sully and the uncredentialed George Beauvais. Both are now working directly for you, yet their appointments have not been confirmed."

So that's how Welsh wanted to play. Heads swiveled to me and I opened my arms at them. "General Sully and Mr. Beauvais are experienced Indian hands," I said. "They are trustworthy and will report to me alone.

The area they serve – the Powder River – is the most sensitive Indian area in the country. I needed them at their posts immediately and they agreed."

I smiled knowingly at the commissioners. "As you know," I told them, "in the army during the war, General Grant," carefully dropping the sacred name, "and I cut many corners on the way to Richmond. Direct contact, in fact, proved the only route to victory." The commissioners chuckled at the mild joke.

Heads turned to Welsh. "Highly suspicious nonetheless," he harrumphed, "putting your own men in such sensitive posts."

I opened my hands. "Perhaps I am unused to diplomacy," I admitted. "Like General Grant, I'm a soldier. Peacetime is teaching us civilized manners, but only gradually. I pledge to you gentlemen that, with your oversight, I will do everything by the book."

The commissioners frowned at each other, and now it was Mr. Brunot who spoke. "The book," he said, "is sometimes good for reference only. We're businessmen. I'd hate to think how unsuccessful we'd all be if we tried to do it by some book." Bearded heads nodded. "With all respect to your scruples, Welsh, it strikes me that Parker, given his head, can see straight through things with a certain efficiency. I suggest we not tie his hands with excessive oversight. Sometimes the direct route is the best."

Welsh, seeing how the wind blew, shrugged in resignation. "There remains," he said, "our own responsibility. Surely we're not simply to approve all Parker's actions after the fact."

"No-no-no," agreed Brunot. "But use the slack rope. Let him run."

"Hoping I don't hang myself," I added.

"I propose," interjected Commissioner Dodge, "that we appoint Welsh here a subcommittee of one to oversee the supply chain. As it seems an area of particular concern to him, let him be the watchdog."

"I accept," said Welsh, a little too eagerly for me, and the rest of the commissioners appointed him unanimously.

When the commissioners departed, for the most part satisfied they had a competent in the chief's chair, I rose to bid them goodbye, hoping never to see them again. But Welsh, the last one to the door, closed it with himself still on the inside. He leaned against the door, folders of paper clutched to his breast, head cocked, listening to the departing footsteps of the other commissioners. Satisfied we were alone, he returned to the table, put down his papers, and leaned both fists on it. "You cannot fool me, Parker," he said.

"I never intend to, Mr. Welsh," I said, approaching the table.

"You will never convince me – never! – that the Indian is capable of civilization. Not in one generation, not even in ten!"

I opened my hands. "I offer myself as Exhibit One."

"You!" he hissed. "I've known you since I laid eyes on you! I know what you want! You want to sit at our table, take our money, drink our liquor, and debauch our women!"

I clenched my teeth to keep from shouting out at him. "Our women?" I asked mildly.

"Your wife!" he hissed. "How dare you! You're a disgrace and so is she! You should both be banished from society!"

I reached out and took his elbow. He shrank away as if I was about to dismember him. "Take your hands off me!"

I let go his arm and stood aside to let him pass. "Just seeing you to the door, Mr. Welsh. Our business is done."

"Oh, no it's not, Parker. I've got my eye on you. This Sully and Beauvais business? Nothing! Just showing you the instruments. I am your overseer now. I want regular reports from you on every – every! – supply transaction that passes through your hands." He brushed past me toward the door.

"Mr. Welsh," I said, following him. "I will report to you as and if I have something to report." I opened the door, but blocked his way with my arm. "And," I told him, leaning close and whispering into his face, "if you ever mention my wife again, I will strip you naked and scalp you!" The last I saw of Welsh that day he was scurrying down the hallway to the outer door, heedless of the papers that dropped from his hands.

There was no way to avoid Welsh entirely, however, and over the next year, as I made trips to Baltimore and New York to oversee the dispatching of supplies to the western tribes, Welsh would often go with me, joining me unannounced, avoiding small talk on the train, wordlessly trailing me as I went from warehouse to warehouse, checking bills of lading against actual shipments. He sometimes insisted on unpacking entire loads and inventorying them himself on a separate list before allowing their dispatch. After a year of such shenanigans he had not uncovered a penny of mislaid funds or a stick of unaccounted supplies. But he was determined to find something.

Chapter XXII

AS LONG AS THE WHITE MAN DOESN'T WANT THE POWDER

Washington 1870

As I HAD TOLD THE COMMISSIONERS, THE SUPPLY LINK was only part of the bigger chain of the Peace Policy. Another link was ambassadorial visits from tribal chiefs and their entourages. The most significant of these – and the one of greatest importance to me personally – was Red Cloud's visit to Washington in the spring of 1870.

In 1868 George Beauvais and General Sully had helped negotiate a treaty with Red Cloud that promised his Oglala band freedom from interference in the Powder River area in exchange for the rest of the Oglala accepting a reservation along the Missouri River, where Spotted Tail and the Brulé were now located. Spotted Tail's group were becoming models for the Peace Policy – confined to their reservation, disarmed, equipped with food and farming supplies. Schoolhouses had opened, and the first year of the Spotted Tail agency was a moderate success. There were two problems, however. The first was the continual, nagging issue of supplying distant reservations from warehouses in the east. When a spring flood washed away the Brulé's new-planted corn, the seed had to be replaced from Baltimore, arriving barely in time to get the crop in the ground. The second problem was that many of Red Cloud's Oglala had not come in to the Missouri reservation, preferring to stay in the Powder River hunting grounds several hundred miles away. Idled by lack of supplies, Spotted Tail's young braves looked longingly west to Red Cloud's hunters.

So we invited Red Cloud to Washington, where we would so shower him with gifts and attention, so scare him with guns and graves, that he would have no choice but to come in to the reservation. Despite his oft-expressed distaste for "show business," President Grant was complicit, knowing the importance of show when it could avoid war.

George Beauvais was a bluff intermediary, carrying Grant's messages to Red Cloud and bringing Red Cloud and fifteen other Oglala east. On May 26, 1870, Beauvais telegraphed from Fort Laramie that all were on board a special Union Pacific coach, bound eastward. I shook my head at the telegram. Three years ago, when Beauvais and I rode from North Platte to meet Spotted Tail, end-of-track was almost 300 miles east of Laramie, many days' ride. Now Laramie was another whistle-stop on the transcontinental railway, whisking sixteen Sioux from Laramie to Washington quicker than Beauvais and I had ridden a fraction of the distance. On June 1, after stops in Omaha and Chicago, Red Cloud's party arrived in Washington.

I met them at the station, and what an array they were! Some in buckskin boots, others in new leather shoes from Omaha. One Sioux woman wore a feathered headdress while her companion sported an equally feathered piece of millinery she probably bought at Field & Leiter in Chicago. Different tribes, different feathers. Beauvais strode in his buckskin jacket along the platform in front of them and greeted me heartily. To my surprise and delight, Indian Charlie was with him, seventeen years old now and considerably taller.

"Quite a change, Mr. Commissioner!" said Beauvais, flicking my cravat.

Behind him most of the Sioux men gathered in a knot, inspecting the white passers-by as much as the whites inspected them. "They're still getting used to the crowds?" I asked.

Indian Charlie eyed them. "Not the way you think. Thing is, they can't get a handle on how many white folk there are. They imagine the same white crowd has followed them – from Omaha, to Chicago, now here." We watched the Sioux point out features of various white men.

"See?" said Beauvais. "They're trying to figure out if that's the same fella they saw in Chicago."

Beauvais stepped to the Sioux and respectfully touched the elbow of one of them, who stepped forward to stare me in the face. "Red Cloud," murmured Indian Charlie in my ear.

Red Cloud was as motley as the rest of them, with a white shirt and loose scarf around his neck, a black vest and buckskin trousers. A single feather sprouted from the back of his head. He was almost a head shorter than me, and he stared up at me with frank wonder, his copper brow furrowed. He spoke something that Charlie shook his head at and replied to.

"What?" I asked, my eyes on Red Cloud.

Charlie kept his face straight. "He thought you were Grant the Great Father," he explained. "He's impressed that the Great Father is an Indian."

I smiled and held out my hand, which Red Cloud shook once, snapping his head in a single nod. "I am only the Little Father," I told him. "The bridge between you and the Great Father. You notice my face?" I pointed to my face and Red Cloud nodded. "Among the whites there are many races and colors," I said. "How far you rise depends not on the color of your face, but the content of your heart."

Red Cloud nodded as Charlie translated the diplomatic lie, then touched two fingers to the spot above my heart. "Your heart is what I am here to test," he said.

"And I yours, and those of all your people." I swept my arm to include all the delegation, who swarmed around me as I escorted them out of the station. It was quite a sight, the sea of white folks parting as the Seneca Moses led his followers to the land of guns and butter.

We got them settled at the Washington House on Third and Pennsylvania, where the Beveridge family catered regularly to Indians. Although the Sioux had stayed in hotels in Omaha and Chicago, they weren't used to it. Amanda Beveridge sized up the group and decided on a four-room suite for the sixteen of them. I was horrified at such crowding, but Beauvais and Charlie assured me it was fine. In fact, after viewing the spacious rooms, the Sioux all moved into three of them, taking turns on the beds, most of them sleeping in blankets on the floor.

As I left them, Red Cloud stopped me with a request that no Sioux had likely made before: "Telegraph my people that the train arrived safe."

Next day we took the group to the Senate, to the Navy Yard and Arsenal. The sequence was not lost on Red Cloud. "Tell your chief," he told Charlie, "that I understand. You are like us. You dress in nice clothes, you convene in great council chambers, you talk and talk. When talk fails, you have ships and guns. And your guns are more and bigger than ours."

When we looked across the Potomac at the rows of crosses in Arlington Cemetery, Red Cloud started to count the graves but soon gave up and looked a question at me. "Over fifteen thousand," I told him. When that figure puzzled him, I quoted figures from last year's Indian census. "More than all your Oglala. More than Spotted Tail's Brulé. Many more than both of you combined. All dead in one war of four years. And there are many more such cemeteries through our land."

"You kill the way your railroad gulps the miles," said Red Cloud.

I took the Sioux to the White House that night for the president's reception. When I found, however, that Beauvais had ordered fancy dress clothes for them I vetoed it. "Tribal wear," I told him. "More impressive." It took me back to my first visit to the White House almost a quarter-century ago, me in my vest and new shoes, but my country cousins Isaac Shanks and John Blacksmith, who knew exactly what they were doing, dressing exotic.

The East Room, having not yet undergone the Grant transformation of 1874, remained as it was when Dolley Madison still haunted it. When I escorted the sixteen Oglala into the waiting diplomatic reception, Grant had done them the honor of arriving before them. He exchanged formal handshakes with all of them, singling out Red Cloud for special treatment and promising a private meeting before the visit ended. The rest of official Washington, in finest finery, put on frozen smiles and endured the Indians' presence as I toured the room with them. The buffet tables particularly impressed the Sioux, and after a few tentative bites they plunged in, Red Cloud downing numerous helpings of strawberries and cream. Indian Charlie translated his ironic question to me: "We may expect strawberries and cream if we come in to the reservation?" I didn't reply that "eating strawberries" is Seneca for death.

My job, however, was not all sightseeing and parties. Late that night, in my office at home, I sat for the hundredth time at my desk, a map of Wyoming and Dakota territories at one hand, the 1868 Laramie treaty at the other, my eye on the bottle of wine my wife had thoughtfully uncorked for me. I poured a small glass and sat back, sipped and sighed.

Minnie, sitting near the fireplace with a book, heard the sigh. "Satisfaction or resignation?" she asked without looking up.

"Resignation," I told her. "Mine, if I can't solve this."

"Will talking help?" she asked.

"Nothing else has," I said. She rustled over to sit in the chair across from me. I never tired of watching her move, gliding as if she had no feet. She was twenty-one now, but so wise and confident I often felt like a bumpkin. I showed her the map. "Here," I said, pointing to the Powder River country in Wyoming Territory, "is land that, according to Article 16 of the treaty, 'shall be held and considered to be unceded Indian territory,' and 'no white person or persons shall be permitted to settle upon or occupy any portion of the same,' in exchange for which 'the military posts now established in the territory shall be abandoned, and the road leading to them and by them to the settlements in the Territory of Montana shall be closed.'"

"Well and good," Minnie agreed. "That's where the Fetterman fight was, yes? So the Indians get it back."

"Yes," I agreed, "except that in Article 15, 'The Indians herein named agree that when the agency house and other buildings shall be constructed on the reservation named, they will regard said reservation their permanent home, and they will make no permanent settlement elsewhere; but they shall have the right to hunt, as stipulated in Article 16 hereof.' That's the stipulation that lets them hunt on the Powder."

"How perfectly clear," muttered Minnie. "No forts in the hunting territory. A permanent reservation elsewhere. And where is this 'said reservation'?"

I traced the designated reservation for her, a trapezoid that, in today's terms, extended from the Wyoming – South Dakota border east to the Missouri River.

Minnie nodded slowly. "The Indians get to hunt in the west while learning to live on the reservation in the east. What you call a 'transition to civilization.'"

"Yes," I agreed. "But to transition to civilization, they must be supplied with goods and teachers. The treaty calls for that." I read excerpts to her. "Physician, carpenter, farmer, blacksmith, miller, engineer. Schoolhouse, gristmill, sawmill, shingle-mill. Each farming Indian to have over 300 acres of land. One hundred dollars per Indian per year for tools and seed. Clothing specified for all adults and children, to be delivered annually to the agency headquarters. All goods, in fact, are delivered to agency headquarters. That's where all the main buildings are too – schoolhouse, hospital, mills, smithy . . . ."

"And these supplies are to be delivered where?" asked Minnie, standing up now, her hands flat on the map.

I traced my finger east from the Wyoming border to where the 46th parallel intersected the Missouri River, halfway across Dakota Territory. "According to the treaty, 'at some place on the Missouri river, near the center of said reservation,'" I quoted.

"But, good heavens," said Minnie. "That's . . . how many miles from the hunting grounds?"

"About two hundred," I acknowledged.

"But that's impossible!"

"No," I said. "Difficult, but not impossible. What's impossible is this." I traced my finger steadily southeastwards, down the Missouri, steadily away from the hunting grounds, until it reached Fort Randall, on the Nebraska border. I tapped my finger there. "That's where the reservation buildings are. That's where supplies are to be delivered. Closer to Chicago than to the Powder River!"

Minnie sat back down. "Whose bright idea was that?"

I shrugged. "Nobody knows. Red Cloud swears that he never agreed to 'on the Missouri River,' just to 'near the center of said reservation.'"

Minnie looked at the map again and agreed. "He's right. The Missouri is nowhere near the center of the reservation. It makes no sense."

"It does if you interpret it the government's way," I said. "According to us, the 'center' can mean the north-south center or the east-west center. We chose the north-south center, then moved it still further south, closer to the railroad. Easier to supply, you see?"

"Where does Red Cloud want his supplies?"

I grinned and traced my finger westward, following the Union Pacific all the way to Fort Laramie, where I tapped my finger. "Easy to supply, right on the railroad, close to Beauvais, who can supervise delivery. Nothing wrong with it, except . . ."

"Except the treaty says something else."

I blinked at her, looked at the map and grabbed up the treaty. "No," I said, the glimmer of an idea dawning. "The treaty doesn't actually *say* something else. The treaty says nothing at all about Fort Laramie."

"But Fort Laramie is outside the reservation," protested Minnie.

I was looking back and forth between the map and the treaty. "Fort Laramie is also outside the hunting grounds," I said. "*Just* outside them."

I began to see a way out.

"But the treaty says . . ." insisted Minnie.

"The hell with what the treaty says," I said, sitting back and exhaling. "It's what it *doesn't* say that might save Red Cloud. Pour me some wine, wench!"

The wench poured me some wine, and then some more, and we took another bottle up to bed, she carrying it while I carried her. She withheld her favors until I confessed my plans, then rewarded me with such favors that, next morning, as I headed blearily to the office, I was not at all sure whether my plan, so darkly hatched by moonlight and so rewarded by squirms and squeals, would get such a bubbly reaction from government men in the light of day.

But the meeting must go on. My boss, Interior Secretary Jacob Cox, chaired the gathering, and all the usual crowd were there. Beauvais, Indian Charlie as translator, Red Cloud and six other chiefs, the rest of the Sioux having apparently gone shopping. An uninvited and unwelcome presence was William Welsh, bustling in late with apologies, taking an unobtrusive seat in the corner away from the table. I shot a glance at Cox, who rolled his eyes. Once he was in, we could not exclude him without calling attention to him.

Jacob Cox was a rarity in Washington, a genuinely honest man with no political ambitions. As a result his stay in office was even shorter than mine. He was, like me, a general, although that didn't count for much in the postwar promotion boom. It amused us to call each other "General" in private and also in public when it seemed politic to do so. From genteel Ohio, he knew little of Indian matters and wasn't afraid to say so. This led him to give me my head, but it also made him susceptible to the likes of Welsh, who claimed to know more about Indians than they actually did.

Cox stood at the head of the table, with me and Red Cloud seated at his right and left. Indian Charlie sat between Red Cloud and Beauvais. Red Cloud has chosen motley for the day – vest, cravat and white shirt, but his hair worn long with eagle feathers in it. Beauvais was, unusually for him, in formal dress, his long blond hair slicked back and pomaded.

Cox began the meeting with the usual blandishments about the wisdom of the Indians, the power of the white man and the conviction that the Indians' wisdom, seeing the white man's power, would see the advantages of civilization. He concluded, somewhat surprisingly, by putting his hand on my shoulder. "Here is the Commissioner of Indian Affairs," he said, "who is a chief both among his own people and among us. His people lived here long before the white man came. He now has power among the white men, who obey him because of the great power he has earned. Let him be an example. We will be your brothers, your followers even, if you follow his example and learn our civilization."

Red Cloud then spoke, impressively. "I know the white man's power," he said. "In my lifetime I have been driven from where the sun rises to where the sun sets. Now you offer us a permanent home, but you don't say where. You offer us hunting grounds in the Powder River, but you give us no supplies. You ask us to learn reading and writing, but that only helps us better understand the lies you tell us. Please, Mr. Cox, let us dispense with pussy-footing. As to Chief Parker, whom we know as Do-ne-ho-ga-wa," I felt my face glowing but said nothing, "let us see if he is one of us or one of you – or perhaps the bridge between the two of us. Let us turn to the treaty."

I stood, the treaty on the table before me, along with a map of the territory. "Here's the sticking point," I said, pointing to Article 16. "Supplies are to be delivered and a reservation established 'at some place on the Missouri river, near the center of said reservation.'"

Red Cloud was immediately on his feet. "I never agreed to the Missouri!" he said. "I have said this over and over. That is not the treaty that was read to me at Fort Laramie. Those are not the words I signed!" There was a murmur of assent from the other chiefs.

"He's right, you know," said George Beauvais. The trader, despite his transformation to diplomat's garb, lifted a saddlebag onto the table. "I have it right here, the transcription of what was telegraphed to Fort Laramie." He pulled out a sheaf of papers and found a handwritten sheet, which he unfolded and spread out. "Here it is, nothing about the Missouri, just that the reservation is to be established 'near the center of said reservation.'"

The white men and I, including Welsh, who crept forward from his seat in the corner, looked back and forth between Beauvais's handwritten transcription and the actual treaty, as engrossed and passed by Congress. There was no question – the treaty as passed contained the words 'on the Missouri,' which had not been in the original.

Seeing us compare the drafts, although unable to read the words, Red

Cloud read our faces clearly enough. "It's true!" he cried. "The Missouri is not there!"

"It appears not," agreed Cox, holding up both papers.

"Then it is clear, no?" said Red Cloud. "The version that we signed at Laramie is the correct one. Your Congress made a mistake. Your Congress must fix it!"

Cox sighed and looked at me to explain it. "It's clear what happened," I told Red Cloud. "In transcribing the treaty, the congressional staff added what it thought was a clarification. 'On the Missouri' was where they thought the reservation was to be."

"They were wrong," said Red Cloud triumphantly. "Tell your Congress to fix it!"

I looked at Cox for support, but clearly I was to break the news. "I learned many years ago about Congress," I told Red Cloud. "Bad white men tried to take our Seneca land by forging names on a treaty. They had names on the treaty of men who were not chiefs, who had no power to touch the pen for the Seneca. But the treaty went to Congress, and Congress approved it."

"And what did you do then?" asked Red Cloud

I looked around for support but found none. William Welsh, in his seat in the corner, was picking his fingernails. "We submitted," I admitted to Red Cloud. "When Congress speaks, it has the force of law. This," I said, holding the ratified treaty in my hand, "is the treaty. This," I indicated the draft in Beauvais's hand, "is just a piece of paper."

Red Cloud looked at me for a long time after Indian Charlie translated his defeat. Then he said to me, "This is the white man's way? This is the way you have learned? I'll take my chances on the Powder River." He made a little circling gesture with his finger, and the other chiefs stood and followed him toward the door.

"Do something Parker!" hissed Cox, seeing an Indian war beginning in his own office.

"Go to the Powder!" I called to Red Cloud. "We can supply you there!"

Red Cloud stopped, his hand on the door. "How?" he said. "Your treaty says nothing about supplying us on the Powder. It forbids white men to enter the Powder River country. At least your Congress got that right!"

I held out my hand to him. "Come. Sit. Look," I said, aware too late I

325

was speaking as if to a dog. Red Cloud stayed where he was, but removed his hand from the door.

"Here, look at the map," I said. "We can supply you from Fort Laramie."

Red Cloud frowned. "The treaty says nothing about Fort Laramie."

"Exactly," I said, and Beauvais, getting it, rose and pulled the spread-out map to him. He chuckled and nodded his head. Behind him, William Welsh left his chair and crept forward.

Red Cloud returned to the table, frowning, and I showed him. "We will supply you at the hunting grounds from Fort Laramie," I said, tapping the map. "It is both outside the hunting grounds and outside the reservation." I explained to the whole room. "The treaty forbids us to *enter the hunting grounds* or to *supply the reservation* from anywhere but the Missouri. But it does not forbid us to *supply the hunting grounds* from *outside the reservation*, and that is what I propose to do."

Cox had his arms folded, chin in hand, nodding. Red Cloud looked at the assembled white men. "This you can do?" he asked.

Cox continued nodding. "With the president's approval," he said.

"Sophistry!" sputtered Welsh, crouched at the table, looking from treaty to map, as if for a loophole. "You can't do this, Parker! It's clearly not what Congress intended!"

"I don't know what Congress intended, Mr. Welsh, and neither do you," I countered. "All we know is what Congress wrote and what it didn't. If you want Congress's intent, go and ask them. Meanwhile . . . ."

"Meanwhile," chimed in Cox, moving past me to confront Welsh directly, "Sit down and be quiet, Mr. Welsh. You are here as an observer." Cox moved forward and, without actually touching Welsh, backed him into his corner chair, where he sat with a thump. Turning to me, Cox motioned Indian Charlie not to translate, smiled, and said to me through his teeth. "We're out on a limb, Parker. Can you get the president's approval on this?"

I smiled back, not letting my doubts betray me. "I hope so," I said.

There were further discussions and an elaborate leave-taking. I promised to speak to the president and arrange a meeting between him and the Indians, which was on our agenda anyway. Left alone in the conference room, after gathering papers, I sat back in a chair and let my breath out as if I had been holding it the whole time. I chuckled to myself. Halfway there. I had Cox's approval, though I had sprung it on him. I had

Red Cloud's. All I needed was Grant's. I fished my watch from my pocket. The president would be just finishing lunch. No time like the present, so I went to the door and found William Welsh lurking outside.

"A word with you, Parker," he hissed. "Inside, if you please."

We closed the door, and Welsh turned on me. "That was a trick, Parker! You should have informed Cox, you should have informed me, before taking this step! It's a violation of the treaty! It's illegal! It's contrary to our entire Indian policy!"

I shrugged. "The president will decide if it's against the law," I said. "I was under no obligation to inform you. As to General Cox, he seems to have no objection."

"You ambushed him!" sputtered Welsh. "You gave him no time to think! That's your Indian way, is it? Take power and force others to follow. Is that what you expect these other Indians to learn from your example?"

I smiled at him. "Mr. Welsh, it was a white man's trick, a lawyer's trick. And why not? The treaty was Congress's trick. I just tricked a new meaning out of it."

"You'll never win this way, Parker," Welsh insisted. "We do not want Indians to be sophisticated, but docile, Christian and on reservations. What you've done is left a band of wild Sioux, roaming free on the Powder, infinitely and forever supplied by you at Fort Laramie!"

I leaned back against the table and folded my arms, trying to calm him. "Mr. Welsh, nothing is forever, particularly where Indians are concerned. We supply Red Cloud this way for a few years and see what happens. There will be other struggles, other treaties, other white men moving west. Red Cloud can't stay forever on the Powder. He'll be a reservation Indian soon. Just give him time. And leave him his dignity."

"Dignity!" said Welsh. "Give him dignity and he'll fight! Deprive him and he'll surrender. Your way takes too long and causes trouble."

I shook my head. "Mr. Welsh, we'll never see eye to eye on this. Let's agree to disagree." I pointed out the window toward the White House. "Let's see what the president says. I'm on my way to see him right now. I'm sorry you can't join me."

I walked past him to the door, leaving him alone in the room. "I'm watching you, Parker," he said to my back. "Never forget that."

Grant retained his ability to see through things and get them done. When I corralled him after lunch it took him no time to agree to my scheme, puffing on his cigar, nodding, even chuckling a little. "If it's not forbidden by the treaty, it's legal," he said. "That your point?"

"And if not forbidden by any other law or treaty," I added. "I have people working on that right now. But I don't think it is. The silence of the treaty gives you discretion to act in areas the treaty doesn't."

"M-m-m," said Grant, eyeing me. "Gives me authority to trust your discretion, eh? Well, it's never hurt before. Cox agrees?"

"Yes, sir."

"Another nice victory for Red Cloud," he said. "Can we afford it?"

"It's temporary," I said. "He'll lose in the end."

"'Let 'em down easy,' that what we're doing?" I was silent. "Very well," he sighed. "I'll meet Red Cloud tomorrow afternoon."

It was a happy crowd that gathered in Grant's office next day. When I showed Red Cloud the office, I was impressed anew at how businesslike it had become since Polk's – even since Lincoln's – day. Gone were the comfortable couches and chairs, gone the table Lincoln worked at, replaced by actual desks and file cabinets. Visitors no longer entered the office directly, waiting instead in a reception area, whence they were rationed to the president. In a room off the anteroom I showed Red Cloud the telegraph, the "talking wire" that could communicate with Fort Laramie in a heartbeat. I did not tell him how recent it was – that even Lincoln, atop a massive war machine, had to walk several times daily from his office to the War Department to find a working telegraph.

Red Cloud and the other chiefs accepted cigars from Grant, a nice touch, which also allowed him to end the meeting when the cigars were out. "You have a good friend," Grant told Red Cloud, "in Do-ne-ho-ga-wa here. He will keep his word. I will keep my word. You are free on the Powder River for as long as . . ." he looked at me. "How long, Parker?"

Red Cloud blew smoke and interjected, "As long as the rivers run and the grasses grow?" he asked sarcastically.

I smiled at the old, disgraced phrase. "As long as you remain peaceful and abide by the treaties," I said.

Red Cloud extinguished his cigar. Grant, taking the cue, rose to let him depart. "As long," said Red Cloud, "as the white man doesn't want the Powder River."

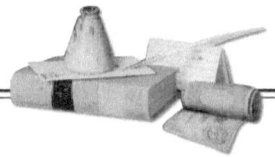

Chapter XXIII

TAKE THE MONEY!

Washington 1871

IMING, TIMING, TIMING. THAT'S WHAT MAKES HISTORY. If Baldy Smith had attacked on a June afternoon at Petersburg, the war would have ended in 1864. If Joe Bowers had got to Appomattox on time, I might never have been "Grant's Indian".

Now it was another June and Grant's Indian was history's fool. On June 1 Congress appropriated money to fulfill all Indian "obligations" *then in existence*. Also on June 1, Red Cloud arrived in Washington. Not until June 10th did we recognize a new "obligation" to supply Red Cloud at Fort Laramie. Red Cloud was chugging back to Fort Laramie, and I wanted supplies to be there when he got there. But Congress had not authorized such supplies and would not meet until July to authorize a supplement.

"So you finagle," murmured Quentin Winslow in his State Department redoubt, files and books protecting him.

"Finagle?" I asked.

"The German mnemonist Feinagle," Quentin explained patiently. "A trick of remembering things by skipping a step here and there. That's what you do now. You skip some steps. You have your full primary appropriation already?" He licked his thumb and turned over a paper.

"Of course," I said. "But none of it earmarked for Fort Laramie. That will be in the supplement."

"You skim from the primary here and there," said Quentin, continuing to turn papers, squaring corners as he went. "When Congress passes the supplement in July, you replace here and there. It all evens out."

"There won't be time for bids," I said. Indian contracts required competitive bidding.

Quentin lifted a shoulder. "They have bid on the primary appropriation already. Use the same contractors, the same bids. On the supplement, let them re-bid. Then replace what you've taken for Red Cloud by means of the supplementary supplies you contract for via the re-bid."

I shook my head. "I've never operated that way. I don't know how to do it."

Quentin blinked up at me from his papers. "Yes," he murmured. "But you're the only one in Indian Bureau history who hasn't. Study. Learn how they do it. Go thou and do likewise."

I rapped my knuckle on his desk, causing him to jump a little, and rose to go. "Parker," he said, finger to his lips.

"Of course," I said. "I was never here."

It took more skimming and finagling than Quentin predicted. I was able to divert enough outbound supplies to Fort Laramie to provide for Red Cloud's immediate needs – food for horses and hunters, powder and shot, medical supplies. This, however, left a shortage in supplies for reservations, notably the new Oglala reservation "on the Missouri." Far more Oglala than expected had come in to that reservation, and they now sat on the banks of the Missouri, awaiting beef and flour, clothing and farm implements, to see them through the summer until their harvest came in. In desperation, I approached a trusted supplier, James Bosler, who agreed to supply the Oglala on credit until Congress passed the supplement. It was a private, no-bid contract, technically illegal, but desperate times need desperate measures. When, on July 15, Congress approved the supplement and bids were solicited publicly, I was relieved that Bosler's was low, and I was able to reimburse him one-for-one.

The result was a peaceful summer and fall of 1870 along the Missouri and Powder Rivers. Red Cloud peacefully hunted, the reservation Sioux peacefully farmed, and I began to see that, by accident or design, Congress had done well to place the reservation "on the Missouri." So far from Red Cloud's hunters, the reservation Indians had no call of the wild from the faraway west to summon them to further mayhem.

I was on the road much of the summer and fall. In September and October, I followed the supply route to Chicago and St. Louis, then attended what amounted to a constitutional convention in Oklahoma, where the tribes who had settled there drew up a constitution and bill of rights. In November, Secretary Cox was replaced by Columbus Delano, also of Ohio. I was sorry to see Cox go, for he was both honest and a supporter of my policies, whereas Delano was pure politics who would support me only in a fair wind.

I was thus both unprepared and unreinforced when the storm broke in January 1871. My wife first brought me news of it at breakfast one fine morning, with sun glinting through the frost on the breakfast room windows. She came in looking oddly pale, holding something behind her back. "Are you finished eating, dear?" she asked.

I flung down my napkin and pushed back my chair. "Done and done!" I exulted, patting my lap. "Come on and kiss me, Kate."

Instead, she sat in the chair next to me. "Take my hand," she said quietly. Perplexed, I did. "There's bad news," she said.

"Who's dead?" I asked.

"Nobody, yet," she said. "Mr. Welsh has written a letter to Secretary Delano. It's in the newspaper. It's about you, Ely."

I grabbed the paper that she held out to me and read the letter, which appeared on the front page. Soon I was standing, pacing the room, unable to believe my eyes, barking phrases aloud to anguished Minnie. According to Welsh, I was guilty of "fraud and improvidence in the conduct of Indian affairs." He had uncovered my finagle with Bosler, claiming that "a few adroit manipulations of contracts and purchases have made at least $250,000," implying that the money had lined my pockets, not mentioning that the $250,000 credit Bosler had given me in June was repaid from the supplementary appropriation in July. He blamed President Grant for entrusting Indian affairs to me, "who is but a remove from barbarism," and demanded a full congressional investigation.

"He sent the letter to the newspapers!" I sputtered. "The low, lame, little rat!"

"Ely, Ely," Minnie soothed. "Sit down."

I couldn't. My face was hot and my brain was boiling. "What can I do?" I demanded of the air.

"Go," she said. "Go now. Go to Delano. He'll know the whole thing is phony."

But Delano was no help. He was a small weasel of a fellow, with a beard twice too big for him, that seemed to grow like an animal down his shirtfront. A complete contrast to Cox, Delano hardly knew me and was scared to death of scandal. He kept me waiting a half hour in his outer office, then busied himself with paperwork as I confronted him. He heard me out and clucked in sympathy.

"All these contracts happened before I got here, Parker," he shrugged. "I can have no opinion of the charges' truth or falsity. I just got the letter myself this morning. Simultaneously with its appearance in the newspapers."

"No, no, no, Mr. Secretary," I informed him. "Not only is the accusation false, but its appearance in print is completely irregular."

"But now that it's there, it's there," he replied, examining a strand of his beard and petting it into place. "We're rather helpless, aren't we."

"No, sir!" I retorted. "It's our move." I ticked off items with raps of my knuckle on his desk, each of which made him wince. "First, you denounce its appearance in the papers. Second, you express full confidence in me. Third, you demand Welsh's resignation from the Board of Commissioners. Then, only then, do you even think of investigating the charges, such as they are."

Delano lifted his weak shoulders. "But suppose I'm proved wrong. Where would I be if I defended you and Welsh proved to be right. I would have offended one of our finest citizens."

"Right now, Mr. Secretary," I said, rising from my chair, "you're coming mighty close to offending me. In the army we knew how to deal with such things. Defend your subordinate, attack the enemy, don't give him a chance to dig in. If you need to investigate, you investigate after the battle, not before. This is an attack not only on me, but on your department."

"Which," said Delano, seeming to shrink into his chair, "is exactly why I must defend myself. From Welsh and from you. It's well and good for the army to act as you say. But not for me. I just got here. I don't know you. I don't know Welsh. I must suspend judgment and let the investigation sort things out."

"Investigation?" I said, sinking back into my chair.

Delano raised his eyebrows and lifted a paper from his desk. "Yes," he said. "This arrived after Welsh's letter. The House Appropriations Committee has decided to investigate the charges."

"Already? Give me that," I said, damning protocol and reaching across his desk to grab the paper from him. It was exactly what he said it was. "The little bastard!"

"Yes," agreed Delano, almost sympathetic. "It seems he didn't strike until his congressional ducks were in order. I'm afraid you're in for a rough winter, Parker. I wish I could help."

He could, of course, but he wouldn't. My next stop was the White House, where I sought to see Grant. Again I waited in the anteroom, and it began to feel like the '40s and '50s all over again, waiting here, waiting there, watching the more powerful come and go, seeing the doors close behind them, seldom opening for me. Horace Porter and Orville Babcock – once my fellow staff members, now Grant's secretaries – scratched their pens and avoided me.

When at length Grant agreed to see me I noticed for the first time how thicker in body and thinner in spirit he seemed. As someone at the time described him, his face wore "a puzzled pathos, as of a man with a problem before him of which he does not understand the terms." Gone was the head-into-the-brick-wall look of the war years. He heard me out, but shrugged almost as helplessly as Delano.

"I'm discovering, Parker," he admitted, "that I have damn little power. This . . . thing of yours can't be put back in the bottle. It's public and will take on its own momentum."

"Like war by different means," I said.

Grant gave that old little lift to a corner of his mouth. "That's it, Parker. Just understand the reality of it and let it take its course. If you resist it, try to divert its flow, it'll break you."

"Unlike the Mississippi," I said, standing to go.

"Hm," said Grant. "I never diverted the Mississippi, though people think I did. I just used its current. See what you can do, Parker. I, of course, must stay out of it."

"Above it," I suggested.

"No. Out of it."

Congressional investigations are so routine by now that my little scrape is just a footnote. At the time, however, it absorbed me completely. Grant was right, it was like war, and I had to give myself over wholly to it. My job was no longer to be Indian Commissioner, but to be a defendant, complete with a defense counsel, who dutifully whispered behind his hand to me as I answered the congressmen's questions. Also complete with a

Grand Inquisitor, the ubiquitous William Welsh, whom Congress, over our objections, allowed not only to attend the sessions but to ask questions. The stakes were high, because I was accused not just of incompetence and mistakes, but of fraud and criminal corruption. The stakes were not just loss of job and office, but loss of reputation and, possibly, of freedom. What an arc – from the Tonawanda to the *juzgao* in a generation – a typical path for a politician.

It was a winter in hell. January was spent preparing our case and lining up witnesses. February was the trial itself, in one of those odd basement hearing rooms in the Capitol that I'd come to know so well. Secretary Cox agreed to testify, but he was more harm than good. Yes, he remembered our meetings with Red Cloud. Yes, he remembered the agreement to supply the hunters at Fort Laramie. No, he didn't exactly recall the details. No, he didn't remember being informed about the interim purchase of supplies from Bosler. He examined a copy of a letter I'd sent him on the subject. But, beyond agreeing it was a letter from me to him, he didn't remember getting it, as much as suggesting I'd never sent it.

James Bosler, on the other hand, was forthright. Although the timing of the transaction was slightly off, he said, there was nothing else irregular about it. The price was market rate. When sealed bids were retroactively solicited and opened, Bosler's was the low bid anyway. We also summoned other suppliers who agreed that the transaction and the price were proper – and these were men with nothing to gain by supporting me, for I had bypassed them in approaching Bosler. Bosler added further flavor by revealing that William Welsh had both been investigating and courting him. Finding Bosler's business in order, Welsh had gone on to slander me to him. I was a drunk, Bosler reported Welsh saying, a debaucher of white women, a naïve barbarian easily duped by wily white businessmen who would rob the Bureau blind, because I "lacked the moral courage to withstand temptation." Asked if Welsh had any evidence of my naïveté and corruption, Bosler said no. The committee asked Welsh, in turn, why he had uttered such slanders, and he said he was merely "trying to draw Mr. Bosler out on the subject of the commissioner's character. That Mr. Bosler knew none of these things did not mean they were not true." You see how it goes.

Welsh was in his element, waving papers at me and other witnesses, demanding "Is it not true that . . .?" "Do you have any evidence that

Commissioner Parker did *not* . . .?" "Are you asking the Congress to believe . . .?" as if he'd been in bad country courtrooms all his life. As with his first strike in the newspapers, he knew that the point is in the question, not the answer. If you make an elaborate enough accusation, that's what sticks in the public mind, even if the answer is "No." As Mark Twain says, a lie makes it round the world while the truth is still pulling on its boots.

The words that Welsh hurled stuck to me even as they were being disproved: "naïve, irregular, shady, corruptible, barbarism, drunkenness, debauchery." He dragged in my appointments of Sully and Beauvais, and his questions, "Who appointed Sully?" and "Who promoted Beauvais?" hung unanswered in the hearing room and the newspapers. He even managed to insinuate that a man who'd miss his own wedding wasn't likely to be a stickler for dates and deadlines. When my attorney got the idea to bring my wife to the hearings, Welsh only changed tactics, now accusing me of being so "understandably concerned with his home and society" that my "neglect of office is understandable, though perhaps not forgivable." The words "Welshing" and "Welshism," though out of fashion today, entered the vocabulary for awhile as synonyms for guilt by insinuation and character assassination.

Though I kept a bold public front, I was miserable. My wife bore the brunt of my moroseness, but she knew how to deal with it. She tiptoed tactfully about, bought me little presents, left an open wine bottle and two glasses on my desk when I came home, an invitation to invite her in if I wanted. I often did, and we'd sit quietly by the fire, not talking much, but not depressed either. I think we grew more as a couple in our silences that winter than we had in all our previous gaiety. She'd smile and nod at me, now and then whispering, "Forsaking all others, Ely."

"Contrition," suggested Quentin Winslow one day when I slipped into his corner for advice.

"But I've done nothing wrong," I protested.

He inclined his head an inch. "Of course not. That doesn't matter. What you've done wrong is to be investigated. There is a dramatic course to such things that has nothing to do with guilt or innocence."

I shook my head.

"Ritual, Parker, it's a ritual. Don't you Indians have rituals?"

"Of course," I said. "But . . ."

Quentin shook a finger. "No but. The point of a ritual, in religion or politics, is completion. This one cannot be complete without contrition."

"President Grant says it's like war," I offered. "You must give yourself over to it."

Quentin raised an eyebrow. "The president continues to impress. He knows war is ritual. There must be mustering, attack, sudden victory, surprise retreat, counterattack, surrender, handclasp, turn and face the camera."

"And this ritual requires contrition?"

"Exactly." Quentin's finger made a circle on his desk. "You're almost at the end now, Parker. You've had accusation, outraged denial, investigation, public hearing, damsel in distress, beleaguered public servant, implacable inquisitor, earnest and bemused congressmen. Now you need contrition. Show them you're sorry. 'I have done the state some service,' sort of thing. Because it's the next step. There are only two thereafter."

"What are they?"

Quentin raised a finger. "Exoneration." Another finger. "Resignation."

"I've been afraid of that," I said.

Quentin shrugged sympathetically. "It's been inevitable since the beginning. Make a graceful bow. That's your victory."

So the next day I sat in the committee room, a piece of paper in my hands, the document of contrition my attorney and I had agreed on. "Gentlemen," I told the congressmen, "at no time have I pretended to be an expert in the management of Indian affairs. I entered the office of the Indian Bureau with the duties perfectly new to me, and it may be that mistakes have been made. In looking back I can see many things which I would change. But I do say, in as solemn a manner as I am capable, that I have never profited pecuniarily," – Minnie particularly liked that word – "or otherwise by any transaction in my official capacity. I have never sought to defraud the government out of one penny, or have knowingly lent my aid to others with that view."

And, as Quentin predicted, what followed, after a fashion, was exoneration. I trudged to my office on an early March day, the sky looming low over the low Washington structures, as if slowly flattening them. Before lunchtime the snow started and brought a congressional messenger, who shed snow from his shoulders as he dropped a packet of papers on my desk.

I stared at it for awhile, as if I could avoid the beast inside it by waiting it out. But it lay there inert, just a stack of paper, the committee report on Welsh's charges and the subsequent investigation. I sighed, reached for it, and flipped through for the conclusion:

> To the committee, the testimony shows irregularities, neglect and incompetency, and, in some instances, a departure from the express provisions of law for the regulation of Indian expenditures, and in the management of affairs in the Indian Department. But your committee have not found evidence of fraud or corruption on the part of the Indian Commissioner. With much to criticize and condemn, arising partly from errors of judgment in the construction of statutes passed to insure economy and faithfulness in administration, we have no evidence of any pecuniary or personal advantage sought or derived by the Commissioner, or anyone connected with his Bureau.

Not so bad. I could have done without the "incompetency" and "errors of judgment," but I had given them the opening. Just an incompetent Indian, not nearly smart enough to derive "any pecuniary or personal advantage." At the end was a recommendation, for what's a committee report without a recommendation? It suggested that Congress pass a law giving Welsh's Board of Indian Commissioners more power than it had before, including "joint supervision with the Commissioner of Indian Affairs over every expenditure of the office."

Well, that tore it. I put my feet on my desk, looked out the window and considered my options. The snow was swirling now, and I could barely see the White House through it. Soon Grant's mansion disappeared entirely. Let me see, should I stay in office, limply exonerated, incompetent but uncorrupt, every expenditure fine-penciled by schoolmarm Welsh? Or should I – what? Appeal to Grant for a different appointment? Fight the bill in Congress – with an interior secretary who wouldn't take his fingers out of his beard to help me? Retire to Tonawanda, admitting the white man's world was no place for me? The snow swirled deeper and deeper, till I was thoroughly alone in the midst of it, the windows rattling.

Somewhere out there, beyond the White House I could no longer see, lay the riverside path where I'd walked all those years ago with John Blacksmith and Isaac Shanks, my white man's leather shoes squelching in the muck the two other Indians trod with ease. The same place where the flat rock lay, where I'd screamed my lungs out three years ago, the night before I didn't get married, the rock from which I'd leapt to kill myself, ending up knee-deep in the muddy Potomac. Also out of sight was the Willard Hotel, where I'd sat and considered my fate the next morning – to join Stanley in his search for Livingstone? This very winter, while I'd sat in hearing rooms and lawyers' offices, my character and my life overturned like slimy rocks, with insects crawling out from underneath, Stanley had reached Zanzibar and disappeared into Africa like Sherman into Georgia, not to be heard of till he surfaced with Livingstone in his teeth. Maybe I'd head for Africa and try to find Stanley.

But I was beyond such childish things. Instead I acted manly. I hefted my feet off the desk, bundled into my overcoat and trudged through the snow to the Willard, where I ate too much, drank too much, and kept my eye on the door, hoping Welsh would walk in so I could give him a war whoop, douse him with hooch and ignite him.

It was late afternoon when I got home, the snowfall now a complete blizzard, knee-deep and blowing pedestrians blind. As I stomped my feet on the porch, Minnie glided open the door, urged me inside, put her hands to my face, stared and threw her arms around the wettest, most God-forsaken Indian she ever saw. Her petticoat telegraph had told her of Congress's report, so she knew silence was the best remedy. She peeled my wet coat off, removed my boots, brought me slippers and ushered me into the study, where a fire blazed and a bottle of port gleamed. I looked down at her, my eyes wet with gratitude.

"I know," she said, leading me to my comfortable desk chair and settling me down. "Shall I stay?" I looked up at her, wanting to be alone, but unable to tell her. My chin dropped onto my chest, and tears overflowed my eyes. She put her arms around my head and held my cheek to her bosom, which usually perked me up pretty well, but now even that tender touch only made me weep more. She peeled herself off me, put a glass of port in reach and tiptoed to the door. "I'll be in the kitchen with Martha," she whispered as she left.

I sat there in the dark, the only light coming from the fire, an oil lamp and a gas jet in the corner. This was my room, containing bits of memorabilia, citations, souvenirs. On the wall, framed, along with the pen I used that day, was Grant's first draft of the Appomattox surrender document, with inserts in my own handwriting, an ironic reminder of the glory days. Also on the wall were the Red Jacket medal and General Sully's fanciful sketch of me in uniform on the plains, thoughtfully watching the Sioux buffalo dance. Hell, I was never a hero. I was just a scrivener who'd got lucky. No more luck, no more Grant's Indian. Farewell the plumed troops and the big wars.

I drank a bit, not too much, and must have dozed, for I awoke to a muffled pounding on the front door. I arose and went, gesturing to Martha and Minnie, who appeared in the hallway, that I'd get it. The opened door admitted whirling snow and revealed a huge figure standing there, swathed head to foot in a greatcoat, scarf and hat, a satchel clutched under its arm, the snow piling up around it.

"For God's sake, Parker, let me in," said a muffled voice. The figure stomped across the threshold and continued to stamp snow off itself as I shouldered the door closed and turned to observe Henry Flagler slowly emerging from the huge, snowy coat he dropped on the floor, the frozen six-foot muffler he unwound from his face, the giant slouch hat he tipped from his head, spilling snow onto the floor, leaving a puddling pile of clothing almost as high as he was. As Lincoln said of Alexander Stephens, it was the biggest shuck and the littlest ear you ever did see. Icicles dripped from his mustache.

"Give me fire, man! Where's your manners!" he cried, arms aspread, and I ushered him, carrying his dripping satchel, into the study and got him seated by the fire. I peeked out the door and saw Minnie looking from the kitchen, but I mouthed to her that all was well.

"You look like Father Christmas," I told Henry, pulling up a chair for myself as he leaned forward, rubbed his hands at the fireside and smoothed his hair. The wet satchel, near the fire, began to steam.

He looked at me sideways-up, his lavender eye glinting. "I may just be, Parker. But all in good time. Ah, my thanks," as I handed him a glass of port and refilled my own. I settled back to let him recover and start explaining.

"Oh, that's good. Thanks, Parker." He sat back, drank deep, and I gave him more. He glanced at the port and around the room. "No," I said. "There's no whiskey."

"Ah, yes," he said. "Very safe."

I let him get comfortable and warm. Soon he sat back further, handed me his glass for another refill and slapped his hands on his knees as if calling the meeting to order. "I heard of your troubles," he said. "I'm in Washington on other business, of course, but I was hoping to come to the hearings and buck you up."

I nodded. "Thanks for the thought," I said. "It's all over now."

He raised his eyebrows. "The result?"

"Complete exoneration."

His smile flashed and he raised the filled glass I handed him. "Well, good! Sometimes the righteous actually win!"

"Feels more like losing," I told him. He clucked and shook his head as I went through the sorry mess for him. Somehow, with him there, the story became more of a tale that I almost began to enjoy telling, imitating Welsh's and other voices, adding embellishments. Maybe I could actually put this behind me and make a good story of it. He laughed at Welsh's shenanigans, at the solemnity of the congressmen, and showed genuine admiration for my eleventh-hour contrition.

"Brilliant!" he said. "I couldn't have managed it better myself! And what's for you now?"

I shrugged. "I honestly don't know, Henry. I'm exonerated, but disgraced. It's like a 'not guilty' verdict – not quite the same as innocent."

He slapped my knee. "Well, a few more days and you'll be over it. Especially in the company of that delightful little thing I glimpsed in the hallway."

I grinned. "Enough about me, Henry. What brings you to Washington?"

"Big doings, as usual," he said, rising and beginning to pace the room, turning over knickknacks as he talked. "You've heard some of it, no doubt."

I had indeed. Since I had last seen him, in the summer of 1867, Flagler and Rockefeller had made news. Cleveland was now the largest oil refiner in the world, much of it the property of Rockefeller & Flagler's Standard Oil. The railroad-rebate scheme Flagler had started in 1867 kept their freight costs below others, so they succeeded in busting and buying out many smaller refineries. Then, in January 1870, just over a year ago, Flagler had sprung his corporation scheme, incorporating the Standard Oil Company of Ohio, with stock of one million dollars, in shares of one hundred each. It was the largest incorporation up to that time, which is why it made news, but the shares were not offered publicly. Instead, they were restricted to Flagler, Rockefeller and a few associates, who now used Standard Oil stock instead of money to buy up the refineries they'd driven to bankruptcy. The one-two punch spread the Standard stock and its makers' names across the land, along with the distinctive five-gallon cans that Henry had shown me in his Cleveland office. In five years Flagler had risen from bankruptcy to second in command at Standard Oil, the world's giant.

"We've saved the whales, Parker!" Henry exulted. "In 1845 there were 800 whaling vessels. Now there's less than a hundred. We can drill oil free from the ground, refine it and ship it around the world ten times faster than a single whale ship can get out of port and back. Unbought barrels are splitting their staves on the Nantucket docks, whale oil returning to the sea whence it came!"

"Dear me," I said. "What will Minnie do for corset stays?"

Flagler looked startled. "That hadn't occurred to me, Parker." He stroked his mustache. "Hm-m-m-m, we'll think of something. Gutta-percha, perhaps. I'll get somebody to work on it. Parker, you're wasted in government. With your odd ideas you'd make a fortune in business! In fact, you already have."

"What do you mean?"

Flagler raised a finger to his lips and tiptoed to the door, which he opened and looked out of. Satisfied, he softly closed it, stopped at the gas light and turned it down. This left only the oil lamp on the desk and the firelight. He picked up the leather satchel and moved to the desk, where he set it upright, undid the straps and flipped it open with a flourish. "Look inside," he said.

I did. A long look. Then I looked at him. "Money," I said. "How much?"

Flagler stood with his arms folded like a proud papa, a finger stroking his mustache. "Count it," he said.

I slowly shook my head. "How much, Henry?"

"Fifty thousand dollars."

"What are you planning to do with it, Henry?"

"Give it to you, Parker. What else do you think? It's yours, after all."

"Mine?"

"Your two thousand dollars from all those years ago! Did you think I'd forgot?"

I peered into the briefcase. I'd never seen so much money all at once. It was more than ten times my annual salary. "I can't take this, Henry," I said.

"Nonsense! Nonsense!" he said, clapping me on the back and leading me to the fireplace, where he pushed me down and sat knee to knee with me. He talked low and looked into my eyes, tapping my leg with his finger. "I told you it was an investment, and it was. You were one of the original shareholders of Standard Oil, Parker. The stock was in my name of course, but it was always yours. You went in with twenty shares at a hundred dollars each. They're now worth twenty-five hundred dollars each. The money is yours fair and square! Take it."

I sat back and folded my arms. "You wouldn't want anything in return, would you, Henry?"

Flagler slapped his chest in shock. "Of course not! Don't insult me, Parker!"

I continued to look into his lavender eyes, which held mine, then slowly dropped, as he shook his head in defeat. "Oh, hell, Parker. I can't fool you. Of course I don't want anything. Not directly. Just, when the time comes, that you should remember your friends." He nodded toward the briefcase. "There's more where that came from, you know. I kept your hand in our little game."

My arms stayed folded. "And when might that time come?"

Firelight flickered on his face. "You've heard of the Northern Pacific Railroad?" he asked.

"Yes," I said evenly. "Jay Cooke."

"Indeed," he said. There was a proposal to build a second transcontinental railroad west from Lake Superior to Puget Sound, through Minnesota, the Dakotas and Montana, the investment instrument being Northern Pacific Railroad bonds, which financier Jay Cooke, almost exclusively, was selling.

"It's stupid," I said. "Why build a second transcontinental railroad? The first was finished only three years ago."

Flagler shrugged. "It's not the railroad I'm interested in, but the land."

I began to see. The proposed railroad would go directly through reservation and other Indian lands that I had negotiated myself, including the Oglala reservation on the Missouri and the Powder River hunting grounds. Land that might have oil under it.

I shook my head. "I can't help you, Henry," I said. "Those are treaty lands. My treaty. I gave my word."

Flagler smiled. "Ah, well," he said. "No harm in trying." He looked around the room as if for eavesdroppers, then looked at the floor, like a little boy afraid to meet a grownup's eyes. "There's, um, oil in Oklahoma," he said, wincing as he squeezed out the words.

"More Indian territory."

"It was discovered in 1859, same year as Drake's well in Pennsylvania. It's never been exploited. It can't be. Regulations."

"Indian territory," I repeated.

Flagler sat back. "Hang it all, Parker, have you nothing to offer but integrity?"

"No," I said, standing. I'd let this go too far. "Wait here, Henry. I'll be right back."

I found Minnie in the kitchen and, without saying a word, took her by the wrist and led her back to the study. When I opened the door, Flagler was on his feet, examining the framed Appomattox document. "You should get Grant to authenticate this, Parker," he said. "It could be worth something some day."

"Minnie," I said, ushering her forward. "This is Henry Flagler."

"Oh, good heavens," said Minnie, as Flagler took her hand. "Mr. Flagler, I feel as if I've known you forever. What on earth brought you here in this storm?"

"Mrs. Parker," he murmured, holding her hand to his chest.

I pried Minnie from him, though she continued to hold his gaze as I led her to the desk, where the leather satchel stood open. "Look inside," I told her.

She did, looked up at me, looked again, touching the satchel gingerly, as if it might burn her fingers. "My word!" she said. "What is it?"

"An investment," I told her. "Remember I told you I invested some money with Mr. Flagler a while back. Now he's repaying it with interest – self-interest. Standard Oil wants to invest in me."

"A bribe," said Minnie, stepping back from the briefcase, hand to her chest. She looked scandalized, but also dazzled at the sudden intrigue. She looked from Henry to me. Henry looked at the floor like a caught little boy. "How much is it?"

"Fifty thousand dollars," I said, reaching for the satchel. "I wanted you to see me return it to Henry." I closed the straps and prepared to hand it over, but Minnie suddenly stepped between us and faced Henry, smiling brightly.

"Mr. Flagler," she said. "I've forgot my manners. You must be very hungry. I'll have Martha fix you something in the kitchen."

"Why no, not at all . . . ," Henry protested, but Minnie took his arm and steered him to the door.

"Martha!" she called, and when Martha arrived, delivered Henry over, watched them go and closed the door, leaning against it and looking steadily at me.

"What?" I said.

"Sit down, Ely," she said, pointing at my desk chair. As I did, she pulled a chair up and leaned an elbow on the desk. The closed satchel was between us.

"Let's talk about this," she said.

"There's nothing to talk about," I said. "I've just been disgraced by a scandal. Now I'm being bribed. Impossible. Do you know what he wants me to do?"

"What?"

"Help him acquire Indian lands in Dakota. Failing that, help him drill for oil on Indian lands in Oklahoma."

"Well," she said. "You can't do that."

"No," I agreed. "So what is there to talk about?"

Minnie's fingers were slowly undoing the satchel's straps. "Fifty thousand dollars," she said. "That's something to talk about. Shall we look at it?" She had the straps undone and looked inside. "It appears to be in hundred-dollar bills," she said. "Quite a lot."

"About five hundred, I should think."

"An investment, you said." Minnie pulled out a stack of bills, bound with red ribbon, and riffled them with her thumb.

"Yes. In me."

"No, before that. You invested money with him. Two thousand dollars. He invested it in Standard Oil, yes?"

I nodded.

"Do you think this is a proper return?"

I shrugged. "I have no idea. The stock doesn't trade. It's worth whatever the principals say it's worth."

Minnie pulled out another stack of bills and laid it carefully on top of the first. "I've never seen a hundred dollar bill before. Look, Ely, they have Lincoln's picture on them." She handed me a stack.

I hefted it and looked at Lincoln's picture. "He looked different in person," I said. "Nobody could quite believe how odd he looked."

Minnie extracted a bill and held it to the oil lamp so she could see through it. "Should we burn them, do you think?"

"No," I said, curious at her whimsy. "I think we should return them to nice Mr. Flagler."

"But he has so much already, according to the papers." Minnie continued to examine the bill in the lamplight. "No, Ely. I think we should keep it."

I was balancing a stack on the back of my hand. "Of course not," I said, flipping it up and catching it on my palm. "It's a bribe."

"It's not a bribe if you're not in office."

"But I am." Minnie ignored me, removing more bills from the satchel and stacking them on the desk. She balanced a stack on her head. "What are you saying, Minnie?"

She took the stack off her head and sat back in her chair, the money in her hand. "Just this. You've always known you wouldn't be Commissioner forever. Now they've tried to hound you from office and you've beat them. But you're wounded. Why not leave now? Resign, like your friend Quentin says you will."

I frowned. "Eventually, I will," I said. "But not now. I can't give them the satisfaction."

Minnie cocked her head. "Satisfaction? What about your satisfaction? What good is staying if you can't do any good?"

345

"I can still do the Indians some good," I protested. "I can . . . well . . . I don't know. I can save them from men like Flagler."

"Oh, to blazes with the Indians!" Minnie shot out of the chair and leaned over the desk, brandishing the money in her fist. "Think of yourself for once!"

Her fire took me aback. "What do you mean?"

"Just this. Ever since I met you you've been such a good Indian. A model, a paragon, the Indian who succeeds in the white man's world. Who reaches out to his red brethren with a helping hand. Who lifts them up, sends them food, makes treaties with them, talks their language and the white man's too. Maybe you could just stop being an Indian, stop being a white man, and just be a man!"

My face was hot. "You're saying I'm not a man?"

"Oh, my darling," she said, coming around the desk and hugging my head to her chest. Now the touch of her breast felt pretty good. "You are such a man! But you don't have to be everybody's – or anybody's – man anymore. Stop being Grant's Indian, stop being the Indians' white man. Nobody wants you to be. Congress doesn't trust you. Red Cloud barely does. They all want you to leave. Well, do it! Just be a man like everyone else. Take the money, move away, start a business, travel with me, do anything you want. You don't have to be a government clerk anymore."

I stroked her arm. "It's all I ever wanted," I said. "I told Flagler years ago that government could work if good men made it work. Now I'm helping to make it work."

Minnie was holding my hand. "No," she said. "You're not anymore. Now you're just like the rest of them. Investigated, humiliated. But before that you were a success! You won! Now, take the money and tell them all to go to hell!"

I started to see it. "Declare victory by moving on," I said. "Like Grant in the Wilderness."

"Yes, Ely!" she said, shaking my hand up and down. I looked up at her. My, she was beautiful! "There will be more battles. Declare this one over. You're going to resign some day. Make tomorrow the day!"

"Tomorrow?"

"Yes!" she said, flinging her arm to point at the door. "While Mr. Flagler's still in town." Her eyes gleamed with conspiracy.

"Minniesackett, you're the devil!" I grabbed the stack of bills from her and swatted her face with it. Money was piled all over the desk. "What shall I do with you?"

"Anything you want!" she said, and started dancing around the room, arms outstretched. "I'm so sick of this town. It reeks of death and corruption. But this!" she swept stacks of bills into her arms and danced with it. "This is freedom! Take it! It's years and years of life!" She stopped in front of the desk. "I want to live in New York, don't you?"

"The city," I said.

"Yes," she said, dropping the bills on the desk and floor and rushing to me. "With a little house in the country. Where we can have children. I don't want children in this pesthole."

"I like New York," I said. I stood up, took her in my arms, and twirled her around. "Can we really do this?"

"We can do anything we want, darling," she said, kissing me all over my face. "I'm pretty, you're smart, and the world awaits us. Shall I summon Mr. Flagler?"

I was shaking with astonished laughter, a grin splitting my face. What a day! "Yes. I can't wait to see his face."

Minnie opened the door. "Oh, Mr. Flagler!" she called.

Minnie and I picked up the money from the desk and floor and replaced it in the satchel. Henry emerged from the kitchen hallway, pulling a napkin from his throat. When he came in, Minnie picked up the satchel. "My, so light for such heavy doings," she said, and handed it to Henry, who stood dumbfounded. "Mr. Flagler, we cannot possibly accept this money. Please take it away with you."

Henry looked at her, at the bag, at me. "Is this final?" he asked.

"No," said Minnie. "I'm sure if you bring it back tomorrow night you'll find us more receptive."

Chapter XXIV

I'VE SAT HERE TWENTY YEARS

New York 1885

I ARRIVED AT GRANT'S OFFICE EARLY THE NEXT MORNING. The snow had stopped and was gleaming in the sun, the roadways shiny underfoot, the trees and eaves white-bearded and sparkly. I was whistling as I entered the outer office, where my former mates and scriveners Orville Babcock and Horace Porter toiled, their pens scratching.

"Good morning lads," I told them. "The boss in?"

Porter looked at me over his glasses, the friendlier and more trustworthy of the two. Both had been with me on Grant's staff in the last year of the war and had stood in the Appomattox farmhouse while I scribed the surrender. Porter would survive the Grant scandals unscathed, but Babcock was a great arranger of things – he had brilliantly improvised the Appomattox meeting. Already implicated in the 1869 Black Friday, he would crash in the Whiskey Ring of 1876 and drown in 1884 while inspecting lighthouses in Mosquito Inlet, Florida.

"You're cheerful, Parker," said Porter. "Do you have an appointment?"

"Commissioner of Indian Affairs," I responded. "But not for long."

At this, even Babcock looked up. "You're not getting fired, you know," he said.

"Thank you for the vote of confidence," I said, trying to glance at what he was writing. He covered it with his arm.

"Go right in, Parker," said Porter. "He'll be delighted to see you."

Grant did me the honor of coming around from behind his desk to shake my hand and sit with me in adjoining chairs. This did not make it any easier to do what I had to do, but when I told him he nodded in understanding. I handed him a one-paragraph letter of resignation.

"I'm glad I put you there," he said, smoothing the paper. "For my own selfish reasons."

"Sir?"

"If I'd kept you here on staff I'd have grown dependent on you. I'd be unable to spare you. I'd be too cowardly to let you resign. As it is, you're free to go, and my conscience is clear."

"It's a good time," I said. "Congress's report is just out. Delano is just in. He doesn't trust me. Let him get his own man."

Grant stood and paced, hands in his pockets. "His own man," he muttered. "I'm losing most of my own men. First Cox, then you. Cox was big and so are you. Delano will only want someone smaller than himself. Crocks and cronies." He shook his head. "Rawlins is gone. I have Porter and Babcock out there, but Porter's the only one I trust." He rounded on me. "You didn't hear that," he said. "I know how it goes. Grant and his cronies. Doesn't mean I don't know 'em for what they are. Enough of that." He leaned back against his desk, his belly out, no longer the cocky little guy with his arm against the tree whose slouch so many men affected. "What will you do?"

"My wife likes New York," I said.

"Mine too," he said. "I almost wish I could go with you. But I'm stuck here."

"Stuck?"

"After a fashion," he said. "You realize, Parker, I'm history's captive. Nothing I do is as important as the fact that I'm doing it. I tell people to look out there," he pointed out the window, down the vista to the Potomac. "Instead, all they do is look at me. Look, the president is pointing. Ah, well."

It was about as philosophical as I'd ever heard him. We talked a bit more then ran out of steam. Before I left, I handed him the draft of the surrender document and asked if he'd write something on it. He was touched – he looked at me sharply, his eyes glistening – and he walked around to his side of the desk, thought a minute and wrote:

> The document below is one of the
> original impressions from the manifold on
> which I wrote the terms of surrender of Gen.
> Lee's army, at Appomattox Court House,
> Apl. 9th 1865. It is one of three impressions
> taken by the manifold. U.S. Grant.

"Simple and to the point," I said, reading it.

"Just like I used to be," said Grant.

That night, Henry Flagler returned with the satchel full of money. In the clear light that morning Minnie and I had both feared that, hearing of my resignation, he'd renege. Instead he was delighted that he'd got hoist with his own petard.

"So the joke's on me, isn't it, Parker? Well played! Although," he added, looking at blushing Minnie, "I have a sense I wasn't outmanned, only outnumbered."

"What about Dakota? Oklahoma?" I asked.

He fingered his mustache. "Dakota? Oklahoma? Oh, I have other satchels for that." As evening fell he swung off down the drive humming to himself. A few weeks later, an envelope arrived containing the "few more shares" of Standard Oil stock Flagler had retained for me "to keep my hand in." "Whatever you do," Flagler wrote, "Do not sell these. Borrow against them, sell your house, your horses, your shirt, your firstborn, but not these until I tell you."

The next months were filled with house-hunting in New York and packing in Washington. Minnie attended a round of farewell parties, and we gave a few of our own in our slowly-diminishing household. In the end, we bypassed New York City as a home and settled in Fairfield, Connecticut, on the water and the railroad line to New York. Minnie dubbed our house the "Robin's Nest," although the nest remained empty.

On the New Haven Railroad, one could buy a "commutation ticket," allowing shuttles back and forth to New York City. I rented an office on Wall Street and "commuted" several days a week, driven to the station by Minnie in a pony cart, met by her in the evening along with other wives in stylish vehicles and becoming apparel. It was a good time. I discovered an ability to pick investments and get rid of them in time, unaffected by the sentimentality that pins men to their hopes rather than to the numbers on the ticker. I joined several other investors in buying one of Mr. Edison's Stock Tickers, which gave prices instantaneously rather than relying on the runners, or "deer," who raced around the street with quotes and orders. At first it was only our own money that I invested, Flagler's fifty thousand dollars plus profit on our Washington house. Soon, however, I was investing other people's money too, and did fine for all of us for a few years.

One Thursday in September 1873 Minnie and I were at a matinee at Edwin Booth's new theater on Twenty-third Street at Sixth Avenue. Booth had built this theatrical palace in 1869, reviving extraordinarily well after his brother killed Lincoln. Minnie reveled in the outrageous design, the busts of Garrick and Kean, with Lear and Hamlet on the walls, the stage machinery that moved huge sets without a creak or wobble. Mr. Booth was playing Benedick in *Much Ado About Nothing* that afternoon, and Minnie was rapt, because she thought of us as Beatrice and Benedick. I preferred Othello and Desdemona, but Minnie thought Desdemona a simp and me "smarter and whiter than Othello and lacking poetry and self-pity." It amazed me that Booth, so struck by fate, who, when you saw him on the street, had clouds of gloom on his shoulders, could play not only tragedy but comedy as well, so lightly he might have been another person. Booth was forty that year – five years younger than me – but his Benedick was full of youth and wit and ardor.

When we emerged on the street in the late afternoon, there was much ado about something, an unusual scurrying in the streets, men hailing cabs and rushing for the elevated railway, all of them headed downtown, rather than north to Grand Central Terminal. Horses and cabs were jostling and crisscrossing each other. Even those who found a cab were unable to move in the jam. I stopped a portly gentleman in a top hat and asked him what the trouble was. "God only knows," he said, breathing hard. "A bank failure. Jay Cooke, they say!" He hurried off, waving for a cab.

I turned suddenly cold. "Minnie," I said, taking her arm and steering her down Twenty-third Street away from the crowd, "You'll have to go home alone. I have to go to Wall Street."

She put her hand to my face. "What is it, Ely?"

"Panic," I told her. "I have no money in Jay Cooke, but other things will be affected. I'll have to see what I should sell."

Minnie, always competent, made her way to Grand Central and home. I joined the crush of frightened tradesmen in the downtown flight. Of course I had no money with Jay Cooke and his Northern Pacific bonds, but other investors did. Surveys of the proposed railroad route took three summers, 1871-73, made more difficult by actual or imagined Indian attacks, yet track was being laid, lines stretching from east in Minnesota and west in Washington, closing in on Dakota and Montana, last refuge of the Sioux. The surveying expeditions included hundreds of men, wagons, and animals, plus a military escort. The 1873 expedition was particularly treacherous and well-documented, led by George Custer, who made sure his exploits got to the eastern papers. Custer's stories greatly exaggerated the Indian attacks, scaring off potential bond purchasers.

I crowded onto an elevated train to Wall Street and fought my way through the crowds to my office. Jay Cooke's bank had, indeed, failed and closed. My suitemates clustered around the ticker, which was falling further and further behind, showing a full-scale plunge. It was impossible to get sell orders filled – nobody was buying. When the market closed, my holdings were down a quarter.

I telegraphed to Minnie I wouldn't be home, then worked through the night preparing for the market's opening. Other men spent the night shuttling between gas lit offices, discussing strategies, working out what to sell and what to buy. But the second day was worse than the first. The market closed that night down considerably further, and I had been able to sell very little. A few brave souls, convinced that the market had bottomed, started to buy, but too few followed to reverse the trend.

It was then announced that the market would stay closed until midweek, so, with nothing left to do, I took the last train Friday to Fairfield and walked home. After the two-day frenzy of smoke and flying paper on Wall Street, Fairfield was uncannily ordinary, enjoying a nice fall night. On the town green, the band was playing late and people ate ice cream. The leaves were just beginning to turn. Families gathered on their front porches to watch the moon and stars. My neighbors waved cheerfully as I trudged home.

"Are we ruined?" asked Minnie, over cold chicken and ale in the kitchen, me in my shirtsleeves and suspenders.

I chewed on a drumstick. "No. But bruised and battered. I'm more worried about the others' investments than my own."

Minnie covered my free hand with hers. "We'll do the best we can," she said.

I grunted and drank ale. "Oh," she said. "A telegram arrived this morning from Henry Flagler. Here." She took it from her pocket. " 'Whatever you do, don't sell Standard Oil.' "

I smiled. "I can't sell anything. Nobody's buying."

We finished the meal in silence, but I was soon restless and remorseful, slumping back in my chair. "Oh, Minnie, I'm so sorry."

"Why, Ely?" she said, frowning with concern. "What have you done?"

I shook my head. "If only I'd seen this coming a few days ago, I'd have sold everything. We'd be out and clear."

She smiled. "How could you see it coming? Slay a bear and read its entrails? See a hawk soaring west?"

She failed to cheer me. "Everything we've worked for," I said. "All up in smoke. We're back where we started."

Minnie shook her head and punched my arm. "You're such a white man, aren't you?'

"What do you mean?"

" 'Everything we've worked for.' As if money was everything we've worked for."

"Well," I said. "It's a big part of it."

She shook her head. "It's a very small part of it. We've worked for our marriage, for our home, for our friends, for our happiness. A market failure doesn't turn back that clock. We've still got everything we've worked for. And we have far more to work on. We're going to have a baby, we're going to go to Europe, we're going to take the train to San Francisco, I'm going to learn Italian . . ."

"What?" I said, as her words suddenly hit me. "We're going to have a baby. Minnie!" I jumped up to embrace her, but she fended me off, laughing.

"No, silly," she said. "Not yet. I just wanted to see if you were listening."

I sat back down, happier. "Well, that's something we've been working on too."

She took my hand. "No, my dear. We've been making love. We'll work on having a baby when I say so."

But for awhile it was no time for babies. It was soon the full-fledged Panic of 1873. I kept me and my investors afloat, which only meant that few dropped below their original holdings. Those that did I reimbursed from my own, which themselves suffered less than most. Henry Flagler resurfaced in another telegram suggesting a shady exit for me. He pointed to a New York law, passed to protect Indians from unscrupulous businessmen, which held that no contract for money could be enforced against an Indian for a monetary payment. I telegraphed back to him, reminding him of the fifty thousand dollars, and suggested he was one white man who needed such a law to protect him from an unscrupulous Indian and his wife. "Whatever you do, don't sell Standard Oil," he telegraphed back.

Booth lost his theater in the Panic. I barely survived. The original fifty thousand was nearly intact, as were our house and the Standard Oil stock. The Tonawanda farm continued to pay rent. We could make ends meet, but not forever. As the panic deepened into a Depression, prices of goods rose, but stock prices didn't, jobs were few, and our financial future grew worrisome. I paid off all my investors and no longer went to Wall Street except to see old associates and sniff out job prospects.

In January 1875 I got a telegram from Fred Grant, who was ten when I had first met him in Galena before the war. He had graduated from West Point in 1871 and served in the west, part of the expedition protecting the Northern Pacific survey in 1873. In October 1874 he had married Ida Honore in Chicago, and was now making a wedding progress through the states. I met the happy couple for lunch at the St. Denis Hotel, at Broadway and Eleventh, bustling in on a crisp winter day, to find Fred and his new wife already seated in the flower-filled dining room, which gleamed with crystal and gold and white napery. After introducing me to his bride, a strong-faced Midwesterner, he turned to the fourth member of the party, still seated, and said, "Ely, surely you remember General Smith."

"No longer General, thanks very much." William F. "Baldy" Smith rose and took my hand. "I'm glad to see you, Parker."

"*Mister* Smith, then," I said, returning his handclasp warmly. He had got nicknamed "Baldy" at West Point, though his forehead was only high then. I had met him first in the rain, then in the woods at Chattanooga, where he oversaw the building and deploying of the pontoons that opened the "cracker line" to the besieged troops. He was responsible for getting me into the pontoons on their nighttime drift downstream toward the only actual battles I fought.

"Soon enough, I'll grow into my nickname," he said now, sitting and running his hand through his thinning hair. His schnauzer mustache and beard were now white. "And you, Parker, how are you?" His blue Prussian eyes gave me a once-over.

I accepted wine. " '*Non sum qualis eram,*" I told Smith, "*bonae sub regno Cynarae.*'"

Fred, a glass to his lips, almost choked.

"I beg your pardon," said Smith, frowning. "Seneca?"

"Horace," I told him. Smith looked helplessly from me to Fred.

"Latin," Fred explained to him and Ida. "Ely's great with obscure languages."

"What's it mean?" asked Smith.

"'I am not what I was,'" I intoned grandly, "'under the rule of good Cynara.'"

Smith nodded. "Cynara being General Grant, I suppose," he said, glancing at Fred. "We all were better off under him. Peacetime has not brought clarity."

"You would prefer war, Mister Smith?" asked Ida.

"I'd prefer the clarity, not the killing," he said. "In business, you don't know who the enemy is. He could be sitting right next to you."

Fred chimed in. "Even the army isn't that clear. I was on the Yellowstone expedition in '73 and last summer in the Black Hills. I swear I never knew who, exactly, we were working for. Nominally, it was General Custer, of course. But we also had the railroad surveyors and the press, both of whom Custer coddled outrageously. Not to be insubordinate, but I often wondered if it wasn't Custer who was the enemy, blustering about that way. Some thought he caused most of the Indian attacks he fended off."

Not eager to discuss strategy, we wandered into friendlier subjects. Fred, it turned out, was on extended leave, on his way to Europe for the winter. Smith had retired as president of the International Telegraph Company and had just been sworn in as one of the Board of New York Police Commissioners.

Their grandiose plans left me morose. When it came my turn, I tried to make a good story of it – bourgeois Indian seeks employment – but my tongue was so loosened by wine that what I intended as an entertaining monologue turned into a confession of failure. I saw sympathetic faces in this table of friends and frankly told them that, with the Depression setting in, and no end in sight, I was out of a job, eating up my capital and didn't know where to turn. "I've had careers," I told them. "Translator, diplomat, chief sachem, engineer, scrivener, commissioner, stock broker. I no longer need a career. What I need is a job."

There was sympathetic, embarrassed, silence around the table and the clink of cutlery. Then Smith frowned suddenly, as if an idea had struck. "Are you serious?" he asked.

"Yes," I shrugged. "An honest day's work for honest pay."

"I have jobs," said Smith. "I'll give you one. Come see me tomorrow morning at 300 Mulberry Street."

I did. 300 Mulberry Street, at the corner of Bleeker, was New York City Police Headquarters, a four-square, four-story edifice with granite stairs leading up to an arched doorway. In muddy Bleeker Street, two open patrol wagons were departing, one east, one south, each drawn by a pair of horses. Face-to-face in the back sat eight helmeted patrolmen, in two rows of four facing each other, jammed knee-to-knee. The wagon would drop each one off at his appointed sector, replacing him in the wagon with the man he'd relieved. These wagons patrolled the city night and day.

Baldy Smith met me in the lobby and introduced me to a square, solid gentleman of about fifty, with a square beard and bald head, so that he might have changed names with Baldy. But no, this was George Washington "Wash" Walling, Superintendent of Police.

"The commissioner wants me to give you a tour. Come along," said Walling, nodding to me once and setting off down the corridor at a brisk pace. Baldy Smith kept lagging behind, like a tot with a new toy, opening doors here and there and raving about the contents. On the ground floor was the central telegraph office, in which Smith took particular delight.

"It's divided into five sections," you see, said Smith, showing me what he called the "switchboards," where five operators worked around a pentagonal central console. "Messages come to the central switchboard, and, by means of switching, we connect the sections, sending general alarms to all five sectors of the city. We also connect to the fire department, the police headquarters of other cities, with railroads, prisons, banks, hospitals, asylums, factories, public schools . . . , all the places where emergencies are likely to arise. Over eighty thousand messages went over these wires last year."

In the Photograph and Record Department, file drawers held photographs of over ten thousand criminals worldwide. A single room was dedicated to the "Rogues' Gallery", containing the photographs of what Walling called "the best people" arrested in New York.

"When we catch one of the professionals," Walling explained, "he is photographed and fifty copies are made, with his pedigree on the obverse. Copies go to the Rogues' Gallery, to all the precincts, and the remainder are used by patrolmen and dispatched to other cities. Look here." He handed me a photograph of a dashing young blade with a smirk and thin mustache, a head of wavy hair. He reminded me of a young Henry Flagler. "Whiskey Short," the description ran. "Claims to have graduated from Corpus Christi College, Cambridge. Speaks five languages. Learned to distill whiskey from swill in Sing-Sing prison. Currently at large."

On the second floor they showed me the Museum of Crime, where likenesses of shoplifters, burglars and other crooks glared from the walls. A glass case contained the tools of "French Gus," drills, telescoping jimmies, keys, wax impression molds, which Gus mass-produced and leased out to his fellows. Elsewhere were bogus gold bricks, an eighteen-chambered pistol belonging to Mike Shanahan, lithographic stones for printing counterfeit railway tickets and a box in which Charlie Adams had sunk $216,000 in bonds beneath the Delaware River.

On the third floor, Smith opened a door. "Here," he said. "What do you think of this?"

It was a spacious office, with nothing but a few file cabinets, a desk and chair. Tall windows looked out onto Mulberry Street. Moving to them, I saw a collection of seedy-looking fellows loitering on the steps of the building opposite. "Spies?" I asked. "Thieves? Beggars?"

Smith and Walling joined me at the window. "A little of each," said Walling. "Police reporters for the newspapers. They wait there to see who goes in and out, then grab a story on the fly. They have offices on several floors there, call it 'The Shack'."

Walling consulted his watch. "I'll leave you, then," he said briskly. "A pleasure, Mr. Parker. Commissioner Smith."

"Good man," said Smith when Walling left. "No nonsense, no small talk." He waved me to the chair behind the desk. "Sit! Sit! What do you think of it?"

The chair creaked to welcome me, and I adjusted my bottom to it. It had a cushion and a swivel, so I could face the desk, the door or the windows. I tipped it back to see how it held my weight. "Comfortable," I said. "A well endowed chair."

"It's yours, if you want it," he said.

"Does a job go with it, or is it just a chair?"

"Oh, no," said Smith. "There's a job. But damn if I can remember its name." He searched his pockets and found a piece of paper. "Requisition Officer for the Committee on Repairs and Supplies of the Police Board of Commissioners."

I chuckled. "Will all that fit on the door?"

Smith looked at the door. "Just 'Supply Officer' then."

I nodded. "I like the officer part. And the chair is comfortable. I'll take it."

I've sat here twenty years.

Well, not the whole twenty years. My job takes me out and about. I am the middle-man between the commissioners and the contractors. The commissioners draw up requisitions for repairs and supplies, I submit them for bids and hire the contractors, inspect the goods, the ongoing projects and finished products and report to the commissioners. This takes me to warehouses and construction sites, to half-finished police stations in the far reaches of Manhattan. In the mid-80s, when we wired the department for telephones, that was my job. It is power without responsibility. I have no authority to approve requisitions or pay bills – that's the commissioners' problem. My job is execution, pure and simple. It's a small version of what I did as Indian commissioner, but with less pressure and almost no accountability. I'm a government man again. I guess I always was. Except for Wall Street, I've worked for governments – Seneca, New York State, United States, now New York City.

When not outdoors I sit in my comfortable chair, read the papers, watch the street outside my window, watch the world go by and find I don't miss it. I sat here while Grant's second-term scandals unfolded, leaving my little Indian Bureau farrago in the dust. The Whiskey Ring, the Indian Ring, Credit Mobilier – these and others soon eclipsed "Welshism" in the language with "Grantism," synonym for graft, incompetence and corruption.

I was sitting here on a hot June day in 1876, when the telegraph chattered out the news that Custer and 196 men had been "massacred" by Lakota Sioux near the Little Bighorn River. I didn't even need a map to know where that was, in the far reaches of the Powder River country, where I'd got Red Cloud leave to hunt in 1870. Red Cloud was long gone from there, squeezed into a reservation north of the Platte in the Wyoming-Nebraska corner. But other Sioux had remained, chiefly Sitting Bull and Crazy Horse. When I saw the name of Crazy Horse, I knew how the fight had gone. Custer had been lured into a trap as surely as Fetterman had been lured, by the same Crazy Horse, out of Fort Phil Kearney in the deadly Christmas of 1866. Just as Fetterman's stupidity had palled the Christmas of 1866, so, on a grander scale, did Custer's foolishness darken the nation's centennial of July 4, 1876. No longer was the cry for Old Glory and freedom, but for Indian blood and revenge. The Custer fight finished the Plains Indians' doom that had started with the slaughter of the buffalo, the discovery of gold and the transcontinental railroad. A year later Crazy Horse, promised sanctuary, was killed with a bayonet at Fort Robinson at what was now the Red Cloud agency. Two years later, with Nez Perce Chief Joseph's vow to "fight no more forever," the last of the Plains Indians were confined to reservations. Grant's Peace Policy had brought peace only for the victors.

I sat here and read of Henry Stanley, whom I'd met among those very Plains Indians, who then found Livingstone and went on to travel the "Dark Continent" to the source of the Nile, to establish the Congo Free State and to rescue Emin Pasha of Egypt.

I sat here while Grant left office after two terms and spent more than two years traveling with his wife around the world. I, along with Minnie and most of the country, followed their travels in the papers. James Russell Young traveled with Grant, sending regular dispatches to the *New York Herald*, reporting Grant's visits to Queen Victoria, to Bismarck, to Jerusalem, up the Nile, across the Indus, down the Ganges, audience with the Emperor of Japan. When Grant returned in the summer of 1879, people had forgotten the failures of President Grant – he was once again "General Grant" of Appomattox.

I sat here while, in the winter of 1877, Congress took the presidency from Governor Tilden of New York, who won the popular vote, and gave it to Governor Hayes of Ohio, who "won" by making a deal for the electoral votes of Florida and two other southern states. In exchange, troops were withdrawn from the south, Reconstruction was over, and the southern blacks, like the western Indians, learned the meaning of peace. Republican hegemony was secure for a generation. The next president, James Garfield, whom I met at Chattanooga in the war, was in office only four months before he became the second shot president. Robert Lincoln didn't miss this one – he was standing next to Garfield when he went down.

I sat here in the fall of 1880 and read that the Grants had followed me to New York, occupying a town house that subscribers had bought for them at 3 East Sixty-sixth Street. Grant also followed me to Wall Street, where he opened an office, and even followed me down. In May 1884 the firm of Grant & Ward failed, and the public was treated to the spectacle of ex-General, ex-President Grant stumping up the steps of William Henry Vanderbilt's house to ask for a loan to bail his company out, a recourse unavailable to me in the Panic of 1873.

I read of Henry Flagler's fortune too. Unable to bribe me or anyone else, he had steered clear of the Northern Pacific Railroad, nor, as far as I knew, had he sniffed out oil in Oklahoma. He stayed closer to home, consolidated and expanded. By 1872 Standard Oil controlled most of the refining capacity in Cleveland; by 1878, most of the capacity in every American refining city. By 1884, Standard Oil had a national monopoly on the transportation of crude oil, first through the old railroad-rebate scheme, then, in the early 80s, by long-distance pipelines that connected all the refining centers of the east to the oil-producing lands of the west. To the growing complaints, Flagler replied, in his words to the Ohio legislature in 1879:

> With the aggregation of capital and business experience, and the hold upon the channels of trade such as we have, it is idle to say that the small manufacturer can compete with us and, although it is an offensive term, "squeezing out" has happened. It is a competitive world.

I have not seen Flagler since that winter day in 1871, and have no need to. His "competitive world" is not mine. At every market downturn, however, Henry has sent a telegram. In the Panic of 1884, the telegram was from his new house, "Satan's Toe," in Mamaroneck, New York; in the Panic of 1890, from the Ponce de Leon Hotel which Flagler had built in St. Augustine Florida,. The most recent, in the Panic of 1893, was from the Royal Poinciana in Palm Beach Florida, which Flagler had also built. He also has built a railroad down the east coast of Florida. All the telegrams said the same thing, "Don't sell Standard Oil." I haven't. It sits secure in a bank vault for Minnie and our daughter Maud. I'll get to Maud presently.

Flagler and Rockefeller must, in 1878, have got a scare when Charles Brush invented a way to distribute arc lighting from central locations, and electric lights started lighting stores and streets in Boston and Philadelphia. The same year, Edison, of the Stock Ticker, patented the incandescent lamp, and I wondered if Standard Oil might follow whale oil into oblivion. But engines need oil, and I've read in recent years of an "automobile," pioneered by Daimler and Benz in Germany, and now something called the Duryea Motor Wagon has appeared at an exposition in Bridgeport.

I did see Grant once more. In the fall of 1884, rumors arose that he was sick, and, indeed, he hadn't appeared in public since he left his summer home in Long Branch. In December the rumors were confirmed in a letter Grant wrote to a friend that was published in the papers. "A painful throat" had kept him home all fall. By winter's end the pain was confirmed as cancer. It was also revealed that Grant was at work on his *Memoirs*, writing against his own, literal, deadline.

Not all my news comes from the telegraph and the newspapers. The first day in my office, Baldy Smith pointed out the reporters that hung around the stoops and occupied the building opposite Police Headquarters. I was a curiosity to them, as they were to me, and we began trading news and gossip. When the weather was bad, I'd sometimes shout out the window for some of them to come up and out of the rain. One of the first to accept was a young Danish immigrant named Jacob Riis, a reporter for the *New York Tribune*, an intense young man with a high forehead and thin blond hair that shot out of his scalp as if by electricity. He liked to talk, partly to practice his English – which was pretty good, actually, with a soft lilt to the vowels – mostly because words just tumbled out of him. He had suffered a lot as an immigrant, he said, sometimes homeless so that he spent nights sleeping in police stations, which naturally led to police reporting. He seemed to consider me a fellow immigrant, fellow minority, fellow sufferer, and no amount of convincing could persuade him what a bourgeois I was, with a house in Connecticut, a commutation ticket and a wife who drove me to the train.

One morning in April 1885, as I ascended the steps of 300 Mulberry, Riis dashed across the street and grabbed my elbow. "Mr. Parker," he panted, "General Grant is dying! Come, let's go up there!"

I let Riis bundle me into a cab, and we clattered north to East Sixty-sixth Street. By the Central Park wall across from the Grant house a crowd was gathering, and we joined it in staring at the house. There was nothing to see, just a front door and four stories of windows. Occasionally an official-looking person would arrive in a carriage, hurry up the front steps to be admitted, then emerge a half hour later, re-enter the carriage and drive off, answering no questions. About noontime, a seedy-looking fellow in a brown tweed suit and bowler hat slipped out of an alley across from the Grant house and joined the rest of us at what was being called the "Grant death watch." Reporters crowded around him.

"Any news, Jim?"

"No," said Jim, brushing his bowler with his sleeve. "Quiet as the tomb."

"Jim," Riis informed me, "has befriended a chambermaid in the house opposite and gained admittance to the upper floors, hoping to see the dying Grant through the window."

Nothing happened that day, or the next, or the next, as the death watch grew, then diminished, then disappeared. Grant recovered, either through the ministrations of doctors or clergy, or from the medicinal brandy Fred said he slipped him. Fred had quit the army and was helping his father with the *Memoirs*, moving into the house with his family. I telephoned every few weeks – we could do that now – but each time Fred told me Grant wasn't seeing anybody.

The crowds that gathered at East Sixty-sixth Street were just a fraction of the crowds that followed Grant's decline in the newspapers. His death was a national event. All through the year of his illness, he was the lead story, eclipsing Gordon at Khartoum, the election of Grover Cleveland and the arrival of golf.

Finally, one day in late May, came a call from Fred Grant. "We're going away for the summer," he told me. "Come right now, Ely."

I slipped out the back of 300 Mulberry to avoid the reporters and took a cab to East Sixty-sixth Street. Fred himself opened the door, and he looked so much like Grant I almost called him "Captain." That is to say, he looked like a refined version of the Captain Sam Grant I'd known in Galena. That Captain Grant, however, had been seedy and stooped and furtive, with a permanent week's growth you couldn't really call a beard, while Fred Grant had a well-trimmed beard and an air of success. Yet as he stood there at the door, one arm leaning against the jamb, hand on his hip, half a smile on his face, he was his father all over again. At thirty-five, he was just three years younger than the Grant I'd met in Galena.

"Ely," he said. He pulled me inside and checked outside the door for peering eyes. "Come in, come in." He ushered me into the front parlor, sat me down in a red, tufted wing-back chair, and perched on a footstool in front of me, talking low and urgent. "My father is dying, Ely. You know that. The world knows that."

"I'm sorry, Fred," I said.

He nodded. "We're taking him away for the summer. I doubt he'll come back."

"Where?" I asked.

Fred looked at the floor and shook his head. "Damndest thing," he said. "Everyone's got an angle on him."

"Who this time?" I asked.

"A hotel man named Arkell," said Fred, his mouth sour. "He's built the Hotel Balmoral and some cottages up on Mount McGregor, north of Saratoga. He's offered one of the cottages, and Mother and Father have accepted."

"You're against it?"

"Completely. Arkell wants to use him as a draw, to fill his hotel. He'll be a tourist attraction, Ely! Dying in public!"

I reached out and touched Fred on the shoulder. "He's been a tourist attraction since Vicksburg, Fred. Remember those days?"

Fred smiled. "Do I ever. Clarity, victory. What an education I had! I was thirteen. Biggest Fourth of July party ever."

"Let him do it his way," I suggested. "He always has."

Fred looked up at me, shrugged, consulted his watch and looked at the door. "You can spend fifteen minutes with him, Ely. He has some questions for you. Don't let him talk too much."

He led me up the front staircase, which angled abruptly as it reached the second floor. An alcove was cut into the wall at the angle, what they called a "coffin corner," so that a coffin could get past the bend. Better Grant should die in the country than be shouldered down a staircase. Fred put his finger to his lips, opened the door to the front room, then nodded me in. Grant sat behind a wide table that faced the door, writing intently on a piece of paper, chewing his lower lip, his beard now partly white. He paused, looked up as if for a thought and saw Fred and me standing there. The only difference between this and other rooms where I'd seen Grant busily writing was the lack of smoke. No more cigars.

"Fred," he rasped, and I saw how painful speech was for him. "Good, you're back. Hello, Parker."

"Good morning Mister President," I said.

He looked sharply at me. "No more of that," he muttered. Fred motioned me to a chair opposite Grant, who returned to his writing. Soon, he looked up, turned over one paper, then another, looked in a book he had flattened on the table. "Now, where did I put . . .? Ah," he said, spying the book he wanted on another table. Without rising fully, he got out of his chair, stoop-walked to the other table, got what he wanted and stoop-walked back. It was the same stoop-walk I'd seen in the war, where he would fetch papers and write out orders, never standing straight, as if standing up wasn't worth the effort. He'd lost weight, and though I knew it was the cancer, it brought him back to what he used to be – a little, scrappy guy darting here and there, absorbed in the task.

Yes," he rasped, without looking up. "Parker. How long did we stay in that house after Lee left?"

I was startled. Grant was back at Appomattox in 1865, while I was on East Sixty-sixth Street twenty years later. I looked at Fred, who smiled, and back at Grant, trying to put my memory where his was. "We stayed there for some time, I think," I said.

"That's what I think," Grant rasped. "So where's all this other stuff come from? Me standing on the porch lifting my hat to Lee?"

I had read the same accounts. Everyone who was at Appomattox, and many who weren't, had written of that day, repeating the story of Grant lifting his hat. I thought I remembered it myself. It had been repeated so often that, as Grant says about something else in the *Memoirs*, "I had come to believe it." But it couldn't be true.

"I didn't go onto the porch," I told Grant. "And you were with me the whole time after Lee left. We were writing letters. One to Secretary Stanton, telling him of the surrender. I dispatched it to the telegrapher."

"I have that one." Grant lifted a slip of paper. "Sent at 4:30 P.M. We must have been still in the house."

"Yes, sir," I agreed. "Another letter appointed surrender commissioners. One went to Meade ordering him back to . . . What was the name of that town?"

"Burkeville," growled Grant. "That's what I thought. I couldn't have been on the porch, tipping my hat to Lee, and at the same time in the room with you, dictating orders. No matter what they say, I couldn't be in two places at once." He started to laugh, but the laugh turned into a horrible, dry, wrenching cough that went on and on, turning his face red. He grabbed for one of many handkerchiefs on the table and held it to his mouth, his chest heaving as the cough took control, like John Rawlins on his deathbed. I half-stood and looked at Fred, who looked alarmed but motioned for me not to move.

When the coughing subsided, Grant looked exhausted, breathing hard, and tears were running into his beard. He picked up a small medicine bottle, tipped it to his lips and swallowed gently, waiting in suspense as the cocaine took effect. "Thanks, Parker," he wheezed. "You've been a great help. I'll just leave it out then." He returned to his writing.

I looked at Fred, who rose, and I rose with him. I extended my hand across the table. "Goodbye, sir," I said.

Grant took my hand, his own hand so thin I feared I'd break it. "Goodbye, Parker," he mumbled, held my eyes briefly, then dipped his pen and wrote. That's the last I saw of him.

A few weeks later, on June 16, passengers hurrying to trains across the lobby of Grand Central Terminal were startled to see an old man in a gray overcoat and carpet slippers shuffling through the waiting room, surrounded by a solicitous entourage. "My God," whispered somebody. "It's General Grant." So it was. The curious crowd closed in then made a pathway for him all the way to the private railroad car, lent by William H. Vanderbilt, that would take him to Saratoga Springs and Mount McGregor beyond. All along the way, crowds gathered at local stations to watch the dying general pass. Arriving at the Mt. McGregor cabin, Grant abjured the study that had been prepared for him and established himself on the broad porch, where, at a little writing table, he continued his work, pausing to greet visitors, waving and nodding at the crowds of tourists he had, inevitably, drawn to Mount McGregor. He was, as Fred had expected, dying in public. Unexpectedly, he seemed to enjoy it.

He made the last entry in the *Memoirs* on July 14 and died less than two weeks later, July 23. Many copies of the *Memoirs*, which appeared in the fall, had been sold in advance by Mark Twain's salesmen, who fanned out across the country with facsimiles and signed up subscribers from Maine to California. Minnie bought one – number 887 of over three hundred thousand two-volume sets – and I see a set on a table or in a bookshelf in almost every house I visit. Grant undertook the job not only to write history but to ensure his family's future. I understand his wife has received over $500,000 in royalties. Grant mentions me once – on page 491 of Volume II, where he details the surrender and omits the hat-doffing – but Fred asked, and I gladly gave, permission to make a facsimile of the draft surrender document that I still possess. The facsimile is folded between pages 496 and 497 in all 300,000 of the original volumes, on yellow paper like my original, with the interlineations in my big, round hand. My wife and daughter dote on it. There's glory for you.

Chapter XXV

INDIANS ON
TOP OF THE WORLD!

New York 1890

I HAVE MENTIONED JACOB RIIS, THE YOUNG DANISH newspaperman who haunts my office. Around January 1890 he began to disappear for weeks at a time, and when he did show up, he was haggard and secretive, his tired eyes blazing as if with a fever. When I worried about his health, he'd give a shy little smile and raise his finger to his lips, promising "Big work, Mr. Parker. Be patient." As summer arrived he began handing me pages of this "work," which proved to be a growing book titled *How the Other Half Lives*. Starting with his own immigrant past, Riis scoured the city, documenting the lives of the undocumented poor, the "other half" whose stories are absent from history books and whose names are unmentioned in the newspapers unless they commit a crime or die grotesquely.

One innovation of *How the Other Half Lives* is "flash" photography. Riis claims that his book will be the first to include unposed, candid photographs of life in tenements, on the streets and in the back alleys where the poor of New York City live. I followed his work with great interest, reading in manuscript his chapters on "The Italian," "The Bohemians," "Chinatown," "Jewtown," "The Color Line," "The Street Arab," "The Working Girls". The photographs are sometimes heartbreaking, as of street children huddled in a pile, sleeping like stray kittens, sometimes brave, as an "English coal-heaver's family" stares at the camera, children on their parents' laps, often ritualistic, as Bohemian cigar-makers bend simultaneously to their tasks, as orphans pray on their knees, in identical white nightshirts, in a charity house.

One day in September, Riis panted into my office and announced his book "finished," plunking a box on my desk that contained his complete manuscript and pictures. "They have been typesetting it as I write, of course," he said, in his soft accent. "But there is much left to be done. Proofreading, the photographic duplication process, *et cetera*. But, for essential purposes, it's done. Farewell, my book and my devotion!" He fell back in a chair, exhausted and pleased with himself.

I paged through the manuscript, impressed again with the details of the research, the clarity of the photographs, the meticulous architectural drawings that revealed the scant dimensions of a tenement apartment, its lack of air and light. Riis told me he had come close to setting some tenements on fire with his flash photography.

I now asked him the question I had been mulling since he started the project. "Where are the Indians?"

He didn't understand. "There are few," he said. "In the tenements, at any rate. There has been little immigration from India."

"No, Jacob," I said quietly. "American Indians. Like me."

He looked thunderstruck, his blue eyes bugging out. "Good God!" he exclaimed. "How could I misunderstand?" He then frowned. "But I found none, Mr. Parker. I was not specifically looking for your people, but I found none in the tenements. If they are in New York, they are not in the slums." He slapped his knee. "But you are right! I must look!"

He dashed out of my office to start work then and there, although I had intended the query as a mild joke. He returned bedraggled a week later and slumped down in my chair. "There are no Indians," he reported. "You, who settled this island, have vanished." He drew his press notebook from his pocket and consulted it. "There are Montauks, of course, and others on Long Island, but none have reached New York City. An Algonquian named Stephen Talkhouse was famous for walking from Montauk to Brooklyn and back in a single day. But he died in Montauk in 1879." He licked his thumb and flipped more pages. "Um-m-m, yes. There was a settlement called 'Shorrak-Kappok' on the very north tip of Manhattan, an Indian village on the shore. There is almost nobody left there. Just an old Indian woman and her family. They have a little store where they sell tobacco, beads, other things. She has no idea where other Indians are. She thinks they are mostly upstate, where your people are." He looked up at me apologetically. "That's all, I'm afraid. I found nothing else."

I patted a palm at him. "Don't worry, Jacob. I was just curious. If we've left Manhattan, what we've left is smoke and grime and poverty. Let the white man have it."

But I remained curious, and when my daughter Maud came to visit me after school that day I presented the problem to her. Oh, yes, Maud. I've been so busy keeping up with national events that I've failed to keep you up on my family. Maud was born in 1878, three years after I took my job at 300 Mulberry Street, when I was fifty and Minnie twenty-eight. By that time Minnie and I had moved part-time to the city, fulfilling Minnie's dream, with a place on West Forty-second Street, walking distance from Grand Central. With my job, we managed to keep the Fairfield house, mostly for summers and occasional fair-weather weekends. Before Maud started school, she and Minnie spent more time alone in Fairfield, but then Maud decided she wanted to go to school in New York. Even at five she was decisive and headstrong, though I suspect her mother put her up to it.

Now twelve years old, Maud went to school on Forty-sixth Street, but had the run of the city much as I had the run of the woods as a child. She knew streets and alleys as I used to know paths and streams, trams and buses as I knew horses and canoes. She's no Indian, in fact or in looks – tribal inheritance descends through the mother, remember – but she can run like a deer, outrunning most boys her age and older. In fact, running is her default gait. When her mother and I walk, Minnie at a gay saunter, me chuffing along, Maud encircles us like a sheepdog, making ten paces to our one. She is also quite tall – taller than her mother already – and nobody thinks she's a twelve-year old tot as she trips the light fantastic on the sidewalks of New York.

That day in September, Maud came to visit, as she often did. She never arrived unannounced. First, the jingle of harness and the clang of the bell as she darts across in front of a cab, followed by "Hey Maudie" from the press boys gathered across the street. Soon, a clomp, clomp up two flights of stairs – half as many clomps as there are stairs – then Maud sweeps through the door, pigtails flying, dumping schoolbooks on my desk, collapsing in my visitor's chair, pulling her blue-striped dress down over her pantaloons.

"Hi, Father," she gasps. "I'm pooped!"

"Ah-weh-ee-oh," I called her, which she hates. "Beautiful flower. You look like a drooping rose."

She shook hair out of her face. "We read about Appomattox today," she said. "You're not mentioned in the book."

"I'm not surprised," I told her. "Indians travel unrecognized. Unlike you, who break every branch in the trail as you pass. You'll never escape the trackers that way."

"I don't have to," she said, chin high. "I can outrun them."

We bantered for awhile. She was getting to be almost as much fun as her mother. In 1890 Maud was twelve, Minnie forty, me sixty-two. They keep me young. I told her about Jacob Riis's book and his inability to find Indians in the city.

She had her knees up under her chin, feet flat on the chair. "Of course there are Indians in the city," she said.

"Who? You, me, who else?"

"You mean you don't know?"

I frowned. "There's an old Indian woman who sells trinkets up by Spuyten Duyvil."

"Mm-mm," she said, shaking her head. "Closer than that."

"Where are they then?"

She circled the air slowly with one hand, her voice turning spooky. "They're in the air, Father. They're over your head, watching you as you walk."

I played along, my eyes wide. "Do they fly?"

"Almost," she said, spinning her fantasy. "Some people think they do. They're up in the air, clinging to the fabric of things. Some people say, when they let go, they don't fall, but float to another perch."

"What do they do up there all day?" I asked.

"They build castles in the sky!" She jumped up abruptly, came around my desk to me and took my hand. "Come on, Father. I'll show you."

"I have work," I protested.

"No you don't. Mother says you nap half the day. Come on!"

It was close to closing, so I took my hat and followed her downstairs, though at my more sedate pace. She led me south on Mulberry Street as I continued to question her about her "Indians," wondering where her fantasy would lead her.

"Are they in trees, these Indians of yours?"

She was in front of me, walking backwards. "No, silly. There are no trees tall enough for them in New York. Or strong enough."

"So how do they stay aloft?"

"They build their own trees, Father. Taller and stronger than the forest trees. They build them from metal that's found underground. They draw it out of the earth and melt it in furnaces so hot they light up the night sky!"

We crossed busy Houston Street and hopped west to Lafayette, continuing south. For a little girl on a wild goose chase, she had a definite idea where she was going. We crossed Canal, with the towers and lacing of the Brooklyn Bridge looming up ahead of us. I had watched the bridge grow, from the first stones of the Brooklyn tower in 1872, to the completion of the bridge, the highest structure in the world. On May 24, 1883, Minnie, Maud and I paid our one penny each and walked across the bridge on opening day. When we reached the center, I paused and thought of John Rawlins, in the summer of 1869, the plans for this very bridge spread out on his deathbed as he tried to determine how high the central arc must be. I know it was Roebling's bridge, but I always thought part of it was John Rawlins's.

"Do you want more hints?" asked Maud, as we passed under the shed near City Hall at Chambers Street, which housed the trains for the Brooklyn Bridge and the Third Avenue Elevated.

"Yes, I do," I said. "I'm not even warm."

"You're so warm you're hot!" she said. "The Indians you seek are at the top of the world!" She flung her arm upward.

I shook my head. "Then why aren't we at the North Pole?"

She folded her arms, impatient. "Not the top of the earth, father. The *World*!" She flung her arm upward, and I realized where we were. We were standing where New York's tallest building was rising on Centre Street. It was now a steel skeleton on its upper floors, with red sandstone beginning to sheath its lower portion. At twenty-six stories high, over three hundred feet, it would be the first New York building to top the spire of Trinity Church. I had walked past it many times as it went up, marveling at how steel construction could support a building of such height, looking at designs for the Otis safety elevators that would make stairs unnecessary and, not incidentally, wondering what kind of men could work so high in the air as the building scraped the sky.

I looked at Maud, who was grinning up at me. "The Pulitzer Building?" I asked.

"It's the *World* Building, Father! Pulitzer's newspaper. The *World*! And the Indians are at the top of it!"

Then, astonishing me and many passers-by, Maud raised her head to the sky, her hand to her mouth and let out a warbling war-whoop of the sort I had never heard from the civilized Iroquois, but only from the wild Sioux in the midst of their buffalo hunt. "HOO-woo-woo-woo-woo-woo-woo! HOO-woo-woo-woo-woo-woo-woo!"

She shielded her eyes and squinted toward the top of the *World*. Almost instantly came answering cries from all over the naked scaffold. "HOO-woo-woo-woo-woo-woo-woo! HOO-woo-woo-woo-woo-woo-woo!" Then, as if by levitation, figures emerged from within the skeleton to the outer edges of the *World* – a dozen men, then more, who started descending the steel posts, hooking ropes around it from their waists, leaping down, hooking the ropes again as they went. So fast did they descend that it seemed as if they were running down the outside of the *World*.

"Who are they?" I asked Maud, looking up, craning my neck and shading my eyes.

Maud's eyes were gleaming. "Isn't it wonderful Father? Mohawks! The keepers of the eastern door! Come in and meet them."

She led me across the street, through the construction barriers and into what would be the lobby of the *World*. The Mohawks finished their descent and crowded around us, dusting their hands on their shirts and pants. "Ah-weh-ee-yo," said one of them to Maud. "Beautiful flower. Have you brought him at last?"

"Father," she said to me, leading me forward by the hand like a stunned bear, "this is Mountain Eagle."

I found myself shaking hands with a swarthy young man of about twenty-five, clearly an Indian like me, with broad cheekbones and flat nose. The handkerchief that he yanked from his head revealed long black hair pulled behind his ears and tied in a tail. He pumped my hand in great enthusiasm. "John Mountain Eagle," he explained. "Your daughter likes to romanticize us. And you are Do-ne-ho-ga-wa!"

"Ely Parker," I said. "I'm sure Maud will let us drop the tribal names. How did she find you? What are you doing here?"

John Mountain Eagle laughed. "You sound like your daughter. Questions, questions. All in good time Mr. Parker. You are keeper of the western door, we of the east. Come, meet the rest of the Iroquois League."

John introduced me around to more than two dozen men, clad in a motley of blue and gray shirts and coarse cloth pants. Some wore handkerchiefs on their heads, others were bareheaded, their hair cropped close. All wore sturdy boots that probably cost more than the rest of their outfit combined. None of them was older than forty.

The Mohawks backed off while I spoke with John and a few others. Behind us they soon had a loose ring of crates and barrels gathered into a rough circle and spread a cloth in the middle, on which they started unwrapping bundles they retrieved from corners of the unfinished lobby.

"I walk by here at least once a week," I told John Mountain Eagle. "This is an astonishing structure, tallest in the world. I used to build buildings. I love them. But I've never seen you. Where have you been?"

"I told you, Father," said Maud, standing proprietarily next to John. "They were in the sky! At the top of the *World*!"

John smiled and tugged her pigtail. "We came when the snow melted," he explained. "In the spring, when the foundation was dug and the columns started to go up. We work the high steel. When it got above five stories, only Kanienkeha'ka worked the heights." He used the name, "people of the flint," that the Mohawks call themselves. Mohawks is what other Iroquois taught the white man to call them before we joined them in a league. It means man-eaters.

"I found them when school started," explained Maud. "A few weeks ago. I was saving them as a surprise. I can't believe you asked me about them first."

"Come," said one of the older Mohawks, Jefferson Deer. He led me to a seat in the circle of crates and barrels, where a small feast was being set out. "Sit with us. Eat with us."

I stared at the bounty being prepared. "Is this in my honor?" I asked, amazed. "Did you know I was coming?"

"Oh, yes, Do-ne-ho-ga-wa," said one of the younger men with great solemnity. "We listen to the wind and ask it, will he come today? Oh, speak to us, west wind!" He cocked his head as if to hear the wind. The other Indians nodded and chuckled.

"It's teatime," explained John Mountain Eagle. "We do this every day. It's a long, hard day up there, and many of us have far to walk home. A little sustenance helps. Also lets us count our numbers and give thanks that we survived the day."

On the cloth in front of us now, opened parcels revealed part of a wheel of cheese, a basket of apples, flat circles of cornbread and several earthen jugs. Jefferson Deer hooked a jug with his finger, balanced it on his upturned elbow, took a long swig and wiped his mouth with his sleeve. "Ah," he said, wincing, "firewater."

I frowned in disbelief. Surely these Mohawks didn't end their workday with a whiskey jug.

Jefferson handed me the jug. "Cider," he assured me. "No drinking on this job. Makes you sweat, sweat gets in your eyes, you fall. Hands get slick, you fall."

"Get dizzy with a hangover," added a young man, Keith Diabo, "better you don't go up at all."

I swigged from the jug, which was indeed cider, and delicious. One of the men found a cup, wiped the inside with his sleeve and poured it full for Maud. We settled back and ate thoughtfully. "Where does this all come from?" I asked, waving at the feast.

"We bring it back from Caughnawaga, on the Saint Lawrence," explained John Mountain Eagle. "We have regular shifts going back and forth – always some of us here, always some of us back home, on our way home or on our way here. Bosses don't care, long as the number of men on the steel stays constant. Those apples were picked in Caughnawaga last week. The corn came down too. We make the bread here."

"Right here?" I looked around the cluttered construction site.

"No," laughed John. "In our homes here. I stay on Canal Street, but many are across the bridge in Brooklyn. The bread is *ka-na-ta-rok*, Mohawk boiled bread. It has kidney beans inside. Bread, cider, cheese, gets the Brooklyn boys across the bridge with full bellies. It's sort of our bridge, you know."

I had been thinking of it as John Rawlins's bridge. "How so?" I asked, as Maud handed me a piece of corn bread.

"Panic of '73," said Jefferson Deer. "No jobs upstate. None in Canada. Indians are last hired, first fired. We spread out, looked for work. I was young, about twenty. Came down here, saw big towers going up, went in and asked for work. Fewer and fewer men were willing to go up the tall towers, unwilling to walk the thin swing bridge that connected them. I said I'd do it."

"You weren't afraid?" I asked.

"Afraid? Hell no! So shit-scared I had to change my britches!" Maud, sipping cider, choked in delight.

I smiled at her and rubbed her back. "But you went up," I said.

"Had to," said Jefferson. "I needed the money. Went up there, did the job. Went up the next day, did the job. A man fell. I didn't. End of the week I got my pay, foreman asks, 'Any more at home like you?' I sent a telegram, got men down here quick. That's how it started. Panic of '73 was worse than panic on the bridge. We finished the thing, now we walk home over it."

"My father worked on that bridge," said John Mountain Eagle. "He's up on Canal Street now, in the flat. I'll take you to him later, if you like."

I nodded. "I'd like that." I shook my head as I munched cornbread. "I watched that bridge go up. I never thought of Indians on it."

Behind the circle, one of the Indians was tuning a guitar, another a fiddle. A concertina wheezed. They started playing softly as we ate and talked. "Have you always been good at heights?"

"Hell, no!" said Jefferson Deer. "We learned like everyone else. But there were more of us, see? The others were just single fellas – an Italian here, a Greek there, a Portagee. But we were a tribe. We helped each other out, taught each other tricks. How to use the wind, how to feel the beam like a broad road under your feet, how to focus on the horizon. When you walk on the outside, you lean in – more places to grab if you fall. Always look for a way out, just in case." Deer shrugged and picked at a piece of cheese. "Anybody could learn it, but we're the ones who did."

"In 1886," continued John, picking up the story, "Canadian Pacific wants to build a cantilever bridge over the Saint Lawrence, one foot of it in our Caughnawaga reservation. 'Sure,' we said. 'But you gotta hire us too.' First we was just day laborers. Later, though, we started climbing, just to show them we could do it. Then we learned riveting, which we hadn't used on the Brooklyn. Pretty soon we're the only ones on the high bridge. When we go away on jobs, we always take some vets, some new hands, teach them like apprentices. Back home, we still use that Black Bridge for practice. I ran across the beams while it was still building.

Indian boys run out on it at night, throwing stuff off. It's a rite of passage. Like your first girl. Oops," he said, looking at Maud.

"No Indian boy's going to get me," said Maud. "I'm too fast." This sent a nice round of laughter around the Mohawk circle, as they looked at me for signs of disapproval. I gave none. I just looked at her sitting there, proud and poised and easy, and realized Minnie was just fifteen when I'd first met her at City Point. Three years older than Maud, who sat here so friendly and complacent among the Mohawks. I saw that young Keith Diabo had taken a seat next to her.

"We did mostly bridges," said Jefferson Deer. "Then a big skyscraper went up in Chicago. But it was too far away. We heard about this one. Some of us came down here, offered ourselves to contract the high labor. They'd heard of us, you see. Word got around. There was bad luck on the Chicago job, they say it's because no Mohawks were there." He laughed. "The white man has many superstitions. One is that Indians bring good luck. The other is that we are unafraid and have a great sense of balance, we walk the heights like they were broad, sea-level roads." He laughed again. "Let the white man believe what he wants. We walk the heights, we stay careful, we pass it along. Can't say more than that."

The party broke up into small groups. John Mountain Eagle unlimbered a fiddle and joined the band, another Indian shook a can of pebbles like a rattle. The music was familiar Anglo-American tunes, "Sweet Betsy from Pike," "Woolwich Arsenal," "John Barleycorn," "Arthur McBride," even "Lorena," maybe for my benefit, sweet and nostalgic, the tune we'd heard on the piano in the Virginia farmhouse the night before Appomattox. We stayed maybe an hour, then the band was packing up to go. The Mohawks gathered around to shake hands with me again, some of them looking directly at me, then stooping to kiss Maud in front of me, as if they were counting coup and daring me to object. Soon there was just Maud and me, John Mountain Eagle, Keith Diabo and a few others.

"The Canal Street contingent," explained John. "Walk with us. You can meet my father and mother. And my wife."

"You're married!" exclaimed Maud.

John laughed easily. "Of course I am, Ah-weh-ee-yo." He ruffled her hair. "I had no idea you were out there or I'd have waited."

Maud punched him gently in the ribs. We walked through the gathering dusk up Centre Street. Looking south I could see pedestrian traffic cross the Brooklyn Bridge, the Rawlins Bridge, the Mohawk Bridge. Our companions, the windwalkers, were on it somewhere, indistinguishable in the homebound crowd.

We turned west on Canal for a block, walking through crowds, vegetable stands, peddlers with pushcarts, then entered a nondescript brick building. Ah, I thought, with mingled dread and curiosity. A chance to see firsthand one of Jacob Riis's tenements, where "the other half lives" in squalor. I saw no squalor, however, on the broad staircase we ascended to the third floor. John opened a door and ushered us into a large parlor, with broad windows looking north over Canal Street. The other men disappeared through doors toward the back of the flat, Keith Diabo blowing Maud a little kiss.

As I turned around in wonder at the neat and spacious flat, John put down his fiddle case and brought two people forward from a table in the corner. Both were younger than me, but clearly John's elders. "Mr. Parker," he said. "These are my parents, Isaac and Sarah. Mother and Father, meet the famous Indian from Appomattox, Mr. Ely Parker." Maud cleared her throat and stepped out from behind me. "Oh. And his daughter Miss Maud Parker."

Isaac shook my hand warmly. "Oh, we know you from old, Mr. Parker. Great-nephew of Red Jacket, sachem of the Seneca and the Six Tribes. Welcome to our home-that-isn't. Sit down."

I joined the elder Mountain Eagles at a table in the front corner. The room was big enough to hold a small and large table, several bookcases, easy chairs and a grand piano. Photographs of other Mohawks on the upstate Caughnawaga reservation adorned the walls. Worn but elegant Indian rugs carpeted the floor. The table at which we sat was covered with a white cloth, and on it were strips of cloth with elegant beadwork woven into them.

John's mother, who wore glasses, spoke for the first time. "Beadwork. It's what we do to keep from worrying about the men on the columns," she explained. "Worry beads. My eyes are going bad, but I can't stop. It brings in money, too. We sell them in the little stores here, also up in Caughnawaga."

"Your son tells me you walked the girders, too," I said to Isaac.

He smiled. "Yes, long ago. On that damn bridge down there. Scared like hell every day. Never was so happy when Sarah told me to stop."

I looked around the apartment. "You live here?" I asked. "You said 'home-that-isn't'."

Sarah smiled like sunshine. "We commute," she said. "The flat is tribal. Many of us live here from time to time. There are three bedrooms in the back. Now Isaac and I have one, John and Mayann the other, Keith and the other boys bunk in the third. When we go, others move in. It's like the longhouse – never anybody's, never empty."

John returned from the back room with his wife Mayann, who was short and compact. Maud accepted an introduction very coolly, but Mayann sized her up and led her to the piano. Soon the two of them were sorting through sheet music, eventually plunking out some simple duets and laughing at their mistakes.

What a comfortable evening we spent then, and how many comfortable evenings thereafter, as I returned to the Mohawk flat often, to be greeted by a revolving population, always friendly, hospitable and comfortable in their skins, always with fresh or smoked venison, eggs, apples, squash and other delights from their upstate garden. They brought white cornmeal from the north to make *o-nen-sto*, Mohawk corn soup, with red kidney beans like the Mohawk bread. The Mohawks once cooked it in a bear's skull or a pig's skull, but now they use a pot. I brought the Red Jacket medal and showed it around. Minnie brought cookies. Sometimes the boys brought out the fiddles, sometimes Maud played the new "ragtime" that Mayann taught her. The Seneca of the western door had met the Mohawks of the eastern door in a secret enclave in the midst of our former home of Man-hat-tan!

Of course I told Jacob Riis about the Mohawks, and of course he insisted on visiting them and taking their picture. "But what can I do with them in my book?" he exclaimed. "They are so bourgeois and prosperous! They're not the other half at all!"

"They're a third way," I told him. "They'll fit in your book."

And so they do. On page eighteen, with no further explanation, is Jacob's flash photograph of "Mountain Eagle, an Iroquois, and his family." No reference to them in the text, nothing to explain what they're doing there. Jacob even did his best to make them look like tenement dwellers. Instead of showing the spacious living room, Jacob crammed them around the corner table near the window, Isaac and Sarah with their beadwork, Isaac with his strong hands and Sarah with her glasses. Mayann also holds beadwork and smiles winningly at the camera. Behind Mayann, facing the camera, John sits in a tilted-back chair playing his fiddle. At first glance it looks like a poor family in a cramped one-room flat. But look closer and you see how wide the window is behind them, with a translucent shade pulled halfway down. The walls are not smoke-and-water stained, but decorated with a twisting pattern of wallpaper roses. Mayann sits on what looks like a cushion but is actually John's suit-jacket, which Jacob made him take off so he'd look poorer. Playing his fiddle, John leans back against the corner of a mahogany bookcase, an unlikely fixture for a tenement. He's wearing his expensive, cloudwalking boots. Their shirts and aprons are crisp and white. The family are happy and direct, looking in welcome at the camera, except for Isaac, who attends to his beads, stolid and camera-shy. Jacob says the old ironworker objected to having his picture taken weaving beads, women's work. It's not a picture of poverty like the rest of Jacob's book, but of comfort and success.

"The problem is," said Jacob. "You Indians fit in nowhere!"

Epilogue

"AB-SO-LUTE-LY DEE-LIGHT-ED!" SAID THEODORE ROOSEVELT

New York 1895

I DREAMED OF APPOMATTOX AGAIN TODAY. I WAS IN MY old Mulberry Street office, which I've commandeered so I can write this in peace. I go in a couple of days a week, and they tolerate me. Today I was retrieving the Appomattox surrender draft and the Red Jacket medal from the walls, packing them to take to Fairfield, along with Sully's sketch of me watching the Sioux buffalo dance. I even took the Appomattox pen from its case to write these last words, and it works fine. As I looked at my mementos, the Red Jacket medal of my one world, the Appomattox draft of the other, Sully's portrait of both, I dozed and was back in the forest. I couldn't tell which forest – Tonawanda or Appomattox – but then I heard the noise of heavy boots and knew it was Appomattox.

"Parker! Attention!" It was Grant's voice, and I struggled awake, trying to remember which hand to salute with. Before my desk stood General Grant, just as he was at Appomattox, grizzled beard, half smile, cigar clamped in his teeth.

I was halfway to my feet when Grant patted a palm at me and said, "At ease, Parker." I looked around and wasn't in the forest any more, but at 300 Mulberry Street. I could see buildings outside the window. But Grant stood in front of me. Was I dead?

"Ely, Ely, wake up. It's me," said Fred Grant.

"Fred," I said, sinking back into my chair, my face cold with sweat. "You gave me a fright. I thought you were him."

Fred Grant chuckled and sat down in my visitor chair. "Yes. I get a certain mileage out of that," he admitted.

I hadn't seen Fred since his father's death ten years ago. I'd followed his fortunes, of course. He had become U.S. Ambassador to, of all things, Austria-Hungary in the Harrison administration. On his return, I had just read, he'd been appointed one of the New York City Police Commissioners. That's what brought him here.

It was welcome to see an old friend alive, after writing about those who've died. I was about, in fact, to write an obituary for the nineteenth century, my century. I had the pages on my desk, stray thoughts scribbled here and there. How we'd gone from the clean truths of the Iroquois League and the Constitution to the dusty volumes of civil and criminal code and case law, from the clean lines of Palladio and the Federal era to the dark, horsehair sofas, the heavy velvet drapes and deep-fringed dark and smoky lampshades of Victoriana. The city streets, the federal government, Henry James's prose, my own arteries, are turgid and clogged, layered and overstuffed. Governments and corporations and trusts and directorships overlap, interlocked into paralysis. Purgatives and laxatives and diuretics dominate advertising, but nothing seems to unclog us. We eat too much, drink too much, wear too much clothing, pass too many laws and make every man a clerk – like I was – daily diminishing a stack of paper that vanishes at closing time to be restacked on someone else's desk tomorrow, while another stack (perhaps his) appears on mine.

Fred Grant would be forty-five now, two years older than his father at Appomattox, and so like his father I couldn't take it in, the same furtive look, the same slouch, the same ability, as I'd just learned, to appear someplace without making an entrance.

"Stay here," said Fred now. "There's someone I want you to meet."

He slouched out the door and down the corridor, returning with someone he introduced as the new President of the Board of Police Commissioners. And when this new fellow entered, it seemed the whole twentieth century strode briskly in, its eyes gleaming, its teeth flashing, rubbing its hands together and radiating energy that blew the cobwebs from the corners and scrubbed the dirt and grime and varnish from the walls, letting in the sun and the air and setting the dust motes dancing. This new man is a man so unlike me and Fred's father, so unlike Fred himself, so unlike even Henry Flagler, that he might be from a different planet. If a new century will begin with more than the turning of a calendar page, it's men like this who will form it, a man with such aggressive hope in his eyes that they seem to shoot beams of their own, illuminating the dark corners, piercing through waste and cant and corruption, a man with such physical and intellectual energy that he doesn't seem merely to stand, but to hover in the air, bristling with strength, as if he might fly out the door or out the window or orbit into space. He could exhaust you just by being in the same room.

He shook my hand so hard he might have torn it off and put it in his pocket. "Dee-light-ed, General! Ab-so-lute-ly dee-light-ed!" said Theodore Roosevelt.

AUTHOR'S NOTE

"My family is American, and has been for generations," Grant famously starts his *Memoirs*. So is mine. My great-grandfather Charles Johnson fought in the Civil War. His son, my grandfather, another Charles Johnson, was born in 1868 in Whitehall, New York. At age seventeen, he bought one of the 300,000 original two-volume sets of Grant's *Memoirs* published in 1885. It's stamped #8883. I have those volumes as well as other Civil War memoirs my grandfather collected as they appeared – Sherman, Sheridan, McClellan, Hancock, Jefferson Davis, Longstreet, Joe Johnstone. I have his other books too -- von Moltke's history of the Franco-Prussian War (great maps!) -- ending with Theodore Roosevelt's *African Game Trails* from 1910, when my grandfather was 42. To start *Grant's Indian* with Grant and end with Roosevelt was destiny.

I grew up with Charles Johnson's books in my parents' bookshelves in Wenham, Massachusetts. His son, my father, collected more Civil War books, including Douglas Southall Freeman on Lincoln and Lee. My father, also born in Whitehall, New York, has the unlikely name for a New York boy of Robert Lee Johnson, because his father and grandfather thought Lee was the war's best general. Lee also survives in my sister Nancy Lee. My grandfather's name survives in me, Peter Charles Johnson. I owe my birth to my father's ability to survive plane crashes during World War II. In 1944, still in the navy, he and my mother Betty (born, believe it or not, Elizabeth Jane Smith) drove from Lake City, Florida to Boston on what turned out to be D-Day, stopping at gas stations to listen to news of the invasion. My seven-month-old sister Nancy Lee was with them, and so, I suspect (since I was born nine months later), was I.

I've read most of my grandfather's and my father's Civil War books. The first thing I remember reading after *Mister Bear Squash-You-All-Flat* was a boy's book about Appomattox, where I probably first met Ely S. Parker. I've been reading about the Civil War all my life, so the sources for *Grant's Indian* are numerous. I won't list them – they're the ones on everybody's list – but three are worth special mention: two biographies of Parker, *The Life of General Ely S. Parker*, by Arthur C. Parker (1919) and *Warrior in Two Camps*, by William H. Armstrong (1978); and *League of the Iroquois*, by Lewis Henry Morgan (1851), whose dedication page reads "to Ha-sa-no-an-da (Ely S. Parker), a Seneca Indian, this work, the materials of which are the fruit of our joint researches, is inscribed: in acknowledgement of the obligations, and in testimony of the friendship of the author." People interested in the historical Parker should read those works.

Grant's Indian is fiction, but I have tried for historical accuracy, to the extent that Parker and other historical figures were mostly where I put them, doing mostly what I have them doing at the time. Anachronisms and whoppers abound, however, most of them intentional. I incorporate by reference Jack Finney's "Footnote" from *Time and Again* on getting the small stuff right and faking the big stuff when you must. As Mark Twain advised Rudyard Kipling, "Get your facts first, and then you can distort them as much as you please."

Peter Johnson
New York City 2009

PETER JOHNSON is an award-winning author, actor and lawyer. A graduate of Harvard and New York Law School, he has written many legal articles, including *Can You Quote Donald Duck? Intellectual Property in Cyberculture* and *Pornography Drives Technology: Why Not to Censor the Internet*. A professional stage and voice-over actor, he has performed plays in New York and nationwide and narrated over 500 audiobooks. *Grant's Indian* is his first novel. He lives in New York City.

www.ingramcontent.com/pod-product-compliance
Lightning Source LLC
Chambersburg PA
CDIIW031420240626
47154CB00001B/132

* 9 7 8 0 9 8 1 9 8 4 2 0 9 *